MW01609637

KALE'S

PAROXYSM

BY

NINA R. SCHLUNTZ

Kale has spent years in a volatile relationship with his ex, Martin. Convinced he will come back, even after a conflict that results in Kale being incarcerated and suspended from his law firm, Kale begins a no-strings-attached relationship with the man he meets in jail.

Eli has always kept his romances with men temporary. He hasn't always been honest about being gay and he prefers to keep the secrets of his past hidden. Kale's obsessive nature makes it difficult though, and soon their relationship is edging toward something more. Kale's possessiveness appears to have no limits, nor do his fits of rage, and Eli worries, as Kale's affection shifts from Martin to Eli, that he may become Kale's next victim rather than his lover.

This is a work of fiction. The characters depicted in this story are completely fictitious, and any similarities to actual events, locations or people, living or dead, are entirely coincidental.

No part of this publication may be reproduced, in whole or in part, without written permission from the publisher or author, except for the brief quotations in reviews.

This book was previously published by MLR Press under the same name in 2016.

Kale's Paroxysm
Copyright © 2016 Nina R Schluntz
All rights reserved

Issued 2021

CHAPTER ONE

The cell door clanged ominously as officer Bower closed it. He grunted and tugged on his belt as it worked overtime to keep his pants up.

"Don't forget my phone call," Kale said. He crossed his arms in an effort not to touch anything in the cell. He doubted anyone ever cleaned them, and he was bound to get a bacterial infection if he remained here for too long. Bower offered him a grunt in response.

Kale refrained from spewing a line of profanity. Upsetting the guard wasn't going to earn him any favors. At least the county jail only had one other occupant. Kale looked at his companion.

A slender man slumped against the wall and stared at his shoes. Kale wasn't able to get much of an impression of him, other than his clothes were from a local thrift store. Kale went to the opposite side of their cage and sat on the bench.

He moved to rub his face and paused at the sight of the blood still on his hands. The arresting officer had allowed him a quick wash in the bathroom but it hadn't been enough to get the blood from the creases in his skin. His knuckles were swelling, but nothing a few days rest and an ice pack wouldn't fix.

He stared at the blood—Martin's blood. And Wayne's. Mostly Wayne's blood. Red spots decorated his name brand shirt. The stains would never come out. He'd have to toss it.

"You kill someone?"

Kale looked over at the only person the words could belong to, his cellmate. He was looking at Kale, pale blue eyes boldly staring at his blood-splattered clothes.

"No," Kale said. At least, they'd all been alive when the ambulance had shown up.

"It's not your blood though, is it?"

He couldn't tell if his companion was curious or concerned. The man took a small step forward and the light exposed his features better. A silver loop earring glinted on his left lobe. His hair was so blond it was nearly white. Natural too, his eyebrows were the same frosty shade. His pale skin was perfect, not a single blemish. Kale guessed he was at least a decade younger than him, barely out of high school, although the perfect skin could be deceiving.

"No, it's not," Kale replied. He stared back, both of them gawking like schoolgirls with a crush. The man's complexion blushed red, an arousing look on him, and he looked away from Kale.

"Sorry, it's none of my business."

Kale kept staring. He wondered if his fellow jailbird turned that same color when he was in the throes of an orgasm. *Now which of us is poking their nose where it doesn't belong?* Kale forced his eyes away and clenched his fists, despite the ache of pain it caused to pulse in his knuckles.

"I put three people in the hospital," Kale said.

"Car accident?" The words seemed to topple out as if he couldn't stop them.

A car was damaged, Kale thought, the irony not lost on him. "No," Kale replied. "Damage was all me." He raised his arms to show off his swelling hands.

"Three against one? Doesn't sound like a fair fight."

"It wasn't," Kale agreed.

"And yet you won." The man shifted his weight and studied a spot on the ground.

Kale considered pointing out that he'd taken his first few hits with the assistance of a tire iron and that his victims weren't exactly fighters.

"Imagining you kicking three people's butts is kind of hot," the man said, keeping his eyes focused on anything but Kale.

"You weren't there," Kale said, the full implication behind the man's words initially escaping him.

"Wish I had been. I could have evened the odds, not that you needed it."

Their gazes met again and Kale saw the look of lust in his eyes. "It's really not smart to promote the fact you're gay when you're in jail," Kale said, slightly harsher than he intended.

"Yeah, but it's not likely I'll ever see the people I meet in jail outside of jail."

"It's still a good way to get your ass beat by a heterosexual homophobe who's heard one too many stories about getting butt raped in prison."

"Point taken," his companion said, shifting his gaze to the bars of their cell. His complexion turned bright red again, contrasting beautifully with his blond hair. Kale adjusted himself on the bench. He waited until the man's color had returned to normal before attempting to trigger it again.

"Lucky for you, I happen to be gay," Kale said. If possible, his cellmate turned even redder this time. Kale's pants were becoming uncomfortable at this point, but he couldn't help watching the man struggle to regain his composure.

"Lucky me," he said, his voice slightly cracking.

Kale said nothing more, deciding to give the kid a chance to recover, and lesson his own arousal.

"So do you, uh, want to take me out? You know, when we get released," the man asked. He sounded more sure of himself than Kale would have expected. *And who picks up a date in county prison?*

"I'm in a relationship," Kale said.

"Oh, right, yeah." He tapped his knuckles on his forehead. "I should have asked that first. Guess he's luckier than I am."

"I definitely wouldn't say that," Kale said. "Considering he was one of the asses I was kicking tonight."

The man's eyes widened and his pupils turned into black saucers, the blue nearly gone. This kid's bodily reactions were the most entertainment Kale had had in weeks. A half-smile broke his composure, and he decided to cut the kid some slack by opting to explain.

"I caught him cheating on me. I didn't react well."

"He was cheating on you? With two guys?" His expression was nearly cartoonish at this point, his jaw gaping.

"No," Kale said. He shook his head, feeling a kink starting to form. "One of them was a Good Samaritan trying to do the right thing and pull me off."

"Wow. Guess he got what he deserved. Well, your boyfriend that is. Shame about the guy who tried to help."

"No he—" Kale clenched his jaw and forced the words out. "We've been on a break for four weeks now. I wasn't handling it well. I'm still not."

He looked away from the guy, not wanting to see his expression any longer. He'd said too much, the story now too personal.

"He always comes back," Kale added, ignoring how lame the line sounded.

"Right."

The silence that enveloped them wasn't nearly as comfortable as before. Keys jangled in the hall and Officer Bower appeared. He unlocked the cell.

"Time to make your call, Kale," Officer Bower said. Kale jumped up, a few joints popping as he did. He followed Bower down the hall to the pay phone reserved for inmates.

He called collect to his secretary. It was late, he wasn't even sure the exact time, but she always answered. She accepted the call, no hint of judgment in her voice. This wasn't the first time her boss had called her from county jail.

"Charlotte," Kale said. "I need you to call the other partners at the firm and have them contact the courts to get my bail arranged."

"What happened?"

"Three assaults. They went to the emergency room, Augustus Memorial, I think. I'm not sure their status. I'll probably have to go in front of a judge to get my bail amount set, and I doubt they'll release me until all three have been discharged from the hospital."

"I'll have Rich call Judge Harper. I bet he can get him to agree on a bail price tonight so we can get you out of there. It probably won't be cheap though. Three people, shit, Kale."

"One was a bystander," Kale said, as if that made the story any better.

"I'll make the calls and get the funds transferred as soon as I can."

"Thanks Charlotte." Kale hung up the phone. His law firm was one of the best in the county, and he was a co-partner with three other men. Waking up a judge on a Thursday night wasn't going to earn him any favors, but they would set his bail. Their firm held enough weight to make any judge's life miserable if they wanted—refusing to settle and taking the most basic cases to court in an effort to waste a judge's time by arguing over the smallest details.

Judge Harper had been victim to such a ploy when one of the firm's partners, Rich, had gotten upset over having to spend an entire weekend in jail after being arrested for unpaid parking tickets. Ever since, Judge Harper had been very cooperative.

Officer Bower led him back to his cell, where his cellmate seemed to be sleeping. Kale let him rest and closed his own eyes, but images of his night's activities kept flashing in his mind.

§§§

Kale jumped, nearly falling off the bench. He must have nodded off at some point. His cellmate watched him. Kale rubbed his eyes, wondering how long he'd slept.

"What are you in for?" Kale asked, deciding to make idle conversation to pass the time.

"Petty theft and possession," he stated matter-of-factly. Kale wished he'd had the forethought to offer such a cryptic reply when he'd been asked why he was here. Would have saved him from spilling his secrets to a stranger.

"Not so smart to go shoplifting with illegal drugs on you."

He rolled his eyes. "They weren't my pills. I was wearing my friend's jacket. I didn't know they were in there. They're prescription pills she takes. The mall cop acted like he'd caught me with a kilo of heroin. The real cops didn't act any better when they showed up. I think they were mostly pissed to have been bothered."

"Who was the arresting officer?"

His eyes searched the ceiling for a moment. "Loraineson, Jekles, something like that."

"Lorainekson?"

"Yeah, I think so."

"He's prejudiced against homosexuals. Considering how open you seem to be, I'm sure he noticed and did all he could to make your life a bit harder. Mention that to your lawyer. He can use it to have your sentence lessened. If you can get your friend to write a testimony about the pills, those charges should be dropped as well. Who's your lawyer?"

"Whoever the court appoints."

Even one of them should be able to handle a case this simple. If he got one of the good ones. Kale would have to hope he did. He wasn't about to volunteer to do his case. He was already behind on his current workload and this incident wasn't going to help matters.

"See if you can get Stunsky," Kale said. "Is this your first arrest?"

He nodded.

"You can probably settle out of court and get off on some volunteer work. So long as you weren't stealing anything worth more than five grand."

"I wasn't," he said. He dug his shoe in the ground and Kale wondered if he was going to admit what he'd been trying to steal. "You know all this from your experience getting locked up for assault?"

"Something like that," Kale said. He didn't want to admit he was a lawyer. It would lead to him having to talk his way out of not taking the kid's case.

Officer Bower rattled the keys as he fumbled with the lock, stopping the kid from asking something he seemed about to say.

"Kale, your bail has been paid."

He wasn't sure he wanted to ask how much it had been. He quickly slipped out of the cell and glanced at the clock on the wall. It was a few minutes after midnight.

His cellmate pressed himself against the cell bars and thrust his hand through to offer Kale a handshake.

"Name's Eli Pendza, spelled with a z not an s. Look me up if you decide you want some companionship during your separation from your boyfriend."

He debated if he wanted to offer his full name to the man. Befriending criminals wasn't exactly on his to-do list even if he did want to experiment further with Eli's blush factor. He shook his hand, professional instincts forcing him to.

The warm hand took his and an array of tingles ran up his arm. He gave Eli a firm shake and pulled away. Eli's reddening complexion told him he'd likely felt a spark of something during their contact as well.

He followed Officer Bower down the hall and realized too late that he'd failed to say anything in response to Eli's introduction.

He signed for his belongings and watched Bower pull them all out of a plastic baggy.

"I need to show you this. You've been served," Bower said. He handed a folded up paper to Kale.

"I bet you've been dying for a chance to say that to me." Kale rolled his eyes and took the paper. He unrolled it. A new restraining order, prohibiting him from going within five hundred feet of Martin. The same judge who had agreed to grant him bail had signed the restraining order. He skimmed the contents. It was impressively detailed. A knot formed in his stomach as he realized Martin had likely been preparing this document with a lawyer for weeks. And tonight Kale had finally pushed him too far.

"What is Eli's bail set at?" Kale asked.

"Two grand," Bower replied.

"Why so high?" Kale raised his eyebrows and looked at him. "Petty theft and possession, right?"

"He's a flight risk. No current address or job. Judge doesn't think he'll show up on his court date."

Kale bit the inside of his cheek as he considered making a very bad decision. But he'd made quite a few of those already tonight. He grabbed his checkbook that Officer Bower had just returned to him and wrote a check for two thousand dollars.

CHAPTER TWO

Kale checked the posted schedule at the covered bus stop. A bus would be arriving in ten minutes. He exhaled as he sat on the bench. He could have called Charlotte to pick him up but he didn't want to be that asinine of a boss to demand her to leave her home at one in the morning.

Calling a taxi had crossed his mind as well, but he didn't want to risk getting a chatterbox driver that might pry into his business. He'd taken the bus from the county jail before. It only took one transfer for him to reach his home and the schedules usually lined up well enough that he'd only have another ten minute wait at the next stop.

Plus, this position gave him a good vantage point to see who came to pick up Eli. He watched every car that passed, eager to see which pulled into the lot.

"You posted my bail," Eli said. He stood next to the wall of the bus stop. He leaned on it and peered in at Kale. Kale had been so intent on watching the traffic he'd neglected to see Eli approach.

"Yes, I did."

"Why?"

Kale intentionally waited a few moments before replying. He was hoping Eli would offer up some hypotheses. Kale would enjoy watching Eli squirm as he asked if Kale expected sexual favors.

"Because your bail was set at a ridiculous amount and I'm not sure how much longer you would have survived in jail," Kale said. Both were true. "I also hoped it might earn me some good karma to make up for what I did earlier tonight."

Also true. He had not, absolutely not, bailed the kid from jail on the slim chance of getting to experiment with his blush factor in the bedroom tonight. Martin was coming back. But not likely tonight since he was probably spending the night in the hospital. And Kale couldn't go visit him, not with the newly issued restraining order. He had no desire to end up back in prison.

"Believable," Eli said. "And something you definitely need."

He turned his body away from Kale but remained near the bus stop.

"Someone coming to pick you up?" Kale asked.

"Why? You want a ride?" Eli looked over his shoulder and raised one eyebrow. Kale was tempted to fall for the cheesy line and say yes, that he would love for Eli to take him for a ride. Perhaps he'd get to see that lovely flare of color again. Although, the lighting outside wouldn't do it justice.

Kale had paused too long. Eli shook his head. "No, no one is coming. It's too late to bother anyone."

"My thoughts exactly," Kale agreed.

"If I'm lucky my car will still be at the mall."

That would require some luck. The mall usually towed any cars that remained overnight. The bus pulled up and Kale boarded first. He tossed a handful of change into the depository and asked for a transfer ticket. Eli counted his change and dropped his coins in the receiver one at a time. He asked for a transfer ticket as well, even though this bus stopped at the mall. Maybe Kale was thinking of the wrong mall.

Or maybe he was hoping he'd be able to use the transfer ticket to reach a different location. Kale bit back the thought and picked a seat in the middle of the bus. Eli sat in the row ahead of him. He turned and rested his arm on the back of the seats.

"So now that we're both out, how about you let me take you out for coffee? So I can thank you for posting my bail."

"That's all I get? Coffee?" Kale did his best to make his tone sound offended.

"No, of course not." He flicked his wrist in the air. "Name the place and I'll take you there."

"Paris."

Eli frowned and shook his head. "Fine, you know what? You do only get coffee. And the cheap stuff too. I'm taking you to a gas station, that's all you get."

"As long as it's in Paris," Kale insisted.

Eli muttered something and slumped down in his seat, his legs resting on the seat next to him. His sass was entertaining. Martin's snarky remarks were often the reason Kale lost his temper. Sometimes Kale felt like Martin was intentionally trying to make him punch a wall. He didn't get that impression from Eli. Eli was more playful—less infuriating.

"What are your plans tonight after you get your car?" Kale asked. He leaned forward so he could see Eli's face.

"Not sure. Find a job and start saving for a trip to Paris, most likely."

Kale grinned. "Would you like to come back to my place? I happen to have a coffee maker that's from Paris. I might be willing to settle."

Eli's eyes shifted dark, the blue turning to slivers. Kale wondered how he dilated his eyes on demand like that, and looked forward to finding out what forms of stimuli could trigger it.

§§§

Eli's heart thrummed so hard in his chest he worried it might fall onto the floor of the bus. Kale was gay and interested and had invited him back to his apartment. The entire night had become surreal once he'd seen a man escorted into his cell who looked plucked from one of his fantasies.

The bus lurched to a stop at the mall. Eli could see his car, sitting alone in the outskirts of the parking lot. *So the fantasy continues,* Eli thought.

"It's still here," Eli said. He got up and hurried to the exit. He didn't look back to see if Kale was following him. Any wrong move might jinx tonight's possibilities.

His legs tingled as he walked down the steps and onto the pavement. He'd been at ease when it was just teasing and he knew there was zero chance of becoming involved with Kale. Now that it was a reality, he was a tense bundle of nerves.

His stomach lurched. *Don't throw up*, he scolded himself. *No one wants to make out with a guy who just vomited.* He hurried across the dimly lit parking lot. Kale's footsteps followed him.

He reached his car, a four-door sedan that was as old as he was. He unlocked the passenger door before going around to his side, since keyless entry was not something his car featured. He got in and took a deep breath of stale car odor, grateful his car, although old and rusty, was at least clean.

Kale settled into his own seat. He flexed his hands and Eli considered asking him if they hurt. *Of course they hurt, he'd spent a good part of the day using them to beat three people.* Eli bit back his comment.

"Where too?" Eli asked. He put the keys in the ignition and the car roared to life, filling the silence of the early morning.

"I need to do something first," Kale said, his deep voice sent a shiver through Eli. He'd met few people with a voice that low, and he loved it.

"What?" Eli waited for an answer or some indication from Kale that would tell him his intentions. The streetlights cast an array of shadows across his face. Kale had one of those five-o-clock shadows that never went away. It was black, thick, spanned his entire lower face and continued down his neck. Eli hoped to discover whether his facial hair connected directly to his chest hair.

He looked like a lumberjack; he was only missing the plaid shirt and axe. He was the hottest man Eli had ever dared to ask out. He was not only out of Eli's league, he belonged to an entirely different sport.

Eli wasn't sure how long he waited, time seemed to pass in bumps and spurts around Kale. A hand snaked behind his neck and pulled him across the center console. His senses heightened at the touch. The fingers on his neck pinched his skin hard enough to pull him into the moment.

Lips collided with his. Kale's beard was sandpaper against his face. It was nearly painful when combined with the force of his kiss. Kale's tongue flicked across Eli's lips; he opened, readily accepting the intrusion. Kale's tongue dove deep, testing his gag reflex.

Eli squirmed but managed to hold his ground. He flailed slightly and to hide it he put his hands on either side of Kale's face. Barbs of hair pricked his fingers as he stroked Kale's cheeks.

Kale pulled back, releasing his mouth. His face scraped across Eli's as he sealed his lips around Eli's pierced ear. Kale sucked the loop in his mouth. Shudders of pleasure rippled through Eli's body.

Eli cried out an unintelligible rambling of words. Kale's lips traveled down his neck. Eli could barely tolerate the bursts of pleasure shooting through his body. Their lips reconnected briefly before Kale pulled away, sagging back into his seat.

Eli's mouth remained open as he struggled to recover, his mind buzzing.

He'd never been kissed so aggressively.

"Do you know where Busch Road is?" Kale asked.

"Yes," Eli replied automatically.

"Head there."

He turned away from Kale and took a few deep breaths. *How am I supposed to concentrate on driving after that?* He looked back at Kale.

"I want to blow you first, right here, right now," Eli said. He couldn't wait. He wanted more. Busch Road was at least twenty minutes away.

"I don't have any condoms on me," Kale said.

He wanted to use a condom for a blowjob? Eli knew he shouldn't take offense, but he did. He put the car in gear and pulled out of the parking lot. He tried to dismiss the apparent insult. *He met me in jail, of course he wants to use a condom. It's not like a person meets the healthiest people in lockup.*

Still, no matter how he tried to justify it, he couldn't shake the feeling that Kale thought of him as dirty.

Their conversation stayed to clipped directions from Kale. Eli wondered if he'd ruined things. Wanting to blow him without a condom probably reinforced the idea that Eli was a festering cornucopia of diseases. If only he'd been able to recover by saying he had a stash in the glove box. Although that might have made him look like a sex fiend who frequently had sex in his car with strangers.

The itches of doubt only got worse as he pulled into the apartment complex Kale directed him to.

"Park here, space thirty-two," Kale said. Eli did as told. He cut the engine and gawked at the cars around them. They were all luxury editions, high-end models, costing more than Eli had made cumulatively in his entire life. His car did not belong here, someone was likely to see it and report it.

"My car's going to get towed," Eli said, the words slipping out.

"No it won't. You're parking in my space," Kale said.

"Where's your car?"

"Probably impounded," Kale said. "I wasn't exactly legally parked when I was arrested. Come on."

Kale opened his door and exited. Eli did likewise but hesitated. He closed his car door and stared at the intimidating three story apartments. The parking lot encircled the buildings; there were six main structures, probably six apartments per building, if they were all one floor apartments.

The monthly rent for this place was more than what Eli's car was worth the day it came out of the factory. Kale checked something on his phone, waiting for him at the intersection of sidewalk that led to the entrance.

Kale was more out of Eli's league than he had initially thought. He couldn't help but feel like some street trash that Kale was bringing home. Eli didn't belong with people like Kale.

"Maybe we should do this some other time," Eli said. "It's late and you probably have to work tomorrow."

Kale's eyes darted up from his phone. "What's wrong?"

"Nothing," Eli said. He pulled his door open, his stomach bunching up in knots. The car door slammed shut, nearly catching his fingers in the process.

Kale kept his hand firmly pressed against the door, not letting Eli reopen it.

"You don't like my neighborhood?" Kale asked. Eli didn't know Kale well enough to tell if his question was serious or sarcastic.

"It's a great neighborhood."

"Then what?"

"It's just not my kind of neighborhood," Eli said. "I don't belong here."

"This is a one-night stand, Eli. Your social class has nothing to do with what I'm interested in right now."

A one-night stand, Eli was relieved to have a definition to associate with what they were doing. He'd never done casual sex with a stranger before, but he supposed Kale was right, one's income hardly mattered if all they were going to do was a quick roll in the hay.

No strings attached, no follow-up phone calls. Kale had an ex to win back and Eli had no business asking for more.

Kale pressed his lips against his, filling Eli's mouth with his taste. Kale wedged Eli between the car and his body, his erection pressed against Eli's stomach. He was hard and big, of course he was big, everything about Kale was big.

"Come inside," Kale said, letting up enough to allow Eli to catch his breath.

He couldn't manage to find his words but he nodded. Kale threaded his fingers with Eli's and pulled him with. Eli had to trot to keep up. Kale seemed in a rush. Perhaps he was worried Eli would change his mind and try to leave again. This man really wanted him. The idea sent tingles of arousal through Eli's body.

They went up two flights of stairs, second floor. Kale let go of his hand so he could unlock the door. He pushed it open, flicked on some lights and held the door for Eli.

He'd had a few moments to prepare himself for the expensive furnishings likely to be found inside Kale's apartment. What he wasn't ready for was the nearly antiseptic feel of the place.

The foyer connected to the kitchen. There was no clutter. Not a single item sat on the counters. It was almost like no one lived there. Two bar stools were tucked under the marble island, the sole indication the place might have occupants. A silver fridge hummed softly, not a single magnet on it.

"Nice place," Eli said, barely biting back what he really wanted to say. *Where's all your stuff?*

"Are you hungry?" Kale asked. He turned on a few more lights in the kitchen. "I don't know how long you were in lockup but I know the food is shit."

The invitation surprised him. He'd envisioned the sex to commence immediately upon entering his apartment.

"Food would be great," Eli said. Kale looked at his hands. His eyes met Eli's.

"I need to shower," he said. He raised his hands to show the dried blood still residing in his knuckles. His boyfriend's blood. A trickle of trepidation tingled down Eli's spine. *I should call someone and tell them where I am.* "Help yourself to whatever you want. I'll be back."

He left Eli alone in the kitchen. The immaculate kitchen that probably didn't have a single fingerprint on any surface. *He has OCD and is prone to violence. Yeah, this is a real smart idea, Eli.* He eyed the door for a moment and considered fleeing.

Get a grip, Eli. He's not a murderer. Unless one of the people he'd put in the hospital died. His stomach twisted, and he pulled open the fridge.

He relaxed slightly at the sight of the contents. It looked normal enough. It wasn't organized by color or in alphabetical order. So at least Kale wasn't that crazy. He gathered up the needed items to make a sandwich.

§§§

Eli was three-fourths finished with the sandwich when Kale came back. His short hair was still damp and he was freshly shaved. Eli figured it would last all of five minutes. He grinned at his internal joke.

"What?" Kale asked. He opened the fridge, surveyed the contents, and pulled out a single sized container of orange juice.

"Nothing, I've just never seen someone shave at two in the morning," Eli said. He took another bite of his sandwich and tried not to think about whether he'd made a mess of Kale's kitchen.

"I figured it was too rough for your skin," Kale said. He picked up a dishtowel and began wiping down the counters, even the ones Eli hadn't touched.

"Thanks," Eli said. He pushed the plate away and stood. "I appreciate it."

"Finished?" Kale asked. He nodded. Kale picked up the plate, dumped the contents in the trash under the sink, and placed the plate in the dishwasher. Kale wiped the counter one more time.

"Sorry if I made a mess," Eli said. Kale tossed the towel in the direction of the sink. His lips were on Eli's in the next moment. His skin was smooth and soft, he smelled of soap and aftershave. The kiss was better without the scratchy beard. Eli pulled on Kale's bottom lip and ran his fingers through his damp hair.

"I'm ready for that blowjob now," Kale said. He pulled back. "But only if you want. I don't want you to feel obligated. You can sleep on the couch if you'd rather."

"No, I want to."

"Good."

Kale led him down a short hall to his bedroom. It was equally antiseptic. Nothing hung on the walls or sat on the dressers. The sheets were a light gray, a nice touch to the already depressing atmosphere. The blinds were closed, no curtains. Kale went directly to a bedside table and pulled out lube and a handful of condoms.

The condom thing still bothered Eli but he was starting to get a better idea of why Kale insisted on it. He seemed to need everything neat and clean.

Kale pulled off his undershirt, giving Eli a full view of his chest hair. It covered his entire front, only his shoulders and upper arms were bare. He undid his fly, neatly piling his clothes on a chair near the dresser.

"Are you sure I can't give you the blowjob without a condom?" Eli asked. "I promise I don't have anything."

"I'd prefer you do," Kale said.

Eli crossed his arms. Even with the knowledge of Kale's germ problem, Eli couldn't help but be offended. "Why do you think I'm so dirty?"

Kale's eyebrows arched. "It's not personal." He approached Eli and put a hand on either shoulder. "I've been with Martin for five years and I still make him wear a condom too, for everything."

Considering that Martin was cheating on him, it was probably a wise decision. Maybe Kale had trust issues intermixed with his OCD and need for cleanliness. Kale kissed his neck, hard enough to leave marks, and Eli consented. Sex wouldn't be as good with condoms but he could touch other parts of Kale with his lips. And if Martin hadn't been able to get Kale past this crutch after five years, Eli doubted he could make any progress either.

CHAPTER THREE

The incessant ringing of his phone roused Kale from sleep. He lay on his stomach, his face buried in the pillow. He turned his head but didn't open his eyes. He ran his fingers across his side table, searching for his phone. He skimmed the entire surface but it wasn't there.

Warm fingers pressed the vibrating, ringing phone into his hand. He almost muttered a thank you to Martin, but his brain locked up as an image of slamming Martin's head into the rear window of Wayne's car flashed in his mind.

Before his brain could do more processing, he pressed the answer button and held the phone to his ear.

"Where are you?" Charlotte chirped.

He forced his eyes open and looked at the digital numbers on his alarm clock. It was fifteen minutes past eight. Kale was supposed to be in the office at eight. And Kale was never late.

"At home," Kale said. "I spent most of the night in jail, remember?"

"The Blumburg case is today at ten."

A spark of adrenaline rushed through him, pushing away the clouds of sleep fogging his mind. The Blumburg case was a million dollar case. *Fuck Martin for his shitty timing. Why did Martin have to instigate a fight the day before such an important case?*

"Have Steve gather my papers. He's familiar with the case. He's been helping me prep."

"He's an intern," Charlotte objected.

"And he's perfectly capable of carrying my things to the courthouse. I'll be there in plenty of time."

"The other partners want to speak to you afterwards. There are some stipulations to your bail. Did you know Wayne is in a coma?"

"Do you want to talk about Wayne or do you want me to get to the courthouse?" Kale asked.

"Get to the courthouse. I'm just giving you a heads up. Things aren't pleasant around here. Rich is pissed you aren't here."

"No shit." He hung up and dropped the phone into the bed sheets. He buried his face in the pillow and debated if he could get a few more minutes of sleep before he needed to get up.

"Was that your work?" Eli asked. A hand rubbed his back, ending by ruffling the hair on his neckline. Eli was still here?

Kale pushed up on his elbows and stared at the man lying next to him. Sheets covered his lower body; his chest, which barely had a happy trail on it, caught Kale's eyes.

"You're late because of me," Eli said it, not as a question but a blunt statement. "I should get my things and go."

"Can I bother you for a ride?" Kale asked. He didn't have time to get his car from impound and he didn't like the idea of calling Charlotte back to pick him up. Having Eli take him would be easier and faster than waiting for a cab.

"Yeah," Eli said, his expression somewhat surprised. All night he'd kept looking at Kale like he expected his welcome to wear out at any moment. It was that weariness that had inclined Kale to let him stay the night. He'd still figured Eli would slip out at some point while Kale slept.

"You can shower down the hall, if you want," Kale said. He climbed out of the bed, ignoring the stiffness of his joints, and went to the adjoining bathroom.

He went through the motions of prepping for the day, while trying to recall what he could about the Blumburg case. An employee had been skimming programs and projects from the company and selling them to competitors. The guy managed to make five million before the company caught on and fired him.

If they were able to prove everything, which Kale knew they would, then Blumburg would be going to jail for a very long time and the company would lay claim to all of Blumburg's finances. He put on a black suit, slipped on his black dress shoes, and finished adjusting his gray tie as he walked down the hall.

The whirr of the coffee grinder welcomed him as he entered the kitchen. Eli jumped like a kid caught with his hand in the cookie jar.

"I found your coffee maker and figured you could use some," Eli said. Kale wasn't a fan of Eli snooping in his kitchen, but he was grateful for the coffee. He couldn't manage a thank you, since he was annoyed, so instead he pressed his lips to Eli's, smothering him in a kiss.

He tasted of coffee, with a slight twang of morning breath. Kale didn't care. Eli was an amazing kisser. Every time Kale kissed him his mind went beautifully blank. Eli's skin was still slightly damp from his own shower. Kale felt his pulse racing as he touched his neck.

"Put it in a thermos, we need to go."

"Right, okay," Eli said. He looked wide-eyed at the cupboards. Right, Eli wasn't Martin. He didn't know where everything was. Kale opened the bottom cupboard near the fridge and pulled out a thermos. He paused for a moment and stared at a red lidded to-go cup with a Texas football team's emblem on it—Martin's cup.

He grabbed the cup and thermos. He gave both to Eli. "You can use the red cup. Keep it."

If Martin was going to leave him for months at a time, he should expect some of his stuff to go missing in the meantime.

§§§

Eli had been baffled that Kale asked for a ride. He kept expecting Kale to be embarrassed of him, or at least of his car. He pulled the car up to the curb directly in front of the courthouse. He was shocked Kale hadn't asked to be dropped off a block or so away.

"Thanks for everything," Eli said. Kale was eyeing the building, perhaps reconsidering his drop off location. "If you want to do it again sometime, let me know."

Kale's dark brown eyes fixed on Eli. "Yes, I would. Pass me your number. I want to help you with your criminal charges as well."

Eli's mind whirled. When exactly was the clock going to strike midnight and change his glass slippers back into worn sneakers?

"Um, yeah, sure," Eli mumbled. Kale pulled his briefcase from the back of the car and pulled out a pad of paper. Eli scribbled his number as legibly as he could with his trembling fingers. "I can't afford a lawyer, though."

"I won't charge you," Kale said.

"You're a lawyer?" Eli asked. He'd assumed Kale did some sort of government work, since he was dropping him off at the courthouse. Lawyer did make sense.

"I'll have one of the interns take care of it for you," Kale said.

"You don't have to do that. You've already done—"

Kale reached across the car and grabbed Eli's neck, pulling him into another kiss. In broad daylight, in front of a courthouse Kale worked at. Eli looked out the windshield at the pedestrians on the sidewalk. People were glancing in their direction. Between his rusty car and the fact he was illegally parked, and now two men were inside it kissing, they were drawing a fair amount of attention.

Kale pulled away. "I want to."

It took Eli a moment to piece together that Kale was defending his stance regarding helping Eli's legal needs. Kale opened the passenger door and exited. He shut the door without further comment.

Eli put the car in gear and pulled away, eager to escape the prying eyes of the strangers on the street. It wasn't until he was waiting at his second red light that he noticed Kale had left a business card in his passenger cup holder. Eli still didn't know Kale's last name.

He picked up the card and read the name. For a moment he forgot to breathe.

Kale Sokoloff of Moroz-Kempt Legal Advisors. Kale's name wasn't part of the company's name, only two of the partners were, but Eli thought there were four partners now. They were the biggest law firm in the county, which encompassed three major cities. He'd seen them on the news more than once. Usually they did cases involving commercial business lawsuits. He thought one of the partners might do something with criminal cases on a personal level, but nothing on Eli's small scale.

The car behind him honked, and Eli looked up to see the light had turned green. He needed to buy a newspaper. If one of the Moroz-Kempt partners had assaulted three people last night, that was bound to be front-page news.

§§§

Kale sat next to Steve in the prosecutor's booth. Steve's face was flushed as he shuffled papers. He glanced up at Kale.

"Oh thank God you made it. We only have ten minutes before the judge comes back," Steve said. The courtroom was currently on break between cases.

"Of course I made it. Do you think I'm incompetent?" Kale asked.

"No," Steve said.

"Do you have all the papers?"

"Yeah, I think so."

Kale flipped through the documents as people trickled back into the courtroom.

"Are the rumors true?" Steve asked.

"What rumors?" Kale skimmed the papers, refreshing his memory.

Steve slid a newspaper across the table. Kale glanced at it. The headline included their law firm's name.

"You beat up a professor at the community college," Steve said.

"I didn't know he was a teacher. He was in the wrong place at the wrong time." He must have been the Good Samaritan who had tried to break up the fight.

"I heard Rich saying they are going to suspend you," Steve said. Kale's eyebrows perked up.

"They can't suspend me. I have three big profile cases. No one is prepared to pick them up for me."

"It's just what I heard," Steve said. Kale ground his teeth and tried not to think about it as their client took a seat next to him.

Two hours later, after making as much headway as possible in the trial for one day, Kale strode into the law firm's lobby. They were on the second floor of a twenty-story building. Ten offices lined the wall, one for each partner and for some of the junior partners. Desks filled the rest of the floor, mostly secretaries and interns.

Charlotte stood up at her desk, her curly red locks bouncing. Her gaudy jewelry glittered in the fluorescent lights. Today she had a turquoise necklace with gems that had to weigh enough to hurt her neck. Her earlobes sagged from the weight of the rocks dangling from her golden earrings.

"How'd it go?"

"I think the defendant is ready to settle," Kale said. "I heard I'm getting suspended."

She frowned. "You punched a professor at LCC in the face."

He tried to recall the blur of the fight from last night. Someone had come up behind him and tried to pull him away from Martin. Kale had jerked his arm back. "I think I back-elbowed him in the nose."

She flinched. "Rich is waiting for you. Good luck."

"Do you know how Martin is doing?" Kale asked.

"I'll call the hospital and see what they'll tell me," Charlotte said with a terse nod.

Kale walked down the pathway between the desks and knocked on Rich's door. He was on the phone but waved Kale in. He sat across from him and waited. Rich rubbed his too pointy nose and ruffled his comb-over, sending a few stray locks askew. Rich finished the call, and waved to someone behind Kale. Kale looked over his shoulder and saw the other two partners enter, Andy and Luke.

"Why does this feel like an intervention?" Kale asked.

"It kind of is," Luke said. He unbuttoned his suit coat and put one hand on his hip. "You made the papers, Kale."

"I didn't know he was a professor," Kale said. "He got in the way."

Andy slumped in the chair next to Kale. His Asian features sagged, making him look as unhappy as the Buddha on his desk. His slanted eyes looked everywhere but at Kale.

Luke leaned forward, his military hairstyle and upbringing taking charge as he confronted Kale.

"You did this in a public place. We can't make this disappear," Luke said.

"There's videos on the internet," Andy said, his tone sounding bored.

"It wasn't smart attacking him on a college campus," Rich said.

"Oh, I'm sorry," Kale said. "My other options were a daycare and a Catholic nunnery. I figured the campus was the lesser evil."

"That's not what I meant and you know it," Rich said.

"We already worked a deal with the judge. So we can keep this from going to trial," Luke said. "We talked them down quite a bit."

"I heard I'm being suspended."

"Twenty hours of anger management therapy. Ten hours one on one with a counselor and ten in group therapy," Rich said. He slid a paper across his desk. "Fifty hours of community service. You're suspended until you complete the community service and therapy. The counselor needs to give you a clean bill of health and say you aren't a danger to anyone."

"If she doesn't," Luke said, crossing his arms. "You'll need to attend a month long camp for anger management training."

"And," Andy said, "you'll be paying the medical bills of everyone involved, including the damages to the property."

"I have to buy Wayne a new car?" That part outraged him the most. He didn't want to buy that prick a new car for him to fuck Kale's boyfriend in.

"Yes," Luke said. "You will buy Wayne a new car. Unless you'd rather he press charges and take you to court so you can buy him a new house."

Kale clenched his fists, sending a burning ache through his knuckles.

"Who's taking my cases?"

"Luke will take your high profile cases. Norton will take the rest," Rich said.

"Norton Shadwick?" Kale asked. He was a lazy oaf. He'd do nothing but put Kale's cases in a desk drawer, if he bothered to touch them at all.

"He's the only one who has a caseload light enough to handle them," Rich said. "Your intern will help him."

At least Steve was capable. Hopefully he'd make sure things got accomplished.

"None of your cases are scheduled for court in the next two weeks. If you put some effort into it, you should be back by then," Rich said. "Luke should just need to do the prep work."

It was feasible. Since he wasn't able to work or speak to Martin, thanks to the restraining order, he'd have no distractions to keep him from completing the therapy and volunteer work.

"Okay, yeah, it sounds doable."

"Spend the rest of the day getting Luke and Norton up to speed on your cases, then get out of here," Rich said. "Keep out of trouble and do your community service. We can put this behind us, Kale."

"I know that," Kale said, slightly harsher than he intended.

The three of them departed Rich's office and Kale bee-lined for Charlotte's desk.

"Martin?" Kale asked.

"He was released last night. So was the professor. I couldn't get much, it sounded like some fractures and bruises, nothing too serious. The professor's face is pretty busted up, so I imagine we'll see him on the news."

"I probably broke his nose." He hated to ask but knew he needed too. "Wayne?"

She took a deep breath. "He was in a coma overnight. He woke up a few hours ago. He's in pretty rough shape."

That was going to be the problem. Wayne. Hopefully, Martin could prevent Wayne from refusing the deal Rich had arranged. The professor would have the sympathy vote, but in the larger picture he would get nothing. He was an idiot who had voluntarily charged into a fistfight. He knew Martin wouldn't press charges himself, and in a few weeks he'd be back and this would all be behind them.

"I hit Wayne pretty hard with a tire iron," Kale said, leaving out that he'd hit him about a dozen times before Martin had managed to pull him off. "Can you put me together a list of volunteer places? I have to do some, part of the settlement."

"How many hours?"

"Fifty."

She nodded, keeping a firm expression like she'd find him the best darn volunteer work possible. He spent the rest of the day going over cases with Luke first, then Norton. He didn't waste much time with Norton since he knew nothing would be accomplished. He told Steve to do his best to keep Norton on track.

He stopped by Jesus' office last. He was a junior partner, and he'd probably never be more than that. He preferred to help the small businesses and underdogs. Kale knew Jesus would never make it far in their business with that kind of attitude.

"Jesus?" Kale asked, knocking on the door.

"Hey, come in," Jesus said, closing a binder and pushing it to the side. Jesus was a devout Catholic, emphasized by the Virgin Mary statue sitting on top of his shelf behind his desk. Kale eyed it warily before he sat. Jesus' parents were immigrants from Mexico. Kale figured that was why Jesus had such empathy for the poorer class. He did more pro bono cases than the rest of the firm combined.

Kale normally avoided him. Although Jesus was friendly to everyone, Kale included. He'd been cornered a few times and forced to endure the "your lifestyle is sinful" speech. Kale hadn't paid enough attention to know which part bothered Jesus the most. The homosexual nature of it, premarital sex, or the abuse he inflicted on his partner.

"I need your help with a case," Kale said. He pulled out a scratch paper he'd transferred Eli's name and number to.

"I thought Luke and Norton were taking all of your cases," Jesus said.

"They are. This is something else. I met a guy last night while in lockup." He paused but saw no judgment on Jesus' face. "He was arrested by Lorainekson and I think he is exaggerating the charges to be more than they should be because the client is homosexual."

Lorainekson not only hated gays, he hated anyone who wasn't white. Jesus had worked a few cases where he'd gotten charges dropped because Lorainekson was targeting people for their nationality. Jesus might think all gays were doomed to go to hell, but he sympathized with them in this area.

"Gotta love Lorainekson," Jesus said. He took the paper. "What are the charges?"

"Petty theft and possession. He was wearing a friend's coat that had prescription pills in it. His bail was set at two grand."

"That's crazy high," Jesus said.

"They think he's a flight risk."

Jesus shook his head. "Any priors?"

Kale realized he hadn't asked. "Not sure, but I think it was his first time in jail."

"If it is, then I can probably get this case dismissed. Sounds like he was being harassed. I'll throw around some accusations, like he might have had the stolen merchandize planted on him, and I bet the merchant backs off. Do you know what he was stealing?"

All good questions Kale should have asked. "No. I didn't ask."

Jesus nodded. "I'll find out."

"Thanks," Kale said. He stood to leave.

"Hey, Kale. Get better," Jesus said.

"I'm not sick," Kale said, trying to keep his tone light.

"I know. But you should use this incident as an opportunity to improve yourself. Don't just go through the motions."

Kale forced a smile and thanked him again. Improve himself. He resisted the urge to ask if Jesus thought he should hit up a homosexual reform camp after anger management camp.

Charlotte handed him the list of volunteer sites as he prepared to head out.

"I also scheduled your first appointment with the court appointed therapist for Monday." She handed him an appointment reminder card.

"Thanks." He tucked it in his pocket and tried to recall if he'd forgotten anything. His car. "Can you give me a ride to the impound lot?"

"Of course, I'm about to head out myself." She busied herself with arranging items on her desk, tucking everything away for the day. She picked up her coat and paused, her brow creased. "How did you get in this morning without your car?"

"A friend gave me a ride."

"At nine in the morning?" She tilted her head, knowing full well that his limited amount of friends all had day jobs. Not to mention most of them had stopped talking to him after his last fight with Martin had resulted in their breakup.

"You don't know all of my friends," Kale said. She narrowed her eyes, as if she hoped to pluck the information from his mind by sheer force.

"A new friend?" she asked, her tone hopeful.

"I wasn't aware I needed to run new acquaintances by you," Kale said. She smiled, amplifying the laugh lines on her face.

"I'm glad. You need a new friend." She grabbed her purse and he followed her out, grateful her inquisition was over.

CHAPTER FOUR

Kale dove wholeheartedly into his volunteer work. He spent his Friday night sorting cans at a food bank, right up until they closed. Five of his mandatory fifty hours done.

He signed up to help with the setup for a marathon race Saturday afternoon, an easy three more hours. That left his morning free to do what he wanted.

He went to Tasty Treats bakery in the Chambers Mall. A different mall than the one Eli had been arrested in. He stood patiently in line until it was his turn. A white aproned, freckled teen asked to take his order. Kale surveyed the pastries as if he was interested in them.

"Is Brandi working?" Kale asked, as nonchalant as possible.

"She's in the back," freckle boy replied.

"May I speak to her?"

The boy hesitated.

"I'm a family friend. If she's busy I can just go back to her," Kale offered. He moved around the counter, pushing past the waist high door meant to keep customers out.

"I don't think you're allowed back there," freckled boy said, too late to stop Kale. Kale walked into the back of the bakery, next to the rows of ovens. Brandi rolled some dough on the stainless steel table, her blond hair bundled under her hairnet. She looked up at Kale with the same blue eyes Martin had. She was Martin in female form—they were fraternal twins.

Fear sparked in her eyes, quickly replaced by anger. "Get out," she growled.

Kale crossed his arms. "I just want to know how he's doing. I know the restraining order was your idea, by the way."

"How he's doing is none of your business. He wants you out of his life, Kale. What will it take for you to understand that?"

"He always comes back," Kale said.

"Not this time, you went too far. Now, get out." She approached him with a rolling pin in one hand. The idea of her actually striking him with it was ludicrous.

"Tell me how he is and I'll go."

"Go or I'll call the cops."

He narrowed his eyes, his temper rising at her threat. "I can do a lot of damage before the cops get here."

"So can I," she countered, holding the wooden rolling pin like a bat. He stepped forward to the challenge and grabbed the pin as she swung, yanking it from her grasp. She tossed a handful of flour at him like an angry child.

"You bitch," Kale said, wiping the flour from his face. She stepped to the side, near the ovens. She stuck her tongue out at him like she wanted it.

Maybe she was egging him on, hoping he'd strike her so she could add it to the charges already piled against him. Brandi would try to file charges, but Martin would talk her out of it. Watching the skin on Brandi's face swell from his fist would be worth whatever added community service hours he had to do.

He swung. And the sneaky bitch was ready for it. She swung open the oven door, using it as a shield. Pain erupted in his hand and glass sliced into his wrist as he punched through it. He instinctively yanked his hand back, cutting it worse on the fractured glass in the process.

Blood gushed from the wound freely. Kale stared at it in shock.

"Kenny, call 911," Brandi shouted. Kale wondered if Kenny was the freckled kid. Brandi wrapped a towel around Kale's arm. He flinched as she pressed on it. "I think you cut an artery." Her eyes were wide, a new kind of fear in them. "I didn't think you'd break the glass."

§§§

The ambulance took Kale to a hospital an hour away since Martin's boyfriend Wayne was in the closer hospital. Kale was in surgery for two hours. Bits of glass were embedded in his arm and he'd severed a main artery. Three fingers were broken in his hand, in multiple locations. At least six pins were implanted in his wrist and fingers, two of which would remain permanently. He awoke, late Saturday, with a plaster cast up to his elbow. The doctor advised him he'd be in it for a week.

"We'll remove the temporary pins next Monday. The swelling should be down by then so we'll resize you for a different cast. At two weeks, we'll remove your external stitches and hopefully we can put you in a functional cast. We can release you tonight if you have someone to take care of you. Otherwise I'd like to keep you in the hospital until Monday," Dr. Erickson said. He pushed his wire-rimmed glasses up higher on his nose. He looked like every other doctor Kale had dealt with over the years. Overworked and exhausted, with black circles under his eyes for emphasis.

Spending the entire weekend in the hospital for a wrist injury seemed crazy. He hated hospitals, something he figured he shared with the general populace.

"I have a friend who can stay with me. No problem," Kale lied.

"They'll need to pick you up and sign a release form," Dr. Erickson said.

Kale picked at the tubes in his arm and glanced at his roommate, some poor fella with his leg hung from the ceiling in a full cast. He really didn't want to stay here and endure the guests and friendly banter his roommate would likely require.

"Not a problem," Kale said.

"Good. I'll have the nurses prepare your paperwork." Dr. Erickson exited the room. Kale wasn't sure what all drugs they were pumping into him, but at the moment his arm didn't hurt. It was hard to keep his eyes open though. He scrolled through the contacts on his phone.

He tried Martin's number. Perhaps Martin would come back if he knew Kale was injured. Brandi was certain to have told him about the incident. The call went to voicemail. He considered calling Charlotte, but she wasn't going to lie for him, and she had a husband who wasn't going to be keen on letting Kale spend the weekend with them. Anyone else from the law firm was likely to suggest he stay in the hospital.

He scrolled through his short list of friends, all of which had taken Martin's side in the last argument they'd had. He tried a few numbers, but no one answered.

He took a deep breath and tried to organize his fuzzy thoughts. He doubted his jailbird friend would dedicate the weekend to taking care of him, but Kale might be able to convince him to pick him up at the hospital. And subsequently lie to the doctors and claim to watch over him for the weekend. Kale had paid his bail, and likely gotten his criminal charges dropped. He'd earned the right to bum one more ride from him and solicit a small white lie.

§§§

Eli read the playbill for the sixth time. He shifted uncomfortably in the plastic seat and looked at the curtain concealing the stage, wishing the first graders' play would start already.

He'd arrived early to impress Jackie. The downside was the extra twenty minutes he had to sit in the torturous chairs. The play was five minutes away and most of the parents were just now arriving. The gymnasium, which doubled for a theatre if the occasion called for it, was half full, most of the folding chairs taken. He counted a hundred people, easy.

Jackie wore the biggest grin he'd seen in a long time as she walked down the aisle and spotted him. Her thick brown locks were pulled back in a ponytail. Her figure was still a good fifty pounds under her ideal weight, but she concealed it beneath baggy clothes. Despite it all, tonight she glowed with a healthy energy.

She gave him a strong hug, taking his air away for a moment. She released him and took the seat next to him.

"You made it. Anabelle is going to be so excited," Jackie said. She wasn't wearing any makeup, she rarely did anymore. He missed that. She'd used to put so much effort into her appearance. She'd been radiant. At twenty-two she looked nearly forty; deep lines were permanently etched in her face, most of which Eli blamed himself for.

"I know how important this is to Anabelle," Eli said. She offered him a warm smile and Eli leaned back in the seat, trying to hide how uncomfortable he was.

"So how have you been?" She took off her jacket and covered the back of her chair with it.

"Good." He decided against telling her about his brief stint in county jail or his one-night stand with a lawyer who had been in the paper. No doubt she would have loved the gossip, but tonight was not about his misadventures.

His phone vibrated in his pocket. He pulled it out as the lights flickered in the gym, indicating the play was about to start. Parents hushed each other and some pulled out their phones so they could use them to record their child's performance.

"Hello?" Eli said, not bothering to check the incoming caller's number.

"Eli? It's Kale." His words were slightly slurred like perhaps he was drunk.

"Kale?" He replied stupidly, immediately hating himself for the idiotic response.

"We met a few nights ago," Kale said, evidently assuming Eli had forgotten him.

"Yeah, I know. I remember you." *Oh yes, this conversation is improving.* "Can you hold on a minute?" He looked at Jackie who had raised an eyebrow. Her green eyes sparkled with curiosity. He mouthed an "I'll be right back" to her and ducked out of the gymnasium before the play started.

After he'd received a call from a lawyer other than Kale, but from Kale's workplace, Eli had taken the hint that Kale wasn't interested. Kale's slurred speech indicated that perhaps Eli's status had been raised to drunken booty call. He had more self-respect than that, no matter how hot Kale was.

"Listen Kale, I'm at an event right now. Can I call you back?" Eli said. He wanted to add, "Can I call you back in the morning when you're sober?"

"I'm in the hospital," Kale said. His words were so slurred it took Eli a moment to decipher what he'd said.

"Are you okay?" He tightened his grip on the phone, eternally grateful he hadn't spouted the accusation about Kale being drunk.

"My arm's messed up. Doctors won't release me unless someone comes to pick me up. Need a ride. Hate to ask you, but I was hoping."

"Which hospital?"

"Saint Mary's."

"Okay, um." He looked at the doors of the gym and considered his options. Would Kale mind waiting a few hours so he could watch the play? "I sort of have a prior commitment though. Would you…" Images of Kale from their night together flashed in his mind. He shivered and his throat clenched. The idea of Kale, injured and in need of his aid cut him to his core.

"I'm not going anywhere," Kale said. "Take your time."

"Are you sure?" Eli asked. Kale sounded pretty drugged, so even if it took Eli hours to get there, he doubted Kale would realize.

"Yeah, it's fine, thanks," Kale said. The call disconnected. Eli stared at it for a moment. Was there no one else for Kale to call? Maybe not, if beating people up was a regular thing for him.

He slunk back into the gymnasium and avoided looking into Jackie's inquisitive eyes.

§§§

Eli reached the nurse's station at slightly after nine that night. It'd taken him longer than he'd wanted to get there. Jackie had berated him with questions when he'd said he needed to leave to get a friend at the hospital. The way she'd emphasized *friend* had indicated she suspected there was more to the story.

He'd refused to give up any information.

He waited for one of the nurses to notice him. One with dark bags under her eyes glanced up. "Yes?"

"I'm here to pick up Kale." His mind blanked on Kale's last name. The nurse raised an eyebrow and stared at him, waiting for him to finish. "Give me a second. I have a business card here somewhere."

"Are you Martin?" a different nurse asked. She had a pen tucked behind her ear and looked a decade older than the first nurse he'd spoken too.

"No, I'm Eli," he said. "But that sounds like my Kale."

"Hot tempered cantankerous ass?" the nurse asked with a grin.

"Definitely my Kale," Eli said. He didn't know why, but he loved the sound of calling Kale his. He would gladly stand here all night and reassure the nurses of his claim.

"He's been babbling about a Martin," she said. "I'm glad someone came for him. I've been slipping him a few extra pills to keep him amiable."

"Fine by me," Eli said. She placed a stack of papers on the counter.

"You'll need to fill out these release papers. Let me know the pharmacy you want to go to and we'll call in his prescriptions. Will you be staying with him over the weekend?"

"Um, no. I'm just giving him a ride." Kale hadn't mentioned anything more than that. Kale had to have someone else to take care of him, right? "I'll make sure someone else is with him before I leave though."

"Good enough for me," the nurse said. She looked to the younger nurse. "Cindy, go get Kale ready."

He filled out the paperwork and slid it back to her. "What happened to him?"

"He broke several bones in his hand, fractured his radial, cut an artery that had to be surgically repaired, and received about eighteen stitches total. Story is, he punched through a glass window. He'll be in a cast for six to eight weeks."

Whose window? Eli didn't ask, but he wondered if it had to do with Martin. She handed him a slip of paper.

"These are the drugs you'll be picking up, an antibiotic, a pain inhibitor, and a muscle relaxer. I'd prescribe something to help you deal with his temper but I'm no miracle worker. You can go see him, room 214."

"Thanks." Eli tucked the paper in his pocket and headed to the directed room. He knocked on the door and entered. Cindy was helping Kale put on his shirt.

"I've got it. I'm fine," Kale said. The anger in his tone rooted Eli to the ground. The nurse stepped to the side and crossed her arms. Kale floundered with the shirt. He had it on one arm and over his neck. The arm through the sleeve had a cast up to his elbow.

"Kale?" Eli asked. Kale looked up, his good arm still clutching the shirt.

"Eli?" Kale asked. His brow wrinkled and he stared at him. "What are you doing here?"

"You called me for a ride."

"Oh yeah." He slumped, looking defeated. "When they said someone was here to get me, I thought it was Martin."

Eli forced himself forward. "Let me help you." If he could dress a six-year-old he could get a grown man dressed. He rolled up the shirt and guided Kale's arm through the sleeve.

"I'm sorry about having to call you."

"It's no problem," Eli said. Cindy reclaimed her position in assisting Kale and put his right arm in a sling.

"I'll get a wheelchair," Cindy said. She darted out of the room.

"You look good," Kale said. His words were slurring again like they had on the phone, as if his flair of anger at the nurse had cleared his senses for a moment and now they were succumbing once more to the drugs.

"Thanks."

Kale's good arm reached up and grabbed Eli behind the neck. He mashed his lips against Eli's. The kiss was sloppy and hard. His beard had grown back and scratched Eli's chin. Kale groaned and slipped his tongue into Eli's mouth. Kale pulled back enough to let Eli catch his breath.

"I missed you." Kale kissed him again before Eli could reply. "Taste so good."

"Kale, we shouldn't—" Kale bit his lip and pushed against his mouth harder before he could finish. Eli wasn't used to displaying this kind of affection in public. In fact, he wasn't used to anyone finding him this irresistible. He wanted to tell himself it was the drugs Kale was on, but Kale had acted similarly the last time he'd seen him.

The nurse cleared her throat and Kale released him.

"Sorry," Eli mumbled, stepping back from Kale so he couldn't grab him again.

"Love making you blush," Kale said.

The nurse thankfully ignored Kale's comment. "You can pull your car around to the south entrance. I'll bring him there."

Eli nodded and quickly exited the room. His entire body twitched as he walked to the parking lot. *You're just giving him a ride home,*

Eli. Martin is coming back and Kale's high right now. You can't believe anything he says. But still, Eli couldn't help but soar from his own high at the fact Kale had missed him.

§§§

Cindy helped Eli get Kale into his car. He offered his thanks, since Kale didn't seem about to. He got in the driver's side and reached over to buckle Kale in.

Kale took the opportunity to trap him in another embrace. Eli pulled away, hoping he wouldn't offend.

"I need to get you home," Eli said.

"Why is kissing you so good?" Kale asked. He pulled on Eli's hair, trying to force him back.

"Probably not as good as kissing Martin," Eli said. He didn't want to get attached to Kale, and listening to Kale ramble about how much he wanted Eli was too much for him to endure. He saw pain flash in Kale's cloudy eyes. He didn't reply, but released Eli's hair.

Eli put the car in gear and pulled away from the curb. They drove in silence for a few miles and Eli thought perhaps he'd fallen asleep. He got on the freeway and considered turning on the radio.

"We need to get off on exit fourteen," Kale said, his voice clearer than before.

"Why?" They needed to stay on the freeway for another eight exits to reach Kale's apartment.

"Just do it."

"Not unless you tell me why."

The exit in question was quickly approaching.

"It's where we need to go."

Eli tried to think of what could be at that exit. He saw the exit ramp and Kale's arm reached across to grab the steering wheel. Eli's heart missed a beat as Kale jerked the steering wheel and pulled them onto the ramp. Eli laid on the horn and slammed on the brakes, pulling them to the side of the road. Luckily, traffic was thin and only one car honked back and swerved around them.

Eli turned on the hazard lights and put the car in park. "What are you doing? You're going to get us killed."

"Not if you go where I say."

"Tell me why? Is this about Martin?"

Kale slumped back in his seat and crossed his arms as best he could with his sling.

"He needs to know I was in the hospital. If he knows I'm hurt, he'll come back," Kale said.

"If I recall properly, Martin is injured himself. He's in no condition to take care of you."

"Then who's going to?" Kale looked at him, fear and pain evident on his face. "I need him." He wiped at his face. Eli tensed. *Was he crying?*

"I will," Eli said. His mind jumbled as he mentally tried to rearrange his schedule so he could spend the rest of the weekend with Kale.

"I can't ask you do that," Kale said.

"But do you want me to?" He turned in his seat so he could face Kale. He waited for an answer.

"You're just helping me because you feel obligated to, because I paid your bail."

"And you got my criminal charges dropped. Jesus called me."

"Just drop me at my apartment. I'll figure the rest out." At least their destination was back on track.

"I like you, Kale. I want to help you because I like you, not because of any obligation."

He swore though if Kale said that line about still being with Martin, he might leave him right here on the side of the road.

"Okay," Kale said. He touched his sling with his fingers. "My arm hurts."

"I'm sure it does. Whose window did you break?"

He waited for a response, but when he didn't get one he put the car back in drive and pulled onto the freeway. They drove the rest of the way in silence. Eli clenched his jaw and hoped Kale was too drugged to remember any of their conversation.

CHAPTER FIVE

Eli pulled into the same parking spot he'd used last time. Kale's eyes were closed and Eli assumed he slept. He turned the car off and stared at his steering wheel for a moment. He wasn't sure how involved he wanted to be in Kale's drama.

Eli took a deep breath and exited the car. He opened Kale's door. He really didn't want to wake him, but they couldn't stay in the car all night. He gently nudged Kale's shoulder.

"M-martin?" Kale asked.

"We're at your apartment," Eli said, not bothering to correct him. Kale blinked his eyes and rubbed his face with his good hand. He flinched and touched the cast on his right arm.

"I'm sorry," Kale said.

"For what?"

"Almost getting us killed on the freeway."

"Apology accepted. Can you walk? We need to get you into your apartment."

Kale climbed out of the car, moving in slow motion and grabbing the roof of the car for stability.

"Let me help, lean on me," Eli suggested. Kale draped his uninjured arm over Eli's shoulders and slumped against him.

"You're better," Kale said. Eli figured he'd misspoken and was trying to say something like, "you'd better."

"Better what?" Eli asked.

"Better at kissing than Martin is."

Eli's cheeks burned and he was grateful none of Kale's neighbors were outside. Kale wasn't exactly whispering in his drugged state.

"Sure. I bet you're just saying that to get me to take care of you," Eli said. They started toward the apartment entrance and Eli wondered how well Kale would handle the steps.

"I'm not. You're better." Kale leaned more against him and Eli nearly stumbled. His lips found Eli's and smothered him in another sloppy kiss. Eli managed to free himself enough to speak.

"Later, okay? I promise to give you all the kisses you want, once we are inside your apartment," Eli lied. He planned to quietly make an exit and sleep on the couch once he got Kale to fall asleep.

They took the steps one at a time. Kale gripped the railing at Eli's insistence. They reached the landing between the first and second floor and Eli paused to settle his nerves.

The smell hit him first. Someone had overindulged in perfume. It reminded Eli of when he'd visited his grandmother in the nursing home.

"Well, it's about time," a woman said from above them. An older woman, perhaps in her seventies, descended the stairs. She wore a long blue dress with a pattern that Eli thought might be flowers but was too faded to discern. Her pearl necklace glinted in the light as she passed under one of the bulbs.

"Mrs. Abbott," Kale said.

"It's nice to see you coming home in a cast for once. I'd like to shake the hand of the man who finally knocked you down a peg." She put her hands on her hips and surveyed Kale, probably looking for signs of more damage.

"Mrs. Abbott lives above my apartment," Kale said.

"Indeed I do. It's the perfect vantage point to bear witness to the terror you've put Martin through." She looked at Eli, her blue eyes piercing into his. "You've no idea the horrors I've heard through these walls."

"I'm sure you're quite popular at Halloween. You do tell a good tale," Kale said.

"You and I both know—"

"That you're an old has-been who pokes her nose where it shouldn't be," Kale said. "Keep walking, Mrs. Abbot, lest you fall down these stairs."

"Impudent child." She gaped at him, more insulted than afraid. "If you ever struck me I'd have you in jail for life."

"Not if you're dead." Kale stepped toward her, all grogginess from the drugs seemingly gone. Eli stepped between them and pushed on Kale's chest.

"Leave her be," Eli said. Kale's eyes went from Mrs. Abbott to Eli.

"He hasn't struck you, yet, has he?" Mrs. Abbott asked. "You wouldn't be so bold to jump in the path of his fists if he had."

Eli pushed Kale back, not hard but enough to make him move so Mrs. Abbott would have room to pass.

"You should really be on your way," Eli said. "Before I decide to push you down these stairs myself."

Eli would never actually do such a thing, but since insults from Kale didn't seem to faze her, he hoped one from him would. For all he knew, Kale would follow through on his threats and Eli wanted to prevent that.

"Disrespectful lot, aren't you? I hope Martin doesn't come back this time. This one is much more your taste, Mr. Sokoloff."

Sokoloff. Eli repeated the name in his head, trying to memorize how to pronounce it. She passed them. Eli used his body as a barrier between them, until she was safely at the bottom of the stairs.

"I can't believe you said that," Kale said. Eli turned back to him.

"I needed to get rid of her," Eli said. "Come on."

He tried to ignore the wide-eyed expression on Kale's face. He wasn't sure how to interpret it. Was Kale shocked and horrified? Or impressed? He doubted Martin would ever threaten an old lady. They reached Kale's apartment and Eli took Kale's keys to unlock it.

Eli couldn't help but breathe a sigh of relief once they were inside. He pulled the prescription drugs from his pockets and put them on the counter.

"I need to take a shower," Kale announced.

"I think it would be better if you took some of your meds and went to bed."

"I have hospital germs on me. I'm not sleeping in my bed until I'm clean." Kale tugged on his shirt as if the germs were causing him pain. "You'll need to help me."

The spark in his eyes told Eli there was likely to be more than washing involved in the shower.

§§§

Kale awoke to intense pain. His right arm throbbed and burned as if fire ants were chewing his skin down to the bone. The noise he uttered didn't sound human. His eyes bulged and he grabbed his injured arm with his good, an instinct to apply pressure to the wound.

Touching it did not help.

He cursed and stared at the white cast that encompassed his forearm. He tried to move his swollen fingers and they barely responded. Tremors of pain shot up his arm and he squirmed in his bed.

Footsteps came from the hall outside his bedroom.

"Martin?" Kale asked, even though he knew that was unlikely. He blinked his eyes, clearing the tears from his vision.

"Eli," the man standing in his doorway said. The casual way he corrected Kale made him wonder how many times he'd endured being called the wrong name.

"Why are you here?" Kale asked. Eli moved forward, his eyes focused on Kale's arm.

"You need to elevate it," Eli said. He gently put a hand under the cast and urged Kale to raise it. "We need to get the blood to drain out of your hand."

Eli raised Kale's hand over Kale's head.

"Can you hold it here? I'll get you your pills," Eli said.

"Yes."

Eli darted from the room. Kale tried to recall what had occurred yesterday but the drugs they'd given him had done a number on his memory. Eli returned, holding an icepack in one hand and a glass of water with a straw in the other.

Eli arranged a pillow above Kale's head so he could rest his arm on it. He packed the ice pack on top. Eli placed four pills in Kale's hand.

"What are these?"

"Two are pain inhibitors, one is a muscle relaxer, and the other is to prevent infection," Eli said. The words were an undecipherable blur to Kale's ragged mind. He took them anyway.

Eli wiped at Kale's forehead with a damp cloth. Kale was covered in sweat. He wasn't sure when Eli had retrieved the towel. Kale decided he must still be loopy from the drugs.

"I need to call my secretary. I have appointments on Monday that I need to cancel."

"I can call her if you want, just pass me her number," Eli said.

"I'd rather call her myself," Kale said. "Can you hand me my phone?"

"It's four in the morning on a Sunday," Eli said. He put the cloth on the side table and peered into Kale's eyes. "How are you feeling? Do you want something to eat?"

"Why are you here?" Kale asked.

"You called me when you were in the hospital. You asked me to give you a ride home."

"And you're still here because?"

"I couldn't leave you alone. The doctors said someone should stay with you and you weren't able to tell me who I should call."

"Martin," Kale said. "Give me my phone and we'll call him."

Eli frowned. "I don't think he's going to answer."

"Well, we won't know until we try."

"It's four in the morning, Kale."

The drugs were making him tired. He struggled to keep his eyes open. "You shouldn't have to do this."

"I don't mind. What's your secretary's name? I'll call her when it's a more decent hour."

"Charlotte," Kale said. He gave in to the sleep tugging at him and closed his eyes. "Give me my phone and I'll unlock it for you."

He forced his eyes open as Eli placed his phone in Kale's hand. He punched in the code and handed the phone back to Eli. He managed to mumble a thank you before he fell asleep.

§§§

Eli settled back on the couch in Kale's living room after he was confident Kale was asleep. He clicked through the channels on Kale's television. He kept the volume low enough that he would hear Kale if he awoke again. At eight, he called Kale's secretary.

"Hello?" A woman answered.

"Uh, hi, is this Charlotte?" Eli fumbled nervously with the television remote.

"Yes, who is this?"

"Eli. I'm a friend of Kale's. He asked me to call you." This was answered with silence so Eli decided to continue. "I'm sorry for calling you on a Sunday. He said you were his secretary and that you could cancel his appointments for Monday."

"Why does he need to cancel them?"

"He was in an accident last night. He'll be fine. He injured his wrist and he's on some heavy painkillers for a few days."

"Was Martin involved? Is Martin okay?"

Eli's stomach twisted. He hadn't thought of that. He'd considered that Martin might have been part of the window breaking, but it hadn't occurred to him that Martin might be worse off than Kale.

"From what I understand, Kale punched a window. Kale wasn't arrested so I don't think anyone else was involved, but I don't know."

"I'll make some calls and make sure. What did you say your name was?"

"Eli Pendza."

"Are you with Kale?"

"Yes." He shifted on the couch, unsure of the multiple interpretations her question and his answer could have.

"I'll call you back when I know more, and I'll make sure his appointments are canceled. Will he be able to attend them on Tuesday?"

"I don't know. He just mentioned the ones on Monday."

"Ask him."

"He's asleep right now."

"Who did you say you were?"

Eli rolled his eyes and leaned back on the couch. Everyone seemed hung up on the same thing, this "Martin" guy, so Eli decided he could either embrace it or be buried by it.

"Eli. I'm the new Martin," he said. He grinned at his own joke. The grin broadened into a smile as he heard something that sounded like an object being dropped on the other end of the line.

"I see, um, so you're…um." She struggled for words and Eli almost felt sorry for her.

"Having sex with Kale but not yet being hit by him, correct," Eli said. "So you'll call me back later when you know more about what happened, yes? And I'll let you know if Kale can make his other appointments. Okay?"

"Yes. That sounds, fine. Thank you. For calling me, I mean."

"No problem." Eli hung up before their conversation could become anymore awkward. Saying those things to Kale's secretary hadn't been his wisest decision, but he figured once Kale had his senses about him Eli wouldn't be around to see the repercussions anyway.

He went into the kitchen and searched the pantries for food. He figured a little free food was the least Kale could do in payment of his babysitting him.

The pain woke him again. Kale had dropped his arm at some point during his slumber. He managed to keep from crying out this time. He lifted his arm, using his good one to help. He placed it back on the pillow by his head.

He opened his mouth to call for Martin. No. Not Martin. He took a deep breath.

"Eli?"

Footsteps shuffled down the hall and his blond-haired, blue-eyed keeper appeared in the doorway. He already held another icepack and this time an entire pitcher of water.

"Feeling better?"

"Yes," Kale said. Eli handed him some pills, but Kale waved them away. "Half the dose for the painkillers."

"Are you sure?"

"I don't like how loopy they are making me."

Eli nodded and handed him three pills. Kale swallowed them and finished the glass of water. He realized he needed to urinate. "I need to use the bathroom."

"Okay, do you want me to help you?"

"No."

Kale pulled back the sheets and sat up. He waited a moment until the room stopped spinning.

"Leave the door unlocked, okay? In case you fall or something."

"Are you a nurse?" Kale asked. He realized he'd never asked Eli what his profession was. Eli's skin flared crimson and Kale's heart quickened. Even with disheveled hair and creases on his face from having just awoken, Eli was attractive.

"No. I've taken care of people before, though."

"Lucky them." Unable to resist, Kale grabbed Eli's shirt collar and pulled him in for a kiss. "I'm glad you're here."

"Me too," Eli said, his breathing hard. Eli's eyes darted down to Kale's crotch and Kale fought the urge to grin. "Do you want me to get you something to eat?"

"What do you suggest?"

Eli grew redder. "Some broth."

Hmm, so not going there, although it was evident Eli's mind was. "Sounds good. I'll be out in a minute."

"You don't want to eat in bed?"

"No." Memories of Martin trying to bring Kale soup in bed when he had the flu rushed to his mind. Those events had almost always ended badly. Martin was clumsy and although he doubted such was the case with Eli, he didn't want to take any chances.

"Okay, I'll get some ready." Eli left the room. Kale took his time crossing the bedroom to the bathroom. He relieved himself and spent longer than intended staring at his reflection in the mirror above the sink. He considered shaving, but dismissed the idea. It wasn't like he would be seen in a courtroom anytime soon. The idea of attempting to shave with his non-dominate hand while groggy from drugs didn't sound like a good combination.

Putting on a shirt wasn't a task he was up for. He put on the sling though; his arm felt like a dead weight and the effort to lift it himself was cumbersome. He put on a pair of flannel pajama bottoms before walking down the hall to the kitchen. Eli had a bowl of soup set up for him at the dining room table. Kale sat down and gently placed his injured arm, cradled in the sling, on the table. Eating soup with his non-dominate hand wasn't going to be easy, but he refused to ask Eli to help him. If Martin were here, he would have ordered him to.

Eli sat across from him with nothing to eat in front of him.

"You aren't eating?" Kale asked.

"I ate earlier. I hope you don't mind I helped myself to your food."

He did actually, but he forced the irritation down. "Of course not. Thank you for staying and helping me. You didn't need to."

He picked up the spoon, testing how to grip it in his fingers.

"I couldn't leave you. You were in a rough state."

"I'm sure I was a jerk. I apologize for anything rude I may have said."

Eli nodded. Kale tried his first spoonful. Most of it dribbled out before it reached his mouth.

"You don't have to stay," Kale said. "I'll be fine."

"I don't mind staying. If you want me to leave, though, I will."

Kale considered his options. "I don't want you to stay out of obligation."

Eli shifted in his seat. "I'm not."

"Or pity."

"I'm not." Eli rolled his eyes this time. He leaned forward on the table. "I like you. Your food and cable are a nice bonus. I'm happy to stay if you'll have me." Eli looked at the soup. "And you can drink that if you want. There's no need to try to impress me."

Was he really okay with letting a man whom he'd met in jail stay in his apartment with him while he was drugged? Eli was supposed to be a one-night stand, nothing more. Martin was coming back.

"Okay. No pay-per-view orders, though," Kale said. Eli grinned.

CHAPTER SIX

Eli kept his eyes on the road, but every so often, he stole a glance at Kale in his passenger seat. It would take a bit before he got over his anxiety from when Kale had tried to steer the car on the freeway. Kale stared out the side window of Eli's car as they drove to his doctor appointment.

Kale was only taking a half pill of the Vicodin every six hours by Monday. He substituted an over the counter pain reliever to ease the worst of the throbbing.

Charlotte confirmed no one else had been injured in Kale's incident, but said nothing more. She'd also told him Kale's car was back in the impound lot. Until Kale decided to get it out, Kale's unemployed friend with benefits, Eli, offered to give him rides. Eli took a deep breath and repeated his self-imposed relationship description to himself again. *Not boyfriend, you may not fall for him.* A swarm of butterflies stirred in his stomach, as if to voice their difference in opinion on the matter.

"We need to make a stop on the way to the doctor's office," Kale said. Eli glanced at the clock on the dash. They had a good thirty minutes to spare.

"Where?"

Kale gave him directions, but didn't say where they were going. They pulled into the parking lot of a mall.

"Park at the north entrance," Kale said. Eli found a spot, put the car in park, and cut the engine. Kale exited the car and started for the entrance before Eli could ask for more of an explanation.

Eli jogged to catch up to him. Kale had his arm in a sling and was sweating. Eli really thought he should be taking more of the painkillers than he was. They entered the mall and Eli continued following Kale until they reached a bakery.

"I need you to go inside and order me a coffee," Kale said. He handed Eli some money. "You can get yourself whatever you want."

"We passed other bakeries on the drive here," Eli said. "Why did we have to go to this one?"

"I like this one," Kale said. "I'll wait over there."

Kale went to a two-seater round table across from the store, but viewable through the windows of the bakery. Eli folded the money and tucked it in his jean's pocket. He entered the store and inhaled the sweet aromas of baked goods.

He was third in line. He scanned the goods in the glass display case as he waited. He figured he should get something to eat, since Kale was buying.

"He's here," the male cashier said in a singsong voice. Eli glanced up at him, wondering who had caught their attention.

"Where?" A woman bustled through the doors that led to the kitchen and surveyed the occupants in the store.

"Outside, sitting," the cashier said. He took a deep breath. "I suppose we can't call the cops on him for that."

The lady in front of Eli stepped to the side and looked at Eli. "I'm not ready, go ahead."

The cashier handed a cup of coffee to the person at the register and looked at Eli. "What can I get you?"

Eli stepped forward. "Two cups of coffee, black, and a bran muffin."

The woman moved to retrieve the muffin from the case. "I can't believe he's back already," she said. She handed Eli the muffin in a brown bag. Eli handed the money to the cashier and took the bag.

"Who are you talking about?" Eli asked. His mouth went dry as he feared he already knew the answer.

"That asshole sitting outside," the cashier said. He handed Eli his change. "He was in here two days ago and broke our oven."

"With his fist," the woman added. She placed two to-go cups of coffee on the counter for him.

"Huh," Eli said, all other words escaped him. He balanced his goods and beat a hasty retreat from the bakery. He clenched his jaw as he approached Kale. He discarded the bought items on the table and glared at him. "We need to go, now."

"Why? What happened?"

"You didn't tell me this was the store where your 'accident' happened. You can't be here, Kale, they're going to call the police."

"I'm not doing anything wrong."

"You could have at least warned me what we were doing. Why are we here? What's so special about this place?"

Kale took his cup of coffee and fumbled with the lid, unable to remove it with only one good hand.

"Kale?" Eli insisted.

"What is this?" A woman's voice cut across the hall to them. Eli turned to see the woman from the bakery storm toward them. "You're hiring people to spy on me?"

Eli backed away, removing himself from in-between them as she approached. She stopped a few feet from Kale and smacked the coffee away from him. The lid popped off and spilled on the table. Kale's face turned red and he stood, his figure towering above her.

She boldly stood her ground. Eli tried to swallow but had no spit to work with.

"Eli," Kale said, his tone low, "meet Brandi, Martin's sister. You owe me a new coffee, Brandi."

"Get out."

"Did you tell Martin what happened?" Kale asked.

"Martin is no concern of yours. Get out of the mall before I call security."

"Kale, we should go," Eli said.

"He has a right to know what happened to me," Kale said.

Her face turned into a sneer and she spat in Kale's face. Eli watched in horror as the spittle landed on Kale's cheek.

Eli wasn't sure what drove his next actions but he dove between the two of them and shoved Brandi away, not hard enough to knock her over, just enough to move her out of Kale's range. He whirled and put both hands on Kale's chest. He wasn't certain he could actually restrain Kale if he charged Brandi, but he was going to try.

Kale stared at Eli, stupefied.

Eli turned back to Brandi and saw a similar expression on her face. The eruption of anger they'd all expected hadn't occurred. Eli grabbed a napkin off the table and thrust it in Kale's hand.

"Clean yourself off," Eli said. He turned to Brandi. "Go back in your shop and get us a replacement coffee. If you refuse, I'll call security myself, because from what I just saw, and the security cameras will support me, you assaulted him. Or do you want to lose your job?"

Eli crossed his arms and he stared into Brandi's eyes until she relented. "I'll be right back."

Eli turned back to Kale. "We're leaving."

Kale nodded.

They waited outside the bakery until Brandi brought out a new coffee. She handed it to Eli.

"Thank you," Eli said. He wanted to apologize to her, but he worried any display of sympathy might destroy the spell he seemed to have cast over Kale.

Why wasn't he pissed? *Why didn't he strike me or knock me out of the way so he could resume his eventual assault on Brandi?*

They walked in silence to the car and neither spoke a word the rest of the drive to the hospital.

§§§

Kale signed in at the front desk at the clinic. The receptionist handed him a stack of papers to fill out. He settled into a seat next to Eli, who had started thumbing through some of the ancient magazines littering the tables. Kale glanced at the two other people in the room with them, an elderly lady with her arm in a cast and a middle-aged man with an ace wrap on his wrist.

Kale held the pen in his left hand, knowing full well he would be unable to fill out the paperwork. His fingers on his right hand were too swollen to hold the pen and he wouldn't be able to write anything legible with his left.

If Martin were here, he would be able to fill out the paperwork for him. He would have all of the information memorized. As it was, Kale would have to verbalize everything for Eli, meaning their two waiting room companions would be listening. Kale didn't even want Eli to know him on the personal level this paperwork would require.

Kale looked at the receptionist. Maybe he could ask a nurse to help him fill it out instead, once he was taken to a room.

Eli tossed the magazine back on the coffee table and glanced at Kale.

"I hope I didn't overstep any boundaries back at the bakery," Eli said. Kale looked at the questions on the documents, trying to decide what to do.

"You didn't," Kale said. "I'm sorry for taking you there."

He placed the pen on top of the papers and sat them on the coffee table. He would have the nurse fill it out for him. Eli leaned forward and snatched up the clipboard and pen.

"Do we need to fill this out?" Eli asked.

"Yes, but—"

"But what?" Eli raised an eyebrow at him and waited. "You have some secret medical condition you don't want me knowing about?"

Kale's face burned and he yanked the papers from Eli's hands. The pen went flying under the coffee table. His world blurred red for a moment and he wasn't certain what he ended up doing with the papers. Eli was repeating his name and Kale's arm throbbed. The two senses combined and brought him back to the surface.

"I was kidding, Kale? Kale?"

Kale wiped his face and focused on the elderly woman sitting across the room. Her eyes were wide as she stared at him. The other man was gone.

"Kale?" A different voice spoke this time. Kale looked up to see a woman dressed in smocks looking into the waiting room.

"Yes," Kale said. He rose, ignoring the fact he'd lost the papers. They could print more. He glanced back at Eli but didn't look at him. "Wait here."

A gut curdling twang shot up from his stomach and throbbed through Eli's body as Kale exited the room. He'd messed up. His stupid smart mouth had bit off more than it could handle. Eli gathered up the forms and pen from the floor. He handed the crumpled mess to the receptionist with an apology. Her eyes avoided him as she took the documents.

Eli settled back into his seat and ruffled his hair. All signs indicated he would need a new couch to sleep on tonight. He texted Jackie, *I think my babysitting job is ending today.*

Her reply was instant. *Good, I was worried you may not make it Wednesday.*

Wednesday. He tried to remember what was happening on Wednesday.

Another text arrived. *My mother is flying in tonight.* Eli cringed. He would find a different couch to sleep on. Jackie's mother hated him.

Understood and yeah, I'll be there Wednesday. He sent the text as the nurse appeared in the doorway. "Eli?" she asked.

He stood and approached. "Yeah, that's me."

"Kale said to tell you not to wait for him."

"But I'm his ride," Eli said.

She shrugged. "I guess you're not anymore. He said you can leave."

So this was it. Not even a proper goodbye.

"Okay, thanks," Eli said. He wasn't about to start some scene with the nurse. If Kale wanted him gone, then fine, he would leave. He walked back to his car and tried to recall if he'd left anything in Kale's apartment. He'd been living out of his car. He kept a supply of clothes in the trunk and he'd been swapping out the clean for dirty. He'd intended to ask Kale if he could do a load of wash, but that wasn't happening now.

He got in his car and stared at the steering wheel. "Good job, Eli." He pinched his nose and tried not to let the emotions of rejection overcome him. His phone chirped.

He blinked back the tears and picked up his phone. A text from Charlotte. *Is Kale really okay to drive? He said he's picking up his car from impound.*

His stomach twisted. So that was Kale's plan. He replied. *I'll follow him home and make sure he's safe. What's the address?*

"He's not your problem anymore," Eli said aloud to himself. But he still programmed the address into his phone and drove there.

CHAPTER SEVEN

Kale pulled his car along the sidewalk, driving slowly by the front entrance to the community college. He had ten minutes before Martin's class would end. He drove up and down the rows of cars until he found a spot that provided him a good vantage point of the exit Martin normally used.

He turned the car off and waited.

A tapping on the passenger window sent his pulse racing. Had someone spotted him already? He impulsively put his hand on the keys in the ignition. Ripples of pain shot up his right arm from the gesture. He glanced at the window and saw Eli looking in at him.

Eli waved and pointed at the lock on the door. Kale pressed the unlock button with his left hand and sagged back in the seat. Eli opened the door and sat. He pulled the door closed and the ensuing silence was palpable.

"I'm sorry I told you to leave," Kale said.

"Did you send me away so you could come here alone?" Eli asked.

"This is where Martin goes to school. His class gets out in ten minutes."

"This is also the place where you beat up a professor. You shouldn't be here, Kale," Eli said. Kale gripped the steering wheel, needing to squeeze something.

"I didn't ask you to come here."

"I want to be here. I want to help you, Kale," Eli said. Kale looked ahead, watching the students trickle out of the building. Fingers brushed his arm. He jerked and looked at Eli, but Eli didn't pull his hand back. "Let me help you."

He looked in Eli's eyes for the pity, but saw something that scared him more. Care, possibly love. It hit him hard and he had to look away.

"I have to come here. I need to know he's okay."

Eli pulled his hand back. Kale refused to look at him but knew he was still there. Kale straightened in his seat as he spotted classmates from Martin's class.

"Do you see him?" Eli asked. Kale shook his head. "You roughed him up pretty badly last week, right? Are you sure he'd be back in class this soon?"

"He's attended class in worse condition," Kale said. His eyes roved from head to head, but Martin was not to be seen. His hand went to the doorknob. "I need to ask one of the classmates if they know how he is."

He pulled the latch and the door opened. Hands, stronger than he expected, grabbed his right arm, above his cast. He glanced back at Eli, who was on his knees in the passenger seat, clutching his upper arm in a death grip.

"You can't get out of the car, Kale. Those students saw you beat up three people last week. If they see you now, they'll call the police. You know that."

"I have to know how he is."

"I understand, but not this way."

Kale shifted his weight and closed the door. He kept his eyes on Eli, wondering why this man would try so hard to help him. He didn't deserve it. Especially not after the way he'd just treated him.

"We can go back to the bakery tomorrow. I can ask his sister about him, okay? How does that sound?"

Kale nodded.

"I don't want you coming here alone," Eli said. "If you want to come here and watch, that's fine, but I want to be here with you."

No one had ever offered such a thing. People told him he should leave Martin alone, that he was causing trouble. No one ever tried to negotiate his stalking tendencies into a more placid form. Or volunteer to help him do it.

§§§

Eli wiped his sweaty palms on his jeans as he entered the bakery. What he was doing was insane and self-destructive and he knew it. He was helping his new boyfriend stalk his old boyfriend. And he was falling for him hard. What would he do when Martin came back?

There was no one in line so Eli went straight to the register. The same man from Monday stood behind the counter. Eli looked him over more thoroughly today. He had a diamond stud in one ear and custom black eyeglasses.

"Two coffees, black, and one bran muffin," Eli said, keeping his voice deadpan. The man said nothing. He hit some buttons on the register and pointed to the total displayed in green letters on the screen.

"You should get an apple turnover," Brandi said as she came up front from the kitchen. "Kale likes those."

Eli nodded and the total increased. Eli handed the man enough money to cover the bill. Brandi collected the items from the display case and sat them on the counter. Her green eyes looked into his. Eli blinked first.

"How's Martin?" Eli asked. "You don't have to answer, but he wants me to ask."

The cashier sat two to-go cups on the counter and grunted.

"What exactly is your role with him?" Brandi asked.

"I'll let you know when I figure that out," Eli said.

Her expression softened slightly. "Thank you."

"You're welcome," Eli said, figuring she was doing her duty of thanking a customer for shopping at the store.

"He hasn't called Martin since Saturday. I don't know what you're doing, but keep doing it." She raised her eyebrows and turned away from him. Eli ignored the flurry of butterflies her words created in his stomach. He gathered up the items and departed the store. He deposited the coffee and bag on the table Kale waited at.

"Did she say anything?" Kale asked. He took the cup and tried to pop the lid off with only one hand. Eli reached to lift it off for him.

"I think she's warming up to me. She suggested I get you an apple turnover."

Kale's face scrunched up in disgust. "She knows I hate apples."

"I see." Eli sat across from him. "I'm still interpreting it as progress."

Eli sipped his own coffee and waited. Tomorrow was Wednesday. And one way or another he needed to break away from Kale for a few hours.

"What's on the agenda for today?" Eli asked.

"I have my first anger management group therapy and a one-on-one appointment with a therapist. I have to do ten sessions of both before I can return to work," Kale said. He blew on his coffee but had yet to taste it. "My schedule will be the same the rest of the week."

Eli could work with this. Maybe he could slip away while Kale was at his appointments.

"Are you sure you don't have other obligations? You've been spending a lot of time with me," Kale said, as if he could read Eli's mind.

"I have something tomorrow," Eli said. "But otherwise my schedule is completely open."

Kale's eyebrows rose. "What's tomorrow?"

"Family thing," Eli said. "What time are your appointments?"

He regretted bringing up that he had plans. He could tell Kale was curious and Eli knew the more he said, the more questions it would create.

"Some family is in town," Eli said. "I just need to make an appearance."

"Right," Kale said. He crammed the lid back on his coffee. "My therapy appointment is at one all week. The group meets at six. If you take me to my appointment at one, I can take a cab home."

"I can stay and wait for you today. I'll bring a book," Eli said.

Kale said nothing, and the frown that marred his face remained firmly in place the rest of the day.

§§§

Wednesday. Kale stared at the ceiling in his bedroom. Eli had been with him for three days and four nights. The last two nights he'd convinced him to sleep in the bed with him. He loved nothing more than making Eli's face turn that beautiful shade of crimson when he climaxed. Whether doing so made his arm throb from the effort or not, he still enjoyed it.

Today, Eli would be leaving him to go do…something. A something he was being vague and elusive about. It drove Kale crazy. He rolled his head and stared at the blond man sleeping in his bed. His temporary possession until Martin came back.

Martin. Kale clenched his teeth and resisted the urge to dial Martin's number. Kale got up and went through the motions of the day, expelling the majority of his energy in not asking Eli questions.

Eli pulled his rust heap of a car up to the curb at the downtown skyscraper his court appointed therapist worked at. Kale stared at the glass doors and hesitated to exit the car.

"Promise me you won't get into trouble while I'm gone," Eli said.

"You'll be back in time to take me to group therapy?" Kale asked.

"Of course," Eli said. Kale leaned across the center console and kissed him. His normal vigor wasn't there though. His stomach bunched up in knots at the idea of being separated from Eli. He hurried out of the car and into the building before he said something he'd regret.

Twenty minutes later, he sat across from his therapist. She had oval glasses and her graying hair rolled up in a bun. She held a tablet of paper and a pen. She scribbled a few notes and Kale reminded himself that nothing he said to her was confidential. It was her job to report her findings back to the court.

"How are you today?" she asked.

"I'm great, Mrs. Dovetree," Kale said. "How are you?"

She smiled, her pale pink lipstick cracking on her lips. "I'm good. Are you still taking medication for your arm?"

"The antibiotic and aspirin," Kale said. He'd stopped wearing the sling. When the pain was at its worst he would hold his hand above his head. He iced it when he remembered.

"That's good."

Kale stared at the clock. He wondered if Eli was at his destination. *A family thing. What did that mean?*

"You seem distracted," Mrs. Dovetree said. "What's on your mind, Kale?"

He forced his eyes back to her. "I started seeing someone." This was a safe topic right? He couldn't say things like, "he's helping me stalk my ex," but he could bring up the family function without looking crazy, right?

"Are you sure you're ready for a new relationship? Are you over Martin?"

"Of course I'm not over Martin," Kale said. "Things with Eli are temporary. He understands that."

"So you're using him as a substitute. Are you sure that's fair to Eli?"

"He agreed to it."

"That doesn't mean he won't develop feelings for you."

"You're supposed to be teaching me new ways to control my temper, not prying into my personal life."

"You brought it up."

"And now I'm ending it," Kale said. He glanced at the clock. Had this session really only lasted five minutes so far?

"Why did you mention it? Is Eli why you are distracted?"

"He normally waits for me, but today he had to attend a family function. I wasn't invited."

"That's not abnormal for a new relationship."

He glared at her. Did she think he was stupid? "Nothing about me or my relationships are normal."

She smiled again. "So what can we do to make them more normal?"

"You think I should break up with him."

"I think you need to concentrate on you."

- 77 -

CHAPTER EIGHT

Two hours later, Kale paced in his apartment. Three in the afternoon. He'd tried calling Eli three times. Every call went directly to a message that said this person's mailbox had not been set up. His texts were returned undelivered.

Kale was more than panicking. He pulled out his laptop and powered it up. He draped his injured limp arm on top of his head to get the blood to drain. The stitches had begun itching this morning and it wasn't helping his mood at all.

He did a search for Eli. He found a few public records and managed to scrounge up his last known address. He took a photo of it with his phone and called a taxi. He popped one of his five remaining prescription painkillers as he waited for the cab to arrive.

He forced a light jacket on over his cast. Fall had begun in full swing and the first nips of winter were cutting into the breeze. He looked at the leaves littering the sidewalk and realized Halloween would be here in two weeks. The holidays were coming. Martin loved decorating for the holidays. He would dress up to hand candy out to the trick-or-treaters.

He wondered if anyone would bother to knock on his door this year, since Martin was absent. The yellow cab he'd called pulled up and Kale entered. He told him the address and tried to steady his breathing. Everything would be fine. He would find Eli and things would be fine.

Twenty minutes later the cab drove up to a yellow house with white trim and a big empty front yard. Not a single bush or tree resided in it. The building was one story, but looked well maintained. He directed the driver to drop him off a block away.

Kale walked by the house twice before going up the walkway and the three steps to the porch. He paused in his reach for the doorbell when he heard the click of a gun being cocked.

"Stop right there," a deep southern voice said. Kale raised both hands into the air. "Turn around slow."

Kale did as ordered. He turned ninety degrees and came face to face with his opponent. The man was tall and lanky. He adorned a mustache that was wider than the man's face. His steely blue eyes locked with Kale's.

"Can I help you?" the man asked. He had a double barrel shotgun aimed directly at Kale's chest. His mind spun as he tried to recall the rules on owning a personal weapon. Yes, this man had a right to shoot Kale while he was on his property. So long as it looked like a defensive shot. Which meant no gunshots from behind. Kale would need to be facing him.

"I'm looking for Eli Pendza," Kale said. The man's mouth moved, like he was chewing on something.

"You try calling Jackie?" he asked.

"Who's Jackie?" Kale asked.

"His wife," the man replied.

The world blurred for a moment. *His wife?*

"I'm sorry," Kale said. He edged toward the steps. "I think I'm at the wrong house."

He reached the first step and took it sideways, not wanting to turn away from the man.

"Eli Pendza's my son," the man said. "You have the right house. You one of his gay friends?"

Kale paused. *This had to be the wrong house. There had to be more than one Eli Pendza in the city.* The man lowered his rifle and peered at Kale.

"You his boyfriend?" the man asked. The front door creaked and a woman appeared behind the screen door.

"What's going on? Who is out there?" the woman asked.

"I'm so sorry to have bothered you," Kale said. He finished going down the steps. The woman came outside.

"I think this is Eli's boyfriend," the man said. "He's freak'n out a bit. I don't think he knew 'bout Jackie."

The woman was in her forties, maybe early fifties; her entire face lit up.

"Really?" She waved her hand at the man. "Put away your gun, Hank. You'll scare him off. Please, come in, I'm Margarine, you can call me Marge."

She came down the steps and took Kale's good arm in her hands.

"Is Eli here?" Kale asked.

"No, but we'll call Jackie for you. Hank, call Jackie." She looked at Kale. "I can't believe Eli finally invited one of his boyfriends over."

"He didn't invite him," Hank said. "He just showed up."

"Either way," Marge said. "I'm still getting to meet one of them before Evelyn." She guided Kale up the steps and into the house. "Evelyn's son came out of the closet five years ago. He still hasn't brought a single boyfriend home to meet her. She'll turn green with envy when I tell her about this."

Kale blinked as he adjusted to the gloom in the house. The lamps emitted a dull yellow glow. The house smelled slightly dank; he suspected mold would be found growing in the walls. Marge guided him to the couch. Kale hesitated to sit, worried of what mites and spores might fester on the surface. He set his jaw and sat.

"You're Eli's parents?" Kale asked.

"Yes, I'm his mother. Hank there is his father. Hank, are you calling Jackie?" She directed her attention back to him. "What did you say your name was?"

"Kale Sokoloff."

"Oh, I like it. Is that Russian?"

"Yes, ma'am."

Hank pulled out his cell phone. It was an old flip-phone style. He held it at arm's length as he dialed a number.

"Let me get you some milk and cookies, you look a bit flushed," Marge said. She scurried out of the room. Kale did his best to touch as little of the furniture as possible. He wasn't sure he could eat something produced in this environment.

"Hey Jackie," Hank said into his phone. "Is Eli with you?"

Kale couldn't hear the woman's response, but Hank nodded.

"Can you get him for me, please?"

Hank held the rifle in one hand, barrel pointed at the ground. Kale wished he knew more about guns. He really wanted to know if the safety was on.

"Hey Eli," Hank said. Kale's stomach did a flip. "I have a guy here at the house who says he knows you. His name's Kale and he's got a busted up arm in a cast... uh huh... yup... sure did."

Hank lowered the phone and approached Kale. He extended his arm and held the phone out to Kale.

"He wants to speak with you," Hank said.

Kale tried to swallow, but his mouth was too dry. As much as he wanted to speak to Eli, he hoped the person on the other end of the line wasn't his Eli.

He put the phone to his ear, making sure to not let it touch his skin. "Hello?" Kale said.

"Kale?" Eli said. "What are you doing at my parents' house?"

It was him. It was his Eli. Words failed him. His Eli was married.

"Kale?" Eli repeated. Marge returned and sat opposite from Kale. She placed a tray of cookies and a glass of milk in front of Kale.

"You weren't answering your phone," Kale said. His tone was monotone. Despite himself, he couldn't find the energy to be angry. *This had to be what shock felt like.*

"My phone?" There was cracking on Eli's end of the line. "Oh, I see. Yeah, I must have run out of minutes."

"You use a pay as you go phone?" Kale asked.

"Yeah, sorry about that. I can only imagine the things you must have been thinking. I'm so sorry, Kale." The things he'd imagined were nothing compared to the reality he was discovering. "How did you end up at my parents' house?"

"It's your last known address. I did a search on the internet," Kale said. Both of Eli's parents stared at him. "I'm surprised it didn't list your wife's address."

He let that hang there between them. Eli was silent. "Kale, hand the phone back to my dad."

"Where are you?" Kale asked.

"Hand the phone back to my dad."

"Tell me where you are first."

"Kale." There was anger and annoyance in his tone now. "Hand. The phone. Back. To. My. Dad."

Kale held the phone out to Hank, not bothering to say anything more to Eli. Hank took the phone.

"Yup," Hank said. He flinched and pulled the phone a few inches away from his ear. Kale couldn't understand the words but he could hear Eli shouting something. Hank met Kale's gaze for a moment, then stepped into a different room, leaving Kale alone with Marge.

"I'm sure Hank will find out where Eli is for you," Marge said. "What happened to your arm, if you don't mind my asking?"

"I was in a fight with an industrial oven," Kale said.

"Oh. Oh my." She stared at the cast in wonderment.

"Do you have any wedding pictures?" Kale asked. "From Eli's wedding?"

"Oh, of course," she said. She went to a bookshelf, lined with enough dust to bury a person, and retrieved a photo album. She handed it to Kale. He wanted to ask for some rubber gloves, but managed to take the book from her, touching it with only his fingertips.

He placed the book on the table and flipped it open. He covered his face with his cast in an attempt to protect himself from the cloud of dust.

The first page showed a young couple standing at an altar. She wore a white dress, the train spread out in front of them. Eli clasped her hands and stood close, dressed in a tuxedo. It was his Eli, younger, but still him.

"How long?" Kale asked. He glanced up at Marge. "How long have they been married?"

"Four years. They were married right out of high school. They've been dating since they were fifteen," Marge said. She clasped her hands in her lap.

High school sweethearts. Kale wondered if Eli was newly gay or bisexual. And why were his parents not only okay with Kale being his boyfriend, but actually excited?

"When did Eli tell you he was gay?" Kale asked.

"Officially, two years ago, but I always suspected. Unlike Evelyn. She nearly had a heart attack when her son told her. But Eli, he was always staring a bit too much at the boys."

"And he's still with his wife?" Kale asked.

"Well, yes." She opened her mouth but no words came. She tried again. "He—"

Hank came back in the room and Marge fell silent. Hank looked more than a little irritated.

"Eli wants me to take you to him," Hank said.

"Where is he?" Kale asked.

"Splitsville," Hank said. "It's a bowling alley about ten minutes from here."

"I can take a cab," Kale said.

"He said you might say that. And he said you might not show up if I let you go off on your own. So I'm taking you," Hank said.

"He needs to finish his milk first and eat something," Marge said. "Look at how pale he is."

Kale glanced at the milk and wondered if he could stomach it. "I'm quite fine."

"Nonsense," Marge said. She stood and plucked a camera, a non-digital one, Kale didn't know they still made those, off the table. "Hank you need to take a picture of us."

"Why?" Hank asked.

"So I can show Evelyn. She'll never believe me. And she'll never believe Eli is dating someone this handsome. I know her son will never catch a boy this good looking."

She thrust the camera in her husband's hands and sat on the couch next to Kale. Hank propped his rifle against the wall and held the camera to his face. This was insane. Kale felt like he'd entered the twilight zone, or perhaps one of those reality shows where they play pranks.

He flashed a smile for the camera and Hank pressed the button. The camera made a series of grinding noises and Hank handed it back to his wife.

Kale stood. "Thank you for your hospitality."

"No, no, you aren't leaving until you drink something."

Kale eyed the milk. The sooner he drank it, the sooner he could leave. He pinched his nose and gulped the contents.

§§§

The first half of their car drive was in silence. Kale got the impression Hank was upset. His tight grip on the steering wheel and stern expression were good indicators.

"I'm sorry if I caused undue stress to you and your family. If Eli is upset with you because of me I—" Kale began.

"It's not your fault. That boy has been making poor judgments the last few years. He should have told you about his wife." He kept his eyes firmly on the road.

Kale scratched at the plaster on his cast, wishing he could itch the stitches beneath. He considered telling Hank that he'd only known Eli for a week, but considering how much time they'd spent together over that week… Eli had had plenty of opportunities to tell him he was married.

Hank stopped at a red light. He let go of the steering wheel but still looked directly ahead.

"He told us he was gay two years ago. It wasn't a big surprise to any of us. Jackie was heartbroken but I think she always knew."

The light changed and the truck lurched forward.

"Why didn't they divorce?" Kale asked. This was something he should be asking Eli, and he fully intended to, but right now getting answers seemed the most likely from Eli's haggard father.

"Six months into their separation, Jackie got sick." He slowed the truck as the bowling alley came into view. "Eli wasn't about to leave his wife at a time like that, I raised him to be a better man than that. So he stayed to help her through it." The truck came to a stop at the main entrance to the bowling alley. Hank turned his head for the first time the whole drive and looked at Kale. "Problem is she's never going to get better. He needs to stop putting his life on hold."

Eli was married and his wife was sick? Memories from his first few nights with Eli came back. He recalled asking him if he'd been a nurse. Eli's response had been something about having experience with taking care of sick people.

"I hope you don't hold any of this against him," Hank said. Kale was too confused and overwhelmed to be angry. That would come later.

"Thank you," Kale said. He opened the door, reaching across with his left hand.

"Next time you plan to come by, call first."

"Will do," Kale said. He stepped outside.

"You want my number?" Hank asked. Kale paused stupidly for a moment.

"Yes," Kale said. He fumbled with his phone and programmed Hank into it as he rattled off his number. He uttered another thank you and closed the door.

Kale looked at the dark tinted double doors and gathered his courage to go inside to find Eli. He held his injured arm to his chest and grabbed the door handle. He pulled it open and took a moment to enjoy the warm air from inside that embraced him.

He entered and scanned the area. The place was fairly empty, aside from a few couples and what looked to be a children's birthday party in the far four lanes. Kale's throat closed up. *What if Eli had kids?*

Twenty bowling lanes were to his right. The food and shoe rental ahead of him and more tables for dining to his left. He didn't see Eli in the bowling area.

"Kale," Eli said. He came from around a corner, the restrooms? His face was pale and damp like he'd just splashed it with water.

Kale's stomach lurched. He took a step toward him, but the movement stopped Eli.

"I need to explain a few things to you," Eli said. His eyes looked Kale over before settling on the carpeted floor. He wiped his palms on his jeans and his Adam's apple bobbed.

Kale crossed the distance between them, doing his best to not be annoyed when Eli flinched at his touch. He put his hand behind Eli's neck and pressed their lips together. He needed to refresh his claim. Eli was his. He forced his tongue in Eli's mouth and caressed Eli's tongue. Some of the tension seemed to ease from Eli's body.

Kale ended the embrace and had to fight hard to not make a verbal declaration that Eli was his. At his first opportunity he needed to mark

Eli somehow, so everyone would know he was taken. He eyed Eli's neck and envisioned a dark hickey.

"I thought you'd be angrier," Eli said.

"Right now I'm too busy being relieved that you're okay."

Eli cussed and looked at the floor. He stepped away from Kale, forcing him to remove his hand from around his neck.

"I can't believe I let my minutes expire. You must have freaked out. I'm so sorry." He ran a hand over his face.

"We'll get you a better phone and put it on my plan, so this won't happen again."

"Yeah, that—wait, what?" Eli tilted his head and looked at him. "Kale, I still haven't explained everything to you."

"You're parents told me about—" Kale started to say. A girl's high-pitched squeal interrupted him. Tiny footsteps came from behind him. He turned in time to see a young girl skid to a halt a few feet from him.

Her eyes, that looked too much like Eli's eyes, gazed up at him in wonderment. She had her light blond hair pulled up in two pigtails. Brown freckles dotted her nose and her cheeks dimpled when she smiled.

"Is this him?" She glanced at Eli, then back to Kale.

"Yeah," Eli said. "Annabelle, this is Kale." Eli knelt next to the girl and draped an arm around her. "Kale, this is my daughter, Annabelle."

CHAPTER NINE

The earth seemed to tilt. Up was now down, his world no longer made sense. The next moment Kale was aware of, he was sitting on a cheap plastic chair. The girl chattered with Eli and both of them kept glancing in his direction. He had no idea how he'd become seated.

"Is he really your boyfriend?" Annabelle asked. Eli looked at Kale, as if seeking guidance.

"He's more like daddy's stalker," Eli said.

"Wha-at?" the girl said, exaggerating the word. Kale stared at her, trying to guess her age. Five? Six?

"He went to Grandpa's house looking for me," Eli said. The girl's eyes got bigger. She looked at Kale with a new layer of wonderment.

"Did Grandpa pull the shotgun on you?"

"Yes," Kale said. The girl clucked her tongue.

"You have to call first," Annabelle said.

"She's right," Eli confirmed. "You have to call first or he'll get the shotgun out."

"Lesson learned," Kale said.

"You look pale," Annabelle said. "You should eat some cake." She looked to her father. "Can I get him some cake?"

"Sure, put it on the table with Mommy. We'll be over in a minute," Eli said. He kissed the top of her head and she skipped away, back to the gaggle of children bowling. Eli put a hand on Kale's knee, still kneeling on the floor. "Are you okay?"

"You're married and you have a kid. No, I am not okay."

Eli squeezed his knee, a little harder than Kale would have liked. "I know. I really messed this up." He retracted his hand. He sat on the floor and put his elbows on his knees, hands to his forehead. "I'll understand if you don't want to see me anymore."

Kale said nothing. He didn't have enough information to make a judgment call on their relationship.

"I want to meet her," Kale said.

"Who?" Eli moved his hand and looked up at him.

"Your wife, who else?"

"Right." Eli grabbed the table and used it to help him stand.

"And I have been promised cake. I'd like to save judgment until after I've enjoyed the festivities." His attempts to lighten the situation had no effect. Eli crossed his arms and led Kale across the establishment to the bowling area. There were tables behind the racks of balls. One was set up with piles of presents and a cake. A second was surrounded by children, the third was occupied by three women, likely parents of the children frolicking.

Two of the women chattered with each other. The third rose as they approached. She was rail thin, her hair an obvious wig, and deep bags settled under her eyes. She smiled and raised a hand to shake with Kale. She frowned as she noticed his cast.

"Oh, I'm sorry," she said, her eyes focused on his arm.

"Kale this is Jackie. Jackie this is Kale," Eli said, giving no title to the introductions.

"It's nice to see you're real," Jackie said. She crossed her too thin arms and hugged herself. "Welcome to the party."

"Whose birthday is it?" Kale asked. If Eli said it was his, he was going to kick him, right in the teeth.

"The girls'," Jackie said. Kale couldn't help but notice the plural usage. He looked at Eli who focused on his shoes.

"Christ Eli, how many kids do you have?" Kale asked.

"Oh no, I didn't mean it like that," Jackie said. "It's just what I call them. Lilly and Jill, it's their birthday. They're Annabelle's best friends."

A plumper woman at the table, who looked like she could eat the entire birthday cake singlehandedly, raised her hand. "The birthday girls would be mine, twins," she said.

"They're always together so I've grown accustomed to calling them the girls. I'm sorry," Jackie said.

"It's fine," Eli said. "This can't really get much worse."

Eli sounded miserable. And Kale had done this to him by forcing himself into Eli's life.

"I don't know what you mean," Kale said. "It's not like you've brought me to a party that's centered on an event I can't participate in." Eli glanced at him from the corner of his eye. Kale raised his broken limb. "Oh wait, I wasn't invited and I have a broken wrist at a bowling party."

The two unnamed mothers giggled, but Eli remained solemn.

Kale cupped Eli's chin and forced him to look at him. "I guess you're right, we should chalk this up as a loss." Some of the color came back into Eli's cheeks. Kale's arousal was piqued. "Can you get me some water? I need to take some of my pills."

Kale kissed him on the cheek, and couldn't wait until later tonight when he could mark Eli's body properly.

"Yeah, okay," Eli said. He stepped away and went to the concession stand. Kale sat at the table and Jackie did likewise. The two mothers excused themselves.

"So how sick are you?" Kale asked. Jackie's eyes widened at the direct question. Annabelle appeared with a large slice of chocolate cake. She placed it on the table in front of Kale.

"Kale, can I sign your cast?" Annabelle asked. He barely listened to the question.

"Yeah, sure," Kale said. She pumped a fist in the air and dashed away, back into the mob of children. Kale focused his gaze on Jackie. "Tell me."

"It started as breast cancer." She pointed to her chest. "We caught it too late." She glanced at Eli, still talking to the cashier. "They removed both breasts, and I've been through chemo three times. I stopped two weeks ago. The doctors say I have four weeks."

"Four weeks until what? You start chemo again?" Kale asked.

"Until I die." She folded her hands on the table. "I haven't told Eli or Annabelle. My mother flew in this week. She's staying until…" She wiped a finger under her left eye. "I'm glad Eli found someone. You'll help him through this, right? This is going to destroy him. Please, please tell me this won't scare you away."

Kale stared at her. His entire world had shifted so much in the last few hours, he wasn't certain he could handle much more.

"If you figure out how to scare me away, there are several people I know who would be interested in learning your secret," Kale said. She laughed, a beautiful, musical sound.

Annabelle returned, armed with a box of markers. A girl with brown hair stood next to her.

"This is Lilly," Annabelle said. "Can she help?"

"Sure," Kale said. He placed his arm flat on one of the chairs and a girl settled on either side. They started with purple and pink markers.

"Whoa, what's this?" Eli said. He held a pitcher of water and tray of nachos. "Annabelle, he broke his arm five days ago. Be gentle."

Both girls paused.

"It's fine," Kale said. The cast would be replaced on Monday anyway, so the temporary pins and stints could be removed. He'd have a fresh, undecorated one before he had to go to work. Only his therapist would see the decorated cast and he figured it might earn him a few good entries in her report.

"Annabelle is a horrible artist," Eli said. "You're going to regret this."

"That's a horrible thing to say," Kale said. He plucked one of the chips from the tray and dipped it in sauce.

"Which pocket are your pills in?" Eli said. He didn't wait for a response and started feeling Kale's side pockets.

"My jacket," Kale said. Eli changed tactics and found the bottle in his breast pocket. He got the pills out for him and handed him the water. He was the perfect bedside nurse, and now Kale understood why.

All the little tidbits Kale had learned of Eli's life made sense now. He had no apartment of his own, because he stayed so often with his wife to take care of her. It also explained the lack of a job. His time was likely consumed with tending to his wife and daughter. The prescription bottle of pills the arresting officer had found most likely belonged to Jackie. And a person would have to be very coldhearted to leave their wife after discovering they had cancer. Kale couldn't think of a better reason for a gay man to remain married to his wife.

He hated that Jackie's story would not have a happy ending. And even more, Kale despised himself for not being the silver lining Eli's family was hoping he was.

Kale's time in Eli's life was temporary. Martin was coming back.

§§§

They left at five thirty so Eli could drive Kale to his group therapy session. Kale said nothing for a few minutes. He watched the scenery race past the side window.

"Your family is nice," Kale said. He glanced at Eli. His eyes remained on the road. "I'm sorry about Jackie."

"It happens," Eli said.

"About your question earlier, I want to keep seeing you. In fact, I think you should move in with me on a more permanent basis."

"What?" Eli shot a quick glance at him.

"You don't have a place of your own, do you? You've been bouncing between Jackie's place and your parents', right?"

"And friends," Eli confessed.

"I have a spare bedroom. I want you to move into it."

"What about Martin? Is he going to be okay with me living with you when he comes back?"

"It's my apartment. I can let whoever I want live there. If he wants to have more of a say in the matter, he shouldn't have left." He would figure out how the dynamics of such a thing would work when and if Martin came back. "I also think you should get a job. I can get you hired at the law firm."

"What? As your secretary?"

"I already have a very capable secretary. I was thinking more the mailroom."

"You want me to move in with you and work for you?"

"And I want to get you a new phone."

Eli laughed. "Am I getting a new car too? And a clothing allowance?"

"Your car is perfectly functional and you can buy clothes with your wages from your new job."

"I know that, Kale, I was joking. You do get how controlling you sound right now?" Eli asked.

"I'm not trying to control you. I'm trying to help you get your life sorted. You're a father. You need to be able to take care of her." Four weeks. The idea hadn't occurred to him until now. Who would take care of Annabelle? Jackie's mother? Eli's parents? Or Eli? And if Eli was living with him, would Annabelle live with him too?

"Did Martin work at your firm?" Eli asked. He parked the car and looked at Kale.

"No, Martin doesn't work. He goes to school."

"Why can't I go to school?" Eli asked.

"Maybe later, right now you need an income. I'm not prepared to support—" He stopped himself. He wasn't prepared for any of this. And yet, he already felt the familiar itch of worry and possessiveness creep toward Annabelle. What grade was she in? First? Second? Were they sending her to public school? That was unacceptable. There was a private school not far from—

"Kale, I'm not asking you to support me," Eli said.

"I know that," Kale snapped. "That's why you're getting a job. We'll stop by my workplace after my therapy appointment tomorrow."

He got out of the car and heard Eli follow him. "I don't want to—"

Kale raised his hand and Eli fell silent. He didn't turn to look at him. "We start with the job, new phone, and you move your stuff from your car into the spare room. End of discussion."

Next, they would figure out custody arrangements of Annabelle. She could stay in the spare bedroom and Eli could move into his room. Would Eli be okay with that or would he worry about how Annabelle might conceive the situation? He didn't want to promote premarital sex to her. *Good Lord, which of us is going to give her the sex talk?*

CHAPTER TEN

Eli woke up before Kale. He lay in the bed and stared at him. Kale hadn't shaved since he'd injured his arm. He nearly had a full beard. Eli wouldn't admit it, but he found it extremely attractive. It was long enough now that it wasn't as scratchy.

Yesterday had been horrible. Kale's reaction to everything had been the best he could have hoped for. His new over-controlling attitude had Eli slightly worried, but he figured it was better than watching his temper flare. He reached across the bed and stroked Kale's furry cheek.

Kale's eyes fluttered open and Eli's stomach lurched. Eli had refused to let himself feel anything for someone ever since Jackie had gotten sick. Taking care of Annabelle was his priority. His needs and a relationship weren't a possibility right now. Kale was supposed to be a one-night stand. Kale had a boyfriend. There was no future to be had with Kale, and yet Eli couldn't stop the growing affection he felt for him.

"Morning," Eli said. Kale groaned in response. Eli considered apologizing for waking him. Before he could, Kale rolled over on top of Eli. His lips entrapped Eli's in a fierce, possessive kiss.

Eli wrapped his arms around him and ground his groin against Kale's stomach. He wished every day could start like this. Kale's lips moved to Eli's neck, trailing kisses the entire way. Eli bucked beneath him, feeling Kale's own arousal pressing into Eli's thigh.

Eli had to bite his tongue to keep from saying the wrong thing. He wasn't sure how Kale would react if Eli said the words consuming his mind. Kale sucked on his neck, hard enough to hurt. Eli realized what he was doing.

"No, Kale, stop," Eli said. He pushed on Kale's forehead, forcing him to let go.

"What?" He lifted his head high enough so he could look Eli in the eyes.

"No hickeys," Eli said.

"I want to mark you," Kale said. "So everyone knows you're mine." But Eli wasn't his, not really.

"No," Eli repeated. Kale tugged on Eli's lower lip.

"Why?" Kale moved to suck on Eli's earlobe.

The words were out of his mouth before he could stop them.

"I'm not going to my wife's funeral with a hickey," Eli said. Kale stiffened and pulled away.

"You're right. I didn't even think of that." Kale rolled off him.

"Kale, I didn't mean we need to stop. I just—"

"Everything is different now," Kale said. He swung his legs off the bed and rubbed his forehead. He held his casted arm above his head. Eli's eyes were drawn to the marker sketches Annabelle had drawn on it. He hadn't been able to decipher what most of the caveman-like images were, he suspected one was a pink pony, another might be a green tree.

"No it's not." Eli pulled his legs to his chest. "This is why I didn't tell you before."

Kale looked over his shoulder at him. "So if I'd tried to give you a hickey before? What would you have said?"

"I would have made something up. I'm sorry. I know this is—"

"Don't. I'm tired of hearing you apologize. You're in an impossible situation. I get it." Kale got up from the bed and went to his dresser. "Don't you think you should be spending more time with her? With Annabelle? Jackie doesn't have much time left. I don't want you to regret spending Jackie's last days with me instead of her."

"We're separated," Eli said. "And I've given her plenty of my time already. If I were with her, she'd be insisting I be with you. She wants me to move on. They all do."

"Yeah, I got that impression yesterday," Kale said, a hint of disgust in his voice. He shut the drawer and turned to face him. "Do you know long she has?"

"She won't tell me, but I know she quit chemo. The fact her mother flew into town." Eli shook his head. "She wouldn't be here unless—"

"I get it." Kale rubbed his face and scratched his beard. "Do you want to borrow some of my clothes? I want you to look good when I take you into the firm today to apply for a job."

A change of topic, shifting things back to what Kale could control. He was like an angel sent to pull Eli through the rough months to come. Unless Martin came back.

An ache stabbed at his stomach and his chest tightened. What would he do if he lost Kale and Jackie at the same time? How would he hold himself together well enough to take care of Annabelle?

§§§

The Moroz-Kempt Legal Advisors law firm was an intimidating building. Despite Kale's insistence, Eli parked in the visitor's area of the parking garage across the street. His beat up car was more than guaranteed to get towed if he parked in an employee spot. He hoped they'd give him some sort of sticker or pass to put on his windshield once he was hired to make his car look more legit.

The building was a twenty-story skyscraper with walls of glass. Eli gazed at it from the sidewalk as they approached. He wondered what window was Kale's office.

"The entire building isn't ours," Kale said. "We share it with fifteen other businesses."

"Okay," Eli said.

"Come on." Kale grabbed his hand, threading his fingers between Eli's and pulled him across the street. Eli hadn't expected Kale to hold his hand in his workplace. Didn't everyone here know Kale was with Martin? Why would Kale want to give the impression he wasn't if Martin was going to come back?

The automatic doors opened as they approached. A reception desk and guard in a typical black uniform stood behind it. He nodded to Kale.

"I thought you were going to be off for a while," the guard said.

"I am. I'm here for something else," Kale said. He continued pulling Eli with him. They entered one of the four elevators as the doors opened to drop off passengers. Once boarded, Kale pushed the button for the B2 with his thumb.

"Should you be using your right hand to do that?" Eli asked. He hadn't worn his sling today and Eli noted his fingers were red and swollen.

"And give you a chance to run off?" Kale asked.

"Where would I go? This place is a maze."

The elevator stopped, and Kale tugged him out the open doors. They went down a hall and into an office with a waist high counter cutting the room in half. Three people busied themselves behind it.

"Hey Jack," Kale said. An older gentleman with soft features looked up from a stack of papers he was sorting. The other two workers, young Hispanic men, glanced in their direction briefly before resuming the application of stickers to envelopes arranged in front of them.

"Mr. Sokoloff," Jack said. "Charlotte said you would be by this afternoon. Is this the new recruit?"

"Yes, Jack this is Eli." Kale finally released Eli's hand. Jack offered his in a handshake. Eli shook his hand with the counter between them.

"Sanchez," Jack said, glancing over to one of the men with the stickers. "Get the forms for Eli."

The man nodded and began collecting papers from various cubbyholes under the counter.

"There're quite a few forms," Kale said. "I'm going upstairs to see how the others are doing with my cases. Come up when you're finished."

"I don't know where your office is," Eli said.

"Jack will give you directions," Kale said. Eli nodded, still unconfident he would be able to find it. Then Kale did the unthinkable. He leaned down and kissed him, as if it were the most natural thing in the world. Why would he do that? In his workplace? In front of what would soon be Eli's new boss? His cheeks burned and Kale grinned, a look of hunger on his face. "I'll never get tired of seeing that color on you."

He kissed him again before turning and disappearing out the doorway and down the hall. Eli forced himself to look up from the floor and at Jack.

Jack looked unfazed by Kale's actions. He slid a thick stack of papers across the counter to Eli. A black pen sat on top.

"Start with these," Jack said.

"Right, sure," Eli said. He took the pen in a somewhat shaky grip and looked at the top document. The very first question on the form asked him to check a box indicating if he were married, single or divorced.

Kale was flaunting their relationship in front of people and Eli needed to fill out forms indicating he was married. Jack noticed his hesitation.

"Is there a problem? Do you need the documents in *Española*?" Jack asked.

"No. I just—I'm married," Eli said. His cheeks burned as he awaited the judgmental look from Jack and Sanchez and whoever the other guy was.

Jack looked at him, his expression devoid of emotion.

"So am I," Jack said. He pointed a thumb at Sanchez. "So are Sanchez and Ricardo. We hire married people here. It's not a problem."

"We even have daycare," Sanchez added with a thick Hispanic accent. "So it's cool if you have kids too."

"Right. Okay." Eli didn't quite understand the rules of this alternate reality he seemed to have entered but he could think of nothing to do but move forward. "Thank you for that reassurance."

§§§

Eli sat across the desk from Melissa Dawery in the human resources department, in a small cubical located in a maze of identical desks. Her fingers moved in a blur across her keyboard as she entered his information in the computer. He'd never seen someone type as proficiently as she did. Her hair was pulled back in a low ponytail, and she wore wire spectacles. He was staring at the sequins on her shirt, trying to figure out if there was a pattern to the design, when she asked him a question.

"I'm sorry," Eli said. He looked at her mascara covered eyelashes and waited for her to repeat the query.

"Will you be filing insurance coverage for your wife or daughter?" Ms. Dawery asked.

"Only my daughter," Eli said. She resumed her typing, gathering most of her information from the documents he'd already filled out.

She turned from the computer and placed a laminated paper in front of him.

"This is our policy on interoffice relationships. I'm required to show it to you, and remind you that if you were to begin an office relationship with someone who works in the building, you'll be required to file a form 522." Her emerald eyes locked onto his. "It's a formality so we can ensure you're never put in a position that might promote an uncomfortable work environment."

He waited for the, "but you're married so you don't have to worry about this" line.

"You have a lot of interoffice love affairs occur with married people?" Eli asked.

"I'm not here to judge." She blinked her eyes at him, her expression telling him nothing.

"Can I fill out a form 522 now?" Eli asked.

"Of course." She opened a drawer and pulled out the form. "She'll need to complete a form as well. What is her name?"

"Kale Sokoloff," Eli said. He didn't touch the form. He wanted to see even the slightest reaction she might have.

"From the law firm?" Her right eyebrow rose.

"Yes."

The glimmer of surprise he saw in her faded. "I'll call his secretary and find out how to contact him. I believe he's been out of the office."

"He's in today," Eli said. Another small flicker of surprise appeared on her face. She picked up her desk phone and dialed a number.

"Hello, Charlotte, this is Melissa from HR... Yes, good and you? Glad to hear it. Listen, I have Mr. Pendza down here. He's requesting a form 522. Is Mr. Sokoloff available to confirm the relationship and complete the form?" She balanced the phone on her shoulder and typed on the keyboard. "Mr. Sokoloff, good afternoon... Yes, a form 522."

She listened to him say something and kept her eyes on the monitor in front of her. Eli wished he could view whatever she was referencing.

"Thank you. Would you like to update your status in relation to Martin Baum? He's listed as your emergency contact, under your address, is covered by your insurance, and is currently receiving a six thousand dollar monthly allotment. Would you like to change any of that information or remove him from the system?"

Eli's mouth went dry. Kale was giving Martin money? Even during their separation? Six grand? That was an outrageous amount. His mind whirled as he thought of all the other things Kale might still be buying for Martin. He was paying his tuition for school, probably his car insurance, his phone... Eli's eyes settled on the form. Eli's relationship with Kale was temporary. There was no longer any point in trying to fantasize otherwise.

"Thank you, Mr. Sokoloff. I'll leave everything as is. Please have Charlotte email me the form 522 when you complete it." Melissa hung up the phone and regarded Eli. "He confirms the relationship. Please fill out the form."

"There's no need." Eli flicked the paper with his fingers, sending it skittering back to her side of the desk.

"Mr. Sokoloff confirmed he's in a relationship with you."

"Well, he's not anymore so there's no need for the document." Eli crossed his arms. He'd take the job and that was it. He wasn't going to stick around any longer and wait for Martin to come back. Melissa stared at him for a moment. She picked up the phone and dialed.

"Hi Charlotte, please tell Mr. Sokoloff to disregard my earlier call. The form 522 is no longer necessary… Yes, thank you." She hung up and straightened her glasses. "Moving on. I'll issue you a parking pass and—"

The phone rang. She reached for it and Eli noticed a slight tremble in her hand as she lifted the receiver.

"Meli—" She didn't finish stating her name before the other person spoke. She kept the phone to her ear and said nothing. Eli couldn't hear the person on the other end. Melissa's composure faltered as her skin paled. She frowned and her eyes glistened as tears formed. Her mouth opened to speak, but she quickly clamped her lips shut.

Eli shifted in his seat as his stomach rumbled. The lecture she was receiving continued for nearly five minutes.

"Yes sir," Melissa said. She pressed a button on the phone and lowered the receiver from her face. "Mr. Sokoloff would like to speak to you."

She turned the phone base to face him and held the receiver out to him. Eli swallowed deeply and took the phone from her.

"Hello," Eli said, after pressing the hold button.

"What changed your mind?" Kale asked. His tone was gruff, but not layered with the anger he expected. Eli looked at Melissa as she dabbed her eyes.

"What did you say to Ms. Dawery?" Eli asked.

"I reminded her of how inept she is at her job and how personal information shouldn't be mentioned in front of others. Now, why are you refusing to complete the form?"

"So you're pissed at her for mentioning your allotment to Martin in front of me?" Eli asked.

"Yes. She should know better and—"

"Fuck you, Kale," Eli said. The words slipped out, louder than he intended. Melissa froze in mid-sniffle. Any background conversations occurring in other cubicles stopped. The pounding of Eli's heart in his ears was the only sound. Even Kale was silent.

Rather than give Kale time to recover from the insult, Eli decided to blunder ahead.

"I'm not filling out a form for a relationship that won't exist by the time your suspension is over." He took a deep breath. "You're still paying Martin because you expect him to come back. But why would he? He's getting everything he needs from you, and now he doesn't have to endure being around you to get it.

"In fact, I think I like Martin's strategy. I'll gladly take a few hits to the face if it means you'll start paying me six grand a month, especially if the arrangement has no expiration and doesn't require my continued presence.

"So no, I'm not filling out the form, because you're in a relationship with Martin, not me." Eli tried to figure out if the jumble of words he'd just uttered made any sense. Eli wasn't sure if his speech was meant to motivate Kale to break up with Martin or coach Kale on how to get Martin back.

"Give the phone back to Melissa," Kale said. His tone was the same as before, all business, no emotion. Eli slapped his finger on the hold button and held the receiver out for Melissa.

"He wants to speak to you again," Eli said. She took the phone from him, nearly dropping it. She clutched it in both hands.

"I can't believe you spoke to him like that," Melissa said. Eli noticed that several heads had appeared peering over the cubical walls. Melissa turned the phone base back to her and pressed the hold button.

"Melissa Dawery, HR," Melissa said. Eli let one side of his mouth curl upwards at the fact Kale had let her finish her introduction this time. She turned to her computer and began typing. "Yes, sir... I can pass—yes. Effective immediately?" She paused. "Two months... Yes, sir."

She hung up the phone and clattered away on the computer. Eli waited. She printed something and plucked it from the printer beside her chair. She laid it in front of Eli on the desk.

"What is this?" Eli asked.

"Mr. Sokoloff wanted me to show you the changes he's requested to his account. I'm emailing this form over to the finance department."

"Just tell me," Eli said. He knew the dozens of ears listening in the surrounding cubicles were curious about the outcome and Eli wasn't about to leave them wondering. He knew Melissa was probably trying to take Kale's advice about keeping personal information close, but Eli didn't care. He didn't have the patience to decipher the form.

"He's stopping the allotment to Martin Baum, effectively immediately. The next installment was scheduled to arrive Monday. He's keeping the medical insurance active for two months." She kept her tone steady but her eyes were huge. "Mr. Sokoloff was insistent that you complete the form 522 before you leave."

Eli said nothing. He picked up a pen and began filling in the information on the form 522. Kale had chosen him over Martin. That wasn't possible. But if Kale had opted to cancel the funds in a ploy to get Martin back, it made no sense to press Eli to fill out the form 522.

Melissa took the form from him. "Thank you. Now, the parking pass." The background warble of voices resumed. The entire room seemed to take a collective exhale, Eli included.

CHAPTER ELEVEN

Eli's nerves were about shot as he walked into the legal office on the second floor. The receptionist in the waiting room smiled as Eli exited the elevator.

"May I help you?" she asked. There were a dozen or so customers seated in the room, a few glanced up at Eli. Even in his borrowed clothes, it was obvious Eli didn't belong amongst the social class who could afford a lawyer at Moroz-Kempt Legal Advisors.

"Hi. I'm here to see Kale Sokoloff. I'm Eli." He rubbed the back of his neck and admired the marble countertop on the desk.

"I'll tell Charlotte," she said. "Have a seat."

"Thanks." Eli turned away from her desk and debated where to sit. The people waiting had all buried their faces in their phones or magazines.

The glass doors leading to the lawyer offices opened. A middle-aged woman in a knee-high silver dress looked at him.

"Eli?" she said. She smiled warmly. Eli approached and she extended her hand. "I'm Charlotte."

Eli gave her a gentle shake, catching a whiff of her rose perfume. She wore a necklace with large turquoise rocks, matching earrings sagged her earlobes. The bright blue eye shadow on her eyelids made Eli think of a peacock.

She surprised him by pulling him into a hug after he crossed the threshold into the back offices.

"I'm delighted to meet you, Eli," Charlotte said. She stepped back, keeping a hand on both his arms and sizing him up from head to toe. "I can see why he likes you."

Eli's hands tingled. "Do I look like him?"

"Like who?" Charlotte asked, her forehead creasing.

"Martin." Eli hadn't seen a single photo of him in the apartment.

"Oh no, I didn't mean that." She waved her hand dismissively. "I meant you're dreamy."

Eli's cheeks burned and he looked away from her. There were no cubicles in the room. Twelve desks were arranged in rows, and offices lined the three outer walls. All the doors were closed and every desk was occupied.

"I don't think you need to worry about comparing yourself to Martin," Charlotte said. His spine tingled at the suggestion in her comment.

"How pissed is he?" Eli asked. A few heads glanced up from their desks and looked in Eli's direction.

"He said you could go straight in. Kale's in Rich's office," Charlotte said, avoiding his question. She guided him down the row, her pale blue pumps clacking on the tiled floor.

She knocked on the office door and opened it for Eli. He thanked her and walked in. A man with a comb-over sat behind a large oak desk. Kale sat across from him, sifting through some papers. They both looked up at Eli. Kale waved Eli to come closer.

"Rich, this is Eli. Eli, Rich, he's one of the partners at the firm," Kale said. Rich stood and shook Eli's hand. He looked directly into

Eli's eyes, but there was no conviction behind the gaze. Their greeting was all business.

"Pleasure to meet you," Rich said.

"Same here," Eli said. Kale stood and Eli took a step back from them.

"Do you want to see my office?" Kale asked.

"I can wait until you're finished," Eli said.

"We're done," Kale said. He threaded his fingers with Eli's and guided him from the office. Eli tried to control the heat rising in his cheeks, but he knew he was redder than a tomato as Kale led him three doors down, to an office with Kale's name on it.

Kale held the door open as Eli entered. Dark chestnut shelves lined both side walls; thick legal books filled them. Windows looking outside were behind the desk, they were tinted dark. Kale locked the door behind them and proceeded to close the blinds covering the windows looking out to the rest of the floor.

"It's a nice office," Eli said. "I'm surprised you don't have a corner office though."

"We only have half the floor, so only two corners. Rich Moroz and Luke Kempt get those, since they are the founders," Kale said.

"Oh, that makes sense," Eli said. Kale was on him then, gripping his chin with his thumb and forefinger. He held his casted arm in the air, keeping it above his head.

"So you want to fuck me?" Kale asked, putting his face inches from Eli's.

"What?" Even amidst the shock of the comment, his body began to react as blood flowed to his privates.

"That's what you said to me on the phone," Kale said. "You said 'fuck you.' So I'm accepting."

Kale leaned forward and tugged on Eli's lower lip with his teeth. His good hand released Eli's chin and snaked down to grip Eli's crotch.

"Kale." Eli sucked in a breath of air as Kale squeezed his growing hard-on. "People will hear." There was a crack of light coming in from under the door, a sure indication that the room was not soundproof.

"That's the idea," Kale said. He stroked Eli and kissed him. "I want you to bend me over my desk and fuck me."

A shiver ran through Eli. The idea was more than tempting. Kale broke the embrace and went to his desk. He unlocked the bottom drawer and retrieved a condom and bottle of lube.

"You must have sex quite often in your office," Eli commented. "Martin would do this with you?"

"No." Kale paused, staring at the lube. "He never would. I've actually never had sex with anyone in my office."

"Why do you have the supplies then?"

"For myself." He scratched his forehead. "Depending on the case I'm working, I'll masturbate before I go to the courtroom, to clear my head."

"You use a condom when you masturbate?" Eli asked.

"Easier cleanup," Kale said. "I won't have to do that anymore, will I? Not with you working downstairs, a quick phone call away."

The implication behind his words sunk in. Kale intended to utilize Eli has a pre-courtroom booty call. Eli knew on some level he should be insulted, but he also found the idea incredibly hot.

Kale unbuckled Eli's pants and stuck one hand inside. Eli's eyes fluttered as his entire body erupted in tingles from the skin on skin contact.

§§§

Eli cleaned his hands on a baby wipe Kale had given him. He did a quick sweep of his privates before zipping his pants shut. Kale collected everything into a baggy and tucked it in his pocket. Neat and clean, just like Kale did everything.

"Thank you," Kale said, giving him a firm kiss on the lips. Eli groaned as he kissed him back.

"Eventually, I'm going to convince you to let me ride you bareback," Eli said. "You've no idea how much better it is."

Kale stumbled slightly as he took a step back from Eli. "That can never happen," Kale said, his expression grim.

"Why? Do I need to get tested and show you the results to prove to you I'm clean?" Eli asked.

"I'm not."

"Not what?"

"Clean."

Eli shook his head. "Kale, you're the cleanest person I know."

"I have Hepatitis B," Kale said. Eli waited for the moment where Kale would say he was joking. He looked at him with nothing but seriousness on his face. "Which is why we'll always use a condom. I won't risk giving it to you."

The puzzlements from before fell into place. His insistence on using the condoms. His total freak out when Eli offered to complete his medical papers.

"I'm sorry I didn't tell you sooner," Kale said.

"I'm sorry I forced you into telling me."

"You didn't force me. I needed to tell you eventually. I know this changes things."

"It doesn't change anything. I don't care what you have. I love you," Eli said. He kissed him, forcing his tongue in Kale's mouth. It wasn't until he noticed the hesitation on Kale's part that he realized what he'd just said. Those three little words he'd been doing his best not to say.

Kale's body relaxed at the same moment Eli's tensed. Eli pulled away, knowing he'd messed up. *Would Kale pretend he hadn't heard? Or worse, feel obligated to say it back?*

"You're just saying that because you want me to start giving you a monthly allotment," Kale said, his tone lighthearted. He kissed him quickly on the cheek, before pulling away.

"Funny," Eli managed to say before Kale opened the office door, ending any chance of continuing the conversation.

Kale didn't hold his hand though. That subtle difference struck deep with Eli. He followed Kale down the aisle, crossing his arms to help ease the void of not having Kale touching him.

Kale stopped at Charlotte's desk, signed a few things, and mumbled words too softly for Eli to hear. Eli said nothing as he followed him out of the legal office, the eyes watching him sent pricks of anxiety through his body. In the parking lot, Kale finally broke the silence.

"Martin has class tonight," Kale said. "We'll need to go to the school after my group therapy."

"Yeah, of course," Eli said, avoiding all eye contact.

"It's been one week," Kale said.

"One week since what?"

"You and I met," Kale said. Eli fumbled with the door handle on his car. *Had it really only been one week?* Eli felt even more like an idiot. He'd confessed to loving Kale after only having known him for a week. He assumed that was why Kale was bringing it up. Eli said nothing as he entered the car.

§§§

Donuts and coffee. Kale gave Eli his best look of puzzlement he could manage as Eli entered the car, clutching both items from a gas station they'd stopped at for fuel.

"It's like a real stakeout now," Eli said, passing the items to Kale. Calling his obsession with Martin a stakeout was better than saying what it really was, so Kale figured he'd play along.

"It is about time you paid up on your promise."

"What promise?" Eli put the car in gear and drove toward the community college.

"On the bus, when we met. You promised me gas station coffee in way of thanks for paying your bail."

Kale watched the grin spread across Eli's face. "Oh yeah, I forgot about that. Glad I could make good on my promise then."

Kale doubted Eli had forgotten, but he let the comment slide. They reached the school and Kale directed him to a spot that wouldn't attract much attention but offered a good view of the entrance Martin used.

Eli turned the car off and cracked his window. The car had manual windows. Kale used his good hand to crank the window down a few inches to let in the fresh autumn air. Eli really did need to get a new car. This thing was a death trap. It didn't even have any airbags. The idea of Annabelle riding in it terrified Kale.

He hadn't figured out the best way to broach the topic of getting Eli a new car. He doubted Eli would let him buy him one and he knew Eli couldn't afford car payments on anything that would be worth the upgrade from what he already had.

"Donut?" Eli asked, pulling one of the glazed treats from the bag.

"No thanks," Kale said. He watched the people trickling out of the building, no Martin.

"You don't like donuts?" Eli asked.

"I'm not as young as you," Kale said. "Those things will go right to my waistline, and I haven't exactly been able to hit the gym with this." He gestured at his cast.

"You aren't that much older, and you look fine. Putting up with that cast has earned you a treat."

"I'm good." He shifted in his seat, thinking he saw someone that might be Martin. The man turned and showed his pointy nose, not Martin.

Eli was silent for longer than normal. Kale forced his eyes from the crowds and glanced at him. He had one foot propped up on the dashboard. He rested the new smart phone Kale had bought him on his thigh. Eli's attention was completely engrossed in whatever he was reading on the phone. Good, at least he was accepting some of the gifts Kale bought him. Maybe offering a car wouldn't be so bad. He could buy it for Eli's birthday or Christmas.

Eli glanced up, perhaps noticing Kale was staring at him.

"What?" Eli asked.

"Nothing. I'm just glad you're using the phone," Kale said.

Eli grinned. "You won't say that when you find out what I'm looking up."

"I didn't ask." Kale looked back to the people outside, searching for any sign of Martin.

"You said you have Hep B."

So we're back on this. Kale's stomach twisted. "Yes."

"It says you can be vaccinated for it."

"I wasn't," Kale said.

"Yeah, obviously," Eli said. "The point is, I was. I think it was for some sport I played in high school. I don't remember, but I know I've had the shots, including boosters, because I remember my mom made a big fuss out of it saying something stupid like, 'Someone like you should be as protected as possible.' I swear she knew I was gay before I did. That or she thought I was going to start doing drugs, sometimes I can't tell what she's thinking."

Kale rolled his eyes and took the moment Eli paused to breathe as an opportunity to interrupt. "Or she thought you enjoyed having unprotected sex since you got your girlfriend pregnant at fifteen."

"Oh yeah, I never thought of that," Eli said. He was silent for a moment. "It really is better without a condom though. You don't know what you're missing. Well—I mean, I guess you do, since you weren't using one when you got Hep B."

Eli was really good at putting his foot in his mouth today. He'd been a rambling ball of tension ever since he'd bubbled out his love confession.

"I was raped," Kale said. Not his most tactful moment, but he was annoyed by Eli's rambling. And he knew exactly where Eli wanted this conversation to go. Eli would spew some line about how they could have sex without a condom since Eli had been vaccinated. Eli really wanted that skin on skin contact and Kale knew the only way to talk him out of it was to bear all and tell him the truth.

"Oh my God, Kale, I'm so—"

"It was a long time ago," Kale said.

"Yeah, but that kind of thing sticks with you. I can't be—"

He really wasn't going to ever shut up today, Kale thought. "I was in the system for three years. Social services, that is, when I was a kid. I bounced around to five different group homes. The other kids in the homes weren't always the nicest, and I wasn't all that big back then."

"One of the other foster kids raped you?" Eli asked, his tone hushed. Whenever Kale told the story, everyone always seemed to jump to the conclusion one of the foster parents had raped him. But in Kale's experience it was the other kids who made his life a living hell. Kids who had lost their parents and been forsaken by their extended family were generally not a cheerful or friendly bunch.

"Yes. I was beat up a lot too." Kale kept his eyes focused outside the car, anywhere other than Eli. "The point is, being raped by that kid hurt like hell. And now the idea of having sex without a condom—" His body tensed at the idea. "I know it's a mental thing, but—"

"You think it'll hurt, because it hurt when he did it?" Eli asked.

"Yes."

"Have you ever tried going bare? On someone else?"

"No."

"I think that would be the way to start, so you can—"

Kale directed his attention at Eli, his movement more than enough to stop Eli's words.

"You're not the first person I've had this conversation with," Kale said, his tone even with an underlying layer of anger. Eli shrunk back, leaning against the door, his body as far as physically possible from Kale. "The answer is no."

Eli looked away, glaring daggers into his airbag-less steering wheel. He crossed his arms and said nothing more.

Kale's spine tingled and he wondered how big of a deal this was to Eli. Would he eventually leave Kale because he missed having sex without a condom? Kale set his jaw, refusing to pursue that line of thinking. At least Eli hadn't gotten all soft and oozed pity at the idea Kale had been raped.

He wasn't sure how long they sat in silence.

"I don't think Martin is showing," Eli said, his voice flat. "Can we go back to your apartment now?"

Kale noticed the usage of calling it Kale's apartment instead of their apartment.

"Yes."

Kale also noted that Eli hadn't asked why he was in foster care for three years. Maybe he was jaded from having his confession of love played off as a joke. What if he really did love Kale and now he was pissed Kale hadn't returned the sentiment? Or was he really this upset over the condom thing?

Worry gnawed at him on the drive home. Eli said nothing as he parked the car. He got out, slammed his door a bit harder than needed, and stomped toward the apartment. Kale followed after him slowly. Eli had his own set of keys now so he could get in on his own.

He entered the apartment to find Eli in the kitchen. He slammed various cabinets as he arranged the needed items to make something, a sandwich, Kale guessed judging by the loaf of bread he had out.

"Eli?" Kale asked. Eli gripped the counter with both hands. Kale went behind him and wrapped his hand around his waist, pulling him against his body. He kissed his neck lightly. Eli's body shook and Eli covered his face. He was crying? Guilt twisted his guts.

"Come to bed," Kale said. He kissed his neck again, wanting nothing more than to pleasure Eli to the point of oblivion so he would forget whatever conflicts were tormenting him. He considered saying some words of affection, but the moment didn't seem right. "Please."

Eli turned and pressed his lips to Kale's. The kiss was desperate and tasted of salt. It reminded Kale of oh too many kisses he'd received from Martin. He forced the memories from his mind and concentrated on the now, on what Eli needed.

CHAPTER TWELVE

The next day wasn't any better. Kale wanted to shake Eli and force him to confess whatever it was that was bothering him. Sex hadn't been quite right last night and this morning Kale didn't even bother. A wall had formed between them, the emotion and passion Kale usually felt from Eli was buried, hidden from Kale and it hurt.

Eli ate his cereal, not looking up from the contents of his bowl. Kale poured his own bowl, proudly not dropping one flake in his increasingly improved one-handed skills.

"I'm going to spend the day with Jackie," Eli said. *Spoke too soon,* Kale's hand twitched and a few flakes dropped to the counter. "I need to pick up some of my stuff so I can more officially move in, anyway. And I want to tell her about the new job."

So he was leaving, but promising to come back. It wasn't like Eli was his prisoner, and he had mentioned that Eli should spend more time with Jackie while he still could. It still felt like Eli was creating an excuse to avoid him for the day though.

Eli looked up from his bowl, the look he gave Kale chilled his insides.

"Is that okay or are you going to show up on her doorstep?" Eli asked.

"Of course it's fine," Kale said. Eli's mood sure as hell wasn't though. "I'm off the narcotic painkillers so I can drive myself to my appointments. I'll be fine. When do you think you'll be back?"

"I'm not sure, depends on if Jackie's having a good day or a bad one." He held his spoon in silence, the milk slowly dripped from it. "How long can I be gone before you'll be worried I won't come back?"

Did he really portray himself as that obsessive? Kale forced a fake smile and stirred his cereal.

"I'm sure you'll come back."

"Really? You weren't that confident when I was at the birthday party."

He wanted to play hardball, huh?

"That was before you professed your love of me. Consider my confidence boosted." Kale met his gaze and held it in silence for longer than was comfortable. Eli blinked first.

"Fine. I'll have my phone. I'll update you."

"Okay."

Eli left shortly after. The apartment was deafeningly empty. He started mulling about, cleaning up things that were already clean. He put on his shoes and prepared to venture to the mall Brandi worked at. He couldn't go inside but he could loiter outside.

His phone chirped. A text from Charlotte read that one of his cases was going to court today. She was wondering if Norton had told him. Of course he hadn't. Kale groaned and had to put his phone down so he wouldn't break it. Norton probably hadn't bothered to look at the case files.

Change of plans. He needed to go into the office today. He couldn't represent his client, but he could still be in the courtroom as an observer.

Jackie's mom, Loraine, answered the door. She crossed her arms and gave Eli the normal *why are you wasting my time* expression. Eli offered her his million-watt smile in return.

"May I come in?" Eli asked. She pushed the door open and stepped to the side.

"Since when do you not have a key?" Loraine asked.

"I have one," Eli said. "I only use it when Jackie knows I'm staying here."

"Still a drifter, huh?" The disdain was more than evident in her voice. Loraine's dislike of Eli stemmed all the way back to when he'd knocked up her daughter and as Loraine said it, ruined her life forever.

"Actually, I'm moving in with someone. Renting his room. That's why I'm here. I want to pick up some of my stuff."

"Uh huh. In other words you found a new cock to suck in exchange for a roof over your head."

Eli stumbled as he entered the foyer. The bluntness in her words shocked him. Normally, she wasn't quite so rude, but this was a good reminder of why he tried to never be around her unless Jackie or Annabelle was present.

"I take it Jackie's not home," Eli said.

"She's sleeping. Today hasn't been good for her. Annabelle is at school." Loraine stared at him.

"I'll pack up some things and poke my head in her room." He almost added, *if that's okay with you*, but decided against it. He was still married to Jackie and he could see her, regardless of whether his mother-in-law approved. Eli started down the hall to the spare bedroom he kept most of his things in.

"You should know," Loraine said. "I'm trying to convince Jackie to give me custody of Annabelle."

He turned. Her words not shocking him this time, only spurring anger.

"You're what?"

"You can't take care of Annabelle by yourself. If you're honest with yourself you'd know that. I can provide her with a good life."

"She's my daughter. You can't take her from me."

She stepped toward him, her back stiff and expression cold. "We need to do what's best for Annabelle. I know being away from her will hurt you. But you know she'll be better with me."

"Well, you should know the current dick I'm sucking belongs to one of the best attorneys in the state." He had no idea if that was true, but Loraine wouldn't either. "So if you try to take my daughter from me, I'll make sure he does everything possible to stop you."

She scoffed. "You actually think your boyfriend wants a kid running around? I'll be doing you and him a favor."

He realized he hadn't actually had that talk with Kale. Had Kale realized his invite to live with him would eventually include Annabelle?

"Yeah, that's what I thought," Loraine said. She pulled her jacket off the coat rack. "I'm going out to do some errands since you're here. Think about what I said, Eli."

He used the anger Loraine had stirred up in him as fuel to sort through his things and box up what he wanted to take to Kale's house. He wanted to bring over enough items that Kale would think he took the offer to live there seriously. But few enough that he could pack up in a hurry and leave.

Martin was still coming back.

He loaded his car with three boxes, mostly clothes. He opened the door to Jackie's bedroom and knocked gently on the door. She was propped up with several pillows. The television at the foot of the bed played something softly. Jackie glanced at him and smiled.

"I thought I heard someone rummaging around," Jackie said. Her skin was pale, but otherwise she hid any discomfort she was in.

"I was packing up a few things to take over to Kale's place."

He went to her bed and crawled onto the side that had once been his. She still slept on only half the bed, leaving his side untouched as if it was still his. He stayed on top of the sheets, while she was under. He grabbed one of her numerous pillows and buried his face in it, lying on his stomach.

"Life that rough?" Jackie asked.

"Your mother is making it," he said into the pillow. He turned his head and looked at her. "I wish she didn't hate me."

Jackie ruffled his hair with her too skinny fingers. He grabbed her hand gently and kissed her knuckles.

"She's just angry about losing me and you're an easy target," Jackie said.

"I know." He kept her hand and rubbed his fingers across it, trying to warm it.

"So you're moving in with Kale? Things must be going good. We didn't scare him off, huh?"

Her eyes lit up at the idea, the dwindling spark of life in her igniting a bit more at the idea Eli might find happiness after she was gone. She'd insisted for months that they press with the divorce so Eli could move on. He was glad he'd won the battle, especially if Loraine was going to fight him for custody.

"He's ridiculous, Jackie. There's a very good chance he'll show up here today if I stay too long."

"As well he should. You should be with him. He's your future. You don't belong here in the past with your dying wife."

"You talk like you're already gone. You know I hate it when you do that." Eli tried to scowl at her but the silly look she gave him only made him laugh. "He made me get a job at his law firm, in addition to insisting I move in. Oh and get this."

He pulled out the smart phone Kale had bought him and handed it to her. She exaggerated her reaction to the device. "This is an expensive phone." She raised her eyes. "When does the new car get here?"

"Ha ha." Eli snatched the phone back and put it in his pocket.

"I'm serious. And how do I get a Kale?"

"Trust me, you don't want one." He couldn't wipe the grin off his face, though.

She rolled over in the bed and faced him. He did likewise, their noses nearly touching. He remembered spending many a night positioned just like this, both when they were kids and during their marriage.

"So what's the problem? If he's so wonderful why are you over here instead of with him?" Jackie's eyes danced. He loved seeing her this happy. He didn't want to crush it, but he also knew she was seeing past the humor to the worry eating at him.

"He's in love with someone else," Eli said. He stroked her chin, disliking the frown that suddenly appeared. "Things with him are just temporary."

"People can love more than one person. And the things he's doing don't sound like the things you do for a temporary relationship."

"He has this on again, off again thing with this other guy. It's just a matter of time until he comes back."

"Are they good for each other?"

"No. Not in the least."

"Then maybe this time things will be different."

He looked at her neck, unable to meet her eyes. "I think I already screwed it up. I told him I loved him."

"Oh, Eli."

"He didn't say it back. He played it off like a joke. I know it's stupid but—" It hurt. It hurt that he hadn't said it back. Jackie didn't ask anything else. She pulled him into her arms and he let the tears he'd been bottling up fall. He was losing his best friend, and the man he wanted to fill the void with didn't want the position.

§§§

It was dark by the time Eli came home. He carried two of the three boxes up the stairs. He couldn't carry the third in the same trip and he didn't want to make a second trip. He'd get it tomorrow. He sat the boxes on the floor so he could unlock the door.

He pushed it open and a ceramic dish shattered to bits inches from his feet as it impacted the side of the door. Eli jumped back, his heart scrambling to regain a steady rhythm.

"Shit, I'm sorry," Kale said from inside the apartment. Eli took a deep breath and collected his boxes. He pushed the door open again, his shoes crunching over the rubble. He elbowed the door shut and looked into the kitchen.

Kale stood in the center of what looked to be a demolition mission. Bits of broken plates and other dishware filled the floor and countertops. Kale's face was red, his good hand balled into a fist.

"I wasn't aiming that at you," Kale said. His tone was filled with anger like he was just barely holding himself together.

"Bad day?" Eli asked. He hugged the boxes to his chest like a protective shield.

Kale narrowed his eyes. "No. This is what I do when I've had a good day."

Eli let out a slight chuckle. "I'd hate to see what you do on extraordinary days." Eli decided to not stick around for Kale's response. "I'm going to unpack."

He scurried through the dining room, grateful the kitchen island was between himself and Kale. He went to the spare bedroom attached to the dining room and closed the door. He sat the boxes down and went to push the lock on the handle. There was no lock.

"Of course there isn't," Eli mumbled to himself. Kale was too controlling to allow someone the power of locking him out of a room. Eli wondered for a brief moment if there was a lock on the outside of the door. Would Kale have ever locked Martin in a room as punishment?

To distract him from the disturbing direction of his thoughts he went to the closet to hang his clothes. It was larger than he'd expected. His clothes barely made a dent in the void. A soft knock came on his door. *Well, wasn't that polite of him,* Eli thought.

He answered and blocked the entryway, not sure if he wanted the raging Kale in his room.

"Yes?" Eli asked.

Kale's face was still red and he was breathing heavily. *Destroying things must be hard work.*

"How was your day?" Kale asked.

Eli scrunched his forehead and crossed his arms. "It wasn't 'break the dishes' good, but it was okay."

Kale's expression remained unchanged. "Are you gaining custody of Annabelle when Jackie's gone?"

The question wasn't what Eli had expected. He took a step back, but maintained a defensive posture.

"That's normally how it works. I am her dad."

Kale nodded. "I want you to know she's welcome to live here. I don't want you to think it's going to be a problem, because it isn't."

Odd time for him to bring this up, Eli thought. "And what am I supposed to do with Annabelle on dish breaking day? This isn't a safe environment for a child."

"I know that. And this isn't—I wouldn't." Kale huffed and the air blew on Eli's face. "I lost a case today."

"How is that even possible? Aren't you suspended?"

"They gave all my cases to other attorneys at the firm. A junior partner took most of them and he's completely incompetent. He ignored my files and went in unprepared. The defense's lawyer tore him apart." Kale yanked at his beard, as if attempting to pull it out. He dropped his hand after a moment. "This wouldn't have happened if I'd been there."

"So you always break dishes when you lose a case?" Eli asked.

"Sometimes." Kale glanced over his shoulder at the mess behind him.

"How did that go over with Martin?"

"Not well." Kale seemed lost in thought for a moment, then he grabbed Eli's wrist. "Come here."

Eli let him lead him into ground zero. The bigger chunks of plates broke under his shoes. Two cardboard boxes were on the counter. Kale pulled a plate out of one.

"I found these boxes while I was clearing out the guestroom for you. Martin hid them from me." Kale rubbed the surface of the plate with his thumb. "This was his hobby. He would buy expensive plates. Some of these are from Europe. These in particular," Kale paused to look at Eli, "cost four hundred per plate."

"That's ridiculous." Eli gaped at the plate that, to him, looked just like any other.

"Martin would have Charlotte call him if I was having a bad day, and he would try to hide all the dishware before I came home. He would stock it with cheap stuff he'd picked up at discount stores." He twirled the plate in his hand. "But there's something extra satisfying in breaking a dish that costs four hundred dollars and is custom made by hand, as opposed to some cheap factory processed plate that's worth a nickel."

As if to emphasize his point, he flung the plate across the room. It hit the cabinets above the counter and shattered. He turned back to Eli with a grin on his face.

"Have you ever broken a plate that's worth that much?"

"I've never touched one that's worth anything near that," Eli said.

Kale reached into the box and pulled out a plate with a hand painted chicken on it. He held the plate to Eli. "Here's your chance."

Eli took the dish in both hands and looked at the beautiful design.

"Break it," Kale said.

"We should return these to Martin," Eli said.

"He bought them with my money," Kale said. "They're my plates he hoarded. I'm destroying them one way or another. So go ahead, break it."

"I think I'd rather not." Eli gently placed the dishware on the counter, the chicken staring at him innocently.

"Your wife is dying of cancer," Kale said. "She'll be dead before Thanksgiving. You'll have to drudge through the holiday season with that burden on your shoulders. If anyone has a reason to be pissed off and needs to vent some anger, it's you. Break the plate."

Eli bit his lip and gazed at the innocent chicken. That chicken wasn't why his wife was dying, but darn it, that chicken wasn't going to save her either. He grabbed the plate and slammed it against the corner of the counter. It broke in two, the chicken head half still in his hand. Eli flung the remaining half against the wall. A small chip broke off and the plate fell to the floor with a thud.

"Doors and cabinets break them better than the walls," Kale said. He handed him another. "Try again."

Eli gave the rooster on the plate a daring glare, then flung it against the cabinets. It broke into six pieces. Eli panted. This actually was exhilarating. He'd just destroyed eight hundred dollars and something a person had lovingly made.

Kale pulled another plate out. "Takes the edge off, doesn't it?"

"Yeah," Eli agreed. "It does."

§§§

Eli woke the next morning, his butt sore from the night before and his body still sticky. He'd neglected to shower after their activities. They'd need to wash the sheets. Eli didn't care. Maybe they'd soil them again this morning. He rolled over and found the bed empty. He'd never awoken alone in Kale's bed.

He sat up, slightly concerned. He grabbed his boxers off the floor and pulled them on. He padded barefoot down the hall and stopped as he stepped on a pebble.

He cussed and lifted his foot. A tiny piece of white ceramic was indented on his heel. He flicked it off and proceeded more carefully down the hall. He reached the kitchen and found the aftermath of last night's events. They'd broken nearly all the plates in Martin's hoard, only stopping when Kale had decided he wanted to redirect his attention onto Eli's body.

The sex with him had never been better. Eli cringed as he recalled shouting out his love for Kale while in the throes of an orgasm. Kale had replied with a husky, "I know," and moved on.

And now he was waking up alone. He retreated from the kitchen and went to the bedroom. He found his phone on the charger. He didn't recall putting it there. He dialed Kale's number. After five rings it went to voicemail.

Eli decided against leaving a message. He'd been making a big enough ass of himself. He busied himself with bundling up the sheets and putting them in the washer. He was about to get in the shower when his phone rang.

He answered on the second ring.

"Kale?"

"Yeah, everything okay?" Kale asked.

"Where are you?"

"Did you get my note?"

"No." Eli glanced around the bedroom but saw no note.

"I left it in the kitchen."

"I haven't ventured in there. It's still a mess."

"Right."

"Why didn't you answer when I called?"

"I'm working with one hand, Eli, remember?"

"Okay, right. So where are you?"

"At the food donation center, sorting cans. I still have a lot of volunteer hours to finish before I can go back to work."

Eli sagged against the wall. Right, his volunteer work. He was overreacting and he hated himself for it. He'd thought for sure Kale had snuck off to be with Martin, or at least stalk him somewhere.

"Are you okay? Should I come home?" Kale asked.

"No." He cleared his throat and fought back the tears. He was a mess, but it wasn't Kale's job to fix him. "I'm fine. Do your volunteer work. I'll go spend some time with Annabelle."

"Are you sure?"

Did he really sound that bad? He cleared his throat and forced himself to sound more collected than he felt.

"Yeah, I am. I'll see you later."

He showered, cleaned the wreckage in the kitchen and finished the laundry. He ate a quick lunch and went to spend the day with Annabelle, dreading the encounter he was likely to face with Loraine.

CHAPTER THIRTEEN

The weekend passed in a blur and before Eli knew it, he was struggling through his first day of work. He was kicking himself for saying he could start on Monday. Kale was getting his pins removed from his hand today and now Eli was unable to take him.

Kale had insisted it was fine and that his first day of work was more important. So here he was, listening to the ins and outs of sorting mail from his assigned mentor, Sanchez. The day started at five in the morning, thirty minutes before the mail was delivered to the building. The first two hours of the day was spent sorting the mail, the next six delivering it to the businesses in the building. Any free time was used to prep outgoing packages. Eli would learn that part of the job last. Eli's shift was from five to two, which worked perfect with Annabelle's school schedule. He'd need someone to take her to school, but he'd be off in time to pick her up after work. He wondered if Kale could take her. He wasn't certain of Kale's work hours, or if he kept any kind of schedule.

"This is your homeboy's floor, yeah?" Sanchez said as he pushed the mail cart off the elevator onto the second floor.

"Uh, yeah, it is," Eli agreed.

"Cool." Sanchez nodded his head and stopped at the front counter. "This is Suzie. Suzie, meet the new guy, Eli."

"Hi," Suzie said. "I remember you. You're with Kale."

"Uh, yeah, I am." She was the same receptionist who had been working last week.

"We always stop and check with Suzie first, before we go in," Sanchez explained. "Sometimes there will be a VIP client and it's best if we come back later. So, we all cleared, Suzie?"

"Yes, you are. Go ahead."

Sanchez turned back to him and Suzie opened the doors. "I try to come to this floor between ten and one, the VIPs aren't usually here over the lunch hour."

Eli wondered what constituted a VIP client and if Kale ever worked with them. He followed after Sanchez and tried to make sense of the order of desks. Each had a nameplate.

"The lawyers who have offices, we give their mail to their secretary. The interns, it goes straight to them. After a while you learn to memorize where everyone sits, until then, use the nameplates."

They were halfway through the deliveries, about five desks away from Charlotte's desk, when the doors opened and a frenzied Suzie shouted for the man to stop. The name she called paralyzed every muscle in Eli's body.

"Martin, stop! You aren't allowed back here!" Suzie said.

Eli stared at the letters in his hands, afraid to look up.

"Where is he?" a man said. His voice was perfect, light and gentle, even though there was a layer of annoyance.

"He's not here," Charlotte said. "And you shouldn't be either. You have a restraining order out against Kale. That means you can't go near him either."

"He stopped payment." That had to be Martin. "He's never done that before."

Eli looked up from the letters to Charlotte's desk. Martin had his back to Eli. He wore designer clothes, smooth and pressed. His dark blond hair was a few inches long and styled with enough gel to stop a freight train. He was a few inches taller than Eli but shorter than Kale. His body was thicker, more defined. It was obvious he went to a gym regularly. Eli should really get a membership at one as well, especially if his competition did.

"That's something you should have your lawyer contact Kale about. You can't speak directly to him," Charlotte said.

"I'm calling security," Suzie said. She retreated from the room, returning to her desk.

"Are you sure he isn't here?" Martin turned his body, searching the offices; his gaze lingered on Kale's locked office. Eli got his first good look at Martin's face and Kale's handiwork.

His was light skinned, which only magnified the darkness around his left eye. The bruising was a mix of purple and green. Lighter marks were on his neck and there were two butterfly bandages on his forehead, holding a three-inch cut shut.

Eli felt sick. He'd known Kale was violent. He'd read the newspaper article, but it was quite another to see it. What did the rest of Martin's body look like? Martin shuffled a few steps around Charlotte's desk and Eli noticed a distinct limp.

Eli dropped the letter on the desk he was near and covered his mouth as he tasted bile.

"Hey, you okay?" Sanchez asked, placing a hand gently on his shoulder. Eli managed to nod and swallowed back the bile. That would not be Eli's future. He refused.

"Please. Charlotte I need that money. He knows I need it. Can't you call him? I'll remove the restraining order. Do you think that's what he wants?" Martin rambled.

The doors opened and Eli expected to see a guard enter. Instead a tall lanky woman came in. She wore a sleeveless dress that made her thin arms look skinnier and longer than they were. The dress was a straight line as it draped over her chest and stopped above her knobby knees. She towered a half foot over Martin as she approached him. Eli's eyes went to her two-inch heels.

She reminded him of a long-legged spider. The way she swooped in and grabbed Martin's shoulder solidified the image of this woman being an insect-like predator.

"You heard her," the woman said. "You can't be here."

The woman's voice was strong and authoritative. Martin shrunk from her.

"My brother finally has the balls to cut you off and you come crawling back like a slug. Really, Martin? Grow a pair and get out," the woman said.

Martin retreated, backing to the doors. "He owes me that money, and you all know it. It's no different than an alimony check."

The woman put her hands on her hips. "Yeah, except he never married you. Gay marriage is legal and if he wanted to marry you, he would have. But he didn't. So stop sniffing around for scraps and get out."

Real pain showed in the man's eyes. He turned and dashed out the doors.

"Eli?" Sanchez said.

"I'm fine," Eli said, prying his eyes away from the scene. "Kale has a sister?" Why he thought Sanchez would know this, he had no idea, but he didn't feel comfortable asking anyone else. The intern at the desk they'd stopped at replied.

"She's his stepsister. They hate each other," the intern said. That explained the stark differences in their appearances. Kale's sister looked to be mixed with something foreign, her skin a dark chestnut, perhaps Indian.

"Come on, let's keep moving," Sanchez said. He pulled the cart and Eli followed.

Kale's sister leaned on Charlotte's desk, her straight black hair falling into her face.

"So now that I've dealt with that problem for you, how about you do me a favor and tell me where I can find my brother?" she asked.

"Call him yourself," Charlotte said, crossing her arms.

"I did. He isn't answering."

"Such a shame," Charlotte said, feigning sympathy.

"I flew in from New York. He won't answer his phone, he isn't home, and he isn't here. So where is he?"

"He's off this week. I don't maintain his personal calendar. So I don't know."

"I do," Eli said. His heart seemed to have migrated into his chest as he spoke. He paused as they passed Charlotte's desk.

The woman directed her dark brown eyes at Eli. "Why does the mail boy know where my brother is when his secretary doesn't?"

"Because I'm dating him," Eli said. Everyone in the office seemed to stare at them, more so than when Martin had been present.

Her eyes widened, making her look like a skeleton. "My brother broke up with the great Martin and got a new boy-toy?" She narrowed her eyes. "Why is he dating the help? He could do better than a mailroom boy."

"He got me this job, thank you," Eli said.

"He's making you work?" She sounded genuinely surprised.

"Do you want me to tell you where he is or not?" Eli asked. He wrinkled his brow and crossed his arms.

"Sassy boy," she said. Her eyes roved his body. "Please do tell, where is my brother?"

"Harper Drive Medical Clinic," Eli said. "He won't be answering his phone because he's having an outpatient procedure. I can give you my mother's number and—"

"Your mother took him?"

"He needed someone to drive him and I had to work."

"Oh this, this is delightful." She rubbed her hands together like she was an evil villain from a cartoon. "I would love to have your mother's number. What's your name, mailroom boy?"

"Eli." He extended a hand to her.

"Delighted to meet you, Eli. I'm Alexis."

§§§

Removing Kale's six pins was supposed to be a simple outpatient procedure. After taking an X-ray the doctor decided Kale would need a permanent pin placed in his hand through his middle finger and down to his wrist. The procedure was still an outpatient surgery, performed in the doctor's office.

The difference was, it required partial sedation. Kale was regaining his bearings just as a voice echoed in his room. Her shrill tone drudged up memories of the past and put him on edge. He opened his eyes and saw his stepsister standing at the foot of his bed, her arms crossed and her deep brown eyes watching him.

Eli's mother, Marge, cowered in the corner of the room. Either Alexis had already insulted her or Marge was terrified by her mere appearance. Perhaps it was a mix of both.

Kale rubbed his face, pushing away the last bits of sedative. His arm was numb from the shoulder down, a fresh white plaster cast already in place and hanging from a sling.

"Hey brother," Alexis said. Her wide mouth grinned at him like the Cheshire Cat.

Kale groaned. "Why are you here?"

"Tomorrow is Riley's birthday." She sat on the edge of the bed. "I met your new boyfriend."

Those two simple sentences explained volumes. She'd gone to his work searching for him and had found Eli instead. Kale had completely forgotten about Riley's birthday. Remembering birthdays had always been something Martin did.

"He's absolutely delicious," Alexis said. She cast a glance at Marge. "Sorry if that's rude, but he really is." She looked back at Kale. "I don't suppose he swings both ways? I thought he was checking me out but it's not like you to—"

"Keep your mitts off," Kale said. He tried to sit up and the room swayed.

"Touchy. You must really like him." She pulled a cigarette out of her clutch and put it in her mouth.

"You can't smoke in here."

"It's an E-cigarette," she said.

"I don't care. You still can't smoke it in here."

She rolled her eyes and glared at him. "You know I'm supposed to be the one telling you what you can and can't do."

"Yeah, like that's ever worked."

She sighed and tucked the stick back in her purse. "Well, I'm in town tonight and tomorrow." She stood from the bed. "I expect you to fill me on…" She waved her hand at his cast. "All this and the boy-toy. And I'm sleeping on your couch."

Of course she was. He closed his eyes and leaned back on the pillows, wishing they'd given him stronger drugs.

§§§

Eli's mother had sent him a message saying Kale's sister had arrived at the clinic and brought Kale home. Eli wasn't sure if she would still be at the apartment. He bounded up the stairs two at a time, unsure what he would encounter inside.

He unlocked the door and entered. The skeleton woman from earlier sat on a stool at the kitchen island that divided the dining room from the kitchen. She took a drag from her electronic cigarette and turned to look at him.

"Hi," Eli said.

She rested an elbow on the counter and held the cigarette in the air.

"I think we got off on the wrong foot earlier," she said.

"Where's Kale?" Eli asked.

"In his bedroom resting. They had to do surgery again." She stood, moving slightly to block his path. "Before you talk to him I think you and I should have a chat."

Eli crossed his arms. "Go ahead."

"I didn't tell Kale about Martin stopping by the office, and I don't think you should either."

"I don't want to lie to him."

"I'm not saying we do that, but…" She turned the cigarette off and dropped it in a small clutch. "I think we both know how unstable Kale's relationship is with Martin. You heard the same things I did today. Martin puts up with Kale for the money. If Kale is really cutting him off, then this might end for real this time. If we tell Kale that Martin is looking for him, then we lose whatever ground we've gained."

"And if he finds out I kept this from him, he'll be pissed," Eli said.

"I think that's worth keeping them apart for a little longer, don't you?" She held up a phone on the counter. "I've been screening his calls. I'm confident Martin will give up soon."

"He's been calling?" Eli's heart sunk. The end *was* near. "Next he'll show up at the apartment."

"He won't be as brave in person."

Eli knew there was truth in that statement, and honestly, he doubted Martin would put himself in a situation that would leave him alone with Kale. Not until he received some sign that Kale wasn't going to react violently to the encounter.

"All I'm asking is that we not tell him today," she said. It seemed reasonable enough, and Eli could always use the sister as a scapegoat if things went south. It was, after all, her idea.

"Fine."

She nodded, and he quickly passed her. He went to Kale's room and entered without knocking. Kale was sleeping on his back, his injured arm propped up on pillows above his head.

"Kale?" Eli asked as he approached.

"M-martin?" Kale asked, shifting on the bed and opening his eyes. Of all the days to go through this again, Eli was not in the mood.

"No, Eli." He gently brushed the back of his fingers across Kale's forehead.

"Eli," Kale murmured. "My sister's here."

"I know. I met her."

"She's a bitch."

"I got that impression as well." Eli pulled his hand back and Kale suddenly grabbed his wrist with his good arm.

"Don't leave. I don't want to be alone with her," Kale said.

"I wasn't planning to leave," Eli said. "I need to shower and change though. I just got home from work."

"First day," Kale said softly. His body relaxed and he loosened his grip. Eli waited a few moments until he was confident Kale was asleep, before he fully retracted his hand and exited the room.

The night proceeded somewhat awkwardly. Kale slept most of it, forcing Eli to interact with Alexis.

"He didn't tell you about me, did he?" she asked as they ate their delivery pizza, seated across from each other at the dining table.

"Our relationship hasn't proceeded in the most orthodox manner," Eli said. He understood now why Kale had demanded he stay. Eli wanted nothing more than to flee to Jackie's house for the night.

Alexis rested her elbows on the table and formed an arch with her hands. She rested her chin on her fingers and focused on him.

"How about we trade information? I tell you something about me, you do likewise."

Eli hesitated. Did he really want to play a modified game of truth or dare with Kale's sister?

"I'll start. I'm two years older than Kale."

Seemed like an easy enough start. "I'm twenty-two."

She smiled. "I work for Vanity Fair in New York City."

"I've been unemployed for most of the last two years. I started in the mailroom today." Eli realized it would have been useful to play this game with Kale.

"I have two brothers."

"I'm an only child," Eli said.

"Stop interrogating him," Kale said. They both looked to the doorway and saw Kale sagging against it. "I got hungry. Looks like it was a good thing, too."

Alexis rolled her eyes. "I've probably learned more about your boyfriend in the last ten minutes than you have in the entire time you've been together."

Sadly, Eli knew this was close to the truth, at least for him.

"Maybe I didn't want to expose him to you." Kale sat at the table next to Eli and grabbed a slice of pizza.

"I think he should come tomorrow," Alexis said.

"He has to work," Kale said.

"You got him a job at your firm. Pull some strings and let him have the day off."

"It's his second day."

"So what? You had surgery and your sister is in town."

Eli shifted in his seat, disliking the fact they were discussing his fate as if he weren't there.

"What's happening tomorrow?" Eli asked. Alexis and Kale exchanged a look.

"Riley adored Martin," Alexis said. "If we take Eli with us, it might take some of the edge off."

"Who's Riley?" Eli asked.

"My half-brother," Kale said.

Alexis addressed Eli. "Tomorrow is Riley's birthday. We always visit him together on his birthday."

"And you're worried Riley will be upset Martin isn't going?" Eli asked, scrambling to piece together the dynamics of their family.

"Have you told him nothing?" Alexis said, shooting a glare at Kale.

"We've only been together ten days," Kale said. "We haven't swapped family trees."

"Ten days?" Her tone was hushed, like she'd suddenly realized a grave error. "I'm sorry, I-I should—excuse me." She rose from the table. She hastily grabbed her phone and clutch. "I should call home and make sure Henry is okay. I'll be back in a bit."

She left the apartment. Eli stared uncomfortably at his remaining pizza slice.

"Henry is her fiancé," Kale said. "I've never met him. I'm not entirely certain he exists."

"Why did she freak out like that?" Eli dared a look at Kale. He ruffled his hair and hefted his sling onto the table.

"I think she thought you and I are more serious than we are. Sometimes the way you..." He shook his head. "Never mind, it doesn't matter. She's a complete spaz."

Eli couldn't help but wonder what the rest of that sentence was. What exactly was Eli doing that was giving people the wrong impression?

"Do you want me to give you some family history while she's away?" Kale asked.

"No." Eli stood from the table. "It's been a long day. I'm going to turn in for the night."

"It's only seven."

"Long day," Eli repeated. He collected his paper plate and tossed it in the garbage. Although Kale had, in a way, forced Eli to tell him about his family, he disliked the idea of Kale being forced to do the same. And it really bugged him that Kale hadn't felt comfortable enough to finish that sentence.

CHAPTER FOURTEEN

Kale finished putting away the pizza and was wiping down the counters for the third time when his sister came back.

"You really do have horrible timing," Kale said.

"I didn't pick when Riley's birthday is. Where's Eli? Did you fill him in on things?"

"He doesn't want to be filled in, and I'm not going tomorrow."

"Kale."

"Riley would be happier only seeing you." He dropped the dishtowel in the hamper.

"Don't blame me for your messed up relationships," Alexis said. She crossed her arms. "If you're not going, then I'll deal with it, but you should at least explain things to Eli. He seems like—"

"Don't, just don't," Kale said. She took a deep breath, but held her tongue. She walked past him and retreated to the hall bathroom.

Kale stared for a moment at the closed door to Eli's bedroom. He didn't like the idea of sleeping alone tonight. Nor of leaving Eli unprotected while his sister slept on the couch.

He went to the room and knocked gently before opening it. Eli lay on the bed, dressed in flannel pajamas and a white t-shirt. He lowered the book he'd been reading.

"May I come in?"

Eli nodded.

"Good book?" Kale asked.

"Yes," Eli said. He closed it and dumped it in the side table drawer before Kale could read the title. Kale closed the door and sat on the edge of the bed.

"I want to fill you in on things."

"You don't have to."

"I want to. If you're going to live here, you should be informed. None of this would be awkward if our relationship was progressing in a more normal fashion. Do you realize we haven't even been on a real date?"

"Huh, I guess we haven't." Eli pulled his legs up to his chest and leaned against the headboard. "Unless you count spying on Martin."

"Yeah, no, that's not." He ruffled his hair and glanced at his swollen fingers. He was beginning to think his hand would never be back to normal. "When things calm down, I'm taking you out on a real date."

"Things will never be normal for us."

He looked at Eli's solemn face but Eli avoided his gaze. Kale took a deep breath.

"So my dad is Freddie Kruz," Kale said. "Have you heard of him?"

Eli squinted. Kale could almost see the gears turning in his head.

"It sounds familiar. Why don't you have his name?"

"He never married my mother."

"Ah."

"Freddie Kruz is a lightweight boxing champion. He was very popular in the eighties and he was in the running for the world championship three times," Kale said.

Eli nodded. "My dad follows boxing. I probably saw some of his games." Eli grinned. "I can just imagine my dad's expression when I tell him he's your dad." Eli narrowed his eyes. "Wait, did he even raise you?"

"He was in my life off and on. My mother left him when I was eight. He used to beat her to the point where she wouldn't be able to get out of bed for days. He was fairly liberal with the belt on me. When she left him, she made sure he couldn't contact me."

This wasn't the first time Kale had told this story. Per normal, there was no look of surprise on Eli's face. Kale was an abuser, it was common knowledge that sort of thing normally ran in the family.

Now the part Kale really didn't want to tell him. "My mother died when I was twelve. She got a bad cough and we couldn't afford the medicine she needed."

The horror in Eli's eyes was exactly what Kale predicted. "Oh, God, Kale."

Eli was too fragile, his emotions always on his sleeve. Kale raised his hand, to stop Eli from becoming a blubbering mess and smothering him in a hug.

"It was twenty years ago, Eli, I'm fine."

Eli bit his lip and nodded, shuffling back to his previous position, his reluctance was noticeable though. "Continue."

"I went into foster care. I've told you a bit about this part."

Eli nodded.

"When I was fifteen, my father found out what happened. He filed to gain custody of me. When social services went to approve him for adoption, they discovered his household was not only unfit for me, but for the two children already living with him."

Eli watched attentively, but didn't interrupt.

"My father had married an illegal immigrant. She had one daughter already, Alexis, who was seventeen at the time. He fathered another son, Riley, who was only five. Social services couldn't prove Alexis was being abused, but the marks were evident on Riley." Kale paused. This was another part of the story people didn't generally react well too. "He's mentally disabled."

"What?" Eli lunged forward, flipping onto his knees. His hands automatically forming fist. "Your dad was beating his mentally challenged son?"

"From what I understand it was less physical and more neglect and emotional abuse," Kale said.

"But still, that's horrible."

"This was all fifteen years ago," Kale reminded him.

"Right, okay, go on," Eli said. He didn't settle back in his seat though.

"Social services removed Riley from the situation and kept me in the system. When Alexis turned eighteen, she was able to gain custody of me, but not Riley. We've both done what we can over the years to ensure he's well taken care of. He's in one of those group homes now with other disabled people. He's not stable enough to be without supervision."

"What's his situation? I mean, there's different kinds of mental disability, right?"

"His behavior is similar to that of an eight-year-old," Kale said. "He has the same temper as our father and I, though."

Eli flinched. "That must be hard."

"Riley dislikes me because I look a lot like our father. I'm told I act a bit like him too."

"What happened to Alexis' mother?" Eli asked.

"Alexis' mother died when I was twenty-five. She was still with our dad. He was the one driving. They were arguing. He went to hit her and drove the car into a pole. He died instantly, she died three days later from an embolism no one detected."

Eli covered his mouth, holding back his reaction.

"Please tell me that's it," Eli said. "I don't think I can handle more stories of tragedies."

"The three of us don't get along that well, but we're all we have. So on birthdays and holidays we make it a point to be there for each other. Riley took a liking to Martin. This will be the first time in five years Martin won't be with us when we visit him."

Eli dropped his hand, his expression more grief-stricken than Kale ever wanted to see.

"And that's why your sister wants me to go, because she thinks Riley will like me?"

"You're a likeable person," Kale said. He noticed the flicker of pain in Eli's eyes as he spoke. Kale realized too late he should have said loveable.

Eli nodded. "I'll go. Can I hug you now?"

"Absolutely."

§§§

Sleep evaded Eli until nearly dawn. Images of a younger Kale being bullied in a group home haunted his dreams. Kale's lips on his neck sent bursts of tingles through his body, rousing him from the sleep he still wanted. He instinctively pushed into the touch, kissing him back and pressing his body against Kale's.

"What time is it?" Eli asked.

"A little after eight," Kale said.

"What?" Eli perked up, panic hitting him. "I'm late for work."

Kale pressed his hand to Eli's chest and pushed him down. "I already called and told them you wouldn't be in."

"It's my second day."

"They'll understand." Kale suckled on his ear and rubbed his arousal against Eli's crotch. He closed his eyes and tried to enjoy the moment but Kale's back and forth with the status of their relationship still had him rattled.

"Are you sure it's a good idea for me to meet Riley?"

Kale pulled back so he could look Eli in the eyes. "Of course it is. He'll love you."

Love. So Kale was capable of saying the word. "That's my point," Eli said. "Are you sure it's smart for him to get attached to me?"

"Sure." Kale resumed kissing him. Eli squirmed.

"But this is all just temporary. Martin's coming back. Don't you think Riley will be confused? It might be easier to tell Riley that Martin is sick or something instead of trying to explain—"

Kale pulled back again. "Why are you saying all of this?"

"Because I'm tired of giving people the wrong impression."

Kale set his jaw. "This isn't what I meant."

"Then what did you mean? You said the way I look at you gives people the wrong impression. You meant it makes people think our relationship is more serious than it is, right? And if it's not serious then I shouldn't be meeting your family."

"No. That's not what this is. It's not what I meant."

"Then what did you mean? Am I or am I not a placeholder until Martin comes back?" Martin who already wanted to come back and had probably left a dozen or so voicemails on Kale's phone last night. Messages Alexis could only intercept for so long.

"You're not a placeholder."

"Then what happens when Martin comes back?"

"I don't know," Kale said. Eli studied his face for a moment and realized Kale was telling the truth. Kale was in uncharted waters and had no idea what he was doing.

"Let me know when you figure it out." Eli pulled away from him.

"What does that mean?"

Eli collected his clothes and dressed. "It means I've already said I love you more than once. You know how I feel. I can't stay here and get more attached to you and your family. Not if this is all temporary." A lump formed in his throat. He really hadn't expected the conversation to go this far. "My heart is already going to be broken once this month when Jackie dies. I can't—" He couldn't let it happen twice, possibly within weeks of each other.

He was running and he knew it. Kale was never supposed to be something serious. He needed to end it now before he got any deeper than he already was.

§§§

Eli's words floored him. Kale's body wouldn't respond. His legs and arms were useless stumps. Eli stuttered to get his last point across as he dressed.

He's leaving me, Kale thought. Kale hadn't hit him. Hadn't abused him in any way. Yet, Eli was still leaving. *What is wrong with me? Why does everyone leave?* He had no friends left to speak of. His only family was his sister and brother, both of which only spoke to him on special occasions.

He had no one. He couldn't even keep a new boyfriend for longer than a week.

"I can't do this," Eli said, finally getting the words out. "Not until you figure out what you want."

"Martin may not come back," Kale said, his body finally responding. "You don't know what I did to him. He may never come back. You can't leave me over something that hasn't happened."

Eli looked him directly in the eyes, but the love he'd seen moments ago was gone.

"He'd already be back if your sister hadn't intervened," Eli said. "He came to the office yesterday. He wants you back."

Kale's world swirled in confusion. Martin wanted back? It was impossible.

"No. He." Kale rubbed his forehead, the start of a headache itching at him.

"Ask your sister. She's been screening Martin's calls all night. Martin is back, and I can't deal with all of this—" The words Eli was saying were lost in the simple phrase that Martin was back, or at least the idea that he wanted back. Kale was up and out the bedroom door while Eli still scrambled to finish his statement.

He entered the kitchen to a wide-eyed Alexis. She was already dressed, her make-up perfectly applied.

"What happened?" she asked.

"Did Martin go the office yesterday?" Kale asked.

Her lips straightened into a small line. "He was only there because of the money. You have to realize that, Kale. These last few years, it's only been about the money for him."

"Why he is trying to reach me is between him and me. Where's my phone?"

She pulled it out of her clutch and placed it on the counter. How had she come to possess his phone? Why hadn't he noticed it was missing? His focus was blurred around Eli. Sometimes he forgot that a world existed outside of Eli.

"Has Martin tried to call me?"

"Yes."

He considered asking how many times, but decided it didn't matter.

"Kale, Eli cares about you. Don't let your obsession with Martin ruin what could be a good thing," Alexis said.

Kale unlocked the screen on his phone and as if on cue, it began to ring. Martin's number was on the display. Kale stared at it. He'd been telling himself Martin would come back. He'd been expecting this. He wanted this.

Alexis said nothing as the call went to voicemail. The screen went dark. A few seconds later, it chirped to indicate a voicemail had been left.

"Was that him?" Eli asked. Kale looked at him. He was pale and motionless, standing in the doorway of the kitchen. Alexis stared at them both.

"Yes," Kale said. Martin had ignored Kale's calls for six weeks. Kale could ignore Martin's calls for a few days. Even as the rationality of the prospect crossed his mind, he found himself in disbelief. He was going to ignore Martin. It wasn't the first time he'd done it, and as was usual, he was doing it to punish Martin. Sort of.

"Today is about Riley, not my messed up love life." Kale put the ringer on silent and tucked the phone into his back pocket.

Something in Eli's eyes sparked, he almost had a twinkle in them.

"And you're coming with us to meet Riley," Kale insisted. Eli nodded.

CHAPTER FIFTEEN

Alexis rode in the backseat of Kale's car as they drove to the group home where Riley lived. Eli drove. It was the first time Kale had let him drive his car, but Kale's backseat had more room than Eli's. They pulled into a parking spot and Kale cussed.

"What?"

"We forgot a cake," Kale said. Martin always had Brandi make a special cake. He should have ordered one.

"We'll take him out somewhere and get one," Alexis said. She exited the car and stretched her long limbs.

"He's going to be upset we forgot a cake," Kale said.

"We didn't forget. We're going to take him out and let him pick his own. We'll say we planned it that way."

"I can call my mom," Eli said. Kale looked at him. "Several people in her church are bakers. I'm sure they can pull something together last minute."

"I'm glad you came," Kale said. He reached across the center console and pulled him into a deep kiss. For now, Eli was still his, and he wanted to make sure Eli knew it.

"You two go in, maybe give Riley some heads up about me, and I'll call my mom," Eli said.

"Okay," Kale agreed. He exited the car and followed Alexis. Only now did he notice the gift bag she carried. A gift. Another aspect Martin usually took care of. Kale was tempted to utilize Martin's current attempts at contacting him to get a cake and gift for Riley.

He froze partway to Riley's home. Alexis noticed his hesitation and glanced back.

"What?"

"What if Martin's here? He's close to Riley. This is the first time we've been apart during a holiday. Do you think he'd come here?"

She seemed to consider this, her eyes glazing unseeing for a moment. "No. I don't think he'd come here without your permission. Martin still doesn't know if you're angry at him. He won't risk a face to face confrontation until he has an indication otherwise."

Her words made sense. Kale did have every reason to still be mad at Martin. He resumed the walk to the group home.

Six disabled people lived in the one story house, a trained staff member or two were always on shift. Kale rubbed his cast. He hadn't taken any pain medication, but his arm was strangely numb, likely from the shock of everything he'd been forced to digest in the last few hours.

The front door opened to a communal living room, behind it was the dining room and kitchen. They entered the house and Alexis chattered with the nurse currently working.

"I'm glad you made it," the nurse said. Kale had no idea her name and didn't care to learn it. She was slightly overweight and looked about as useful as a post. This is what kind of help his money was paying for?

"Wouldn't miss it for anything," Alexis said.

"Riley's been looking forward to your visit. He's always bragging about his big brother and sister." She looked at Kale. "He was delighted when he saw your name in the paper."

Alexis looked at him. "You were in the paper? For a case?"

"For putting a college professor in a coma," Kale said. Alexis flinched. It was a slight twisting of the facts, Wayne had been the one in a coma, not the professor, but the story held more punch saying it the other way.

"Alexis!" Riley's voice boomed across the house. His short, round form bounded toward them, embracing Alexis in a bear hug. His boyish features grinned. Kale noticed how long his hair was, his bangs covered his eyes. Why weren't they giving him proper haircuts?

"You need a haircut," Kale said, the words warm.

"So do you," Riley said. "You look like a lumberjack." He gestured to Kale's face. The beard, right, he wasn't sure Riley had ever seen him with one.

"Shaving is hard one handed," Kale said. Riley gasped, noticing the cast.

"What happened? Did you do this hurting Martin?" Riley's gentle hands took Kale's casted arm and inspected it. Kale wished he still had the one on that Annabelle had decorated. Riley would have enjoyed seeing her artwork.

Annabelle.

"I brought someone with me today that I want you to meet," Kale said.

Riley's face scrunched up. "Who?"

"My new boyfriend," Kale said.

"I thought Martin was your boyfriend?"

"Martin and I had a disagreement. He won't be around for a while," Kale said.

"Is he still upset about his dad dying?" Riley asked. Kale's mouth went dry. Who had told Riley about that?

"I don't know," Kale said, forcing the words out. The front door opened and Eli entered, pulling Kale's thoughts from the past and back into the present.

Riley still held his cast. Kale wasn't certain how to detach himself so he motioned Eli to join them.

"This is Eli, he's my new boyfriend," Kale said.

"Hi," Eli said. He offered a warm smile. Riley looked him over skeptically, like he was considering purchasing Eli in a store. "It's nice to meet you."

Kale's heartbeat throbbed in his cast as the seconds ticked by. This introduction could go in so many different directions.

"Hi," Riley said, at last. He thrust his hand out in greeting. Eli broadened his smile and accepted the offer. "Be nice to my brother. Martin would make him real mad."

He'd never heard Riley put the blame on Martin before.

"I'll do my best," Eli said. He looked at Kale. "My mother will be in here in twenty minutes." He looked to Riley. "I hope you like parties, because she's probably bringing her entire church group."

Riley's face lit up like he'd been told it was Christmas. "I love parties!"

The awkward greeting over, Riley buzzed with energy. They got the dining room ready for the visitors. The other members of the group home joined in, excited for the company.

When they had a moment to themselves, Eli pulled Kale to the side.

"I hope this is okay," Eli said. "When I started explaining the situation to my mother she got excited and kind of took over. I don't know if you've noticed but she loves gossip."

"Are you saying my having a disabled brother is a positive thing in your mother's eyes?"

"You've no idea," Eli said.

"Look who's here," the nurse from earlier said. She stepped to the side and a group of six middle-aged women paraded into the room. A heftier woman with brown locks led the way, holding a large sheet cake in front of her. The other five all had gift bags and wore polka dotted party hats.

§§§

Kale mostly stayed in the background during the festivities. He watched his brother shine in the spotlight the older women cast him in. They ogled and awed over him, treating him like a chick from their own brood. How they'd thrown together a cake and gifts with twenty minutes of prep time, Kale would never understand.

Alexis sat next to him on the couch and handed him a cup of punch.

"So a little birdie let it slip that Eli has a daughter," Alexis said. She sipped her punch before continuing. "Riley is telling everyone that he's an uncle now."

"What?" Kale stiffened. Alexis smiled.

"He's happy, let him be."

Kale tried to loosen tense muscles but found it difficult. "What else did they mention?"

"Nothing else," Alexis said. "I was hoping you would elaborate for me."

Kale huffed and leaned back on the cushions. Everyone else was in the dining hall or outside in the backyard, no one close enough to overhear them.

"Eli's bi. He got his high school sweetheart pregnant and decided to do her right and marry her. He came out to her two years ago and they've been separated since. Six months later, she was diagnosed with terminal cancer. Again, he opted to do the right thing and stay married to her until the end. She has less than a month left."

Alexis covered her face and blinked her eyes quickly. "Wow, that's a lot to take in." Her voice cracked slightly. "So how did he end up with you?"

"I met him in lockup, after I was arrested for beating Martin and his boyfriend in public."

"You took home a guy you met in jail?"

"It was supposed to be a one-night stand," Kale said. "Then this happened." He gestured at his cast. "And things... I..." He couldn't think of how to phrase it. Eli had been the only one to answer his call when he'd needed help and now he didn't want to let go.

"What was he in jail for?"

"Petty theft and possession of narcotics."

"Which translates to?"

Kale arched an eyebrow. "What?"

"What was he stealing and why did he have drugs on him?"

Kale realized he still didn't know. The topic hadn't been a priority. "I didn't ask."

"You should. Stealing doesn't add up. I can't picture him doing it."

Kale realized he couldn't either. Not even a stick of gum. So it did beg the question, why had Eli been arrested? Even the bigoted officer had to have supporting evidence before making the arrest. Kale needed to find out what it was.

§§§

Kale had to leave for his therapy appointment at one. He took Alexis with him so he could drop her off at the airport. Eli stayed behind with Riley and his family. Kale hesitated to leave them all there, worried what topics would come up, but he didn't have much choice.

After his appointment, another which he dodged most questions and learned nothing in ways to curb his temper, he stopped at the office. He skirted queries from his coworkers, who asked how his arm was and when he'd be back. Charlotte mechanically told him of a few important messages. He noted she said nothing of Martin.

He knocked on Jesus' office. "Can I come in?"

"Of course." He looked up from a stack of files, a broad smile on his face.

Kale shut the door behind him and sat across the desk from Jesus.

"How are things?"

"Progressing," Kale said. "I wanted to ask you about the case you were handling for me."

"Oh yeah, I took care of it. I got the charges dismissed."

"Can you tell me more about the circumstances?" Kale asked.

"Uh, sure," Jesus said. He rummaged through a stack of files on his desk. "I don't think I've filed it away for storage yet, so give me a sec. I want to refresh my memory. If I recall properly, you had a few facts wrong."

He pulled out a manila file and nodded.

"Yeah, this is it." Jesus opened it and skimmed the contents. "You said you met Eli in county jail, right?"

"Right."

"Yeah, I guess you don't meet the most trustworthy people in jail, so it's no surprise the story you told me didn't match up with the official report."

"What do you mean?" When he'd paid for Eli's bail, the officer had confirmed Eli's story: petty theft and possession.

"An employee at the store, Selena, she called the police. She said she caught Eli stealing a video game worth $2. The arresting officer, as we know, is prejudice of homosexuals, so when Selena also happened to mention this, he was more than happy to arrest him.

"When I called the storeowner to collaborate the story, he said he was already planning to drop all the charges." Jesus looked up at Kale. "He said Selena and Eli knew each other and the arrest was all part of a lover's quarrel. I dug a little deeper and other witnesses at the scene confirm the couple were arguing, rather loudly."

Lover's quarrel. Kale was hung up on those words. How many lovers did Eli have?

Eli had slept with him hours after having met him. Why would Kale think that wasn't a normal thing for Eli to do? Kale reprimanded himself for thinking his relationship with Eli might have been special or different from Eli's other relationships.

"What's the name of the store?" Kale asked.

§§§

Kale knew it was a long shot, but his curiosity drove him to the department store in the mall. He went directly to the service desk and asked if Selena was working. He hoped he didn't need a last name.

"Oh yeah, she's in jewelry," the woman said, her speech slurred slightly by adult braces. "Do you want me to page her?"

And force everyone in the store to listen to that lisp? "No thanks, I'll go to her."

There were three jewelry counters in the store. He causally approached each one, glancing at the nametapes on each woman. His money was on the cute brunette. He approached, putting on his winning courtroom smile. Her nametape said Darcy.

He adjusted course and moved to the watches. The woman working there was an older Asian woman. He grimaced, surely Eli wasn't into women that old. He headed to the last counter, where a woman was helping a couple finish their selection. He eyed some necklaces as he waited his turn.

The woman looked his direction, her green eyes sparkling in the extra lights illuminating the jewelry.

"I'll be right with you," she said, her tone warm. She wore just the right amount of make-up to make her look cute. Her hair was pulled back in a ponytail to show off her diamond stud earrings.

The couple thanked her and collected their purchase bag. The woman focused on Kale, giving him his first full body look. She was pregnant. Her short five-two frame was engulfed by a stomach that told him she was ready to pop any day.

His face must have given away his shock because she chuckled slightly and patted her stomach.

"Don't worry, I promise I won't burst until after I've helped you. I just got big early. I'm actually not due for six weeks," the woman said. "So what can I help you with?"

Okay, Eli liked older Asian women, he could deal with that. He opened his mouth to tell her he'd changed his mind when he read her nametape.

Selena.

"So how can I help you?" Selena repeated. There were plenty of reasons why this baby wasn't Eli's. And an equal amount of reasons why it could be. Kale closed his gaping jaw and stumbled a response.

"Watches. Do you have any gold ones?"

"Sure do." She guided him to a collection of gold watches.

"Pardon me for asking, but your husband must be a real hardass to be making you work in your condition. Being on your feet all day must be uncomfortable." Not his most tactful moment, but it was better than outright asking her who the father was.

She chuckled softly, an indication that he was not the first to have asked her that question. She flashed her hand at him. "No husband."

"Boyfriend?"

She grinned and batted her eyelashes. "Depends why you're asking."

He shuffled on his feet. "I don't normally do this, but you seem like a nice girl. I'm a lawyer. If you're having trouble getting the father to step up and claim responsibly, I'd be happy to help you." He fished one of his cards from his pocket and handed it to her.

She didn't look at the card, but she was obviously flattered. "Do you pick up all your new clients with that line?"

He grinned back and leaned against the counter. "Dates too."

"Well, it's definitely effective." She glanced at the card. "Kale."

She frowned. Kale's heart raced. Had Eli told her about him?

"I don't think I can accept your offer." She handed the card back to him.

"Why?"

"A different lawyer from the same firm is already representing the father. Wouldn't it be some violation of interest if we both had lawyers from the same firm?"

Denial was getting harder. He couldn't resist the question. "What's the father's name?"

"Eli Pendza," she said. Kale's heart cracked, sunk, and the world blurred. This wasn't possible. How many surprises did Eli have up his sleeve? "Are you okay?"

Kale wasn't certain how, but he ended up sitting on the floor, his back against the glass display case. Selena and a man who was evidently her supervisor were huddled around Kale, asking if he was okay.

No he was not. He told them the opposite as anger fueled the energy his initial shock had stolen. He rose from the floor and shrugged off their offers to help him.

"I'll be fine, thank you. I just haven't had much to eat today," Kale said.

He made a hasty retreat from the store and pulled out his phone as he walked through the parking lot. His phone vomited an array of missed calls from Martin across the screen.

His anger bubbling over and having no good place to expel it, Kale hit the callback icon. He put the phone to his ear as Martin's voice answered.

"Kale?" Martin said.

"What do you want?" Kale barked. "Your restraining order says no contact. Are you trying to entrap me?" If he could legally prove Martin had initiated the contact then the restraining order was void, but he knew from experience Martin had a knack for evading the clause.

He tried to brace the phone against his shoulder so he could use his good arm to retrieve his car keys. He failed miserably and the phone and keys tumbled to the pavement. Kale cursed and picked up both.

The screen was cracked on the phone but he could still hear Martin speaking a panicky, "Are you there?"

"Yes, hold on," Kale said. He unlocked his car and got in. He put the keys in the ignition but didn't start it. He couldn't drive and hold the phone with one arm. He looked at the screen so he could put it on speaker phone, which he should have done in the first place, but the screen was black. He'd broken it.

"I'm here," Kale said, giving up. He'd stop by a cell phone store later.

"Are you okay?" Martin asked.

"No," Kale said.

"Is there anything I can do?"

"Do you want your money?" Kale asked. There was a moment of silence, then a small yes. "Meet me at the Allison Motel on the Breezeway, you know it?"

"Yes."

"How soon can you be there?" Kale asked. He wasn't feeling patient and he needed the answer to be minutes, not hours.

"Uh, thirty minutes?" Martin said. His uncertainty wasn't a confidence builder.

"Fifteen," Kale said. "You lose a hundred off your normal allowance for every minute after that."

"Okay, I get it. I'm coming," Martin said. He disconnected the call. Kale closed his eyes and took a deep breath. What was he doing? He was going to beat Martin instead of Eli, that's what he was doing.

CHAPTER SIXTEEN

Kale sat in the parking lot. He knew exactly what would happen if he went inside the motel. He used his shattered screen to dial Eli's number. The screen was still black, but he had put Eli's number on speed dial #9 and he made a guess at where the nine was.

"Hello," Eli said.

"I need you," Kale said. He rattled off the address of the hotel and hung up. He waited. A car pulled up next to Kale's car. He listened to a door open and shut. Someone rapped on his passenger window, the events eerily like that of last week when Eli had found him spying on Martin at the college.

Eli slipped into his passenger seat. "What's up?"

"Martin's here," Kale said. Eli glanced at the motel. It was a single level building, doors to the rooms opening outside. The epitome of a cheap motel often found near interstates.

"How do you know?" Eli asked.

"I called him and told him to meet me here. He went in room six." He turned his gaze on Eli. "I booked it over the phone and told him which room to go in. I watched him go in ten minutes ago."

Eli was silent for several minutes. "What are we doing here, Kale?"

"Do you want to know why Martin left me?"

"I want to know why we're here, spying on Martin."

"His father died," Kale said. "Nine weeks ago to the day." Kale watched the bedroom window of the motel room. He already knew Martin wasn't inside. Kale had left the cash on the table in the room and waited in his car. He'd watched Martin come and leave.

"Okay."

"I was working a case, a big one, the Pules-Westshore. Some idiot was selling secrets to China. It was designs for an ink pen. Can you believe that? All this fuss over a pen. The case was worth two million." He kept his eyes forward, not looking at Eli. "The funeral for Martin's father was the same day as my case. I told him I couldn't go. He said he'd go by himself. The funeral was in California. I told him there was no way he was traveling that far by himself. I'd be too worried and the distraction might cost me the case.

"He waited until I'd gone to work. He had his sister pick him up. He went to the airport and didn't even tell me until he'd landed in San Francisco. He sent me a text, apologizing and saying he'd make it up to me. I didn't speak to him the entire time he was gone. Three days. No communication."

Kale looked at Eli, his face deadpan. "I lost the case."

"I wasn't exactly expecting a happy ending," Eli said. "So you broke all his dishes while he was away?"

"I blamed him for my losing the case. I'd told him this would happen and he still went. I was waiting in the apartment when he came home. I'd taken the day off to wait for him. I knew he was going to try to sneak in while I was at work, maybe grab some things and stay with his sister for a few days.

"We argued. His father's ashes had been put in two urns, one for him, the other for his sister." Kale tapped his forehead. "I broke the urn over Martin's head, gave him a two inch cut on his forehead. I made him clean up the spilled ashes and flush them down the toilet. I didn't let him bandage his cut until he was done.

"I beat him and fucked him raw that night," Kale said, his voice monotone. Eli squirmed in his seat.

"You don't have to tell me this," Eli said.

"He didn't wake up the next morning. Turns out I'd given him a concussion. I should have taken him to the emergency room, but instead I left him there. Possible brain swelling and everything. His sister came by to check on him later that day. She freaked and called an ambulance. Told me if I ever tried to touch him again she'd kill me.

"Something she tried to do later with an oven," Kale said, gesturing to his cast. "The night I met you I found Martin cheating on me. I was watching him from afar, as I'd done since the day he left. He got into Wayne's car after class, but they didn't leave, not right away.

"I thought something might be wrong, so I decided to investigate. I still don't remember how the tire iron ended up in my hand but it was there. I broke Wayne's window and pulled him out through it. I hit him twice with the tire iron, then I beat him with my hands. Martin tried to pull me off. It was all a blur of rage. I'd caught Martin sucking Wayne's dick in the car. I was furious."

Images of the event flashed in his memory, the sound of the breaking glass was something he would never forget.

"That's horrible," Eli said. "I'm sorry."

"None of it was your fault," Kale said. They sat in silence for a few minutes. "Tell me who Selena is."

§§§

"I'm sorry?" Eli said. He was still reeling from Kale's confession. The images of Kale being that brutal frightened him. The emotionless tone he was speaking in was freaking him out even more. It took all his courage not to bolt from the car.

"Selena," Kale repeated. "The woman who is carrying your unborn child."

His heart raced erratically at the statement. Suddenly Eli knew why they were here. Kale's goal was to terrify him. He moved to unlock the door but Kale beat him to it. A firm hand gripped his wrist and held him in place.

"She—she's a problem," Eli said. "I'm dealing with it."

"Is it true? Is her baby yours?"

Eli swallowed the lump in his throat. Was this the moment when Kale would hit him? Kale squeezed his wrist, not enough to bruise, but enough to hurt.

"No."

Kale released his hold on Eli and slumped back in his seat. He closed his eyes and sat very still.

"I need you to be honest with me, Eli," Kale said. "I don't like liars. Are you a liar?"

"No."

"Why is she saying the baby is yours?"

"Because she wants it to be," Eli said. "There was a chance it could be, but she did a paternity test and it's not mine."

"How many other women are going to show up claiming to have your kid, Eli?"

"I've only been with two women."

"Men?"

"I can't get them pregnant."

A flicker of a smile played on Kale's lips. "You never wrap that dick of yours up, do you?"

"No. But it's starting to sound more and more like I should."

"You think? Explain to me who Selena is."

Eli glanced out the car window and debated if a beating would be better than the confession Kale wanted.

"I'm giving you something I never gave Martin," Kale said. "A chance to explain and convince me I shouldn't want to hurt you."

Eli laughed, a deep throaty chuckle. "You're going to be disappointed."

"Try me."

"Selena went to college with Jackie. They hit it off and became inseparable. Selena didn't care that Jackie had a kid already. The two of them would go off and do girl things. She was the one friend Jackie had who didn't ditch her because she had a baby.

"One night when I was a bit drunker than I should have been, Selena made out with me. We agreed to not tell Jackie, but ever since, Selena seemed infatuated with me. When I came out of the closet and Jackie agreed to the separation, Selena saw her chance.

"She'd been on the dating scene and knew the game better than I ever could. I'd only ever dated Jackie. So she took me to clubs and helped me pick up men. We'd take them home together." Eli hesitated. "And have sex together."

"You had threesomes with Selena?"

"Yeah. A lot of them. So many that when she found out she was pregnant, six of us had to get tested to find out who the father was." Eli ruffled his hair and considered not telling Kale the last bit. "I found out later she used a condom with the other men. She only went bare with me. She was intentionally trying to get pregnant with my baby. She has this idea that she's perfect for me and she's doing everything she can to entrap me into being with her."

"How could you not tell she was only going bare with you? You were all having sex together."

"I was always a bit drunk and there was a lot going on. Have you ever been in a threesome?"

Kale rolled his eyes, not admitting anything.

"You didn't ask her if she was using birth control?"

"I assumed. I mean, she was always having sex with people."

"Who is the real father?"

"It wasn't any of us that got tested. I'm guessing it belongs to a guy she was with without me. All the men we were with together got tested."

"Why didn't you tell me?" Kale asked.

"That some crazy ex-girlfriend is going around claiming her baby is mine when it isn't? Why would I bring that up? I made Selena swear to leave Jackie out of it and...I said if she did, then I would sign the birth certificate." The heated looked that Kale gave him at that comment made Eli want to die, right there. "I wasn't planning to actually do it. I was just buying my time, putting everything on hold with the idea that the baby won't be here until—" *after Jackie died.* Eli didn't want to finish the sentence. He knew how much of a jerk the comment made him sound.

"But Selena's getting impatient. That's why you were arguing with her the night you were arrested," Kale said.

"Yeah, I think she knows or suspects that I'm not going to follow through on claiming the kid. So she said some crap that if I wasn't going to claim her kid that she'd make sure I couldn't get Annabelle either. So she called the cops and got me arrested."

Kale was glaring at his steering wheel and Eli worried for its safety.

"You should have told me the truth."

- 176 -

"Honestly, I didn't think our relationship would last long enough for any of this to matter."

Kale turned his head to look at Eli, the movement so sudden it was startling.

"Selena doesn't know it yet, but her trying to destroy your name is going to be what saves you."

"What do you mean?"

"If you hadn't gotten arrested I never would have met you. I'm not going to let anyone hurt you, Eli. Tell me how you want this to play out. Tell me what you want, and I'll make it happen."

"What happened to beating me senseless in the hotel room?" Eli asked, only slightly teasing. Dusk was settling and it was getting harder to get a good look at Kale's face. He moved quickly and Eli flinched, expecting pain. Lips pressed against his, kissing him deep and hard.

"I want you to be mine," Kale said. His hand crept up Eli's chest, setting a flurry of tingles shooting through his body. "No one hurts what's mine."

"Except you," Eli said, his voice trembling.

"Correct." Kale's hand shot down and took his crotch in a firm grip. Eli hardened and pushed into the touch. Kale's controlling side was downright terrifying, yet hot, really hot. He prayed Kale never hit him, it would hurt on more levels than Eli cared to admit. "Tell me what you want."

"I want you," Eli said. "I want to be yours."

"And?" His voice was husky and Eli resisted the urge to go groping to see if Kale was aroused.

"I want that whole mess with Selena to go away, and I want Annabelle, full custody."

Kale didn't seem satisfied with his answers. What else did he want him to say? He could ask Kale to save his dying wife and keep her from dying, but he knew Kale couldn't do that.

Kale retracted his hand, but kept his face close. "Do you want me to be part of it? Or just help you get her?"

"Part of?"

"You know what I'm capable of. You would want me around your child?"

Eli wrapped his hands around Kale's neck. "Of course I want you to be part of it. I want us together. A family. I trust you. I love you." Eli couldn't help but say it, even if he knew Kale wasn't going to say it back. Kale kissed him again, perhaps the only way he knew how to show affection. His lips moved down Eli's chin, tracing his jawline.

"Let me mark you," Kale said. "I want everyone to know you're mine."

He figured it was better than the black eye he'd used to mark Martin as his. He'd figure out a way to cover it at the funeral. If Kale let him.

"Okay," Eli said.

"Unzip your pants," Kale said.

"What?"

"I want you to jerk off while I do it."

Fuck. Eli obeyed, turned on, yet uncertain. Where were the lines drawn? How close was he getting to his first view of abusive Kale?

CHAPTER SEVENTEEN

His two-week suspension from work was coming to an end quickly. Kale was four hours short on his group therapy appointments, three short on his one-on-one appointments and fifteen short on the volunteer work. He rambled like a drunk housewife at his last two appointments with his therapist, hoping it would make her think they'd made some breakthrough and she'd give him a positive report.

He'd managed to dodge the courtroom on his sentencing, but there was no such luck this time. His additional incident with the bakery expired what little grace the judge had for him. He would have to plead his case in person before his license to practice law would be reinstated.

At least his office had managed to pull some leverage and get his trial scheduled for the same Monday they wanted him back at work. If the judge ruled him a threat to himself or others though, it would complicate matters. The threat of being sent to an anger management camp still loomed over him. As did jail time.

"I'd nearly forgotten what you looked like freshly shaved," Eli said. He stroked Kale's cheeks as he came out of the bathroom. It had taken him twenty frustrating minutes to accomplish the clean shave, but it was worth it to look more presentable in court.

Kale kissed him and Eli moaned. "I forgot how good it feels to kiss you when you're this smooth too," Eli said.

Kale pushed him away before things could derail and make them both late.

"Why are you still here? Don't you go into work at five?"

"I asked if I could come in late today. I wanted to be here for you."

"You need to stop abusing your privileges of dating one of the partners at the firm," Kale said. He didn't add the tiny fact that after today he may no longer be a partner. "Get to work."

"Yes sir," Eli said, giving him a mock salute. Kale tried to hide the stir of angst the gesture caused. Martin had used to do that, back when he'd still had enough nerve to add a bit of sass to his responses.

Two hours later, Kale itched at the edges of his cast as he waited his turn in the courtroom. Flecks of dead skin fell out of the cast and he had a decent mound forming before the door to the courtroom opened and his name was called.

He didn't have a lawyer with him. Even without his rights to practice law, he could represent himself. He took his seat at the table in front of the judge. He glanced over at the prosecuting attorney. Blarney. Kale had been opposite of him in court cases before.

He was a decent enough guy, and Kale hoped this wasn't going to turn ugly.

Blarney was also alone at his table. The people he'd beat up had all settled outside of court. The judge had still put restrictions on him out of a concern for public safety. Blarney was here because he'd likely lost a bet at the district attorney's office.

"Mr. Sokoloff," Judge Harper said. She pushed her bifocals up on her nose. "Have you enjoyed your time off?"

"Of course, Judge," Kale said. "I cherish any opportunity to give back to society."

The judge looked through the papers Blarney passed her. The man's waxen demeanor glanced apologetically at Kale.

"Not quite enough, it would seem. You failed to complete any of the requirements you were given. Another week should do," she said. She handed the files back to Blarney.

"Judge, if I may," Kale said as he rose. "I suffered an injury. I believe I made great strides toward my punishment given the circumstances. I can complete the remainder of the community service and therapy while resuming my normal work."

"Your injury was sustained in another incident when you failed to control your temper," Harper said. "If an arrest or charge had been filed, I would be increasing your sentence."

"I'm not a threat to society."

"Your therapist doesn't agree." She nodded to the file. "Come back in a week, after you've completed your previous sentence and I'll decide if you should attend the anger management camp."

Kale mentally did the math. The anger management course was four weeks. If he went to it one week from now, he might be at it when Jackie died and Selena's baby was born. The timing was horrible. At least three of his cases would also go into trial at that time.

"Judge Harper, is there an alternative? Being gone a month from my job and family isn't feasible right now."

"I doubt it's convenient for anyone. I'm aware of your current case load, your office sent it over for my review." She looked bored with his plea and about to declare his case dismissed.

"It's not just that," Kale said. "My life partner." God, how he hated that word, but it sounded more grownup and serious than boyfriend. "His ex-wife is dying of cancer and not expected to survive the month. He'll be fighting for custody of that child while arguing against the claim of another. I need to be here to help him both emotionally and for the wellbeing of the children involved."

"I thought your life partner was who you assaulted?"

"He's my ex." The finality of the words nearly crumbled his resolve. The judge narrowed her eyes and seemed to reconsider.

"There's a weekend anger management camp," Harper said. "Attend that this upcoming weekend, complete your volunteer work and continue both group and personal therapy a minimum of three times a week for the next six months."

"I can do that."

"Mr. Sokoloff, your restrictions in practicing law are removed effective immediately. No need to return to the courtroom unless you fail to comply with the restrictions I've given you. Understood?"

"Yes, Ma'am."

Kale made a mental note to be on his best behavior for any cases he may have to present to Judge Harper in the coming months. He owed her. Although her sentence hadn't exactly been light. That was a lot of therapy to work into his schedule.

Kale collected his things and departed the courtroom. Kale paused in the hall and pulled out his phone. Blarney approached Kale.

"You sure can pick 'em, can't you?" Blarney asked.

"I'm sorry?" Kale glanced at him, uncertain.

"Instead of spending your time actually doing your sentence you went and found some guy who could make the judge take pity on you. What did you do? Patrol the hospital halls for a suitable victim after Martin was laid up? I mean, that was a hell of a pity party, Kale. I sure didn't see it coming. And with all that shit going on in his life. He probably welcomes the punches you throw his way."

"Are you trying to get me to break your nose, Blarney?" Kale asked. "Is this your new strategy? Get me to slug you so you can get me sent off to anger management camp? Get me permanently disbarred? I'm not an idiot, Blarney. I know two of my *smaller* cases are being prosecuted by the district attorney. And we both know you'll win if Norton is the one representing my clients instead of me."

Blarney scrunched up his face, making him look very pig like.

"Doesn't matter if it's me or someone else. You're a ticking time bomb, Kale. Without that Martin kid to beat on, you're bound to hit the wrong person and end up in jail."

"Yes, well, thanks for the vote of confidence," Kale said. He pushed past him, doing all he could to ignore the drumming in his ears. He sure hoped that weekend camp offered him some better management methods than the stupid therapist.

§§§

Kale was quickly buried under his workload. The Milton case went to trial Thursday and it seemed nothing had been done to prep for it. That was his biggest profile case in the near term. He had a handful of smaller cases he hoped to settle out of court.

His intern, although he wouldn't straight out say it, had been pressured to focus his attention on other cases, not Kale's. He bit back a few choice words he wanted to have with the other partners at the firm. He worked through his lunch hour, and replied with a snarky, "What?" when someone knocked on his office door.

Charlotte flinched and dug the heel of her shoe into his office carpet. "I wanted to remind you, you still have your therapist appointment at one."

"Shit," Kale remarked. "Cancel the appointment for today and change them all to morning appointments. I want to do them before I come into the office."

"Monday, Wednesday, Friday?"

"Yes, put Monday's on Tuesday for this week," Kale said. He'd still have to do his group therapy at six. He'd grown comfortable with the crowd that showed at that meeting.

He kept his nose buried in his work until two. He'd checked Rich's calendar and knew he'd be free then. He knocked on his office door.

"Welcome back," Rich said. He stretched in his chair and drummed his fingers on the desk. "I heard the judge gave you a hard time."

Kale shrugged. "It worked out. I need to ask you a favor."

"Go on."

"You worked family court before you joined the firm. Are you familiar with custody cases?"

"I am."

"Can you take a look at a case for me? I've never worked one before and I could use the expert opinion."

"Ah, I see." Rich looked at his computer for a moment. "Maybe in a few weeks, next month? Leave the files with Tim and I'll get them when I can."

It wasn't the answer Kale wanted. Jackie would be dead by next month and Kale wanted to get ahead of things.

"It's not something that can wait."

"How important of a case is it?"

Kale knew the real question was, how much money would they earn from the clients?

"Never mind, I'll figure something out," Kale said. He went back to his office, trying to shake off the dismissal. Twenty minutes later, someone knocked on his door and Kale didn't even give a verbal response. He looked up and glared at the intruder.

"Mr. Sokoloff?" The bright blond intern poked her head into his office. She'd been with them for two months and if he recalled properly, she was assigned to Rich.

"Yes?"

"Do you have a moment?"

He didn't. He really didn't, but after his rude encounter with Rich he didn't have the zest to be rude to her.

"A few." He gestured for her to enter.

She didn't sit. She crossed her arms nervously, clutching a folder in one hand.

"I was hoping to discuss a potential case with you."

"Shouldn't you be discussing it with Rich?"

"I did. He said it was too low profile for the firm to deal with."

"Well, there's your answer." Kale thumbed through some papers on his desk, looking for the eyewitness report for the Milton case.

"Oh, okay." Her deflated tone reminded Kale of what he'd experienced only twenty minutes ago.

"Why's it important to you?" Kale asked. He glanced up, worried she'd already departed when she didn't respond immediately. She bit her lip. When she replied the words seemed to tumble out involuntarily. He couldn't recall, but he was fairly certain this was the first time he'd ever spoken to her.

"The client is a friend of my cousin. He owns a restaurant and he thinks someone is stealing his secret recipes and selling them to his competition. He's super paranoid and my cousin is worried he's going to spend all his money on a private investigator. So I said I'd have one of the lawyers here look into it, to see if he even has a case. I thought you'd be able to help because Martin's sister owns that chain of bakeries. So I figured you'd know a thing or two about running a local business and what kind of laws work in their favor. Shit, I shouldn't have mentioned Martin. I know you're not with him anymore, but that's also why I thought this client would be perfect for you. He's also gay. I mean, the client, restaurant owner, he's gay. And maybe, oh God, I'm totally blowing this."

She slammed her palm against her forehead. Kale had his doubts about how far she'd make it as a lawyer if she didn't learn to clean the fluff out of her presentations. He tried to pick the important parts out of her rambling.

"It shouldn't be hard for me to figure out whether or not he has a case," Kale said. "Leave the files with Charlotte."

"Really? Oh, thank you." The relief on her face told him she'd likely been trying to muster the courage to speak to him all day. Kale tapped his foot, an idea working out in his brain as it still tried to recover from her disjointed speech.

"How familiar are you with family court?"

"I minored in it." *Good enough.*

"Can you look at a case for me?" He opened his drawer and pulled out what he'd complied for Eli's case. He jumped slightly when he looked up. She'd moved to stand directly next to his desk, her sudden closeness unexpected.

"I'd love too. I'll get right on it." She beamed at him, dimples showing in both her cheeks.

"Great. Thank you," Kale said, careful not to offer the same to her case. He had no intention of shuffling it to the top of his to-do list.

She sashayed out of his office with a slight skip in her step. If Kale had been a straight man, he imagined he would have enjoyed the view.

CHAPTER EIGHTEEN

It didn't take long for Kale to figure out his workload was going to drown him. He had to leave the office at five thirty in order to make it to his group therapy at six. Arriving at the office at nine, after his one-on-one therapy, still didn't leave enough hours in the day. He arranged his calendar to have him work from seven in the morning until eight at night on Tuesdays and Thursdays. And he feared that he would likely be staying well past his intended departure time.

By Wednesday, he decided he needed to return to the office after his group therapy. He promised himself it would get easier, but with his weekends currently reserved for anger management camp and finishing his volunteer work, the future was quite bleak.

He needed to figure out a better method. Eli was quickly becoming nothing more than a roommate. He was asleep by the time Kale came home and already at work before Kale awoke. He didn't want Eli to think this was the normal routine, but right now pride kept him from asking any of the other lawyers to take some of his cases.

He called Eli as he walked through the deserted parking garage.

"Hello," Eli said.

"Hey, it's me. I won't be home until late. I have the Milton case tomorrow and I need to finish prepping for it," Kale said. Eli was silent for a moment. Was he pissed? Did he think Kale was blowing him off?

"Are you really at the office?"

"Of course I'm at the office. Where else would I be?"

"Selena called me."

Kale stifled the groan burning in his throat. Eli wasn't upset about the neglect. He was worried Kale was out stalking Eli's pregnant ex-lover.

"I'm not stalking Selena, or Martin, or anyone else for that matter. I'm too busy for any of that. You can verify my whereabouts with the front guards if you want. They'll still be on shift when you come in at five." Kale waited at the door as Albert, the guard currently on shift, unlocked it for him.

"Uh huh, you'll probably pay them off to cover for you," Eli said. Kale couldn't tell if it was playful banter or if he was actually upset.

"They can show you the camera footage of me entering and exiting the building," Kale said. He pushed the elevator button and it dinged as it arrived. "Hear that? It's the elevator."

"Okay, okay, I believe you."

"Good."

"I cooked too much supper so I'm going to put some leftovers in the fridge. I'll talk to you later," Eli said. He sounded sad. Kale hated himself for being the cause.

"Thank you. I promise it won't always be like this."

"Right. Bye." Eli disconnected the call on his end before Kale could say more.

Kale stepped off the elevator and stuffed his phone in his pocket. Eli would be fine. He'd figure out a way to make things up to him. Like get him full custody of his kid.

He pulled his keys out and unlocked the glass doors to the firm's section of the building. He stepped inside and left it unlocked behind him. Only every fifth light was on after hours, but lamps were located at each desk in case someone needed to work late.

Kale hadn't told anyone he would be returning. He himself hadn't made the decision until halfway through group therapy. The light was on under Rich's office door, indicating he was in. Rich was a married man who had a family to get home too. It wasn't like him to work late, at least, not that Kale knew of.

The lamp was turned on at one of Rich's intern's desks. It was general policy at the firm to keep the interns to banker's hours. They already weren't being paid, no need to abuse them further.

Kale unlocked his office and dropped his briefcase inside. He strolled to the intern's desk and read the nameplate. It was Carol's. A twang of guilt itched at him. Was she working late to help him with Eli's case? He'd never intended for her to research the case on her personal time.

He put his hand on Rich's office door and tried to turn the handle. He intended to ask him what Carol was doing here. The door was locked. Why would it be locked if Rich and Carol were the only ones here? It wasn't like the cleaning crew would come barging in, and if they did, they had a right to. Cleaning the offices at night was their job.

Maybe Rich wasn't here, Carol either. In which case, the lights had likely been left on by accident. No need to waste electricity. Kale pulled his keys out and slipped them into the door's lock. All of the primary associates at the firm had a universal key so they could enter each other's offices. It was a needed precaution in case something happened and a file needed to be accessed in someone's absence.

The door unlocked and Kale pushed it open, not bothering to knock because logic had already told him no one would be inside. Logic however, was not what greeted him inside Rich's office.

Kale's eyes went first to Carol, lying on her back across the desk. Their gaze locked. She had that wild animal, scared to death look. Tears streaked her cheeks, one dimpled cheek was swollen. She was bent over the desk, arms sprawled at her sides, shirt untucked and unbuttoned.

Her skirt was hiked up, pantyhose destroyed and discarded. Rich was fully dressed, only the important part of him was exposed, the part of him that was violating Carol beneath her skirt.

Images of Kale from years ago, being in a situation all too similar to Carol, blurred Kale's senses. He raised his right arm and his cast impacted Rich's face. Kale felt nothing, unable to tell if he'd broken the man's nose. He shoved Rich back with his good arm, sending him toppling to the floor.

Rich's erect dick, wagged at him, peeking out from his unzipped dress pants. Kale wanted to kick him in the groin, ribs, face, make him bleed and suffer. The words of his therapist rang in his ears.

Aggravated assault. Things are going to happen that are going to piss you off. What if they hit first? Of course, you're going to strike back. The idea is, to only inflect the amount of harm needed to control the situation.

Was Kale in control of the situation? Was Carol safe? Rich disarmed?

He will be if I kick him in the nuts, Kale thought.

Rich looked up, his eyes wide. He let his nose bleed freely and opted to raise both of his hands in a gesture of surrender. Kale was in control of his body, refusing to let the anger surging in him take over, but evidently it did not show on his face.

Rich looked absolutely terrified.

Kale heard nothing but the pounding of his heart in his ears. He saw Rich's mouth moving, but the words couldn't be heard. Rich moved his hands, probably to tuck himself back in his pants.

"Don't fucking move," Kale said. Rich froze. The world came back, just a little, enough that he could hear Carol's sobs.

"This isn't what it looks like," Rich said. "Carol and I have an arrangement."

"Does your wife know about the arrangement?" Kale asked. Rich wiped at his nose and seemed surprised to find the blood there.

"You hit me."

Another wave of rage washed over Kale and he fisted both hands, sending a ripple of pain up his right arm. Kale took a few steps back and picked up Rich's desk phone.

"Who are you calling?" Rich asked.

"The front guard. He needs to call the police."

"What? No. There's no need for that."

Kale put the phone down and glared at him. "Why?"

"Because you don't need another assault charge and the company doesn't need this drama."

"You were raping her," Kale said. He couldn't bring himself to look at Carol or say her name. She was still sobbing, somewhere on the floor he thought. He took the sound of her cries as enough indication that she was alive and well enough to survive until an ambulance got here.

Rich had smartly stayed on the floor, but his face was serious. "You don't want to do this Kale. You have a record. No one is going to believe you."

"They'll believe her."

"Carol won't say anything. Not if she knows what's good for her, and neither will you. You want your friend Eli to get custody of his kids? He won't, not when I'm done dragging your name through the mud. No court will want a child to come anywhere near you—"

Kale wasn't sure the direction the rest of the speech was supposed to go. But Kale didn't care to hear it. If Kale did, Rich would likely be dead in the next ten minutes. He kicked Rich right in his smart mouth. Blood gushed and Rich gagged, his entire body shaking in shock.

Kale had likely fractured his jaw. Good. He needed to shut up.

The situation once again controlled, Kale dialed the front security desk. "Albert, call an ambulance and the police."

"What happened?" Albert asked.

"Just do it," Kale said. He hung up. He forced himself to move around Rich's desk and face Carol. She was huddled against the wall, knees to her chest. "Help is on the way."

Her eyes moved up and met his, then settled on his waist. Was she staring at his crotch? Was she worried he was going to assault her too?

"You're bleeding," she said.

"No, it's Rich's blood."

She shook her head and pointed at his arm with a trembling finger. Kale looked at his cast. His entire hand was covered in blood. Droplets impacted the office carpet, his limb a leaky faucet he'd forgotten how to turn off.

"Shit," Kale said. He lifted his arm above his head, unable to do anything else. He couldn't apply pressure with a cast on it. He must have ripped some stitches open.

§§§

Kale sat on the tailgate of the ambulance. Rich was inside, on a stretcher, his status stable and on IV fluids. A paramedic looked over his hand. Kale watched Carol as she gave the responding police officer her statement. She was draped in a blanket, but looked more in control than Kale had after his rape.

"You'll need to go to the hospital," the paramedic told him. "They'll need to redo your cast and your stitches."

"It stopped bleeding," Kale said.

"But it'll start again if they don't give you new stitches." He scrunched his eyebrows at Kale, a resolve that said he'd had this kind of argument before and wasn't prone to losing them.

The police officer approached, pen and paper in hand. "I know you need medical attention so I'll keep this quick. I need a statement about what happened to put in my report."

Kale wondered what Carol had told him. Kale gave a recount of what he'd seen, leaving his assault on Rich more vague than the rest of the story.

The officer nodded. "This matches with the victim's story. She says you came in and Rich sustained his injuries during your attempt to dislodge him from her. She says he fought back and you only did what was needed to disarm him. He must have gone for your cast." He gestured at Kale's bum arm.

"You believe that?" Kale asked.

He shrugged. "I looked up your rap sheet." Of course he had. "And considering what you saw, I think you showed great self-control. My report's going to reflect that."

This was new. An officer actually on Kale's side.

"Thank you," Kale said. The officer nodded. As he departed, Carol came to join them. They all climbed into the ambulance, including the paramedic.

Carol sat on the small bench with him, close enough he could feel her body heat, not touching. He knew the feeling. After his rape he'd wanted to be close to someone, hated the idea of being alone. But he also hated being touched, in any manner. With this knowledge he refrained from offering Carol any form of physical comfort.

The paramedic focused on Rich. Kale busied himself with thoughts of pulling Rich's IV out and letting him suffer the rest of the ride in pain.

"We'll contact the previous female interns," Kale said. "See if he ever did this to any of them. I bet we can get them to talk and we'll build a case against him."

Carol said nothing.

"Is there someone you want me to call?" Kale asked. She shook her head.

"My parents were convinced something like this would happen. I don't want to tell them."

"A friend?"

She shook her head again.

"They'll have a victim advocate at the hospital that you can talk to. They're good people. They'll get you through this."

"You know that from cases you've worked?"

"No. I avoid assault cases," Kale said. "It's why I went into business law."

He hesitated to tell her the truth. He could easily dismiss her query with an idle lie, but that wasn't what she needed to hear right now.

"I know from personal experience," Kale said.

"I'm sorry," she mumbled.

"It was a long time ago," Kale said. The ambulance came to a stop. Kale's heart thumped in his chest. He'd forgotten to ask which hospital they were going too. "Which hospital is this?"

"Augustus Memorial," the paramedic said. He opened the backdoors and jumped out. Two nurses were there waiting, they helped pull the gurney with Rich off.

"I can't be here," Kale said. "One of the employees has a restraining order against me."

"Extenuating circumstances, I'm sure the court will understand," the paramedic said. He vanished around the side of the truck. Kale gritted his teeth. Right. The odds were slim Wayne would be working, even slimmer Kale would actually see him.

He followed the nurses inside, not noticing Carol stuck next to him.

Two women approached, directing themselves at Carol. She backed away from them, bumping into Kale.

"Ma'am, come with us. We'll take good care of you," the older woman said. A male nurse approached Kale.

"Sir, if you'll come with me," the male nurse said.

"Can't we stay together?" Carol asked. He knew they'd need to do a rape kit on Carol. He couldn't be around for that.

"You don't want to see my gnarled paw," Kale said. "I'll find you when they're done with me."

She nodded and went with the women. Kale had never gone to a clinic after his rape. He hoped it helped Carol. Not going sure hadn't done Kale any favors.

He followed the nurse. They settled in a makeshift station in a hall. Kale sat and waited patiently as the man took his information and vitals. He was starting to think maybe he wouldn't encounter Wayne, just as he heard the man's surly voice.

"No, no, you cannot be here," Wayne said. He always sounded like he had his nose pinched. Kale had often wondered if he needed nasal surgery.

"Medical emergency. It wasn't my choice," Kale said.

Wayne was dressed in a smock covered in various colored balloons. He was a nurse in the ER. Wayne had been the nurse working on more than one occasion when Martin had been brought in. Wayne had convinced Martin to leave him several times. It wasn't until later that Kale found out they were sleeping together.

"Whose face did you hit?" Wayne asked.

"My boss," Kale said. "I caught him—" He stopped short, his encounter too similar to the one he'd had with Wayne. He was going to get a reputation of beating people's brains in whenever he saw them having sex.

The nurse attending to him spoke in a low voice. "He came in with a sexual assault victim."

Kale resisted the urge to punch the nurse.

"Oh," Wayne said. He chewed his lip for a moment. Kale noticed Wayne's hair was cut short. He wore a wrap around his head, probably to hide the scars from Kale's assault. He'd probably had some form of brain surgery as well, since he'd been in a coma. He thought he'd heard something about brain swelling.

"Well, I'm not about to let someone else deal with your horrible bedside manner," Wayne said. "I'll take care of him, Gary."

"I'd rather you not do that," Kale said. The two of them switched seats and Wayne removed the blood pressure cuff.

"Not your choice. Unless you want me to call the police about your being here in violation of my restraining order?" He raised his eyebrows and Kale gave him his best glare.

"If you saw my arm off when you remove this cast, I will kill you," Kale said. Wayne chuckled. Oh how Kale hated that laugh.

"So is your boss still alive?"

"Fractured jaw, I think."

"Lucky him. You went easy."

"I'm trying."

"Anger management classes helping?" Wayne touched each of Kale's fingertips, testing his blood flow.

"Among other things. What kind of car did my settlement money buy you?"

Wayne's face lit up in an exaggerated manner. "A firebird."

Kale rolled his eyes, unsure if he believed him.

"Aren't you going to ask me how Martin is doing?"

"Not my business," Kale said.

"Well, look at you, growing up, are we?" Wayne's facial expressions were annoying. Why hadn't he suffered more long-term damage from his assault? Kale pushed the dark fantasy away.

"Let's do an x-ray to make sure your pins and plates are still in place. Then you'll get a new cast and I'll fix up any stitches you happened to tear."

"Great."

"I do have some bad news though." Wayne pulled a roll of something pink from the cabinet. "The only fiberglass casting tape we have in stock is pink."

"I'm not letting you put that color on me. I want the standard white."

"Sorry, Sugar, all out," Wayne said. He made a pouty face and Kale swore the kid was egging him on, just wanting him to deck him in front of all these people.

Could this night possibly get any worse?

CHAPTER NINETEEN

The slam of a door jarred Eli from sleep. The wall vibrated and shook the bedframe. For a moment, he thought it was an explosion. He heard the stomping of feet in the hall and realized it was Kale.

Eli glanced at the clock and saw it was two in the morning. Kale was just now getting home?

They'd been drifting farther apart as the workweek progressed. Eli was trying to accept that lawyer Kale was a different person than the one he'd known the past few weeks. Workaholic didn't even do Kale justice.

Eli not only understood why Martin had cheated on him, but he also understood why Kale had no problem letting Eli live here. Because Kale didn't. He slept here. And quite frankly, Eli didn't know why. For as little as he was home, he should just sleep on his office couch.

Eli opened the door to the spare bedroom, his sanctuary, and peered out to see the form of Kale in the kitchen. Kale rummaged in the fridge. Eli had to get up in another hour and half anyway, to be at work by five. He slipped out of the doorway and went to the kitchen.

Kale jumped slightly, his eyes wide. He ran his fingers through his hair.

"Sorry, I didn't mean to wake you. I forgot the spare bedroom shares a wall with the front door," Kale said. Judging by Kale's reaction he was surprised Kale hadn't said something more along the lines of, "I forgot you're living here."

"Is this how late you've been getting home all week?" Eli asked.

"No," Kale said. He fumbled with a bottle of water, trying to get the cap off with one hand. Eli saw a flash of pink on his cast as his dress coat sleeve rose up his arm.

"What is that? Did you get a new cast?"

"Oh, yeah," Kale said. He looked at his arm as if just remembering it was there. "Fingers are still numb from the lidocaine. Can you open this?"

He held the bottle of water out to Eli. It took a few moments for Eli's brain to start working again. "You had that done tonight? You were in the emergency room?"

"Yes." Kale narrowed his eyes, still holding the water. Eli noticed the annoyance in his demeanor and he took the water. He removed the lid and Kale quickly downed the contents.

"Why didn't you call me?"

"I knew you were sleeping. I didn't need you. I just tore some stitches." He tossed the empty bottle in the recycling under the sink. He shrugged out of his coat. "The ER nurse said pink was the only color they had. I'm fairly certain they were lying but I was in no position to argue."

He draped his suit coat on the counter and kicked off his dress shoes.

"I still would have liked to know. Even if I didn't need to come down, I want to know about these things. How did it happen? How did you hurt yourself?" Eli stepped toward him and Kale moved to match him, keeping a four foot distance between them. Eli took the hint and backed up.

"You'll hear all about it tomorrow at work," Kale said. "I need to get some sleep before tomorrow, I mean, shit it's already tomorrow."

"I'd rather hear it from you," Eli said.

"I have a trial tomorrow. I need to get enough sleep to be somewhat lucid for it." Kale exited the kitchen and went down the hall to the bedroom. Eli followed.

"Give me the highlights then. Please, Kale."

Kale went into his bedroom and took his dress shirt off, there was blood on it. Eli wondered if it was all his, there was a lot of it.

"I went into the office after group therapy," Kale said. "I didn't think anyone would be there, but there was. We had…" His eyes focused on a corner of the dresser. "A disagreement about how the interns should be treated."

"A disagreement that ended with you tearing your stitches?" Eli crossed his arms. Kale undid his pants and folded them on top of the dresser.

"Yes." Kale went to the bed and fell atop it, draping his cast above his head on the pillow. He closed his eyes.

Something about this wasn't right.

"You came home straight from the hospital?" Eli asked.

"Yes."

The hospital germs. Kale had been half-drugged, in pain and loopy as hell when he'd come home from the hospital the first time. He'd insisted on taking a shower to get the so called hospital germs off. Why the hell wasn't he doing that this time?

"Aren't you going to take a shower?" Eli asked.

"Later. I need sleep, Eli."

Eli stepped closer to the bed. "Kale, what was the argument about?"

"It wasn't so much a verbal argument." He moved his cast to cover his eyes. "I caught Rich forcing himself on one of the female interns, Carol."

It took a moment for Eli to understand what "forcing himself" meant.

"You caught Rich sexually assaulting a coworker?"

The lights were off in the bedroom and the only light came from the hall. Even in the shadows Eli could see Kale flinch and he regretted saying the words. Kale had been raped as a teenager. Eli could only imagine how horrifying it had to be for Kale to see that.

"There was no trying," Kale said. "He was succeeding. I hurt my arm separating them."

"Is Carol okay?" Eli asked.

"She's why I was kept so late. I didn't want to leave her at the hospital. We shared a cab. I had her dropped off first. She has a roommate so she's not alone."

"That's good. It sounds like you did the right thing." Eli wasn't sure what to feel. Pride at the fact Kale had saved her warmed him. Fear and worry itched at the edges as he wondered if Kale was okay.

"Are you okay?" Eli asked.

The answer was small and pitiful. "I wasn't the one being assaulted."

"What can I do?" Eli asked.

"Leave the door open," Kale said. "The light in the kitchen too, leave it on."

A chill tickled at Eli's spine. He always slept with the lights off and door shut. And he always showered before he went to bed.

"Do you want me to stay with you? I can go into work late."

"No, I'll be fine. Go to work. If anyone asks, I'll be at the office in time for the trial."

Eli decided not to press the issue. He walked down the hall, his stomach bound in a tangle of knots.

§§§

The security guard buzzed Eli in the front doors. The mailroom employees were always the first to arrive for the day. The guard on shift was Albert. Eli had worked up a friendly repertoire with him over the past few weeks.

"How's Kale?" Albert asked. Eli tensed. How did Albert know he was in a relationship with Kale? Or did he? He must know they were close to some degree if he was asking something like that.

"He got home late. He seemed worn out, but he's fine." Eli figured that was the answer Kale would want him to respond with. Kale is fine and he'll be in later, Eli decided that would be his staple response.

"I was here when it happened," Albert said. He stood behind the security desk and wrung his hands. Eli slowed his gait, feeling obligated to hear Albert out. "I can't believe it was happening in this building. Practically in front of my face. I'm supposed to keep everyone in this building safe." He ran his fingers through his thinning hair. "I can't help feeling like I failed."

"You make sure only the right people get inside the building. You can't be held responsible for what happens after that," Eli said.

"I should have known though. Looking back, I can see the signs now. I should have known." He shook his head and Eli took the opportunity to keep moving.

Eli took the elevator to the mailroom floor. Jack was at the front counter. Sanchez and Ricardo were bringing packages and boxes of letters in from the mail truck. Eli clocked in and headed to help them.

"I heard what happened," Jack said, before Eli finished coming behind the counter.

"What?"

"Kale punched Rich," Jack said. Sanchez chuckled as he hefted a box onto the counter next to the one Jack was sorting.

"I wish I could have been there to see," Sanchez said. He pretended to punch himself in the face, mocking Rich's injuries.

"If I had to name a person who I would have wanted to be the one to walk in on Rich doing those things to that girl, Kale would be my top pick," Jack said. "I bet Rich pissed his pants when he saw Kale."

"Heard he broke his jaw, they had to put wires in it," Sanchez said. "Rich will be eating out of a straw for weeks."

He broke his jaw? Eli couldn't hide the shiver that ran through his body.

"I'm surprised he didn't kill him," Ricardo said, coming in with another crate of letters. He pointed to a small scar on his forehead. "Kale threw a coffee cup at me once, for giving him a certified letter a day late. I would think sexual assault would be a death penalty in Kale's eyes."

Sanchez grabbed Eli's shoulder and gave it a firm squeeze. "Nah, Kale isn't like that anymore, not since my man Eli took over. You keep him in check, don't you, Eli?"

"More like drugs his coffee," Ricardo said.

"Ha-ha," Eli said. "Can we get back to work? I don't think Kale would want me gossiping about what happened."

"Sure, sure, but I don't think everyone else feels that way," Sanchez said.

True to Sanchez's word, the day unfolded much like the first five minutes of his day had. Every bundle of mail delivered was met with a quandary into Kale's wellbeing and comment regarding Rich deserving what he got. Eli's skin was buzzing by nine in the morning, a mix of shock at Kale's brutality being viewed as positive and pure astonishment at the fact every employee in the building seemed to know Eli was dating Kale.

Kale was the hero of the day and Eli was playing the role of proud spouse. He wasn't proud though. None of them knew Kale's past and the dark memories last night might have dredged up.

Eli pushed the cart on the fifth floor, in the pharmaceutical sales department. Eli thumbed through some of the letters, making sure he gave the right bundle to Ms. Elsinore.

"Eli?" a male voice asked. Eli glanced up at the Asian man approaching him. He wore an expensive dress suit, similar to the ones Eli had seen Kale wearing. He smoothed his tie with one hand and offered his other to Eli to shake. Eli accepted the offer, and tried to determine if he should know the man.

"I'm Andy Blue, one of the primary partners," he said, as if noticing Eli's confusion.

"Oh, hi," Eli said.

"Do you know if Kale will be in today?" Andy crossed his arms, but his entire body seemed to writhe with energy.

"He said he has a big case today. Why? Is he late for it?" An array of horrible outcomes flashed in Eli's mind. Had Kale called Martin? He'd seemed closed off to Eli so it would make since for him to seek his old partner. Or was it worse, had he hurt himself? Gone on a bender? Did Kale drink?

"The trial doesn't start until ten," Andy said.

Eli slumped, the tension and stress from those few moments unraveling. He wanted to punch Andy for stirring up such concern.

"He said he'd be in for it," Eli repeated. "He got home late."

"Okay, good. We expected him earlier. He won't answer his phone so I was hoping you would know."

"Do you want me to call him?" Eli asked. He had no idea if he would have better luck getting Kale to answer. It wasn't like him to avoid a work call. Or was it? He hated how not well he actually knew Kale.

Andy seemed to consider his options. "He said he would be in? He didn't sound like he was quitting?"

"Why would he quit? This place is his life." The idea people in the firm thought Kale would quit made no sense. Eli wondered what pieces of the puzzle he was missing.

Andy lowered his voice. "Rich is threatening to press charges. He wants Kale fired."

"Kale wasn't the one at fault," Eli said, not bothering to keep his tone down. Everyone he'd seen today had sided with Kale.

"We're doing what we can, but the firm can't lose both of them. We can't fire Rich and have Kale quit."

"He's not quitting," Eli said. His hand dove into his pocket and retrieved his phone. He dialed Kale's number and waited. The call went to voicemail after five rings. "I'm sure he's coming."

Eli put the phone back in his pocket, deciding against leaving a voicemail. His phone chirped as Eli removed his hand. He pulled the phone out and answered.

"Hello," Eli said.

"You called?" Kale said. Relief washed over him. Kale was fine.

"Yeah, why didn't you answer?"

"Still only one hand, remember?" Kale asked. "I'm driving. I had to pull over."

"Are you on your way in? Andy is asking about you."

"Tell him I'm going directly to the courthouse," Kale said. "Have my intern meet me there with the case files."

"Okay," Eli said. Kale disconnected the call before Eli could say anything more.

§§§

Eli worked through his lunch, eating his sandwich while wrapping packages. He clocked out at two and decided to stop by Kale's office before he left. He wasn't sure if he'd still be in the courtroom but he wanted to check. Suzie smiled and buzzed him through the glass doors to the Moroz-Kempt Legal Advisors.

He was greeted with a hug from Charlotte, his second for the day from her. The bulky topaz rocks on her necklace dug into his chest.

"Carol didn't come in," Charlotte said, not that Eli had asked. From the stories Eli had heard, he'd gathered Carol was the female intern. Charlotte rubbed his upper arms before she released him, as if he was the one needing comfort.

"Is Kale here?" Eli asked.

She nodded. "In his office. Go ahead, he's not with anyone."

"Thank you," Eli said. He diverted his gaze from the prying looks of those at the desks. He'd hated delivering the mail to their floor today and he fully intended to ask Sanchez if he could cover for him tomorrow. Everyone's eyes seemed full of questions and odd wonderment, like Eli was a magical wizard who could spawn cupcakes if they only knew the right words to ask.

Kale's office door was open. Eli stopped in the doorway and knocked.

Kale had removed his coat and rolled his sleeves up. His pink cast rested on a pile of papers, while his eyes focused on his computer screen. His expression solemn. Eli considered knocking again when Kale's eyes jerked in Eli's direction. His posture slumped, some of the tension easing from his body.

"Hey," Eli said.

"Come in, leave the door open," Kale said as Eli reached to close it. The things he wanted to ask Kale weren't things he wanted everyone in the office to hear, but perhaps that was why Kale wanted it open. So Eli wouldn't ask anything too personal.

Eli sat in a chair across from Kale. His muscles ached from lugging boxes, and he sagged wearily, it was the first time all day he'd sat.

"How did the trial go?" Eli asked.

"Fine," Kale said. His eyes stayed on his computer monitor. They flickered back to Eli when he said nothing. "The trial didn't end. It'll last into next week."

"Oh," Eli said. He shifted in his seat. "How are you?"

"Fine," Kale said. His fingers constricted by the cast wiggled like he might be trying to form a fist. Eli hesitated, unsure his touch would be welcome. He set his jaw and decided to go for it. He leaned forward and linked his fingers with those on Kale's injured limb.

Kale jerked slightly but didn't pull away. Eli tightened his grip, enough to be felt, but gentle, in case Kale was sore from whatever they'd done to his arm last night.

"Is there anything I can do?" Eli asked. He felt as useless as he did around Jackie. He wasn't used to feeling it around Kale. He hated seeing the people he cared about in pain. And every time Kale met his eyes he glimpsed the demons haunting him.

Coming back here, the day after what he'd witnessed had to be hard. Eli wasn't sure he would have been able too, and he didn't have the personal aspects to add on top of it like Kale did.

"Can you check on Carol? We gave her the day off. She wants to come in tomorrow but I want to make sure she's ready. If someone could stop by her place and access her mental status that would reassure me. I would go myself but I'm behind." He looked at the piles of documents on his desk. "I'm not sure who to ask." He looked out onto the office floor as if any one of his coworkers might be capable of the same evil Rich had done.

"Maybe Charlotte?" Eli suggested. "Or one of the other female interns?"

Kale's eyes met his. "I want you to do it."

"She doesn't know me."

"Everyone knows you," Kale said. He pulled his hand back and used his thumb and index finger to delicately hold a pencil. He couldn't apply enough pressure to work a pen, but he could drag a pencil around well enough and leave a somewhat readable mark. He jotted down an address.

Eli repeated those words in his head. Everyone did seem to know him, or at least know of him. He crossed his arms and watched Kale struggle through writing the information.

Kale finished and looked at Eli. "What's the look for?"

"Nothing," Eli said. He shrugged. "I just don't get why you think she'd be comfortable seeing me."

"You asked if there was anything you could do to help me. If you don't want to do it, that's fine." There wasn't any anger in the words, and Eli couldn't help but digress.

"No, you're right. I'll do it." He took the paper.

"What's bothering you?" Kale asked.

Eli stared at the lightly scribbled address. "You're busy, I should go," Eli said.

"I'm not too busy for a five minute conversation with you," Kale said. "Tell me what's wrong."

Eli could see the possessive fire inside Kale's eyes.

"I'm just not used to all of this," Eli said.

"All of what?"

"Of this." Eli shook the four-inch square of paper. "Of being able to stop by and check on someone just because of an association to you. To accept that she'll welcome me in because I'm dating you.

"I've spent all morning fielding questions from people who want to know if you're okay. People who want to tell me how proud they are of you. I'm—I'm not used to people... Usually people look at me with pity because my wife is dying. I've never—I didn't..." Eli floundered to find the right words to express the emotions weighing on him.

"I expected people to continue looking at me with pity. I figured they'd all give me that, 'oh it's just a matter of time before Kale hits him, poor thing.' I didn't think this would become a positive thing. I've never been in a relationship that I wasn't either ashamed of or forced into."

He'd kept his eyes downcast for the entire speech. His thoughts had kind of gone all over the place, but he felt the last sentence got the point across fairly well. He'd been forced into marrying Jackie when she'd gotten pregnant and he'd stayed with her out of obligation when she'd gotten cancer. Every man he'd been in a relationship with he'd been ashamed to have the relationship discovered. He'd been very careful to maintain two separate lives, both of which made him miserable.

Kale had somehow bridged the gap between the worlds, and brought with him an entire building full of accepting people who were thrilled Eli was dating Kale. The HR department treated Eli like a king every time he delivered their mail. The story of his application process had spread like a legend—the great Eli who made Kale apologize for being a jackass. Coupled with this whole "Kale the hero" bit from last night, Eli felt like he was dating a candidate running for president.

The silence dragged on and Eli forced himself to look up. Kale stared at him, his gaze intense enough to make Eli squirm.

"I should go, you're busy, and I'm rambling," Eli said. He stood and so did Kale, matching his movements. Eli turned and hurried from the office, Kale never saying a word.

CHAPTER TWENTY

At five-thirty, the door to the apartment opened and closed. Eli sat up straight, all senses on alert. He muted the television and listened to the footsteps in the foyer. Kale appeared in the entranceway to the living room. This was the earliest he'd been home all week.

Kale dropped his suitcase on the floor, pulled his coat off and collapsed onto the couch next to Eli.

"Hey," Eli said, the knots in his stomach pulled tighter. "You're home early."

"I couldn't stay."

"Why?"

Kale turned his head to look at him, as if his question were stupid. "Because I didn't want to."

"Oh."

Kale shook his head. "The idea of being alone in the office after what happened... I couldn't do it. I brought home as much of the work as I could. I'll finish it here." He stared at the television. "What are you watching?"

Eli took the hint and decided not to pry. "It's one of those criminal investigation dramas."

Despite his declaration of needing to do work, Kale stayed on the couch and watched the television. Eli doubted he was really paying attention to it.

"Is this what you've been doing all week when you get home from work?" Kale asked. Eli couldn't tell if there was disapproval in the question or not.

"I've been spending time with Jackie and Annabelle too." He settled more on the couch, but resisted the desire to touch him. He wanted so badly to curl up in Kale's arms and ease his pain. "I'll admit I've been getting a lot of use out of your cable service, though. It's been a while since I had access to this many channels. What do you normally watch?"

Kale was silent a moment. He wondered if Kale would proclaim that he never watched television. Perhaps the service was there for Martin's entertainment, in which case Eli would have successfully put his foot in his mouth.

"Those reality shows," Kale said. "Where they go into someone's house and find treasures. The ones about hoarders and fighting over deserted storage units and homes."

"Really? Reality shows?"

"Riley introduced me to them."

"Have you ever thought about doing it yourself? You know, go to an auction or something, find some junk that's worth something."

"Riley would love that, but no."

"I should take you to my parents' basement. You two can probably find a lost treasure or two in there," Eli said.

"I'm sure. I got a pretty good idea of the contents of their house."

Eli's guard went up. "When did you see the inside of my parents' house?"

"I went there looking for you, remember?"

"My dad let you in the house?" Eli's stomach went hollow. He'd had no idea Kale had seen that mess.

"Your mom did, yeah. I was only in the living room."

Eli didn't mean too, but he shrunk away from Kale, edging to the farthest part of the couch. "I can't believe you let me move in with you after you saw that. You must be terrified I'm going to fill your apartment with mounds of worthless collectables."

"You were living out of your car," Kale said. "I doubt you have much stockpiled in your car. Plus, you were unemployed. I doubt you could afford to buy anything worthless."

Eli wasn't sure if he should be insulted by the words or not. He was still reeling from the fact super clean, no clutter, not even an appliance on the kitchen countertops—Kale had agreed to let a potential pack-rat move in with him.

"What would you collect if you could?" Kale asked. He turned his head and rested it against the back of the couch.

"Why? Are you wondering what treasures of mine you can break since Martin's dish collection is gone?"

Kale flinched. Eli waited for some half-hearted reply about how he hadn't meant it like that.

"How was Carol?" Kale asked, dodging the sensitive topic and choosing an even worse one.

"She was good. She let me in and we had tea. Her roommate took the day off to spend with her. She seemed well adjusted considering what happened," Eli said, and she'd seemed a little too thrilled to be paid a visit by Eli.

"That's good. I'm glad she'll be okay." Kale closed his eyes for a moment. He opened them, a question seeming to linger in them. "Did you mean what you said earlier in my office? About my being your first openly gay relationship?"

Eli wished the couch were bigger so he could slide farther away. "Yeah. I mean, I'm still married, so I couldn't start anything that serious. People aren't usually fans of all the baggage I have."

"Except Selena," Kale said.

"Yeah," Eli agreed.

Kale reached out with his good hand and beckoned Eli to come closer. "Come here."

When Eli was within reach Kale grabbed his arm and pulled him on top of his lap. Eli straddled him, a knee on either side, his face inches from Kale's. Kale grabbed his collar and pulled his lips to his.

Eli melted into the touch, sliding his legs apart so as much of his body as possible pressed against Kale. Kale pressed his tongue into his mouth, caressing the roof of his mouth. Eli ground against him, his body yearned for the sexual release that had escaped him most of the week.

Eli ran his hand over Kale's chest. Inches from reaching his groin, Kale intercepted and pulled his hand up. So Kale wasn't so far recovered from last night that he wanted things to go that far. Eli could work with that.

§§§

Eli's alarm clock went off way too soon. He slammed his palm against the wretched device and debated if he really needed an hour and half to get ready. Kale rolled on top of him, kissing him deeply and instantly giving Eli's morning wood a firm awakening.

"Take a shower with me," Eli managed between Kale's smothering lips. Kale's body went rigid and Eli realized he'd said something wrong. Then it struck him. Why Kale hadn't taken a shower yesterday. "It happened in a shower."

He hated himself instantly for having said it aloud.

"Yes," Kale said. "It always happened in the shower."

Eli got hung up on the word *always*. Kale hadn't been raped once. It had happened repeatedly, in a shower.

"Oh God, Kale." Eli wasn't sure what to do. He cupped Kale's face in both his hands, hoping his touch was welcome.

"I never told Martin," Kale said. His gaze focused on the pillow next to Eli's ear. His dark eyes darted back to Eli. "About any of it. I never wanted him to see me vulnerable."

"You never told him you were assaulted," Eli said. *Why do I keep repeating the obvious,* Eli could kick himself.

"Correct." At least he'd had the decency to not say, duh. "I want to feel you in me. Do you have time before you go to work?"

Every hair perked up on Eli's body. Even if he didn't have time, he'd make time. "God yes."

Kale rolled off. Eli retrieved the lube and a condom from the side table. Kale grabbed the condom from him and tossed it to the floor. "I said you, not rubber."

Eli hesitated. "Are you sure?"

"It's what you like. I want to give you what you like, Eli."

"You don't have to. I don't want you to feel obligated."

"Never." Kale sat up and pulled him close. "Show me how good it can be. Make me forget how bad it was."

§§§

Kale worked hard to walk with a normal gate as he exited the elevator on the second floor. His rear was still tender from overdoing it this morning. It had been well worth it though. The burn that lingered today was a good reminder that Eli wasn't going anywhere. He needed that. To know his new relationship was secure and wouldn't falter due to a dying wife or obsessive ex.

Suzie glanced up as he passed the reception desk. There was something awry with how quickly she looked away. He pushed on the glass doors as she buzzed him in. He went two steps inside when an eruption of applause froze him.

Everyone stood at their desks, facing him and clapping. Kale set his jaw, mind reeling. Was it someone's birthday? It wasn't his. And normally they didn't celebrate birthdays with this much flare. Carol walked down the aisle, sheet cake in hand, cursive blue frosting spelled out "Thank you, boss."

Luke stepped forward, his demeanor still rigid from his military career. "The girls wanted to put something together to thank you for standing up for Carol," Luke said. He shrugged. "I know public recognition isn't your thing, but you'll just have to tolerate it this time."

Luke clapped him on the shoulder and that spurred the assembly line of hugs, handshakes and murmurs of thanks. You'd have thought Kale had vanquished some unsightly pest from the facility, not punched a senior partner.

Kale settled in his office, a slice of chocolate cake with white frosting balanced on a stack of papers. Luke and Andy entered with slices of their own. Neither of them touched the sugary treat. Luke didn't have an ounce of fat on him and Kale figured he didn't even remember what sugar tasted like. Andy studied his slice as if tempted, but pushed it to the side.

Luke closed the office door. Kale bit his lip to keep from telling him to open it. He wasn't okay with being shut in a room, alone or not. It was one of the many triggers that reminded him too much of his dark days in foster care. Memories that thanks to Rich, were now on the surface.

"We need to discuss how we want to restructure the business," Luke said. "Rich isn't coming back. He's spewing venom and threatening to take his clients with him, but we aren't letting him come back."

Andy slumped in a chair. He dipped a finger into the frosting and sucked it off. "I doubt many will go."

"We need to promote someone to partner, maybe more than one, and hopefully they'll help us buy Rich's part in the company," Luke said. "We have our eyes on a few interns and we thought we'd promote a junior to partner."

"Which interns?" Kale asked. He was still surprised they were keeping him on. After the adrenaline of the situation had ended, he'd thought for sure his career at Moroz-Kempt Legal Advisors was over.

"For starters, yours," Luke said. "Steve did a good job while you were out. If he wants the job, it's his."

"We were thinking he could take most of your cases, and you could take Rich's," Andy said.

"You want to give Andy's cases to me?" Kale stared at them, surely they were joking. Rich handled the highest profile cases in the business. Rich had a decade of experience over Kale. Luke had eight. Andy had joined the firm the same time as Kale, but Andy didn't have all the legal drama Kale did.

"What you think you can handle at least," Luke said. Kale leaned back in his seat as the gravity of the situation settled. "You'll get Rich's interns, Carol and Tim. They're familiar with the cases."

"Carol and Tim?" Kale ruffled his hair. Carol, who had just been assaulted, wasn't going to be of much use. He'd never spoken to Tim so he had no idea of the man's work quality, but he was fairly certain

Tim hated him. He had a hunch it had to do with him being gay. Tim had a day-by-day calendar with a different bible quote for each week.

"You can take on an additional intern if you want," Luke said. "And speak up, if you think someone else can handle one of the clients better than you, we'll make it happen."

"Right, I will."

"We know this is poor timing for you," Andy said. "We heard about Eli's wife. If you need time off, we'll figure it out."

"She's not dead, yet," Kale said, his tone ruder than he intended. "Who are the other interns you want to promote?"

"Ethridge Law," Andy said. "He's been with us two years. I heard he got a job somewhere else, but I think this will convince him to stay."

He was an intern for one of the junior partners, but yes, Kale had heard good things about him.

"Do you want to make anyone a primary partner?" Kale asked.

Luke shook his head. "Not right now. We need to get our own feet under us. Do you have a preference on the order of the names?"

"For what?"

"The new business name," Andy said. "We thought we'd put you in the middle."

"Kempt-Sokoloff-Blue Legal Advisors," Luke said.

"That sounds ridiculous and no one will be able to pronounce it," Kale said. "Take my name out, just use the two of you."

"Not happening," Luke said. He'd been standing for the entire meeting, like he always did. Maybe that's how he stayed in such good shape. He only sat in the courtroom. He approached Kale's desk and loomed over him. "You're a part of this company and our clients need that assurance."

"You think I'm going to quit?" Kale looked from him to Andy and could see the worry in both their expressions. "Why would you think that?"

The two of them exchanged a look, as if the answer were obvious to everyone but Kale.

"What the hell do the two of you know that I don't?" Kale asked.

Luke spoke first. "We know Rich is going to attempt to destroy you. It would be easier for you to uproot and start over somewhere else."

"To hell with Rich," Kale said. "I'm not running away from him."

"What about your personal situation?" Andy asked. Kale's scowl spoke volumes and Andy continued without needing to be asked. "If Eli doesn't get custody of his kid, the grandmother will. She lives in D.C. There's talk that you and Eli will move there, so you can be close to her."

Talk spread fast. He hadn't even considered moving to where Annabelle's grandmother lived. That actually sounded like a peaceful solution to the potentially bloody custody battle.

"I hadn't even thought of that," Kale said. He'd only known Eli for three weeks. He wasn't about to end his career and uproot his life for him. The coldness of that reality hit him. He wondered if Eli would make the same choice if their roles were reversed.

"Our relationship isn't that serious," Kale said. "Eli's decision to move to another state won't affect my job here."

§§§

Reluctantly, Kale boxed up most of his clients' files for relocation to Steve's new office. Luke had insisted Kale move into the corner office, but Kale had refused. Blue would get the office. It would be a while before Kale would be able to set foot in that office without feeling a chill and he didn't want Carol going through that either, since they'd be working together.

Kale's desk was clear for only a few minutes. New files were stacked on it, all of Rich's clients. Carol and Tim sat across from him, notepads at the ready.

Carol smiled at him kindly enough. Tim gave him a steely glare a Nazi would be proud of. Kale imagined the gold cross around Tim's neck was a swastika. Tim's blue eyes and blond hair perfected the image.

"So I'm sure you heard I'll be taking over Rich's clients. I want to go over them all with you. Fill me in on the highlights and feel free to mention if you think one of the other attorneys would be better suited to handle the client," Kale said.

"You mean like, if a client wouldn't want to work with a homosexual?" Tim asked. The air in the room seemed ten degrees chiller. *So Tim wanted to go there, right off the bat, huh?*

"Do you actually have that kind of information at hand?" Kale asked.

A vein grew larger on Tim's neck. "It's not that hard to determine."

"Is my sexual orientation going to be a problem, Tim? If it is, you can leave right now."

Tim uttered one short chuckle. "You need me."

"What? Because I can't read a client's file on my own? Leave this office, Tim, and come back when your attitude improves." Kale waited as Tim obediently departed the office. He turned to Carol. "How familiar are you with the clients?"

"I don't know as much as Tim," Carol admitted.

"We'll work with what we have. What's the next case Rich has that is going to trial?"

Two hours later, Tim knocked on Kale's door. Kale motioned for him to enter.

"I'm sorry about earlier," Tim said. He held a brown folder to his chest. "Can we start over?"

Kale wondered who had talked to him. Perhaps he'd realized if he quit, his only reference from the company would be from a man who would soon be serving time in prison for rape.

Kale motioned to the chairs across from his desk. Tim sat, still clutching that folder like a lifeline.

"Want to tell me what your earlier comments were about?" Kale asked.

"I was being brash. I realize now this is an opportunity. God is putting us together, intertwining our lives for a reason. I can help you, Kale. There are—"

Kale grabbed the thickest book sitting on his desk and chucked it at Tim's face. The man managed to block it with his right hand, knocking the book to the side. The last thing Kale needed was some religious banter about how Kale was doomed to hell unless he changed his sinful ways and became a straight man.

"What was that for?" Tim asked. His eyes dilated, and his hands gave a tremble. And damned if Kale wasn't turned on by it.

"My soul doesn't need saving," Kale said. Tim's jaw dropped slightly. He relinquished the folder he'd been clutching.

"I was talking about the custody case you gave to Carol. My father practices family law. I grew up watching him deal with cases like this. I can help your friend—"

"Boyfriend," Kale corrected. He wasn't about to let the homophobe off the hook, even if Kale had behaved just as poorly in misinterpreting Tim's intentions.

"I can help your...partner get custody of his daughter," Tim said, seeming too uncomfortable with the boyfriend word. Kale decided to accept it, it was progress after all.

"I'm listening," Kale said.

CHAPTER TWENTY-ONE

Kale looked at the Rengate Hotel as Eli pulled his car up to the entrance. The anger management camp was hosted here.

"Sure you'll be okay?" Eli asked. It was court ordered, so Kale would have to be.

"It's two days and one-night," Kale said. "I'll be fine."

He had to be. He worried the firm would go under if he was sent to jail or anger management for thirty days. And he needed to be there for Eli when Jackie died. The weight of responsibilities was getting a bit daunting, but if he could pass this course, everything would be fine. At least that's what he kept telling himself.

"I'll miss you," Eli said. Kale reached across the center console to give him a lip bruising kiss, staking his claim one last time before going a full thirty-two hours without seeing him.

"Same here," Kale said. He wouldn't even be able to call him. Cell phones were confiscated and the phones in their rooms were monitored. Kale got out of the car and grabbed his bag from the trunk. Eli stayed in the car, as they'd discussed. If he'd gotten out and hugged him goodbye, Kale wasn't sure he'd be able to break the embrace.

He walked inside the hotel and to the check-in desk. The hotel was lavish, high vaulted ceilings and a fountain in the center. He checked in, received his welcome kit and was instructed to go to ballroom four.

Kale shouldered his bag and followed the receptionist's directions to ballroom four. At the entrance to the room, a man waited at a folding table in the hall. He handed Kale a nametag to wear and button that said, "team Q."

He looked at the bald headed man and hesitated. "Do I put them on now?"

"Yes, both," he replied. Kale attached both pins to his shirt, wishing he'd worn cheaper clothes that he wouldn't have minded being damaged from the pin.

He piled his bag in the corner with everyone else's. People mulled about, sipping the free coffee and munching on bagels. The room was set up with twenty-four tables, two seats to a table. No one was sitting, but Kale noticed a letter was on a placard at each table.

At nine on the dot, a bell chimed and Mr. Alonso, the life coach leading the camp, gave his introduction speech. He gave an overview of the camp, basic goals, rules, and expectations. He ended with a biography of his own, spending way too long on his list of degrees.

"Be a good team player and you'll all receive diplomas at the end of tomorrow," Mr. Alonso said. "Now each of you have been assigned a letter. You'll be working with an anger buddy for the weekend. Go ahead and find your table and meet your buddy.

"There is a stack of index cards with basic questions to help get the conversations started. After thirty minutes we'll start with the exercises." Alonso gave them a winning smile, his teeth so straight Kale wondered at what age he'd had braces.

He walked slowly to table Q. A woman was already seated there. She had broad shoulders; her hair, a razor even cut with her earlobes, was pencil straight. Kale slid into the chair across the table from her.

She bunched her forehead up as she looked at him, sizing him up as if prepared to arm wrestle. Kale lifted his cast and placed the heavy burden on the table, hoping his injury would diffuse the tension.

"Are you a wife beater?" She squawked in a tone that belied years if not decades of heavy smoking. Her skin was smooth though, aside from small lines surrounding her mouth.

"No," Kale said.

"They normally partner the wife beaters up with women at these camps. Trying to make a point or start a fight, I suppose." She crossed her arms and puffed out her sizable chest. She was in shape, like, nearly body-builder, heavy lifting in shape. Not to the point where she'd lost her womanly curves though, but she had enough bulk he did not want to wrestle her—in any aspect.

"I've never hit a woman," Kale said. It wasn't like he had some moral code that kept him from it. He'd simply never had one upset him enough to feel the need to strike them.

"Huh," she said. "So what, are you more the pick a fight in a bar to defend your woman's honor, type?"

The closest he'd come to that had been saving Carol, and honor had nothing to with any of it.

"No, more the beat my boyfriend, type," Kale said.

Her perfectly plucked eyebrows rose. "Well, holy shit. That's why they put us together. Gave us the damn letter Q too. The shrinks must have got a good laugh at that." She flicked the placard with her fingernails.

Kale glanced at the other tables. Everyone else had a partner who was of the same gender.

"It could have just been an odd numbered class," Kale said.

"I'm a dike and you're queer. It doesn't take rocket science to figure it out," she said. "We've been targeted."

Kale looked at her, wondering exactly what negative impact she was expecting this so called targeting to create. "I think we share a hotel room with our partner," Kale said, recalling that tidbit from the pamphlet. "So this actually makes sense."

His therapist had signed him up for the class, so he didn't doubt certain bits of information, like his sexual preferences, had made it into the hands of the people leading the course.

"You better not be lying about being gay in some attempt to fulfill a lesbian fantasy. My partner and I aren't into that," she said.

"Neither are—" He almost said, neither are we, but realized Eli actually might be. He'd done threesomes with two men, why not two women?

"Neither what?"

"Nothing." Kale put his elbow on the table and ruffled his hair. He read her nametag. "Morley." *Gah, that was a horrific name.*

"You can call me More," she said. She grabbed one of the index cards. "So who's the last person you hit?"

"It says that?"

"Yup."

Kale sighed. "My boss."

"No shit? Why?"

"Does it say that too?"

"Nope, just curious."

"I caught him sexually assaulting someone in the office. I broke his jaw."

"No shit?" She chuckled. It was actually a whimsical sound, he'd expected her laugh to be more of a cowish bellow. "When I was waitressing, I backhanded a guy for pinching my butt. He got a bloody eye and I lost my job."

"Guess we have something in common," Kale said. "So who was the last person you hit?"

"The guy who hit my car. I stopped at a yellow and he rammed right into me. Things got heated."

Kale pulled another card from the deck. "Has your anger ever affected your work?" He glanced at her. "I think we already covered this one."

"Was the incident with your boss why you're here?" Morley asked.

"No, you?"

"It's the only way I'll get my license back. That cast have something to do with why you're here?"

"No, the industrial oven was kind enough to not press charges."

She laughed louder this time, it sounded as pleasant as the first. He glanced at some of the other tables. No one else was laughing, a few actually shot their table dirty looks.

"You a baker then? Did the oven burn the cake?"

"No, my ex's sister owns a bakery. I was pissed at her and she dodged me. I'm a lawyer."

"Really? I could use one of those."

"I'm sure everyone here could." Crap, why had he offered up his job? The last thing he needed was another client who couldn't afford to pay him.

"I own a gym, bi-feet fitness," she said. She pulled a card from her pocket and handed it to him. "You ever want to punch something that won't break your hand, come on by. I can plan a good workout for you taking consideration into account for your broken chicken wing."

She was making it hard for him to not reciprocate the offer, but he already had a backlog of cases even with working fourteen-hour days.

"So is your ex why you're taking this course? Trying to win him back?" she asked, politely changing the topic.

"No, I'm with someone else, actually. He is why I'm here though." Kale went into the story of what he'd done to Martin. Morley chirped with glee. She'd seen the article in the paper. The topic shifted to Morley's own partner, Laney, who Morley praised up and down. Kale then told her about Eli.

"You treat your new partner different?" Morley asked.

"I haven't hit him, yet," Kale replied. "But I was with Martin for six months before I ever struck him."

She nodded. "You think you will?"

He'd be lying if he said no. "It's possible."

"Pardon me for saying it, but it sounds like you're starting the cycle all over again. I've known a few men who hit their wives. First there's the honeymoon stage, then once you've got them fully smitten with you, and you've got them dependent on you, the abuse starts."

"I don't plan it out like that," Kale said.

"So Martin had his own money and friends? He could leave you and be fully independent?"

Kale shifted in his seat. "No. He...he actually tried to come back when I cut him off financially."

"And Eli is already down on his luck. You're playing the hero swooping in to save him. Gave him a job, place to live, helping him get his kid. Won't be long before he'll put up with whatever you dish out, just so he can keep those niceties."

Kale was about to deny it, when the chime sounded, indicating their social time was over and the first exercise was about to begin.

Mr. Alonso broke into a thirty minute lecture, explaining what they had planned for the day. Kale mulled over what Morley had said.

He'd known Eli was vulnerable from the moment he'd met him in prison. The guard had told him he was jobless and broke. Had Kale picked him because he knew it would be easy to make Eli reliant on him? He rubbed his arms, a sudden chill hitting him.

He couldn't abuse Eli like that. Eli had been through enough and he deserved to be with someone who cared about him. Not someone who wanted to control and dominate his entire life. He deserved better than Kale.

§§§

"This is stupid," Morley said. Her statements for the last twenty minutes had alternated between, this is stupid and I really want to win. Kale remained neutral.

The last activity for the day was to complete a five hundred piece jigsaw puzzle with their anger buddy. The first three couples to finish were promised a prize. Kale figured it was a coupon or a mug advertising the camp. He twirled the puzzle piece he'd had in his hand for the last five minutes.

A cheer broke out from table G. Two girls rose and high fived each other, the first ones to complete the puzzle. A pair of men, one of whom had arms covered in tattoos and Kale could easily imagine belonging to a biker gang, stood and knocked his table over. His partner cussed and shoved him. Kale cringed and put the puzzle piece into its proper location to complete the image of two kittens playing in a flowerpot.

"Shit, one couple won already." Morley's brown eyes, that were nearly a bronze color, looked at his with a competitive edge. "We got this."

She tried desperately to fit a piece somewhere and failed. Kale picked another piece and stalled, feeling its glossy surface with his thumb.

"There's one thing I don't get," Morley said. "Why did you stop?"

"Stop what?" Kale said. He put the piece in its home and surveyed the remaining unfinished puzzle.

"Hitting your boss. You said three cops had to pry you off your ex and those other two guys, but you threw two good hits at your boss and you stopped. Why?"

During the last ten hours, and various exercises, Morley had come to know Kale's last month of drama quite well. And he hers. That was the point of it all.

"It wouldn't have done any good," Kale said. "Carol would have been terrified. I would have wound up in jail. Eli would lose his daughter, and have no one to help him when Jackie dies."

"You usually have time to think things through so thoroughly when you're pissed at someone?" Morley asked.

"No."

"So you didn't get as angry as you normally do?"

He tried to recall what exactly had gone through his mind. "Eli would have left."

"He wasn't there."

"He would have left me." Kale snapped another piece in place and shot her a warning look.

"I thought we already established Eli is a perfect mark for your needs because he's vulnerable," Morley said. "So why do you think he would have left?"

"Annabelle." Kale said her name softly. "I may have picked Eli because he was an easy partner to mold into what I need, but I didn't know he had a kid. He'll pick her over me. If I do something that makes him think Annabelle is in danger, he'll leave."

He'd had plenty of time to reach that conclusion during the boring lectures they'd endured that afternoon. He'd also concluded it was only a matter of time until those events took place. He'd hit Eli or do something to spook him and Eli would scoop up Annabelle and run.

"That sucks. You sure he'd do that? Lots of people have kids and still stay with their abusive partner."

"Eli will put his needs second. No matter what he needs, he'll do what's best for Annabelle." He ruffled his hair and moved his aching fingers in his casted arm.

"Sounds like your relationship is doomed for failure," Morley said. She sighed. "Kind of like us and this puzzle."

"At least we aren't losing our tempers. I think the point is to show patience, doesn't matter if we complete it."

"Yeah, but if we complete it, we might get to leave. I'd sure like to hit up the pool if we get out of here early enough," Morley said.

He looked at the puzzle. He hadn't considered the idea that they might get dismissed when they finished it. The couple who had won first place hadn't returned. He stopped dawdling and started putting the pieces into place. Morley sat back, watching his fingers move in awe.

"Since when are you so good at puzzles?"

"I have a brother who is mentally disabled. Doing puzzles is something that calms him. I've done quite a few with him. This one is easier than the thousand plus piece puzzles he does." He had to try a few different times to get the array of pink flowers complete. Morley snatched up the last piece, put it in place, and jumped up.

She yelled, "Done," with the same affliction one would yell bingo. They were given gift cards to a local massage parlor and dismissed for the night.

"See you in the morning, chuckles," Morley said as one of the assistants handed her a room card key in the hallway outside the ballroom.

"More like, see you in five minutes," Kale clarified. "We're sharing a room."

"Oh crap, that's right." She frowned and her eyes settled on his crotch. "No beating off under your sheets while I'm in the room."

Kale rolled his eyes. "Don't worry. My jerking off hand is the broken one."

"Ouch," she said, actually looking like she sympathized. "No wonder you're so worried Eli is going to leave you."

Before he could reply, she grabbed the handle on her rolling luggage and took off down the hall. Kale followed, letting her get far enough ahead that he could take a separate elevator.

§§§

Kale couldn't remember ever sharing a room with a girl. All the foster homes and group homes had been boys only. He'd lived with his sister for a year, but he'd had his own room. The two full sized beds were three feet apart. Kale could hear Morley snoring softly in her sleep.

Staying in a hotel room with a woman. This was one event he wouldn't soon forget. He rolled over, facing the wall. The last few days with Eli had been perfect. Sex with no condoms had been liberating, in more ways than one. Kale felt like he'd finally shaken free of the last of the ghosts haunting him.

But now reality was crashing back down on him. Eli would leave, just like Martin and everyone else. He buried his face in the pillow and pushed the thoughts from his mind. He needed to seal his heart back up before Eli got any farther inside.

He woke up to firm hands shaking his shoulders. He opened his eyes to see Morley staring at him. The lights were on in the room. Her hair stuck out in crazy directions, her cleavage threatening to burst from her low cut tank top. He did not need that image added to the array of nightmares he already endured.

"You were thrashing about and talking to yourself," Morley said. "I almost thought someone was attacking you."

And she'd been brave enough to shake him awake. Shit. She was lucky he hadn't woken up swinging. Martin had gotten more than one black eye from trying to rouse him from a nightmare.

"Who is Roy?" Morley asked. Kale flinched and shrunk back from her. *Not over things as well as I thought.*

"Someone from the past," Kale said.

"He used to hit you?" Morley asked.

"Why would you say that?" Kale sat up and wiped the sweat from his face. Being in a strange room with no warm body next to him, coupled with witnessing Rich's assault, must have triggered the nightmare. He hadn't had it since the first week after Martin left. He'd woken up screaming, fists clenched for seven days straight. Then he'd called his doctor and had him prescribe a sleep-aide. Why hadn't he brought the pills with him? The answer snagged in his brain before he could finish asking it, because he'd stopped needing them since he'd met Eli.

"You were begging him not to hit you, in your sleep," Morley said.

"I was in a group home for three years," Kale said. "Some of the other boys weren't all that kind."

"They would beat you?"

"Yeah." He shivered from the chill his damp skin gave him. Morley did the most shocking thing then. She climbed into his bed and wrapped her arms around him, hugging him from behind. She pressed her cleavage into his back and rested her head on his shoulder. "Pillowcases full of bars of soap, socks with lose change in them. I'd wake in the middle of the night to a group of them over me, welts covered my body the next day."

"Shit." She hugged him tighter and some of the chill loosened in his gut. Roy had been the ringleader. It'd taken Kale a while to figure out why Roy had hated him so much. Later, after the third butt rape, also courtesy of Roy, Kale had realized it was because Roy hated the feelings Kale stirred up in him. Roy wanted to be straight, but he couldn't stop wanting to fuck Kale. He knew because Roy had told him on more than one occasion.

"What'd you end up doing?" Morley's voice pulled him back from the memory of Roy whispering his dark desires into Kale's ear as he squeezed his throat so tight he couldn't breathe. "Did you just put up with it until you switched homes?"

"My dad came back. He wasn't able to adopt me but I started visiting him. I asked him to teach me how to fight. He wasn't a good person, but he was a good fighter. A professional boxer. I took the beatings for a few more months, until I was confident I could take him."

Kale leaned forward and craned his neck so he could look her in the eyes. "I beat him senseless in front of everyone. Got me in a shit-ton of trouble, but it was worth it. No one touched me after that."

"And you've been using your fists to solve your problems ever since, huh?" She quirked an eyebrow at him.

"Something like that," Kale agreed.

CHAPTER TWENTY-TWO

At five pm Sunday, Kale bolted from anger management's rented ballroom, free from the emotionally suffocating weekend. He had his certificate, and that's what mattered. His fellow detainees swarmed the hall with him. They flooded into the hotel lobby. Some bolted straight out the exit, others were welcomed by loving family members.

Kale spotted Eli. He wanted to engulf him, swallow him and never let him go. He reigned in the desire flooding through his body as he noticed Eli's pint sized companion. She clutched her father's hand, but broke free when she spotted Kale.

They'd only met once, but the girl bounded into his legs like he was her best friend. He realized too late he should have kneeled so he could hug her properly, instead she wrapped her hands around his knees, forcing him to stand still.

"When I told her you were at camp, she insisted on coming," Eli said. He shrugged and rubbed his arms, as if uncertain how Kale would react. "She's been asking about you. I hope you don't mind."

He wanted Eli to himself. Wanted to fuck him into oblivion after this stupid weekend apart. So yes, it bothered him that his reunion was going to be forced to the PG level because Eli had brought his daughter. His face must have shown his emotions a little too clearly because Eli cleared his throat and tugged Annabelle's shoulder until she let go.

"How was camp?" Annabelle asked, unnoticing of the tension her presence created.

"Stressful," Kale said.

"I thought camp was supposed to be fun." Annabelle frowned.

"Camp is fun," Eli said. "Kale finds everything stressful." He shot a warning glare at Kale. "She's never been to camp."

Right, so Kale saying camp sucked might ruin any future aspects of sending her to summer camp…and having Eli all to himself for a few weeks. Point taken.

"He's right. You probably would have enjoyed it. We spent a lot of time doing puzzles and games. Even had to make a tower out of marshmallows and spaghetti."

"Where is it? Can you bring it home?"

"It didn't go so well." He could do puzzles but construction was not his strong suit. Morley had traded defeat for the treat of eating the marshmallows. "We can make another one, but you have to promise not to eat the building supplies like my partner did."

"Partner?" Eli asked. His eyebrows raised and his pupils dilated. Touch of jealousy perhaps?

"Anger management buddy," Kale said. He glanced around, wondering if she was still here. They'd exchanged numbers and agreed to keep in touch. Kale still hadn't offered to help her with her legal problems, but he intended to in the future.

He spotted Morley standing with a thin blond woman across the lobby. The two women were both shooting quick glances at him. He waved his hand at them and gestured for them to approach. He was suddenly glad Annabelle was there. She created a filter on not just his behavior, but everyone around them. He didn't want Morley bringing up the fact they'd ended up spooning part of the night. Kale would never forget the awkwardness of waking up with Morley's arms wrapped around him. There had been a layer of intimacy to the embrace as if she was a mother comforting a child.

He did not want Eli or anyone else finding out about it.

Still, the two of them were linked, confessions had been made from both parties, and Kale knew if he ever got in a bind, Morley would be there for him. No more having to call his last one-night stand for a ride from the hospital because everyone else was too pissed at him to answer his call.

When she was within earshot, Kale gestured to Morley. "This is Morley, my anger management buddy," Kale said. Despite her wanting to be called More, Kale found himself inclined to use her full name. "This is Eli and Annabelle."

Morley shook Eli's hand, then knelt to shake Annabelle's as well.

"I'm Laney," the woman with Morley said. She politely extended a hand to Kale, offering him the opposite normally offered so Kale could shake it with his unbroken arm.

He glanced back at Eli in time to notice Eli's eyes were glued to the large chest on Morley. His eyes roved over Laney's body as well as she shook his hand. Eli's skin flushed a light hue of pink and the effort was noticeable as he directed his gaze to Laney's eyes. Kale wasn't sure how to feel about the idea Eli was attracted to women, but his behavior made denying it difficult. Could Eli be happy with only a man?

"Laney's my girlfriend," Morley said, more to Eli than Kale. She probably picked up on Eli's gawking too. Shit, what if she decked Eli for staring too much? Morley wrapped a possessive arm around Laney's waist.

"We think they partnered us together because of our sexual preferences," Kale said.

Eli choked a nervous laugh. Despite Annabelle being right there, Eli blurted a, "You got to spend the night in a hotel room with a lesbian?" His eyes were practically bugging out of his head.

Annabelle tilted her head, looking at her father strangely, as if also noticing his odd behavior.

"Shit, Kale, you have the best luck of anyone I know," Eli said. Suddenly, Kale wanted to tell him more of the details from the night. Wanted to see the flare of jealousy when he told him he'd shared a bed with Morley, even spooned with her.

Annabelle rolled her eyes. "Daddy's so weird sometimes," Annabelle said. She looked at Kale. "What's a lesbian?"

"Morley likes girls instead of boys," Kale said. He assumed such an explanation was okay to give her, since she seemed to have a firm grasp on the fact her daddy liked boys…and girls.

"Women," Morley clarified. "Let's keep that straight." She clapped Kale on the shoulder. "We're gonna go. Was nice to meet you, Annabelle. Good luck rolling your boyfriend's tongue up off the floor." She winked at Eli and he turned completely crimson.

The two women walked away, Eli's eyes followed them. Kale snapped his fingers in front of Eli's face. He twitched and focused on Kale. "I didn't know you liked women that much," Kale said, letting his annoyance show.

"Kale they were—I mean how can you not—they." Eli still seemed unable to form coherent sentences. Too much blood directed at the wrong parts of his body. Kale decided to focus his attention on the currently more composed and intelligent of his companions.

"Shall we get something to eat while your father collects himself?" Kale asked. She nodded enthusiastically. "What kind of food do you like?"

She began a long list of fried goods, ending with a massive list of desserts. Kale plucked the keys from Eli's back pocket, deciding he was in no condition to drive.

§§§

"You really didn't think they were hot?" Eli asked for what had to be the hundredth time as they entered Kale's apartment. He had this spring in his step that Kale found really annoying. Mostly because he wasn't the cause for it.

"No," Kale said. "I'm gay."

"But you still had to notice," Eli said. He held his hands to his chest, gesturing as if he were holding a pair of cantaloupes. "You said she owns a gym?"

"Yes, she said I could come by and she'd figure out a workout program for me."

"We have to go," Eli declared.

"Since when do you workout?" Kale narrowed his gaze at him as he opened the fridge for a bottle of water.

"Since a hot lesbian is offering to coach us. I mean, you're okay with this right? I can look?" Eli wasn't looking, he was drooling, panting, and way too excited.

"How is Jackie?" Kale asked, shifting topics to one he hoped would squash some of that excitement in Eli's eyes. Eli's body seemed to deflate as he read the meaning behind Kale's question.

"Not good. She'll probably be in the hospital before the week is over. She wants to wait until after Halloween though. She wants to hand out candy to the trick-or-treaters. I'll take Annabelle out with some of her friends. You're welcome to come with."

Halloween fell on a Thursday, in theory he could go, no therapy that day, but he didn't know how late he'd be at the office. "Depends on how busy I am."

Eli took a deep breath. "Right."

The silence dragged on for a few minutes. "I should get to bed, early day tomorrow," Eli said. He backed away, retreating to the spare bedroom. Kale didn't want to be alone, not after spending the weekend away from Eli. But he also didn't want to fuck him while there was a very high chance Eli would be fantasizing about his anger management buddy. He chucked his empty water bottle, and grabbed a stack of case files to keep him company.

§§§

Old habits fell into place as the workweek began. The week blurred by, Kale went in at seven, intending to leave before the office was empty. His nose was buried so deep in case files that he was alone for two hours before he noticed. His phobia of being alone in the office conquered, he stayed until ten…every night.

The trend continued. By Friday, Kale caught his first breath of air, his head finally above water. Until two fifteen when a knock came on his office door and he glanced up to see Eli standing there, frowning.

He tried to shift the gears in his head from work to Eli. Tried not to think about the client who was scheduled to be in his office at two thirty. A client he wasn't about to leave waiting, but saying any of that to Eli would likely end badly.

"Worked late last night, huh?" Eli said. His arms were crossed as he entered. He stiffly sat in the chair.

"It won't always be like this," Kale said. "I'm taking over Rich's cases. We're promoting internally and—"

Eli waved his hand dismissively. Kale clammed up. "Yesterday was Halloween. Annabelle wanted to show you her costume."

"Did you tell her I was working?"

"I have a feeling that's what I'm going to spend a lot of time telling her." Eli said the words coldly. Since when was Eli wanting him to be an active participant in parenting his daughter? Kale had never signed on for that.

"I have a career," Kale said. "It's not like I can call in sick and have someone else do my job. My clients would leave the firm if I did that. Some of them are here because they specifically want me representing them."

"You're irreplaceable. Good for you," Eli said. Kale couldn't tell if it was sarcasm or contempt etched into the tone.

"I'm not her dad," Kale said. "You are."

Eli flinched. The shield of anger he'd entered the office with easily punctured and crumbled. He sagged in the seat. The light on Kale's desk phone flashed, the ringer off. He glanced through the glass windows into the office floor and saw Charlotte holding her phone. She met his gaze and mouthed, "He's here."

He needed to reassemble Eli and get him out of his office.

"I'm sorry, I didn't mean—"

"I'm moving into Jackie's house," Eli said. He stared into his lap, shoulders slumped. "Jackie checked into the hospital this morning. Loraine and I are trading off taking care of Annabelle." Loraine? It took Kale a moment to realize that had to be the name of Jackie's mother. "Loraine wants to spend as much time at the hospital with

Jackie as she can. So... I mean, it's not like you're ever at the apartment anyway."

This felt too much like a break up. Kale's entire body ached, his stomach swirled uncomfortably.

"You're moving out?" Kale said, needing the clarification on how this was playing out.

Eli's eyes moved up and searched Kale's. Perhaps trying to read whether the question held any meaning for Kale.

"Everything is in flux right now," Eli said. "Jackie's leaving me the house, but I can't afford the mortgage payments. So yeah, I'll probably live there until I can find a buyer, or the bank takes it."

Kale wanted to remind him that there was no expiration on his invitation to live with him, but the words sounded too much like Eli was a stray puppy he wanted to adopt. His phone lit up again. He didn't dare to look at Charlotte this time.

"I was thinking..." Eli bit his lip. Kale wanted to give him time to assemble his next sentence, but his client ran a billion dollar company and it was two-twenty-eight...

Eli took a deep breath and it took all of Kale's patience to keep from rising from his chair and ushering Eli out of the office with a few standard words of consolation.

"You could move in with us," Eli said. His eyes darted up again, and then the word vomit started, as if afraid to leave a break in-between his words because he didn't want to hear Kale's reply. "I know it's too soon, but you offered to let us live with you, so I thought maybe it wouldn't sound as crazy as I think it does. It just makes more sense for you to move in with us instead. Annabelle has friends in the neighborhood and she likes her school. I don't want to put her through more change than I have too. I know it is an extra twenty minutes on your commute to work and I don't know how comfortable you are with the idea. It doesn't have to be right away, but I wanted to put the offer out there for you to consider. If you—"

Charlotte knocked loudly on the ajar office door and stood in the doorway. She'd kicked Martin out of Kale's office more than once, not to mention a few clients who didn't know how to keep to a time slot. Normally Kale welcomed the intrusion, but the idea of kicking the broken man who was offering to share his dead wife's home with him—an offer Kale wasn't sure how he felt about it—pulled at Kale's gut.

"Mr. Lowery is here," Charlotte said. "Eli, sorry but you'll need to go now."

Eli jumped up from his chair. "Right, yeah, I didn't even think to ask if you were busy."

Charlotte's dismissive tone sent a spear of anger through Kale. She'd said those lines to Martin and Kale had never cared. He knew she was working herself as tirelessly as Kale was, but damn it, Eli was about to be a grieving widow and he deserved better.

Kale got up from his desk, crossed the room in six quick steps, and grabbed the door. Charlotte backed up out of the doorway. "Tell Mr. Lowery I need fifteen minutes. If he's not okay with that, he can reschedule."

Kale shut the door, right in Charlotte's face, nearly hitting her nose. He spun on his heel and faced Eli, who was standing but hadn't moved from in front of his chair.

He crossed the distance between them and took Eli's face in both his hands. He kissed him deeply, slipping his tongue in and caressing the roof of his mouth. He hadn't shared his bed with Eli all week. A mistake he was sorely regretting, especially if Eli was no longer going to be under his roof.

If Rich hadn't put everyone on edge about sexual relations in the workplace, Kale would have rectified their week of abstinence then and there. Eli's body pressed into his, as if trying to blend into one form with him. Kale pulled back first. He needed time to wrap his head around the feasibility of moving into Jackie's house. He wasn't attached to his apartment, but he was used to being the one with his name on the lease, not the other way around.

"I can be flexible," Kale said. "Take the time you need to sort things. Keep your key to my place, you're welcome back anytime." He reconsidered his next request, but damn it, Eli was his and he wanted access whenever he wanted. "I want a key to Jackie's house. I require an open invitation to enter and fuck you whenever the mood hits me."

Eli's body shuddered and he mumbled something Kale couldn't understand. Kale nipped his ear, teeth hitting his earring. "Try again," Kale said.

"I'll leave a key to her place on your counter," Eli said. "Call first though, okay?"

"Why? You planning to have someone else over?"

"No, but I don't want you giving Loraine a heart attack."

Kale cupped Eli's groin, and felt his growing erection. Eli was going to have a damn hard time hiding it when he exited the office. "This is mine," Kale said, a low growl came from his throat. "And I don't need to place an advance order to access it, understand?"

"Tonight," Eli's said. "Need you to fuck me tonight."

"Is that so?"

"Need you." Eli's words were digressing to single words, unable to formulate full sentences. Kale had taken a near break up and spun Eli up so hard he was likely going to need to jerk off in the bathroom before he left. Kale wanted to do likewise but Mr. Lowery was waiting, so he'd have to endure the discomfort.

"Then you better remember to leave the key," Kale said. He stepped away from Eli, glancing down at his pants to see how obvious the erection was. Eli did some adjusting and hid it well.

Eli shook his head, as if clearing a fog from it. He narrowed one eye at Kale. "No wonder Martin had such a problem leaving you. You're fucking intense when you want to be."

"You should see me in a courtroom," Kale said. He opened the door and jerked his head to indicate Eli needed to depart.

"Try to show up before midnight," Eli said, bumping into him as he passed.

"What difference does it make? You'll be asleep by seven anyway."

Eli cast a backward glance at him, probably to make sure he'd correctly interpreted the humor in the words. He rolled his eyes and shook his head.

Kale shifted his attention from Eli's departing ass and looked to Charlotte. Her complexion was flushed and her hands trembled as she fumbled with the pens in her cup. She gave a little huff as Kale approached.

"You have something to say to me?" Kale asked. She stood, still coming a few inches shy of him, okay, more like half a foot shy, *she must have on flats today.* She tilted her head and glared up at him.

"A personal visit should not take precedence over a high profile client," she said. Kale had never put his personal life first, until now.

He'd had no idea that quality meant so much to Charlotte. "This business is already teetering on the edge. The last thing we need is clients leaving because you are giving them the brush off for a quick—"

"Do you have a fucking business major now?" Kale asked, cutting her off before she could dig herself any deeper. "I will fire you and hire someone just as competent for half the pay. Keep that in mind the next time you want to discuss what's best for the company. And don't you ever..." He stepped closer, his hands itching to touch her or pull that God-awful oversized necklace off her neck. "Ever speak to Eli in that tone again. Are we clear?"

She'd spoken rudely to Martin on more than one occasion, and more crassly than she had to Eli today, and Kale had never corrected her. As her face turned bright red, he realized he must have struck another nerve with her, the final one.

"Fuck you, Kale. You're going to destroy this company. I quit." She grabbed her purse and a few other items from her desk. "A few of us thought you might change, but you're the same asshole you've always been. I'm not sticking around to put up with it anymore."

She stormed off. Kale didn't watch her go. He stood there, taking a moment to accept what had just happened. Charlotte had been his secretary for seven years. He never would have actually fired her, losing her hurt worse than losing Martin.

He gritted his teeth as he realized their drama had been very public. Everyone on the office floor had witnessed it. He spun on his heel and went to the glass doors to get his damn client himself, if he was still there.

CHAPTER TWENTY-THREE

Sitting in his car outside Jackie's house at ten pm, Kale rethought his whole not calling first proclamation. Letting himself into a person's house that he'd never been in before didn't sit quite right in the bowels of his stomach. He dialed Eli's number. He picked up on the fifth ring.

"Hello?" His voice was heavy with sleep.

"Hey, it's me, I'm outside," Kale said. He eyed the house for signs of life.

"Could you not find the key?"

"I decided against looking like a burglar," Kale said. "Can you come let me in?"

He heard shuffling and static, like Eli was digging himself out of a mound of blankets. A cold snap had come in but it wasn't *that* cold. Or did Jackie not use a heater?

"Kay, coming," Eli said. Kale hung up and exited his car. The crisp autumn air had a colder nip to it, dipping them down into the forties. He figured it'd be snow weather in a few weeks, perhaps a white Thanksgiving. He grabbed his duffle bag from the backseat and crossed the street to the white picket house. It literally had a knee high white picket fence around the front yard.

There was no gate crossing the sidewalk so Kale went straight up to the four by four cement porch. A cement lion sat on one corner, a paw lifted in friendly greeting. The door opened inward and Eli peered through the screen door at him.

Eli fumbled with the screen door before pushing it open. Kale stepped in. The entire house was dark. He blinked his eyes and waited for them to adjust.

Eli closed the doors, taking away what little light he'd had. "Loraine is at the hospital and Annabelle's asleep. Mind if we wait until morning before I give you the tour?"

Tour? Kale said nothing, still waiting for shadows to start showing up in the darkness so he could move.

"Or were you not planning to stay?"

"What? No, I'm staying if you'll let me. Morning is fine. I can't see shit," Kale said. A few nightlights started showing up, lighting a hall and giving him an outline of a couch.

"Sorry," Eli said. "Annabelle sleeps with her door cracked. If I turn on a light, it'll wake her."

Of course it would. Better for Kale to stub his toe in the dark than Annabelle learn how to sleep with her door shut.

"Come on, I'll guide you," Eli said. He closed his fingers around Kale's and pulled. Disliking the vulnerability of it all, Kale gritted his teeth and followed. The first door they past was cracked open. "Annabelle's room," Eli whispered.

He opened the door across the hall from Annabelle's room and held it open for Kale. He entered, only going a few steps since he had no idea what the furniture arrangement was. Eli shut the door and flicked on the lights.

Kale blinked a few times as he adjusted. Shelves lined one wall, overflowing with all kinds of tacky paperbacks. A futon was folded out into a bed and a desk was crammed against the wall.

"We're sleeping on a futon?" Kale asked.

"Loraine is staying in the spare bedroom and Jackie was in the master," Eli said. A four-bedroom house, Kale was slightly surprised. Exactly where did Jackie get that kind of money? It wasn't the best of neighborhoods, but still, the house couldn't have been cheap.

"You don't have to stay if you don't want to," Eli said, misinterpreting his silence. Kale tossed his bag into the corner and slipped his shoes off.

"No it's fine. It'll remind me of my college days." He undid his fly and dropped his slacks. He folded them neatly and placed them on top of the desk.

"I'm sure those are fond memories," Eli said. He climbed into the bed, burrowing into a pile of blankets and quilts that made him look prepared to endure a snowstorm.

"You've seen how I am at work. I gave my studies the same amount of attention," Kale said. He pulled his sweater off and added it to the pile.

"What? No frat parties and loads of gay sex?"

He didn't think all the blankets were needed but Kale climbed under them anyway. "More like sleepless nights studying and a few bloody brawls."

"A fighter not a lover, huh?" Eli raised an eyebrow. Kale pressed his body against him. His skin was cold. Kale pulled him closer, rubbing against his thigh to get an erection started.

"Shit, I forgot the light," Kale said.

"It's fine," Eli said. "I prefer to watch you."

The blood rushed to his groin so quick Kale felt dizzy. No further foreplay needed. He pulled Eli into a hard kiss and hoped the sex made sleeping on a futon worth it.

§§§

It wasn't. A little after midnight, Kale detached himself from Eli and tried to rub the kink out of his neck. His back already ached from the bar that had spent the last two hours digging into his side. Kale's body wasn't young enough to endure this kind of abuse. Apparently Eli's was, he was dead to the world.

Kale stared enviously at him in the glow from the streetlight outside. Eli was nearly a decade younger than him, and tonight Kale felt every extra year weighing on his body. He edged around the futon that took up most of the floor space in the room and eased the door open.

He'd already showered and dressed in a white shirt and boxers. The house did have a chill in the air. He tried not to think of how it added to the overall morose state of the people living in it. He walked down the hall, wishing he'd put on his socks.

He went to the kitchen and considered getting some water. Opening the fridge to look for bottles would cast a glow of light. He wasn't sure how much light it took to wake Annabelle and he didn't want to risk it. He retrieved a glass from the strainer next to the sink, grateful he didn't have to go searching in the cupboards for one.

He poured a glass from the tap and choked it down, trying not to gag on the chlorine taste. He refilled and padded to the living room. Perhaps he could take a nap on the couch. It had to be better than that futon. He wasn't sure how the other household members would react, but with Eli's early morning work schedule he was confident Eli would be the first to find him.

The front door creaked and a figure slinked in. Kale froze. The person did likewise, probably letting their eyes adjust. Kale debated if he should remain silent and hope they didn't notice him or if he should risk an introduction.

"Eli?" a woman's voice asked. Her eyes adjusted fast. Kale sat his glass down on what he thought was a coffee table.

"No," Kale said. "I'm Kale. Eli invited me over. You must be Loraine."

The woman groaned and unshouldered a bag. She dropped it somewhere near the door. She crossed the room with an agility of someone who knew every inch of the house. She went to Annabelle's door and pulled it closed, then flicked on a lamp in the living room.

Kale flinched and blinked as he adjusted to the light. It was a dim bulb but still a stark contrast to the darkness he'd grown accustomed to.

"And you must be the complication," Loraine said. She looked plucked straight from a politician's arm. Hair done up in a tight bun, terse expression, entire body wrapped in a tan trench coat with matching gloves. Her eyes never strayed from his.

"I'm not sure I follow," Kale said.

"We had a plan," she said. Her tone was steady, maybe she was the politician. "Once everything is settled here, Eli and Annabelle were going to move to D.C. with me. I was going to help Eli set roots out there and help him with Annabelle until he was back on his feet."

Kale realized he wasn't looking at Jackie's mom. He was looking at Mrs. Pocketbook. She was the money behind the four-bedroom house and potentially devastating medical bills.

"I'm sure you have an idea or two as to why Eli is backing out of the plan," Loraine said.

"You mean aside from the obvious bits? This is where he's from, his parents live here, Annabelle has friends here."

"That didn't bother him two months ago," Loraine said. She crossed her arms, blue eyes staring him down. "I think you should leave. My son-in-law's boyfriend is not welcome in my daughter's house."

"This is as much Eli's house as it is hers."

"He stopped living here two years ago when he broke my daughter's heart. He's as much a guest here as you are. Get out." Her tone left no room for argument.

Kale wished he knew exactly whose name was on the mortgage loan and exactly what Loraine's role in everything was. He wasn't sure how much of a problem being a dick to her would create.

"You're a grieving mother, so I'm going to give you a pass on your manners," Kale said. "But you should know I don't like being—"

A shrill scream came from Annabelle's room. Loraine jumped, as if the noise intended to harm her. Another scream followed it and the door to Eli's room was thrown open. Eli bounded across the hall, wearing only boxers, and thrust open Annabelle's door.

The screaming stopped and dissolved into sobs. Eli appeared in the doorway, holding a sobbing purple nightgown clad Annabelle in his arms. He glared from Loraine to Kale. "Which of you shut her door?"

Kale crossed his arms, but bit back his urge to rat out Loraine.

"It was only for a minute," Loraine said. "She was already asleep."

Eli rocked back and forth, stroking Annabelle's hair in an effort to calm her. "You know she's claustrophobic, Loraine." Kale had never heard the tone of annoyance that laced Eli's lips. *Yeah, Eli was definitely disappointed in me offering him a life that didn't include Loraine in it,* Kale thought sarcastically.

"Well, she needs to outgrow it," Loraine said. "We should not have to creep around whispering in the dark just because she needs her door open."

"Oh yeah," Kale said. "Heaven forbid we step outside to have our conversation. The neighbors might have heard." Kale rolled his eyes.

Annabelle's sobbing stopped and she turned her head from Eli's chest. "Kale?"

"Hey, kiddo," Kale said. He offered her a small wave. She unlinked her hands from behind Eli's neck and reached for Kale. His toes tingled at what she was asking. He couldn't think of the last time he'd held a child. Eli's eyes looked at him questioningly. He was nice enough he'd probably come up with an excuse for Kale if he asked. Kale's lack of immediate reciprocation must have been enough of an indicator for Eli.

"Kale has a busted arm, remember? He can't hold you," Eli said. Shit, his arm. Kale glanced at it, he'd grown used to the ache and often forgot it was still a hindrance. His relief at having evaded potential intimacy with a child he didn't yet know if he wanted to be around was squashed by the smug look on Loraine's face.

"I'll take her," Loraine said. "I'm the one who woke her."

"She wants me," Kale said. "I can hold her with one good arm."

He blocked Loraine and approached Eli. He used his good arm as the base and Eli transferred Annabelle to sit on it. He draped his cast behind her in case she fell back. She wrapped her tiny arms around his neck and pressed her damp face into his shirt.

"Apparently, everyone wants you," Loraine mumbled. She went down the hall and into the room Kale assumed was the spare guestroom.

"We don't really get along," Eli said.

- 259 -

"No kidding?" Kale asked. He couldn't imagine a world where a parent would like the man who impregnated their daughter at fifteen, then proclaimed he was gay after he married her.

Eli flushed red and looked away. "Let's see if we can get her back to sleep."

Kale followed him into Annabelle's room. Not a single nightlight. So darkness wasn't a problem for her. Kale made due with the lamp light from the hall and found her bed. She slept on a full twin size. He made out shapes of various stuffed animals in the corners, boxes of toys were neatly tucked away. Eli pulled back the sheets and Kale laid her down but she held fast to his neck.

Considering how soft the bed was, it might actually be a better alternative than the futon. He considered asking if he could sleep in here with her, but Eli was already freeing her arms.

"We'll be right across the hall," Eli said. "We'll leave our door open."

She nodded and snuggled into the sheets. "House feels better now."

Kale scrunched his eyebrows together wondering if that would make sense if he were more awake or if it was simply six-year-old gibberish.

"Why's that?" Eli asked. Kale wanted to ask why the house had been sick in the first place. Was there an infestation? Haunting?

"Kale's here." She pulled a lizard shaped animal to her chest and closed her eyes. Kale must have had the questions swarming in his mind visible on his face because Eli put a finger to Kale's lips, indicating he needed to be silent.

Eli rose slowly and exited the room. Kale followed. Eli turned the lamp off and gestured for him to come back into the torture chamber that was the futon. He wasn't about to risk another ambush from Loraine so he figured his back would have to make the sacrifice.

CHAPTER TWENTY-FOUR

A tingling in his guts and pressure of an impending orgasm yanked Kale from sleep. His eyes jerked open as he climaxed and he flung his arm over his face to stifle his shout. He had enough of his bearings to know he wasn't in his bed and he needed to be quiet. But not enough pistons were firing to remember his right arm was covered in a hard cast. He busted his lip between teeth and plaster. Salty blood touched his tongue.

Eli detached from Kale's erection with an audible pop. "Are you okay?"

Kale grabbed a handful of Eli's fine hair that was annoyingly difficult to get a grip on, and yanked him off. He wiped at his lip with his good hand and glanced at his cast. A single droplet of blood stained the pink. At least it wasn't as noticeable on the neon pink as it would have been on the white. *Thanks Wayne,* Kale thought.

"Sorry, Kale," Eli said as he tried to slink closer. Kale pushed him back.

"What were you thinking? Our door is open. Annabelle could walk in."

"She knows better than to do that," Eli said. Why exactly would Annabelle not enter her parents' bedroom when supposedly they'd broken up two years ago? Kale didn't want to go down the rabbit hole of explanations that comment required.

"She could still hear us," Kale said.

"She wouldn't know what the sounds meant." Eli tried to touch him again and Kale batted him away.

"Loraine would."

"And since when do you care what she thinks?" Eli asked. Kale didn't bother replying to that. "Do you need me to get some ice?"

"No, it's fine." The bleeding had already stopped, but it would be tender for most of the day. He leaned back against the pillows he'd arranged in an attempt to make the futon more livable. "But don't expect me to return the favor anytime soon."

"How long is the no touching decree in place?" Eli asked. Humor, no one should be attempting it at this early hour. The sun was barely coloring the sky.

"If you'll let me go back to sleep, I'll end it now."

"No dice. You have volunteer work at eight. Get up. I'll make coffee."

By the time Kale had showered, shaved, and dressed, more than just coffee aromas came from the kitchen. He entered to find Annabelle seated on a stool at the counter. Still in pajamas, hair in disarray, she devoured a pancake covered in a generous helping of syrup.

Eli flipped a pancake on the stove. He glanced over his shoulder at Kale. "Want some?"

"You cook?" Kale rubbed at the crick still in his back and took a stool next to Annabelle.

"I just added water. It comes from a box." Eli put a steaming coffee mug in front of Kale. "It's not name brand, but..." Eli gave a shrug and Kale realized he meant the coffee.

"It's fine." Kale took a taste of the bitter stuff.

"More college memories, right?" Eli said, returning to the stove.

No, nothing about this situation reminded him of college. He'd never been in a home that felt…quite this normal. Annabelle hummed to herself as she took another mouthful of pancake. Eli sat a plate of two pancakes in front of Kale. They weren't exactly his normal breakfast. His days of eating that many carbs were long gone. He hesitated and Eli frowned.

"Lip still hurt?" Eli asked.

"No it's not that. It's nothing." He put a moderate amount of syrup on them and decided he'd simply have to start hitting the gym again. He needed a reason to visit Morley anyway. "It's fine."

"Are you spending the day with us?" Annabelle asked.

"Afraid not," Kale said. "I'm doing volunteer work today."

"What kind?" She turned on her seat to face him. He wished he had a better understanding of the mental capacity of a child her age. What exactly did she think volunteer work was?

"I'll be sorting cans at the local food bank," Kale said.

"Can I go?" Annabelle asked.

"It's really not that fun," Kale told her. Eli was staring at him, so Kale took his first bite of the pancakes. It'd been a long time since he'd had them, years probably. His mouth started watering at the taste. He didn't know how they rated against other pancakes but to his sugar deprived body they were great.

"We're visiting your mother today," Eli said. "So you're busy too."

"But that won't last all day," Annabelle said. "She gets tired fast."

"How's the food?" Eli asked.

"It's fine, Eli," Kale said.

"Of course it is," Eli grumbled. He took Annabelle's plate and dumped it in the sink.

"Morning," Loraine said. She wore a bathrobe that covered her down to her ankles, where Kale spotted cotton pajama bottoms and pink slippers. She shot a look at Kale that said volumes, mostly, "Why are you still here?"

"Morning, Loraine," Eli said. He grabbed his own plate of pancakes and sat them across from Annabelle. Before he could eat, Loraine grabbed his elbow.

"Can I have a word, Eli?" Loraine asked. She tugged on his arm before he could reply.

"Be right back," Eli said. He followed her out of the room and they went down the hall. Kale groaned and shoved the plate of half eaten pancakes away. He wondered if he should try to dispose of them before Eli returned so he wouldn't be insulted.

"Did you enjoy your sleepover?" Annabelle asked.

"Yeah, it's been a delight," Kale said. He rubbed his forehead. He needed aspirin, lots of it.

"You should stay over more. Daddy's happier when you're here."

He turned his head to look at her, still rubbing his forehead.

"You broke the marathon run of cold cereal," she said.

"Did I now?" Kale asked. She nodded.

"Everyone is so sad, a-all the time," she said, adding extra emphasis on the "all." Her tiny face took on a serious expression. "I don't want to move to D.C. My mom is here. I won't be able to visit her if I live in D.C. with grandma."

"You're not moving as long as your mom is here," Kale said.

"Yes, I am. I hear them talking. My mom is staying here at the Birchwood Cemetery and I have to go with grandma to D.C."

Good Lord, how much did Annabelle know?

"Annabelle—" Kale didn't manage to say anything more, not that he had any idea what he would have said. Eli came back and sat in his seat, frowning, all the life seeming drained out of him.

Annabelle gave him a "See what I mean," look and nod as she glanced from her father to Kale. Yeah, Kale got it. Eli would be miserable in D.C. living with Loraine. She hopped down from the stool and went off to the living room to turn on the television.

"I should get going," Kale said.

"Yeah, I figured," Eli said. He stared at his pancakes, not touching them. Kale hated leaving them like this. He was starting to see what Annabelle meant, this house was sick, and not just from the clutter and cobwebs.

"Annabelle," Kale said. She glanced over and muted the television. "When you're done visiting your mom, see if you can convince your dad to come by the food bank. I'll save some cans for you to sort."

Her eyes lit up, a flicker of hope in them. "Really?"

"There's no age restrictions, so yeah." He looked at Eli, who mostly appeared confused. "I'm there until three."

§§§

The weekend passed in a blur. Kale spent another backbreaking night on the futon with Eli, but decided it was worth it. He did what he could to keep the encroaching depression of the Pendza family at bay and he could have sworn even Loraine lightened up on her dislike of him.

Monday morning came too quickly and the reality of his sinking law firm rose anew. Without Rich, the company was struggling to maintain its clients. He sank into his desk chair and looked out the window to the office floor, his eyes settled on his new secretary from the temp office. A frazzled thing that jumped at the slightest noise and munched Tums like they were candy.

He was fucking doomed.

He buried his face in his one good hand as a soft knock came on his door. "Kale?"

"Yeah?"

He didn't look up as Luke entered. "Two junior lawyers quit. Five interns resigned, and a handful of secretaries. We called the temp office to send over more secretaries and we'll see about getting more interns."

"Are you going to hire anyone?" Kale dropped his hand and looked at him. "We can't keep going like this."

"No clients have left," Luke said. "Some are grumbling, but no one's left. Even the lawyers who quit couldn't convince their clients to go with them."

"We can't handle this many cases," Kale said. "Even if we push to settle out of court, there just isn't enough time in the day."

"I get that." Luke sat across from him. Luke actually sat, shit, Kale wasn't sure he'd ever seen him do that. "We're also getting new clients."

"Why?"

"Because your name has been in the paper twice this month."

"Not for winning cases," Kale said.

"It's better publicity than a banner on a bus."

"You're not putting my name on the new company," Kale said, getting an idea of where this was heading.

Luke raised his hand. "K.A.L. Attorneys at Law. K for Kale, A for Andy and L for Luke."

"And it just so happens to spell my name," Kale commented.

"The new clients aren't coming in for me. And it sounds better than LAK."

"You're an ass, Luke," Kale said. Luke grinned.

"I'm putting some ads out to hire new attorneys. Just keep your head afloat until I can get them in, okay?"

"Why don't you and Andy start working some late nights?" Kale asked. "That would help."

"We're all doing what we can."

"Really, because you seem to be dashing out of here at five on the dot, while I'm here until well after dark. These new clients? You're taking them, Luke."

"They want you."

"I can't fucking handle this shit." Kale gestured at the stacks of files on his desk. "You want me to stay? You're afraid I'll quit and start the mass exodus of our clients? Then start helping me."

Luke's eyes roved the piles on Kale's desk. He replied with a simple, "Okay."

Kale had expected more of an argument. "Thank you."

Luke started staying until seven. He didn't take cases from Kale, but he helped research and prep them. He even gave one of his interns to Kale to use until the end of the year. Andy took a few lower profile cases off his stack and somehow, Kale started seeing a light at the end of the tunnel.

Four pm on Friday, Kale thought he might actually get enough work done that he wouldn't have to come back after this group therapy. His phone rang and he answered on the second chirp.

"Kale Sokoloff," he said.

"Hi, Mr. Sokoloff, this is Christian." The name meant nothing to him. He glanced out at his jittery secretary, Ali, who avoided his gaze.

"I'm the friend of Carol's cousin. She said you would be helping me with my recipe theft case?"

Oh, right. "I'm going to transfer you back to my secretary to make an appointment," Kale said. The call never should have reached him in the first place.

"Actually, I was hoping you'd do an onsite visit. If you come down to the restaurant I can better explain what I think is happening, and there will be a free meal in it for you." His tone was warm and inviting, if slightly nervous.

Kale considered his options. He could stop by this guy's restaurant after therapy, grab a quick meal and listen to him chatter about his problems. His workdays were full and this would be a chance to take care of it out of normal hours.

"I can be by around seven," Kale said. "What's the address?"

"Tonight?"

"Yes, tonight." He considering asking if that was okay, but he didn't want to give the man an option to reschedule.

"Okay, sure," Christian said. He rattled off an address and Kale hung up.

§§§

Kale entered the restaurant at the promised time. He'd expected Christian to be running something similar to a Denny's or IHOP. Not a four star restaurant where every item on the menu was over fifty dollars. A well-collected woman greeted him at the entrance.

"Do you have a reservation?" she asked with a smile that almost looked genuine.

"No," Kale said.

"I'm sorry, we're booked full tonight." The smile never faltered.

"I'm here to meet with the owner, Christian," Kale explained.

"One moment, please," she said. She vanished into the back and Kale took in the scenery. Mood lighting, all the waiters and waitresses dressed in black and white. He moved to a display of expensive wines and surveyed the labels.

"Mr. Sokoloff," a man said behind him. The voice from his phone call.

"Kale is fine," he said, turning to meet him. His dick gave an approving twitch as he took in Christian. He dressed in the same black pants and white dress shirt everyone else did. The only difference was a somber dark red tie. Christian held out a hand for a shake, a gesture Kale wished he could accept but his hand was still casted.

He lifted his embarrassing pink cast as a means of apology. Kale's eyes lingered on the man's long fingers, they had to be eight inches long. The man towered above Kale by a few inches; tall, thin and lanky, he could be a pro basketball player.

And fuck, did Kale want to know what those fingers would feel like jammed deep in his ass. He shook the thoughts from his head. The week had been too long. He hadn't seen Eli in more than a quick passing at work. Normally, a stint of celibacy didn't affect his work, the majority of his clients were fifty-something year old men who hadn't so much as glanced at a gym in decades. Such was not the case with Christian.

He forced his eyes to meet Christian's baby blue ones.

"I see your restaurant is doing well," Kale said.

"Friday nights are busy nights. It's why I hesitated when you said you were coming."

"We can make it quick. I don't need to eat."

"No, I'll have them bring you something, but there're no tables. Let's talk in my office." Christian led the way past the kitchen and into a small office that was not nearly as lavish as the dining area. Kale dropped his suitcase on the floor and took a seat on a bargain chair.

"Sally, bring in a menu," Christian said to a girl who was rushing past.

"Food really isn't needed," Kale said.

"You're doing me a favor. It's the least I can do."

"Actually I'm doing Carol a favor and she's doing one for me in exchange, so we're even," Kale said. He wanted to remark that there were a few other favors he'd rather Christian do for him, but he bit back the comments.

Protests aside, he found himself enjoying a perfectly roasted duck with a mushroom sauce that made it the best fowl he'd ever tasted. He listened to Christian recite how more and more of his family recipes had been turning up at competitors' restaurants over the last few months.

Christian walked through how he kept the recipes safely locked in a safe box. He opened the safe and pulled out a book. "This is where I keep them all."

He handed the booklet over to Kale. He wiped his hands on the cloth napkin and took the book. He'd been expecting some handwritten pages with fading pencil squiggles. Instead, this had a glossy cover, typed pages and... Kale flipped the book over, yes, even a barcode.

"This is a published book," Kale said.

"My grandmother had her collection of recipes made into a book by a local press about twenty years ago. She only had a few copies made, they are all in the hands of family members."

"But it has a barcode," Kale said. He pointed at it. "This book is probably available on the internet. Once you publish something, you can't sue someone for using the information in it."

Kale pushed aside his meal and broke into a narrative of explanations, full lawyer mode. He sighted copyright laws and explained that even if an employee were stealing the recipes, the material was public property, since it was in a published book, even if the book wasn't actively in circulation.

Christian covered his mouth with those enticingly long fingers and his blue eyes darkened. "I guess I should thank you for saving me time, money, and the embarrassment I would have encountered if I'd pursued this."

He knew this was a disappointment for Christian, but Kale was relieved, it was one less case he'd be taking on. He was about to politely excuse himself, but Christian pulled a bottle of wine from his desk.

He uncorked it and poured a glass. Kale hadn't seen where the glasses came from. He pushed a glass to Kale. "I think this is worth drinking."

The occasions where Kale drank were few and far between. He drank very little in college, his studies had been too important. Work was too important afterwards. Drinking clouded his judgment and made him say stupid things. He liked to have all his bearings about him. People never questioned his sobriety, most assumed his anger only got worse if he was drunk.

Kale couldn't remember ever getting angry when he'd had a few too many drinks. He was much more likely to turn into a sobbing idiot.

"Don't make me drink alone," Christian said. He took a drawn out sip of his red wine and Kale's gaze lingered on those delightfully long fingers.

CHAPTER TWENTY-FIVE

A crash from the living room woke Eli. The grogginess of sleep left him as he sprang from the bed. Too many nights of a delirious Jackie, stumbling about in the middle of the night, and a terrified Annabelle crying, had honed his gears to switch from deep sleep to wide awake in seconds.

He was in the hall, flicking on lights minutes after the noise. Two men stood in his living room, only one of which did Eli know. The other was tall, pale, and handsome in the—if you like really tall skeleton men—kind of way.

"Shhh," Kale said, waving his hand at his companion. He looked at Eli. "Turn off the light. You'll wake Annabelle."

"I think that ship has sailed," Eli said. He glanced at the lamp on the floor, its base broken.

"Who's Annabelle?" the tall man asked. "I thought you said it'd just be the three of us."

Kale stumbled toward him and put a finger of the man's lips to shush him. He whispered something too quietly for Eli to hear. *What the fuck, were they both drunk? A drunk Kale?* The idea sent a shiver down his spine. Drunk people with anger problems were normally not a good combination.

Eli took a few backward steps toward Annabelle's room as Kale continued his embrace with the tall man. He glanced in Annabelle's room and saw her sitting up in bed, wide-eyed with her bunny toy clutched to her chest.

"Everything is okay," Eli told her. He turned on her bedroom light. "I need to close your door for a few minutes while I deal with this."

She nodded her head quickly. Evidently, deciding keeping the strange men from her room was more important than the fears she had of her four walls closing in on her. Eli closed the door and turned his attention back to Kale.

Kale pulled away from the other man and regarded Eli.

"Eli, this is Christian," Kale said. The man tipped his head in Eli's direction. "He has the most amazing dick..." Kale looked at him, proud as a child who had spotted Santa Christmas night. "And the things he can do with his fingers will amaze you."

Eli was internally grateful he'd closed Annabelle's door and that Kale was keeping his tone low enough she was unlikely to have heard him.

"You brought me home a man?" Eli asked, confused. Kale took a few wobbly steps to him and grabbed both of Eli's shoulders, likely for support.

"Yes. I want to keep you happy. I know you like threesomes and Christian is perfect." He leaned forward and planted a sloppy kiss on Eli's lips. He tasted sweet—wine? Kale groaned. "Fuck. Forgot how good you taste."

He pushed Eli against the wall and kissed him again. Eli wasn't entirely sure what was happening. Part of him hoped Loraine would walk into the house and interrupt them.

"He is hot," Christian said. Kale released him and seemed to ponder something, or he was fighting a wave of nausea, Eli wasn't certain.

"I don't think I can do this," Kale said. He looked at Christian and tightened his grip on Eli's shoulder, almost to a painful degree.

"Let's not forget what I'm bringing to the table," Christian said. He undid his belt and unzipped his pants.

"No," Eli said, reaching out as if to grab the man's pants and pull them back on. "Please keep your pants on."

Kale pushed into him again, putting his forehead against Eli's. His breathe was rank and Eli resisted the urge to push him away.

"I don't want to share you," Kale said.

"I'm okay with that," Eli agreed. "Let me call Christian a cab."

"Wait? Is this happening or not?" Christian asked.

"Not," Kale and Eli said in unison. Eli pushed on Kale's chest, hoping he could get him to back up. He stumbled a few steps and Eli inhaled deeply, grateful for the fresh air. He went to the kitchen phone and dialed a taxi service. Christian and Kale spoke to each other in hushed tones, standing way too close to each other for Eli's comfort.

Christian nodded and stumbled to the door, opened, and exited. Kale closed it behind him and locked it.

"Where did he go?" Eli asked. "I called him a cab. It'll be here in ten minutes."

"He'll wait outside," Kale said, waving his hand in the direction of the door. "Want you to myself."

Eli resisted the urge to dodge him, not wanting to upset him and worried Kale would end up sprawled on the floor. Kale engulfed him in a suffocating hug and kiss. Eli pried his face free as Kale trailed kisses down his neck.

"Let's get you to the bedroom so you can sleep this off, huh?" Eli said. He guided Kale down the hall and into his bedroom. Kale slammed him into another wall once they were inside. *Shit, I'm going to have bruises in the morning.*

Kale stroked his face. "You're so beautiful. Fuck, I get hard just looking at you. Haven't been this horny since I was a teenager." His hands went to the elastic waistband on Eli's flannel bottoms.

"Kale, why don't we lie down, huh?" He hoped if he got him to lie down he would pass out. Kale gripped his waist and dropped, falling on the futon with enough force Eli worried it would break it. He pulled Eli with him.

Eli struggled to get back on his feet, but Kale wrapped his legs around him.

"Need you to fuck me," Kale said. Eli squirmed.

"Kale, you're drunk."

"Drunk on you," Kale said. "Love you."

"What?" Eli's body stiffened.

"I love you. All of you." He kissed his neck, tugged on his earlobe.

"You're saying this to me now? While you're drunk off your ass and you just brought another man home to have sex with me? This is when you choose to tell me you love me for the first time?"

"Why are you mad?" Kale's words slurred. His glazed eyes searched Eli's.

"You're an asshole, Kale. Fuck you, you're sleeping on the floor." Eli grabbed him and gave his right shoulder a pull, rolling him off the bed and onto the floor with a thump.

Kale didn't move. Eli considered checking him for a pulse. A strangled snore came from his body and Eli sighed. He went back into the hall to check on Annabelle and open her door.

§§§

A pounding headache pulled Kale from sleep. His bladder protested as well. He groaned and pushed himself up on his good arm, the other a dead weight from sleeping on it wrong. He was on the floor, which was actually more comfortable than the futon.

He sat up, cradling his throbbing head. He blinked his eyes at the sunlight coming in the window. No one was in the futon. He remembered Eli rolling him off the bed with an angry "fuck you" comment. He'd never seen Eli quite so annoyed.

Kale got to his feet, the room swayed a bit, but he thought he could walk. His stomach did a few summersaults and he found a new motivation for finding a bathroom.

He opened the bedroom door, scurried down the hall, and slammed the bathroom door shut behind him. He reached the toilet in time and emptied his stomach contents. He gagged, flushed, vomited, and repeated the routine a few more times.

He reeked, the alcohol leeched from his pores and made him feel even sicker. He stripped his clothes off and left them in a pile. He grabbed a garbage bag from under the sink and covered his cast with it. He used a hairband to secure it. He went into the shower and stood under the cooling droplets of water for a while. He searched the assortment of bathing supplies. Most of them were for women, either Loraine or Annabelle. He picked a lavender soap that didn't upset his stomach when he sniffed it.

He tried to recall the events of last night. It came back to him in backwards order, Eli rolling him onto the floor, Kale saying…shit; he'd told Eli he loved him. And Eli's response had been to push him onto the floor. He went back a little farther, ah yes, he'd brought Christian home. Some drunk logic had convinced him that he needed to show Eli he was okay with threesomes, since Eli used to do them with Selena.

And Christian had been a great—Kale paused, suds in his hair, the smell of roses filling the air. No. He hadn't, wouldn't have. Memories of flirting with Christian flashed in his mind, but nothing more.

Kale sagged against the wall of the shower and forced his pounding head to remember if anything else had happened. The night unraveled for him. Short answer, no, some touching, maybe groping, but nothing unforgiveable. He hoped.

He slammed his casted arm against the side of the wall, sending bottles toppling over. This is why he didn't drink. Fuck, he was an idiot. His arm throbbed from the impact, old aches returned to arc up his arm. He steadied his breathing and resumed showering. He grabbed a towel from the rack, not caring if it was previously used or not. He dried and tied it around his waist.

Only then did he realize he had no clean clothes. He stared at the pile he'd removed. They reeked, not only of his own body sweat but he now regarded them with the same disdain he did his actions of the night before.

Eli had been right to shove him from the bed.

He took a deep breath and opened the bathroom door. He'd have to ask Eli if he could borrow some clothes while they washed his. He padded barefoot down the hall. He didn't even have his car here. It was at the restaurant.

Voices came from the living room so Kale headed there. Annabelle sat at the counter, crayons and a coloring book in front of her. Loraine was in the kitchen, busying herself with something, it looked like she was arranging the cups in the cabinet so all the designs were facing outward.

Great, Loraine was going to see him dressed in nothing but a towel. He wasn't in the mood to go hunting for Eli, though.

"Morning," Kale said. Annabelle looked at him first, her eyes going up and down several times. Loraine said nothing. She moved to a different cabinet and thumbed through the containers inside.

"Do you know where Eli is?" Kale asked. Loraine turned to him, holding out a bottle of over the counter pills.

"Judging by the activity last night, I'm guessing you might want a few of these," Loraine said. Kale took the bottle, noting she offered him no water. He dry swallowed two of them. "Eli is out taking care of a few things."

Her eyes roved his body.

"Let me guess, you have no clean clothes?" Loraine asked. Her tone didn't sound as resentful as Kale expected. She sounded more like a mother who was taking care of a neighborhood kid whose own parents had neglected him.

"My overnight stay wasn't preplanned."

"Indeed. I don't think Eli's clothes will fit you." She took a deep breath. "My husband's old clothes should though. Follow me." She strutted past him and Kale had no choice but to follow, and silently curse Eli for abandoning him alone with his mother-in-law.

She went to a door at the end of the hall and opened it. She flicked a switch and revealed a staircase leading down. The house had a basement? Kale hadn't been given a proper tour yet. He'd assumed the door at the end of the hall was a closet. Loraine went first and Kale followed.

The basement was finished, and smelled of mildew. It appeared to be used primarily as storage. Cardboard boxes filled the hall and more were visible in the rooms. A family room took up half the space, with two smaller rooms to the side.

"Why don't you guys use this area?" Kale asked. Loraine moved to a stack of boxes and started opening them.

"Jackie hasn't felt comfortable going up and down the steep stairs for the last few years. The basement was always my husband's domain anyway. And… this is where Eli would…" She paused, not speaking or sorting the box. "Do his more unsavory activities."

Kale wondered what exactly that meant. It could range from watching gay porn to actually bringing men over. He noticed a couch and television in the family room. Loraine pulled out a flannel shirt and cargo shorts.

"See if these fit," Loraine said. Kale took them and gave them a whiff first. They smelled better than the clothes he'd been wearing. He struggled a bit to get the cast through the sleeves and Loraine shocked him by coming over to help him. She rolled the sleeve up past his cast, her touch surprisingly gentle.

"He's a better man with you around," Loraine said. She kept her eyes focused on her work, not looking up at him. "You've no idea the mess he was before you showed up."

She finished and took a step back, meeting his eyes. "Bouncing from stranger's couches, getting drunk, showing up on the doorstep skunk drunk and livid. Try the shorts."

Kale pulled them on under the towel. They fit well enough and he figured he'd rather go commando than wear a stranger's used underwear. He pulled the towel off and she nodded.

"Looks like a good fit."

"It'll do, thank you."

She nodded. "I don't want to take Annabelle from her father," Loraine said. "But Eli isn't a responsible adult. He can't take care of her on his own. You've no idea the temper he gets when he's drunk."

"I don't plan on going anywhere," Kale said. "He asked me to move in."

She rolled her top lip and bit it. "He's happier when you're around. Annabelle feeds off that. I want my granddaughter to be happy."

"I'll keep him straight, so to speak, you have my word," Kale said. She nodded and wiped a tear from her eye.

"I don't know what you're doing to him, but…" She took a deep breath and looked at the wall. "When he said he was gay, I thought for the longest time he was trying to find a kind way to leave Jackie. It wasn't until I saw the way he looks at you that I finally understood." She looked at him, her eyes serious. "He never looked at my daughter the way he does you."

"I'm confident he loves your daughter," Kale said. "He stayed with her all these years."

"He loves her like a best friend," Loraine said. "He looks at you like he can't wait to put your dick in his mouth."

Kale choked, her choice of words shocking him.

"He never lusted for Jackie like that," she said. *Jesus, no parent should ever see a person looking at their kid like that.* He wasn't sure what to think of Loraine's seeming insulted at the fact her daughter had been deprived of it.

"Hey," Eli called from the top of the stairs. "Everything okay down there? Is Loraine chopping you up into small pieces so she can bury you in the crawlspace?"

Loraine rolled her eyes. She looked at Kale. "Take good care of them for me, Kale. Give Annabelle the happy home my daughter couldn't." She stepped to the stairs and directed her voice at Eli. "I'm dressing your boyfriend since nudity is not something I'll allow in this house."

Kale waited until he was certain the blush was gone from his cheeks before he followed her up the steps. Eli met him at the top, a worried look on his face.

"Sorry about last night," Kale said. "You were right to push me onto the floor."

Eli's eyes continued searching his body, as if expecting to find injury. "It's okay, but next time you decide to bring home a strange man, call first, okay?"

"Can do."

CHAPTER TWENTY-SIX

Kale writhed in the bed as Eli trailed kisses down his stomach. Guilt ate at his stomach though. He tugged on Eli's hair, pulling him up.

"I need to tell you something," Kale said.

"I think I know," Eli said. "You slept with Christian."

Kale's chest tightened. "How did you know?"

"You mean, how did I not know? You're a cheater, Kale. All those late nights at the office. I know you aren't working." He pushed up, extending his arms and hovering over him. "You did the same thing to Martin. It's why he left you. How many times did you cheat on him?"

Kale's jaw moved but no words came out.

"How long do you think I'll stick around and put up with it? The abuse? The affairs? You're too broken to love, Kale. I'm only around for the money and the sex."

"You don't mean that."

"Sure I do. It's why Martin was here. Why else would I be here?"

"No." Kale jumped and thrashed in his bed, eyes fluttering open into the darkness. His chest heaved as he tried to steady his heart. It was only a dream. He wiped his damp forehead. Only a dream. "I never cheated on Martin," Kale mumbled into the darkness.

"Kale," Jackie's voice said. His eyes shot open and he looked at Jackie standing at the foot of his bed. But she wasn't the frail woman he'd met in the bowling alley. She was younger, full of life, her cheeks a healthy pink.

"Jackie?" Kale rubbed his eyes. How had she gotten into his apartment?

"You have to take care of them for me," she said. "Eli's not as strong as he seems."

"Right, sure." Kale slouched back in his bed.

"He needs you. Please, promise me you'll take care of him for me. Give him the happiness I never could. Be the strength Eli needs so he can be there for Annabelle. You've been through so much, Kale. I know you can get him through this. No one was there for you, but it doesn't have to be that way for Eli."

"How do you know what I've been through?" Kale glared at her.

"He's never hurt like this before. You have."

"I don't—" A ringing broke the illusion and Kale jerked awake, for the second time. *Shit, a dream in a dream.* He cussed as he rolled over, twisted his arm wrong, cussed again, and lifted his cast into the air to ease the fresh throbbing. He fumbled for his phone on the nightstand.

The alarm clock read two fifteen. Kale grabbed his phone, not bothering to read the caller ID.

"Hello?" Kale closed his eyes and tried to will the pain in his arm to go away.

"Kale? It's Hank," Eli's father said, his southern accent deeper than Kale remembered.

"Hi." Kale could think of nothing else to say. He was still trying to collect his wits.

"Jackie passed away at two oh two this morning," Hank said.

"I'm sorry," Kale said, still trying to grasp the meaning behind the words. Jackie. He glanced at the foot of his bed.

"Loraine called and told us. She's at the hospital with Eli. Marge and I are at Jackie's house with Annabelle. We aren't going to tell her until the morning." Kale refrained from telling him it was already the morning. "According to Loraine, Eli isn't taking the news well. Would you mind going to the hospital and collecting him? I don't want him coming to the house unless he's in his right mind. No need for Annabelle to see him like that."

"Like what, exactly?" Kale asked. He sat up in the bed.

"He should still be at the hospital or close to it. Loraine took his keys."

"Like what, Hank?" Kale repeated.

"He might be drinking. He's a cruel drunk, if he is," Hank said, after a long pause.

"Fine, sure, I'll find him."

"Don't bring him here," Hank said.

"Fine." Kale hung up. He dialed Eli's number and put it on speaker phone. He turned on the lights and pulled a pair of pants from his dresser.

"What?" Eli said, as he answered. Kale buttoned the pants and grabbed a shirt.

"Where are you?" Kale asked. He heard an engine in the background.

"She's duh'ed. I'm a w-id-oh," Eli said. His words were strange, was that some accent he'd never heard or was Eli already drunk? He realized he'd never seen Eli drink alcohol.

"Just tell me where you are."

"My fah-alt."

He didn't see any point in arguing.

"I'm coming to get you. Tell me where you are." He picked up his phone and went to the foyer to get shoes.

"Bah-us saa-top, crah-oss furom la-quor sh-op," Eli said.

What the fuck was wrong with him? "What are the cross streets?" Kale said, hoping he could understand the words well enough, and wondering if Eli could even read at this point into whatever was wrong with him.

"Da-don't come. Bah-etter this wuh-ay," Eli said. The call disconnected. A chill ran down his spine. There was more than just alcohol in Eli's system, Kale would bet money on it.

He dialed a number he never thought he'd call as he locked his apartment and bolted down the steps.

"Hello gorgeous," Wayne said. Kale could almost see his eyelids batting as he spoke.

"It's Kale, don't hang up. Are you working tonight?"

"You know I love the graveyard shift. And I'd never hang up on you, what's up? Gotta message for Martin? How's that pink cast working out for you in the courtroom by the way? Martin laughed for like ten minutes when I told him."

Kale reached his car and started it. He put the phone on speaker and dropped it to his lap so he could steer with his good hand. "Are there any bus stops near the hospital that have a liquor store near them?"

"Yes, there's one about two blocks away, why?"

"What's the cross streets?"

Wayne rattled them off and repeated his query as to why.

"My friend's wife just died. I called him and he doesn't sound right. I think he took something and might be drinking himself to death."

"Shit. Do you want me to send an ambulance?"

Was he overreacting? Did he really want to put Eli in the hospital? For all he knew Eli was speaking weird as a joke or something.

"I don't want to put him in the hospital, but can you meet me there? Don't approach him until I get there. Just make sure he doesn't leave."

"I'll take my break and grab a few things just in case." Wayne hung up and Kale accelerated through a yellow light.

§§§

Kale parked in front of the bus stop, to hell at how illegal it was. A single form sat slumped on the bench in the glass box. Kale left his car running and exited. The night air nipped at him and Kale wished he'd taken a second to grab a coat. Wayne appeared at his bumper as Kale walked around, where the hell had he come from?

He held an oversized man purse at his side, his hair spiked up with green tips. His clown covered smock matched the color well.

"Wait here," Kale said. He entered the booth and called Eli's name. A brown bag sat next to him, its form crumpled around a bottle.

The body moved, thank God, and Eli's bloodshot, glazed eyes looked at Kale.

"Ta-old you nah-ot to ca-um," Eli said. Kale knelt in front of him and could smell the alcohol, or perhaps the booth simply reeked of it on its own.

"What did you take, Eli?"

"She's duh-ed," Eli said. He wiped at his face. "She's fuk-en duh-eh."

"And I don't want you to be, so what did you take?"

He closed his eyes and turned away from Kale, as if looking at him was painful. Kale patted down his pockets. Eli tried to push him away, but the attempts were feeble. He found a prescription bottle in his jacket pocket and pulled it out.

He glanced over at Wayne who hovered at the side of the booth. He tossed the bottle at him. Wayne caught it and read the label.

"How many did you take?" Kale asked.

Eli gave him an annoyed groan in response and tried to shove him away. Kale grabbed the brown bag and shook it, it gave a small slosh, nearly empty. Shit. He yanked the bag down and read the label. Whiskey. Jesus, drinking this much was likely to kill him by itself.

"Should we induce vomiting?" Kale asked.

"I'm sure he'll start doing that on his own in a few minutes," Wayne said. He pulled a syringe from his bag and filled it with something from another bottle.

"Did you steal that from the hospital?" Kale asked.

"I'll fill out the paperwork when I get back," Wayne said. "Claim it as a dose I gave to a homeless walk-in. It's not like its narcotics. That's the stuff the hospital gets all crazy about when they do inventories. This is naloxone. It'll reverse the effects of the opiates he took. Hold him still."

Kale grabbed Eli firmly as Wayne gave him the injection in his right shoulder. Wayne looked at his watch.

"What now?"

"Keep him awake and give him another two milligrams in two minutes if he doesn't start improving," Wayne said. Kale nodded. He figured Wayne had seen plenty of overdoses in the emergency room and knew what he was doing. "I brought a tank of oxygen too in case his breathing starts to get weak."

Eli squirmed more and tried to lie down. Kale held him upright. "What the hell were you thinking, Eli?"

"Iz better this wuh-ay," Eli said. Kale grabbed his forehead and pried one of his eyes open. The pupils didn't react.

"Better for who? Annabelle? You think she wants to lose both her parents in the same night?"

"All-red-ee la-ost ha-r. Ja-en is tah-ak-en ha-r."

"Well, I certainly wouldn't blame her if she does. No court would give you parental rights after this stunt."

"Fu-uck you," Eli said. He tried to shove him off again.

"Loraine told me she's going to let Annabelle stay here with you, but only if you get your act together. You can't do this kind of shit."

"Time for another shot," Wayne said.

"No." Eli thrashed a bit harder. Kale took that as a good sign. He was getting his strength back. Kale held him down and Wayne gave him another injection.

Eli lurched. He grabbed his stomach.

"Told you," Wayne said in a singsong voice. He handed Eli a plastic barf bag. Eli cupped it around his face and retched into the bag.

Kale stayed kneeling in front of Eli. Wayne sat on the bench and watched his watch. Eli threw up a few more times until it turned into a dry heave.

"You can throw it away. I have more if he vomits again," Wayne said. A flash of headlights crossed the bus booth. Kale glanced out to see a blue sedan parking behind Kale's car.

"You fucking called him?" Kale glared at Wayne.

"You'll need help getting Eli home with that busted chicken wing of yours," Wayne said, his voice velvety soft. He was right, but Kale still wanted to hit him.

Kale focused on the pavement at his shoes as he heard the car door shut. He grabbed the vomit filled bag from Eli and went to throw it in the garbage outside the booth. He came back in as Wayne gave Martin a light kiss on the cheek.

Kale fisted both hands, regardless of the pain it caused his arm.

"Kale?" Eli said, his voice trembled. He was hugging his stomach with both hands. Kale pried his eyes away from the couple and knelt between Eli's legs.

"I'm here," Kale said. He cupped his chin and looked in his eyes. Some of the glaze was gone and he seemed able to focus better.

"Let me check his pulse," Wayne said. He grabbed one of Eli's wrists and held it while he watched the seconds tick by on his watch. Kale didn't say anything to Martin but knew he was standing just behind Wayne.

"I think one more shot would be wise. His pulse is a bit slow," Wayne said. He reached into his bag for another syringe.

"I fucked up," Eli said. "Shit-shit." He descended into a chorus of that one word, but Kale didn't care. He was just glad his speech was better. Wayne gave him the shot and Eli pulled his knees to his chest, pulling himself into a tight ball.

Wayne packed his supplies back into his man-purse and stood. "I need to get back. I think he'll be okay. Martin will help you get him home."

"Martin?" Eli's eyes widened and he sat up straight, sobering up quicker than any drug would have made him. "Why's he here?"

"Because my list of friends who will get up at two in the morning to help me pick up a drunk is rather short," Kale said.

Eli hugged his knees tighter to his chest. "Are you back with him? I'll un-under-st-stand if—"

"No, still with you," Kale said. He brushed some of the hair from Eli's forehead. "We need to get you in the car. Can you walk?"

Eli nodded. Kale backed up as Eli attempted to stand. His knees gave out and Kale took an arm as Martin took the other. The excess amount of Old Spice Martin used wafted over to him. He looked up and met his eyes. There was something in them that Kale couldn't quite interpret. It was almost a, "You never would have done this for me," look, but it could have also been a, "Glad you're changing," look. Maybe it was just a, "You better give me another six grand for helping you with this shit," look.

Kale noted the bruises were completely faded from his face. They'd been gone from Wayne's as well. They led Eli to Kale's car.

"Sure you don't want him to ride in mine? I don't want you to get pissed at him if he throws up in your car," Martin said.

"He has a barf bag," Kale said. He opened the passenger door and let Martin ease him in, since he had two good hands.

"I'll follow behind and help you get him in your apartment," Martin said.

"You don't need to," Kale said.

"I want to," Martin said. He met Kale's eyes for a fleeting moment. He shrugged and hunched his shoulders. "Besides if I don't, and he falls down those steps and breaks his neck, you'll probably blame me and—"

"Jesus, stop it, Martin," Kale said. He slammed the car door shut. "The world doesn't fucking revolve around you. If a bunny dies in Asia I'm not going to hunt you down and hit you for not being there to prevent it."

"Only dead bunnies in Europe, right?"

Kale's head and arm throbbed as his blood pressure rose. "Get in your fucking car and try not to rear end me while you follow us. I already bought your boyfriend a new car. I'm not buying you one too."

Martin backed away, as if seeing the punch already coming. "Speaking of which, best sex I've ever had was in that new thunderbird. I'd like to thank you for it."

Kale picked up a rock, too small to actually do damage, and tossed it at Martin. He turned so the pebble hit his shoulder. "Get in your car, you fucking ass."

Kale went around the rear fender and got in his own car. He took several deep breaths to settle his nerves, telling himself he was stalling to give Martin time to get in his own car.

"You two should start a comedy show," Eli said. "The banter you two have is hilarious."

Kale shot him a glare that quickly faded when he saw how horrible Eli looked. His skin was pale and covered in a layer of sweat. He was shivering as if the night air had gone down thirty more degrees. Kale turned up the heat.

"Yeah, we're a fucking riot." Kale pulled the car onto the road and watched in his rearview mirror to make sure Martin was following at a safe distance.

"I can tell you two still love each other," Eli said. He said it softly, like it was the saddest event of the night.

"Yeah, in a wanting to strangle each other kind of way," Kale said. He drove for a few minutes in silence. Eli adjusted one of the vents on the dash. "He only gets that kind of lip on him when I haven't hit him in a few weeks. It's like he forgets what an ass he is unless he has a bruise somewhere to remind him."

"Maybe you should break his arm so it'll last longer," Eli said. In his weak state Kale couldn't tell if he was trying to be funny.

"Trust me, I have," Kale said. He slowly came to a stop at a red light. He took the moment to focus on Eli. "You need to never do that kind of shit again."

Eli shrunk back in his seat. "I know. I wasn't thinking."

The light changed and Kale pulled forward. "Have you done this before? Tried to kill yourself?"

Everyone was being vague about Eli's past, in particular the last two years. Kale was reaching his breaking point on the secrecy.

"Directly no," Eli said. "But I did some drugs when I was with Selena. It got bad, but I was never trying to actually kill myself."

"What kind of drugs?"

"I would...take some of Jackie's prescriptions. It was Selena's idea. She was the one who wanted them, but sometimes she would put them in her mouth and then kiss me and shove it in mine. I'd usually be pretty drunk by then and it was kind of hot so I didn't stop her."

Kale glared at his steering wheel. "I think I need to give Martin Selena's phone number so he can go annoy her for a while."

Eli said nothing. Kale reached across the center console and shook him awake.

"No sleeping, not until more of those drugs are out of you."

Eli groaned and rubbed his eyes.

CHAPTER TWENTY-SEVEN

After they'd gotten Eli settled in the spare bedroom Martin lingered in the foyer.

"Do you want me to stay?" Martin asked.

"It'd probably be best if you don't," Kale said. He ran a hand through his hair and glanced at Eli's sleeping form.

"Wayne said he should be okay, but you'll want to make sure he doesn't stop breathing while he sleeps," Martin said.

"I know. I get it," Kale said.

"You have to work today. I can stay and watch him. Go get some sleep."

He hated that Martin was right. He did have a case going to trial at two that afternoon. There was no one who could cover for him, not if he wanted to keep the client with the firm.

"We'll be fine," Kale insisted. He realized Martin was stalling and it hit him like a slap in the face as he realized why. "How much do you want?"

"How much what?"

"Money, what else?" Kale asked. "I'll have to write you a check."

"I don't want your money, Kale."

"Since when?"

"I used the money you gave me to buy Brandi a new oven at the bakery. I'm working there now, getting back on my own feet. I don't want any more handouts."

"How grown up of you," Kale said. He rolled his eyes.

"This is kind of nice."

He shot him a glare. "What is?"

"Being cordial to each other. There's no reason for us not to be friends."

"Yes there is and we are barely managing civil." Kale opened his door and held it for him. His emotions around Martin kept fluxing from wanting to hit him to wanting to kiss him. He couldn't take much more.

"Call if you need anything else," Martin said. He gave him one of those smiles that made Kale switch back into wanting to grab his face and kiss him so hard he would feel it in his toes. Instead, he put a hand on Martin's back and pushed him out the door. He locked it after, grateful he'd changed the locks so Martin couldn't come back inside.

He stripped down to his boxers and shorts, set an alarm for nine, and lay on the bed next to his comatose boyfriend. Yes, he should stay up to monitor him, but the amount of favors he was capable of was quickly expiring. He closed his eyes and drifted.

§§§

The world was fuzzy and numb. Eli wanted to stay in that place, a void where he could pretend everything was okay. Jackie was alive and healthy. Annabelle had two parents who loved her. Eli hadn't tried to kill himself. He had, oh God he had.

The memory cut him as sharply as the cramps in his stomach. He curled into a ball and wished he'd die. His stomach hurt more, forcing him to acknowledge he was alive. He would lose Annabelle for sure now. Kale too. Who would stay with him? He was a mess.

Martin. He had been there.

The entire night was a horrible nightmare and Eli didn't want to wake up for the sequel. A firm arm shook his shoulder. He balled up tighter.

"Eli." The firm voice left no room for argument. Eli opened his eyes, wincing at the bright light. He uncurled a bit, his abdomen still sending trills of pain throughout his body.

"It's time to get up," Kale said. "I called you in sick to work, but I still need go in. Your parents are with Annabelle. They haven't told her the news. They're waiting for you. We all think she should hear it from you."

Eli forced himself to sit up, despite the discomfort. He pulled his knees to his chest.

"We need to get you cleaned up and see if you can keep anything down," Kale said. This must be Kale in lawyer mode, all fact, no emotion. He didn't see a speck of remorse or anger on his face. He wondered if it was because Kale didn't care or if staying neutral was all he could do to keep the anger from coming out.

"What time is it?" Eli asked. His voice sounded horrible, like he had strep. He didn't feel much better either. He rubbed his throat.

"A little after nine," Kale said. He held a bottle of a red sports drink in front of Eli. "Try to drink this."

Eli grabbed the bottle with both hands and sipped it. His throat burned as he swallowed. He coughed and pain erupted in his throat and abs. *Today was going to be hell.*

His brain was fuzzy as he showered, brushed his teeth, and dressed. Kale helped him, as if Eli were a small child. Eli stood in front of the bathroom sink and let Kale pull a cotton shirt over his head. Everything was numb, his mind, body and soul. He couldn't take it anymore.

He turned to Kale, dressed in a white dress shirt and black slacks.

"I want you to hit me," Eli said. Kale narrowed his eyes and stared at him.

"I'm not hitting you," Kale said. He tugged on the shirt, as if checking to make sure it fit properly.

"I need to know how bad it can be. I need you to hit me," Eli said. He took a few steps away from him and put his hands to his sides. "Hit me."

"How bad it can be? Broken bones and coma, that's how bad. Stop being stupid and get your shoes on," Kale said.

Eli grabbed his forearm, his good arm, and held fast. "No. Not until you hit me. I know it's going to happen someday and I want to know what it will feel like."

He didn't so much care what the physical pain felt like, he knew that kind of pain. He wanted to know what it felt like to be at the receiving end of Kale's anger. Needed to know he could endure it.

"I'm not—" Kale began to say. Eli stopped him, deciding to speed things up. He slapped him, good and hard on the cheek. The sound echoed in the bathroom. Kale's entire face turned red, a vein bulged in his neck.

Things happened faster than Eli expected. Perhaps he was still lagging a bit from the abuse he'd put his body through. His head smacked against the tiled wall as Kale shoved him against it. He saw stars for a moment, then a deep pain cut into his side as fingers pinched flesh, striking on a nerve. His breathe was gone, his world a tunnel vision of pain.

"Is this what you want?" Kale said, his lips near Eli's ear, breathe hot. It hurt, but shit, it felt good too, like he'd succeeded in making it to hell and his punishment was starting.

The hot pain in his side lessened. His body uncoiled as he regained awareness. He threw his hands around Kale's neck and kissed him hard. He bit his lip, teasing at first, until Kale nipped back. Kale pressed him against the wall harder.

Make me forget, Eli thought. He couldn't say it though. Speaking it would bring the pain too close to the surface.

§§§

The temperature in the car slowly dropped. Eli's hands were numb from the chill, but he didn't care. Wouldn't even move his fingers to rub them together in an attempt to warm them.

"Shall we both sit here until we turn into popsicles?" Kale asked. Eli dragged his eyes from the dashboard and looked at Kale. The tip of his nose was red, but otherwise Kale seemed fine. Of course he was fine, Kale had Russian blood in him. The twenty-degree weather was barely coat worthy for him.

The cold snap had arrived this morning, greeting them with a layer of frost. A few more minutes in the car and Eli would be able to see his breath. Kale groaned and opened his car door. Eli didn't move.

Kale opened the passenger door and grabbed Eli's arm, yanking him from the car. Eli's left foot slipped on the frosty sidewalk. Kale held him until he regained his footing.

"I have to go to work," Kale said. "We can't wait any longer."

Eli almost said an, "Of course you do," but bit back the comment at the last second. He was going inside Jackie's house to tell his daughter her mother had died. Now was not the time to lash out at those who were trying to help him.

"Can you stay with me while I tell her?" Eli asked. Kale touched his cheek, despite the bitter air, his hand was warm.

"Of course," Kale said.

Eli hunched forward and jammed his hands in his pockets. It wasn't smart considering how slippery the sidewalk was due to the layer of frost. Risking the peril of falling, he stomped forward, up the walk to the house. He reached the door and paused, uncertain if he should knock or just go in.

Kale must have interpreted his hesitation as another stalling tactic, and reached past him to solve the dilemma. He pulled the screen door open and pushed on the wooden door. Both were unlocked. His parents must have known they were coming.

"You called first," Eli said softly.

"Of course I did," Kale said. "Your father is here. I didn't want him jamming a shotgun in my face again."

Kale went first, blocking the first burst of warm air from the house. Kale stomped his shoes on the rug, as if expecting a layer of snow to have accumulated on them. Eli grinned, amused by the habit.

"Oh, Eli, I'm so glad you're all right." His mother wrapped her arms around him, her hug gentle and light, as if she thought he might break if she squeezed too tight.

He wrapped his arms around her, returning the embrace. His father stood behind her, his eyes searching Eli's body. Guilt ate at him. His father didn't know what had happened, but that look...his father was a good detective, and had worked on the police force for thirty years. Hank could surmise enough to guess accurately at what had occurred.

"We haven't told her," his mother said. She gave him a firm smile, masking the pain. Why was everyone else treating this with such a detached manner? They all acted like he was simply going to tell

Annabelle she'd gotten a bad grade in school. Someone was dead. Where were the tears? The screaming? The anger? He wanted to shout it at them. Tell them to stop acting tough and show some freaking sorrow. How could he be the only one in mourning?

"I'd like to tell her alone," Eli said.

His mother nodded. "Do you want us to leave?"

"Just wait out here." Eli brushed past her, moving to Annabelle. She would cry. If anyone was going to cry with him, it would be her. She was sitting at the television, watching a cartoon he didn't recognize. He watched the green blob dancing with purple rats for a moment. Maybe he would tell her later…

Kale's hand landed on his shoulder and squeezed. "Annabelle?" Kale asked. "We need to talk to you in your room."

Her bright eyes looked away from the screen and at them. He was going to squash that happiness, burn out that joy growing inside her. She jumped off the couch, looking from Eli to Kale.

"Okay," she said. He started after her and felt resistance from behind. Kale was pulling on his coat. Eli turned and noticed Kale had already removed his own.

"Unless you're planning to run off, directly after," Kale said, giving the coat anther jerk.

"No, right," Eli said. He shrugged the coat off and handed it to his mother. He felt more exposed than ever now. He wrapped his arms around his stomach that still ached from what he'd put himself through last night.

Annabelle sat on the edge of her bed, her hands tightly grasping a pink bunny. "Are you okay?"

She was asking him if he was okay. That wasn't how this was supposed to work. Kale shut the door behind them and Eli collapsed to the floor. The energy was gone from his body. Kale had managed to make him eat a few crackers and drink some water. The weight of his malnutrition hit him and he wanted to curl into a ball and sleep.

"Your dad had a rough night," Kale said. *Not as rough as her mother,* Eli thought.

Annabelle looked from Kale back to him. She looked as resigned and accepting as the rest of them. He didn't figure it would last.

"Do you remember how your mother has been sick," Eli asked. Annabelle nodded. "She explained to you how she wouldn't be coming home this time, right?" Another firm head nod. "Early this morning she…" He choked, his throat closed, refusing to let him say the words he needed to.

"Did Mommy go to heaven?" Annabelle asked. This time Eli was the one to nod, but his nods weren't single or firm. He nodded numerous times and closed his eyes, the tears welling up inside. "When is she moving into the cemetery? I want to visit her there."

He couldn't do it. Eli couldn't maintain this façade of calm everyone else was. He covered his face and stifled back the sobs.

"Today's Thursday," Kale said. "The funeral will probably be Saturday."

She didn't understand the days of the week, but Kale wouldn't know that. "Not today," Eli managed between sobs.

He heard a thump and Annabelle's tiny fingers pulled Eli's hands away from his face. "Why are you so sad? Mommy said she won't be in pain anymore after she goes to heaven, and we can still visit her in the cemetery."

Did she understand what this all meant? Did she think the cemetery was some resort? Kale knelt next to them and redirected Annabelle's attention.

"Your father is just upset he won't get to see your mother as much as he used to," Kale said.

"But she's happier now." She looked at Eli, not understanding his grief. He wanted to argue with her, say that Jackie wouldn't be able to talk back. All Annabelle would be visiting was a rock with her mother's name on it.

"What do you think a cemetery is?" Kale asked.

"A place where your loved ones go when they live in heaven. You can visit them and talk to them. They can't talk back, but they'll hear you. Mommy said so. She said if I ever miss her, I can go the cemetery and talk to her," Annabelle said.

Jackie had prepared her well. They'd had a year and half of knowing this day was coming. It seemed everyone else was ready, except him.

"She said I might get a new mommy, too. Someone to help you take care of me. Tommy's dad did that. His mom died when he was a baby and now he has a new mommy."

Jackie wasn't even in the ground and Annabelle was asking about a new mommy? A flare of anger rose in him. Why did no one else care that she was gone? Kale squeezed his shoulder.

"How about a new daddy?" Kale asked. "Your dad said I could move in. Would you like that? I can try to do some of the things your mother did."

What hope Eli had for a mourning partner faded at Kale's proposal. Annabelle's eyes lit up.

"Really? I would love that! Two daddies?" She looked from Eli to Kale. "Yes, yes, you have to move in."

She moved away from Eli and threw her arms around Kale. "But you can't leave," Annabelle said. "Not ever. You have to promise you won't leave."

"I don't have any plans to leave," Kale said. He looked questioningly at Eli.

"Daddy can't take care of me by himself, so you have to promise to stay," Annabelle said.

Eli bit his tongue to keep from lashing out. He wanted to tell her what an impossible demand that was. Kale could get hit by a bus tomorrow and become another person to visit in the cemetery. He wanted to shake his daughter and make her understand how sad and horrible all of this was.

"You have to take care of both of us. Promise," Annabelle said.

"I promise to take care of you," Kale said. Annabelle mouthed, both of you. "Both of you. I won't leave."

CHAPTER TWENTY-EIGHT

Kale made the mistake of assuming Marge and Hank would be staying, or at a minimum that Jackie's mother would be returning. Where was she? By the time Eli had himself composed enough to exit Annabelle's room, both Marge and Hank were putting on their coats.

"You're leaving?" Kale asked. Annabelle clutched Kale's pant leg, as if the very word "leaving" caused her distress.

"We've been here all night," Marge said. She buttoned her coat. "I have phone calls I need to make."

"Thanks, Kale," Hank said. He tipped his hat and opened the front door. *No-no-no, this was not an option.* Kale needed to go to work. Leaving Eli here alone with his daughter was not an option.

"Can't you stay a few more hours?" Kale asked. "I need to go to work."

"You're leaving?" Annabelle asked. The first inkling of anguish reverberated in her voice.

"Just for a few hours," Kale said. He patted the top of her head.

"But you promised you wouldn't leave."

"I still have to go to work." So she could understand her mother dying, but not Kale's need of employment?

"Kale always has to work," Eli said. He slumped down on the couch, his eyes focusing on whatever was on the screen.

"You can't leave, you promised." Annabelle wrapped her arms around his leg and held fast. Marge shrugged and followed Hank out the door. He glimpsed metal and realized Hank was carrying his rifle. Maybe it was a good thing if they left.

Kale tried to sort out an alternate solution. "What if you came with me?" Kale asked. He looked down at Annabelle.

"To your work?"

"Can you sit quietly?" He had no idea if a six-year-old was capable of that. She seemed serene enough. She nodded her head multiple times, sending her hair flying.

Eli looked at him doubtfully. "You're taking us to court with you?"

Eli's eyes were sunken, bloodshot and surrounded by dark circles. His skin pale and sweaty. He was in no condition to sit in a courtroom. What if he fainted or started crying uncontrollably?

"Not you," Kale said.

"Good," Eli said. He relaxed back in the cushions.

"I'm still not leaving you here alone," Kale said. "Annabelle, go get ready."

She nodded and scurried down the hall to her room.

Eli pulled himself from the couch and ran a weary hand through his short hair. "You can't take her to a courtroom."

"Children are allowed, as long as she's quiet. It's a business case about espionage, it's not like she'll overhear anything traumatic."

"Can't someone cover for you?"

"No. Are you wearing that or did you want to change?"

"Where are you taking me if I'm not going to your work?"

§§§

The car pulled to a stop in front of Riley's group home. Eli couldn't believe this was Kale's solution. To have his mentally disabled bother babysit him. Eli turned to look at Annabelle. It had taken them a good fifteen minutes to install the child seat in Kale's car. Kale had suggested they take Jackie's car, since it was already installed in it, but Eli had refused. He wasn't ready to start using Jackie's things as if they were his own.

"Be good for Kale," Eli said. She nodded. Kale exited the car and opened Eli's door. He practically dragged Eli from the car. "We should really take her in with us. It's child abandonment to leave her alone in a car."

"You're thinking of child endangerment and our state doesn't have any specific laws regarding it," Kale said.

"You're leaving a six-year-old alone in a running car," Eli said.

"And if we were in Washington State or Connecticut, I would be concerned."

Dating a lawyer was nearly as annoying as having a retired cop for a father. Eli crossed his arms and followed Kale to the group home.

Kale held the door for him and before he'd finished entering he heard Riley's excited squeal. A warm body embraced him, snuffing out more than the chill from outside.

"I heard about Jackie," Riley said. "I'm so sorry."

"Riley goes to work at six," Kale said. "I'll be back before then."

"You work?" Eli couldn't help but say.

"At Liverpool Resort downtown," Riley said.

"Remember what I told you on the phone," Kale said, looking at his brother. "Eli is currently a code purple."

Riley's eyes got big as he seemed to recall something important. He turned back to his housemates in the living room.

"Code purple guys," Riley said. One of them jumped up, Eli thought his name was Ben.

"Let me lock my bathroom," Ben said. He dashed down the hall.

"I've got the knives in the kitchen," another said, Paul, if Eli remembered correctly.

Eli stepped closer to Kale and asked quietly, "What's a code purple?"

"A suicide risk," Kale said.

"You told them I'm suicidal?" Eli asked, insulted.

"You tried to kill yourself less than twelve hours ago, so yes, you are. It's not a big deal to them. They make a game out of it. Ben has a sister who is in and out of rehab for drug abuse." Kale pointed at the brown haired man who remained transfixed on the television. "Mike has an alcoholic dad. One of them has a cousin who cuts herself, and there's a handful of previous roommates who had even worse histories. They run this drill whenever one of them comes to visit."

Paul returned from the kitchen. He was the thinnest among them. He wiped his brow dramatically. "The kitchen is secure."

"Good," Kale said. "Make sure he drinks and eats something. I'll bring pizza when I come to pick him up."

An exited uproar came echoing the proclamation of pizza. Riley pulled Eli's coat off and hung it on the coatrack. He led him into the living room. Eli managed a quick wave before Kale escaped out the doors.

Eli sat on the couch, Ben on one side, Riley on the other. Various words and mutters of comfort were offered. Paul knelt in front of Eli, fully surrounding him.

"You should never hurt yourself," Paul said.

"We all miss Jackie," Ben said, giving his knee a squeeze.

"We can't lose you, Eli," Riley said. He threw his arms around Eli in a sideways hug. Eli wanted to correct them and point out that none of them had ever met Jackie so it was impossible for them to miss her. Their closeness and warmth filled the void he'd felt since last night when Jackie had taken her last breath and left him.

Eli clutched at whoever was closest to him and let the tears fall. Sobs wracked his body as reassuring pats touched him.

He caught bits and pieces of their words as they held him. "Okay… Get better… We're here."

§§§

Kale got in the car and shut the door. He looked at Annabelle in the rearview mirror. "You sure you don't want to stay here with your dad?"

"I want to stay with you," Annabelle said. "I'll be good."

He couldn't blame her for choosing him over Eli. Even Kale was a bit more relieved than he had a right to be at having a break from the gloom Eli currently carried with him.

"Okay," Kale said. He put the car into gear and drove to the law firm office. It was nearly one in the afternoon, he had an hour to prep before he'd need to be at the courthouse. Snowflakes dotted his windshield and he turned on the wipers. The sky was a dark gray, as if the entire city were mourning the loss of Jackie.

Kale wondered if they'd be able to dig her grave or if the ground would be too frozen. The car lost traction for a moment as he pulled into his parking spot. His front bumper hit the curb and the car stopped. He took a moment to settle his nerves before he exited the car.

He opened the back door and fumbled with the belts on the car-seat. He finally got Annabelle free and she jumped out. He collected her bag and helped her put it on. She wore a knee length yellow dress with a white cat face on the front. She adjusted her black leggings to make sure her boots fit snuggly. Kale held his briefcase in his good hand and gave her his casted arm. She wrapped her tiny fingers around two of his fingers and he led the way to the office.

The sidewalk was getting slicker. Several times Annabelle would have fallen if not for the firm grip she kept on his hand. The doors opened to the lobby and Kale stopped to stomp the snow dust from his shoes. Annabelle watched him, then did likewise, copying his movements.

They remained silent as they waited for the elevator, rode to the second floor and exited. Suzie looked up from the surprisingly empty lobby.

"Where is everyone?" Kale asked.

"Most clients canceled their afternoon appointments," Suzie said. She glanced down at Annabelle but Kale rushed them past before she could address her. Suzie buzzed them through the glass doors into the office. At least people were present in the office.

Kale went to what used to be Charlotte's desk and addressed his temporary secretary, whose name evaded him. "Any messages?" Kale asked.

She looked up, surprise on her face. "We didn't think you'd be in today."

"I called and said I would," Kale retorted, annoyed. "Messages."

She handed him a neat stack of notes with messages scrawled on them. "Tell Tim to come to my office and update me on the case."

He let go of Annabelle's hand so he could take the papers. Annabelle stood on her tip toes and peered at the bowl of candy on his secretary's desk. His temp smiled and handed a butterscotch candy to Annabelle.

"And what brings you into the office? Looking for a good lawyer?" she asked.

"I already have one," Annabelle said, pocketing the candy.

"Do you want me to take her to daycare?" his secretary asked, looking at Kale.

"No, she's staying with me," Kale said.

"I have to make sure he doesn't leave," Annabelle said. "Like my mommy did this morning."

"Oh? Where did your mommy go?"

"Heaven."

The woman's jaw dropped and she stared at Annabelle, at an apparent loss for words.

"She's just a little bundle of joy, isn't she?" Kale said. "Spreading rays of sunshine everywhere she goes."

Kale put the notes in his mouth and grabbed her hand. He pulled her over to his office and unlocked the door. "Sit in that chair," Kale directed. He used the kickstand on his door to prop it open. He dropped his suitcase by his desk and thumbed through the messages.

"We'll be here for a bit so go ahead and get comfy," Kale said.

"Okay," she said. She wiggled out of her coat and backpack. She pulled a coloring book out and sprawled on his floor, going to work on filling in some pages.

Tim came in and gave a slight jump when he saw Annabelle.

"Any updates?" Kale asked. He turned on his computer and waited for it to boot.

"Mr. Poche called. He's not going to make it to court today," Tim said.

"He's our primary witness. We barely have a case without him," Kale said. "He has to be there."

"He said something about inclement weather. It's the same reason most of our afternoon appointments canceled," Tim explained.

"What kind of bad weather?"

"I don't know."

Annabelle looked up from her book. "We're supposed to get four to six inches of snowfall before dark." She looked from Tim to Kale.

"How do you know that?" Kale asked.

"Grandma M. watches the weather channel like it's a religion," Annabelle said, the words likely not her own. Kale turned to Tim.

"Are they canceling any of the trials?" Kale asked. Tim shook his head.

"Anyone who doesn't show, they'll base their testimony off their written word. No rescheduling," Tim said. Poche's testimony made a bigger impact in person. There was a high risk they'd lose the case if he didn't show.

"Call Mr. Poche and tell him to suck it up and get here," Kale said. "We won't have six inches by four and his testimony will be over by then."

Tim lingered, biting his bottom lip.

"What?" Kale asked.

"Can you call him? I already spoke to him on the phone and—"

Kale bit back the slew of profanity he wanted to shout at Tim. "Exactly what good are you to this firm, Tim? My six-year-old has provided me with more useful information than you have. I should hire her and fire you."

"I—"

"Get out," Kale said. He waved his hand and Tim quickly obeyed. Kale logged onto his computer and looked up Mr. Poche's number. He dialed and listened to the ringing.

"Hello," Mr. Poche said.

"Mr. Poche, this is Kale Sokoloff from Moroz-Kempt Legal Advisors. I had you scheduled as a witness today and I was informed you wouldn't be able to attend. Can you advise me why?"

"There's a winter storm coming in."

"There's no road closures," Kale said. "If you're uncomfortable with the drive, I can call you a shuttle service."

"Can't you just use my written testimony?"

"Only if you want us to lose the case," Kale said. Mr. Poche still worked for BlackOre Industries and Kale knew the shareholders were planning to give Mr. Poche a sizeable bonus in exchange for his testimony against a former employer who was accused of using the facilities to smuggle contraband. Kale didn't know if the bonus would be given regardless of if they won the case.

"I'm sorry, Mr. Sokoloff, but it's just not worth it to me. The roads won't be safe."

Anger welled up inside Kale, this stupid employee who waited six months to raise any flags about the illegal activities was now trying to weasel out of testifying.

"Mr. Poche, your testimony is vital to the success of this case. A few inches of snow should not keep you from fulfilling your promise to your employer."

"I know but—"

"But nothing Mr. Poche. I've been up since two this morning with a grieving friend who lost his wife. I spent a good portion of my day keeping him from drowning his sorrow in alcohol and drugs. Instead of being with him, I came into the office so I could represent my client and enable you to testify. I had to bring his six-year-old daughter into the office with me because I was afraid of what he might do while I'm away. So you do not get to tell me a few fucking inches of snow are going to keep you from showing up at the courthouse. Do you understand me?"

Mr. Poche's voice was very quiet as he replied. "Yes, I do."

"I am calling a shuttle service to pick you up. Do not refuse them." Kale hung up the phone, slamming it so hard Annabelle gave a small yelp. He'd forgotten she was there, even though he'd just declared it to Mr. Poche. He wondered how much of what he'd said she understood.

"Sorry about that," Kale said.

"Daddy gets depressed sometimes," Annabelle said. Kale wondered how well she understood the words she repeated.

"Yes, he does," Kale agreed. "Pack up your things. We need to go to the courthouse. If you need to use the bathroom, you should go now."

She jumped up. "Where is it?"

He stared at his secretary, willing her name to come back to him. Kathy? Kitty? Kim? "Kathy!" Kale shouted it and the woman jerked in his direction. She scurried to her feet and appeared in his door.

"Yes, sir?" she asked. He wondered if he'd gotten the name right or if she was simply going along with what he'd called her.

"Can you take Annabelle to the restroom?"

"Of course." She took Annabelle's hand and led her down the corridor. Kale gathered his things and put them in the briefcase. He did likewise for Annabelle's items.

§§§

The bailiff gave Kale a questioning look as he escorted Annabelle into the courtroom. There was no rule against it so he stared the man down until he opened the doors. Kale had arrived during a break. His case was up next. He took Annabelle to the front row and sat her directly behind the prosecution's table.

Mr. O'Donnell, the primary shareholder for BlackOre Industries, was already seated at the table. He twisted in his chair to look at Kale. "What's all this? You couldn't find a sitter?"

His white moustache was twisted into a flip at the ends, making him look like he'd sprung from a western. Kale hoped Annabelle didn't comment on it.

"This is Annabelle," Kale said. "She believes I'm a flight risk."

"Supervising your old man, eh?" Mr. O'Donnell asked. Annabelle nodded.

"Stay here," Kale said. "I'm going to sit with Mr. O'Donnell."

He walked down the aisle and around to where Mr. O'Donnell sat. The brief thirty seconds was all the opening Annabelle needed to share her dreary news of her mother's passing.

"I'm so sorry for your loss," Mr. O'Donnell said. He looked at Kale. "I didn't know you were married."

"I'm not," Kale said simply.

Smartly, Mr. O'Donnell dropped the topic. "Are we sure we shouldn't settle? I hear Mr. Poche isn't going to show."

"He'll be here."

"But it's going to snow." What was with everyone and this storm? He'd listened to the weather report on the drive from the law firm to the courthouse and although it was the first snow of the season, it wasn't expected to be anything disastrous.

"I called him and clarified things. He'll be here."

Mr. O'Donnell shook his head mournfully. "He would save up his sick days for when it snowed. Ever since he lost his wife and daughter in a car accident during a snowstorm, he's never set foot in a car when there's so much as a splattering of snow on the ground."

For a short moment, Kale forgot how to breathe. Had he just belittled a grieving man into facing his fears in order to give a testimony at the trial? He glanced at the doors as the last people arrived before the bailiff would lock the door. A chubby man in a blue coat hurried in at the last minute.

"We're fine," Kale said. "He's here."

Mr. Poche looked pale, like driving here had likely given him the fright of his life. He gave a small wave to Kale and took a seat toward the back, since the proceedings were about to start.

CHAPTER TWENTY-NINE

Kale knew very little about kids, but he knew bathroom breaks were a frequent occurrence. Before they put on their coats, Kale asked her if she needed to use it. Even if she'd said no, he might have insisted she try anyway. He did not want an accident in his car.

They walked down the corridor in the courthouse to the public restroom.

"Give me your things. I'll wait here in the hall for you," Kale said.

"No, you have to come in," she said.

"You're six, you can go in by yourself." No one was going to kidnap her. He was right outside.

"But I can't lock the stall door."

"Why not?" She was tall enough to reach the knob.

"Cause of my closet fear," she said. He stared at her a moment before he remembered her claustrophobia.

"I can't go in the women's bathroom," Kale said. He searched the women passing in the hall for one he might know. How did Eli deal with this? Did he never take her to a public restroom? Or had Jackie always been there?

"I'll have to take you in the men's," Kale decided. He went to the door and peered in, making sure there weren't any unabashed men using the urinals with no sense of modesty. There was one male, but he was practically inside the urinal with the way he stood.

"All right, come in, eyes on the floor," Kale said. He draped their coats over his cast and hugged his briefcase to his chest using the same arm. He used his good hand to steer her, putting it on the top of her head. He led her to the first stall and released her once inside.

"Hold the door from the outside, but don't lock it," Annabelle said. He nodded and kept one hand on the top of the door to keep it closed.

Kale obeyed his own rule and kept his eyes on the ground. Most in the courthouse knew he was gay and the last thing he wanted was for people to think he was trying to catch a quick look at someone in the bathroom.

Several people came and went. "Everything okay in there?" Kale asked.

"Can you turn on the faucet?" Annabelle asked.

Not if you want me to keep holding the door, Kale thought.

"I've got it," someone said. The nearest faucet was turned on.

"Thanks," Kale said. He chanced a glance up and saw Mr. Weyenberg drying his hands.

"Good job today," Weyenberg said.

"Thanks," Kale repeated. He heard a trickle from inside the stall.

"That's too bad about what happened with Moloff," Weyenberg said. "How's the office running without him? I heard you're taking most of his cases."

"Yeah, we're promoting from within, we'll be fine," Kale said. Weyenberg was one of the better lawyers Kale had crossed paths with. He was buried at a larger company that provided little room for promotion. Kale was impressed by how that never seemed to deter how hard he worked.

"That's smart," Weyenberg said. The slight tone of sadness in his voice wasn't lost on Kale.

"We aren't opposed to hiring on new help though," Kale said. "You should drop off a resume." If it was up to Kale they'd hire on five more lawyers tomorrow. He needed the help.

"Really?"

"Absolutely," Kale said. Annabelle tugged on the door and Kale let it open. "Wash your hands."

She trudged over to the sink but was too short to reach. "You need to lift me."

"Here, let me. You still have your bum arm," Weyenberg said. He lifted Annabelle by her waist and helped her wash up. They departed the restroom and Kale put her coat on at the exit to the building.

"I'll stop by next week," Weyenberg said, with a wave of his hand. Kale and Annabelle stepped outside. The wind sent a shiver through Kale's body. The sky was gray with swirls of snow still falling. Kale grabbed Annabelle's hand as he had before and they walked to the car. The snow was three inches deep in areas that weren't salted.

"You need to carry me," Annabelle said. Kale looked down and saw her leggings were getting wet. There was no possible way for him to carry her and his suitcase. Not with his injured arm.

"I can't," Kale said. "It's not much farther."

She shivered and pulled her coat around her tighter.

"You were the one who knew the weather forecast. You should have dressed more appropriate," Kale said.

"You're the adult," Annabelle said. "You're not doing very good at filling in for my mom."

They reached the car and Kale lifted her into the car seat. He took off her boots and leggings, since they were wet.

"I'm still figuring it out," Kale said. There was definitely a steep learning curve that he wasn't prepared for.

§§§

The chorus of "Pizza is here" resonated throughout Riley's house as Kale entered. He balanced a stack of four pizzas. Annabelle carried a bag of breadsticks. He was relieved of the pizzas by an eager Ben who whisked them away to the kitchen.

Kale was grateful to see Eli looking not only healthier but in better spirits. Eli gave Annabelle a quick pat down, as if worried she might have lost a limb. Kale took his coat off and hung it. Eli handed him Annabelle's.

"Everything go okay?" Eli asked.

"It was fun," Annabelle said, making Kale seriously wonder what she didn't find fun.

"Did you win the case?" Eli asked, looking up to Kale.

"They'll announce a verdict on Monday," Kale said. "The judge wanted to review some of the evidence and we'll do our closing arguments."

Riley arrived and swooned over Annabelle, boasting that he was an uncle. Introductions were passed and pizza shared. Kale wasn't sure what had transpired during his absence but it would seem Riley had helped Eli heal in a way Kale couldn't.

The entire time they visited, Annabelle stayed close, never straying more than a few feet from Kale. Her newfound attachment continued after Kale took them home.

"The house seems emptier," Eli said as they entered. Even Kale seemed to notice the foreboding vibe the place now emitted. The place was devoid of life. In his mind, he pictured a puppy bounding up to great them at the door. That kind of joyous never ending energy was just what the house and Annabelle needed.

Eli took off his coat and shivered, as though the chill wouldn't leave his bones.

"Turn up the heater," Kale said. "Where is it?"

"We can't afford to turn it up more," Eli said.

"I'm pretty sure I can afford it," Kale said. He gripped Eli's shoulder. "We're in this together."

Eli nodded and went to the thermostat on the wall. "Get ready for bed, Annabelle."

"Are you going to move into mom's room?" Annabelle asked.

Kale saw the look of horror flash across Eli's face. Kale would love nothing more than to sleep somewhere other than that futon, but he wasn't going to rush Eli.

"Not yet," Kale said. "We'll need to sort through and box up her things."

Sleeping arrangements reminded him of the continued absence of Loraine. The spare bedroom door was closed and no light came from inside.

"I want Kale to sleep in my room," Annabelle said. She stood in the hall with her night clothes bundled against her chest as she prepared to change.

"Go take a bath first," Eli said. She nodded and scurried off to the hall bathroom. Kale approached Eli and wrapped his arms around him from behind.

"How are you?" Kale asked.

"Exhausted."

"Her bed is probably more comfortable than that horrid futon," Kale said. Small yes, but he still thought he'd get more sleep in it.

"Thank you," Eli said.

§§§

The next morning, Kale rummaged in the kitchen, looking for some form of coffee. Grounds, instant, he didn't care. He opened one of the top cupboards and was given a wide display of prescription pills. Jackie had kept them. He grabbed a few bottles and read the labels.

He wasn't sure what they all were, but many had labels that indicated they were of the narcotic variety. He grabbed the bottles, emptying the cabinet. He sat them on the counter. Over twenty bottles of hazardous pills that his lover could easily take if he felt like trying to end his life again.

Annabelle came into the kitchen, rubbing her sleep sand filled eyes. Eli was in the shower. He wondered how much time he had.

"Annabelle," Kale said. "Let's play a game."

"What about breakfast?"

"After the game, it won't take long," Kale said.

"Okay." She nodded.

"I want you to help me gather all of the pills in the house." He held up one of the bottles to show her. "Do you know where your mother kept them all?"

"Some are in the bedroom and bathroom," Annabelle said.

"Search the house, top to bottom, give me all of the bottles you can find," Kale said. She dashed down the hall. Kale opened the bottle and dumped them into the sink. He knew there were regulations about properly disposing of medications, but he didn't have time to drop them off at a pharmacy. He needed to get rid of them now, regardless of the potential risk to contaminate the tap water supply.

He turned on the garbage disposal and emptied bottle after bottle into the roaring blades.

"What are you doing?"

Kale turned the disposal off so he could hear her better. Loraine stood in the entrance to the kitchen, her bathrobe tied around her waist.

"Getting rid of Jackie's medications," Kale said.

"Her body is barely cold and you're already—"

"Already what? Making this house a safer environment for your granddaughter? Keeping her suicidal father from hurting himself? Are these pills some part of a legacy Jackie left behind that I'm unaware of?"

She pursed her lips and stared at him. Some gears must have aligned and her demeanor shifted. "I know where some are kept. She locked some in a safe box. I'll get them."

Annabelle brought him six more, saying she found them in the living room and bedroom. He told her to check all the bathrooms. She dashed off, quick to obey, as Eli entered the kitchen.

"What are you doing?" Eli asked. He picked up one of the bottles.

"Cleaning house," Kale said. "You can help by peeling the labels off."

Eli fondled the bottle for a moment. "I should cook breakfast."

"Actually," Loraine said as she walked back into the room. "I was thinking I'd take us all out to breakfast. I don't know about you, but I could use some comfort food before the wake."

"What time is the wake?" Kale asked.

"It starts at one and lasts until four. Tomorrow morning we'll have the graveside funeral," Loraine said. She sat a dozen pill containers on the counter.

"Eating out for breakfast sounds great," Kale said, assuming he was invited. He grabbed the first bottle and dumped them out. He reached for the second and Eli grabbed his wrist.

"Those are mine," Eli said. He shot an anger filled look at Loraine.

Annabelle dashed in, tossing six bottles onto the counter. "I have to make more trips," she said.

"I'll help you," Loraine said.

Kale waited until they'd both left. "Let go of the bottle," Kale said.

Eli obeyed. Kale looked at the label, sure enough it was for Eli. He was about to give it back to him when he read the name of the drug.

"You don't need these," Kale said.

"Yes, I do. They're mine." Eli tightened his grip on Kale's wrist and held his other hand out, palm open. "Give them back."

"You're twenty-two and from what I've seen you do not need Viagra." A flicker of doubt crossed his mind as he wondered if he was incorrect. What if Eli had been taking these the entire time?

"You don't get to decide that," Eli said. He grabbed for the pills, attempted to force them from Kale's larger hand. Kale unclipped the lid with his thumb and the purple capsules tumbled out, scattering across the counter, sink and floor.

Eli cussed and let go of him. Kale dropped the container and used both hands to restrain Eli. "If you really need them, you can get a new prescription. Tell me why you even have them."

Eli's face reddened, a vein appeared in his neck. He pulled away from Kale and went down the hall. A door slammed a few moments later. Kale was growing tired of Eli's secrets.

CHAPTER THIRTY

The wake was worse than Eli expected. Everyone wanted to pause and pass their condolences. Kale watched over him like a protective mother hen, herding people away when he noticed Eli was about to cry if the words of caring became too much.

Eli stared at the mountains of plants arranged by the casket. There were so many, the forest spilled onto the main floor. The funeral home directors brought in armfuls of more. Eli wondered what he would do with them all. He hadn't bothered to read any of the cards attached to the pots. He wondered if he was expected to send out thank you cards.

Loraine floated from guest to guest, chattering and smiling. She'd put everything together, making sure Jackie's every request was fulfilled. Eli had refused to discuss Jackie's funeral with Jackie. He hated talking about what would happen once she was gone. He was noticing now that those actions had ill prepared him for her death. Everyone else appeared to have come to terms with it. Eli was still struggling.

Annabelle mingled with other children, every so often she'd come over and give him a reassuring pat on the knee as if Eli were the child needing to be cared for. He noticed her eyes often went to Kale. When did his daughter start putting more confidence and reliance in a stranger than her father?

"Here, you need to drink something," Kale said. He held out a paper cup with water in it. Eli took the object and drank the contents. He looked at his watch, time was crawling by, the wake would never end at this rate.

"Be sure to sign the guest book," Loraine said as she passed by him, herding a group of women Eli couldn't place.

Eli groaned and leaned forward, burying his face in his hands.

"Do you want to step outside, get some fresh air?" Kale asked.

"No, I do not. That would require me to pass by all those people attending the wedding," Eli said. Who had a wedding at a funeral home? The establishment had four rooms for rent, two of them were being used by a wedding party. They were directly across the hall. Their chorus of laughter and celebratory nature were wearing Eli's nerves thin.

"All we need is a baby shower in the fourth room and we'll have all the phases of life represented," Eli said. "Maybe we should have..." He was about to say they should have invited Selena to do her baby shower as a joint occasion with the funeral when he noticed none other than her, walking through the entrance.

She paused at the guestbook and scribbled in it. She wore all black, the dress draped over her robust stomach. Even looking like that, swollen with child, she did things to his body he didn't want to admit. The expression on his face gave away too much and Kale looked in Selena's direction.

"Oh hell no," Kale said.

"She has a right to be here," Eli said. "She was friends with Jackie."

"Friends don't sleep with their friend's husbands," Kale said. "I'll get rid of her."

"Kale," Eli said, but Kale was already heading to her. Eli stood and followed, unsure of how he could defuse the possible hostile situation.

Selena finished with the guestbook and surveyed the lobby. Kale stopped in front of her, the two of them locked eyes. Eli stayed behind Kale. He wanted to step between them but also worried what would happen if he did.

"You aren't welcome here," Kale said. Eli opened his mouth to argue, but Selena beat him to it.

"So you were the lawyer representing him," Selena said. "Nice little cover story." Her tone dripped in sarcasm and annoyance. "I have a right to be here, I'm a friend of the family."

"You're no friend," Kale said. He reached for her arm and she backed away from him.

"Don't touch me," Selena said.

"Do we have a problem here?" Eli's father asked. They all heard the distinct sound of Hank's double barrel shotgun being cocked.

"You brought your shotgun? To my wife's funeral?" Eli exclaimed.

"That's not legal," Kale said.

"I have a right to carry," Hank said.

"No one has a right to carry around a shotgun in this state! That's excessive force," Kale said. "You can only carry handguns."

"I used to be a detective," Hank said. He raised the rifle and pointed it at Selena. "I believe Kale said you need to leave."

"Jesus, Hank," Kale said. He grabbed the barrel of the gun. "You're pointing your loaded and cocked rifle at a pregnant woman."

"Dad, put the gun away," Eli said.

"Your family is fucking crazy," Selena said.

Hank tried to keep his grip on the rifle as Kale pulled on it. Eli moved to stand in front of Selena. "You should go," Eli said.

Her lips narrowed into a firm line. "Not until you and I talk. You said you'd claim this baby after Jackie died."

"She just died," Eli said. "I need a few—"

The rifle went off. The gun echoed in the room. Eli's ears rang from his close proximity. Even through the ringing, he could hear people screaming, mostly those from the wedding party next door.

People rushed past, hurrying to the exit. His father gripped the rifle and lowered it to point at the floor.

"Dad, you could have shot someone," Eli said.

"Oh my God," Selena said. Eli looked at her. "My water just broke."

"What?" Eli looked at the floor and saw the dampness pooling around her feet.

"Shit," Kale said.

"Now isn't the time," Eli said, thinking he was complaining about Selena. He glanced over at Kale and saw red spreading on Kale's black suit. The world spun and tilted. Kale dropped to his knees, in what to Eli seemed to be slow motion. Blood poured between Kale's fingers as he pressed against a wound on his left side.

Eli heard someone say they were calling 911. Eli crumbled to the ground in front of Kale. No-no-this wasn't happening. He couldn't lose everything, not all at once. Not like this.

"It's okay," Kale said. He was blinking his eyes rapidly. "It just grazed me. I'll be fine. Need a few stitches that's all."

"It's a lot of blood," Eli said. He wanted to touch him, but wasn't sure if he should. "You can't die. Kale, you can't die."

"I'm not dying," Kale said, his tone laced with annoyance. Everyone but Hank, Selena and his mother had left the room, well, and Jackie inside her coffin. Marge helped Selena to sit and mumbled something about breathing.

"Help me," Kale said. He grabbed Eli's hand and pressed it against his wound. Eli tasted bile in his mouth as the warm blood coated his hands.

"I'm so sorry," Eli said. "I caused all of this."

"I'll be fine."

"No, I—." Eli was only a few inches from him. Kale sat on the floor, leaning to his right, Eli applying pressure to his left side. "I lied."

He couldn't let Kale die without knowing the truth. He'd kept it all from Jackie. He wouldn't do it again. The guilt was destroying him.

Kale narrowed his eyes, but said nothing.

"Selena's baby is mine. I lied to you. I was worried you'd beat me senseless if I said it was mine. You were so terrifying that night. The paternity test confirmed her baby is mine."

Kale's face darkened. Eli was surprised he had enough blood left to make his face that dark.

"And I'm not bisexual," Eli said.

"What?" Both Kale and Selena said in unison.

"I'm not, I don't," Eli struggled to say it. "I'm not attracted to women."

"But my anger management partner," Kale said. "I saw the way you—"

"She had monstrous cleavage, Kale," Eli said. "I'm not saying I don't like looking, but when it comes to performing, I can't get it up. That's what the Viagra was for. I used it when I was with Selena."

"What about when you were with Jackie?"

"I was never with Jackie. Annabelle isn't mine," Eli said. "That's part of why Jackie's mother wants custody so badly."

"Who is her real father?"

"I don't know, neither did Jackie. She snuck into a college fraternity party, got drunk and nine months later she had Annabelle. Jackie was my best friend. I couldn't let her go through this alone," Eli said. The paramedics arrived and Eli recoiled from Kale. "I'm sorry."

Kale said nothing, but his gaze said more than enough. Eli had used up his allowance of lies.

§§§

Eli sat in the back of the ambulance, his feet hanging, dangling past the bumper. The one taking Kale and Selena to the hospital had already left. The medics had insisted on checking out Eli since he had blood on him. His father appeared, his rifle gone.

"I cleared things up with the police and funeral home director," Hank said. Eli looked over at the huddled wedding party. That was the one bright spot in all this, their wedding was ruined, and rightfully so, since they'd opted to have it at a funeral home.

"Loraine took Annabelle home. Your mother and I will drive you to the hospital so you can be with Selena or Kale, or both, whichever," Hank said. "Are you okay?"

Eli swallowed and took a deep breath before speaking.

"No, Dad, I am not okay. My wife's wake was ruined. My boyfriend was shot by my dad and my mistress went into premature labor. So no, I am not okay."

"Yeah, hell of a mess," Hank said. He scratched his head. "I saw what you did back there. Your little confessional to Kale. You pushing him away so you can marry this new woman, now? Do with Selena what you did with Jackie?"

"I'm not pushing anyone away," Eli said.

"Like hell you aren't. This is what you do. You start to admit what you are, but then you get scared. You get scared people are going to judge you for being gay, so you find some reason to go back in the closet. I know you were getting ready to come out when Jackie got pregnant. She gave you an excuse to crawl right back in that closet. Then you came out, only to go back in when Jackie found out she was sick. When she discovered it was terminal, you went looking for your next cover, Selena was more than happy to step up and be your next woman in need. Is the fucking kid even yours this time?"

"Yes," Eli said. Hating how true his father's words were. Eli had known exactly what he was doing with Selena. He had gone along with not using a condom even though he had noticed everyone else did. He wanted to get her pregnant. He didn't want Jackie to know. It would have crushed her. But he planned for Loraine to take Annabelle. Eli would marry Selena, and he would continue to secretly see men, using their marriage as cover.

But then he'd met Kale, and he'd fallen in love, screwing up his whole life plan.

"So which one are you going to visit when we get to the hospital?" Hank asked.

There was really only one option. He was fairly certain Kale would never speak to him again.

§§§

Eli stared in the nursery at the female infant in a bassinet labeled with Selena's last name. The nurse tending to them smiled at Eli and made a gesture to ask if he wanted to see her. Eli shook his head. He wasn't certain he wanted to be a part of her life. He was considering moving to Mexico.

Someone stood next to him. Eli didn't look up, figuring it was the parent of one of the other six babies on display.

"Which one is yours?" Kale asked. Eli nearly jumped out of his skin. He directed his jump away from Kale and held his breath.

Kale wore only his dress shirt, his suit coat likely discarded. He was pale, but otherwise appeared fine, aside from the large bloodstain on his left side.

"Linrens," Eli said, "the girl."

Kale stepped closer to the window, moving with a distinct limp. He put his left hand on the glass and peered inside. "She looks healthy."

"She is."

"How's Selena?" Kale asked. He looked back at Eli.

"She wouldn't let me in the delivery room. She let me sign the birth certificate though, so I'm sure I'll be owing her some child support."

"Most likely," Kale said.

"I think she's pissed I lied to her about liking women," Eli said.

"Most likely," Kale agreed again. He leaned against the wall.

"Wayne stitch you up?" Eli asked.

"Yeah, he got his nurse practitioner license a few months ago and he's eager to show it off," Kale said.

"Are you…okay?"

"Medically yes, they already discharged me," Kale said. "Seven stitches, less than I got when I punched an oven."

"So it was just a graze?"

"Yes," Kale said. The annoyance was back in his voice. "Were the things you said true? Annabelle isn't yours? Selena's baby is?"

Eli nodded. "I'm sort of a coward when it comes to…being gay and…actually doing something that might make me happy."

"Like being with me instead of marrying expectant mothers?"

"Yeah," Eli said, keeping his eyes on the hospital floor. Kale's hand cupped Eli's chin and tilted it up so he would look at him.

"You should know you can't run away from me," Kale said. His lips touched Eli's and he melted at the touch. The potential promise behind it was the lifeline he needed to keep going, keep trying.

CHAPTER THIRTY-ONE

It was the family Kale had never had growing up. Even when he'd joined Martin at his house for holidays, he had always felt like an outsider, viewing the events but not living them.

This year was different. Alexis flew in to join them. She rented a car and picked up Riley. Annabelle was currently living with Eli, but she'd stay with Loraine over summer and Christmas break. The other holidays, like Thanksgiving, Loraine came to them. She sat across the table from Kale, Annabelle next to her. Riley sat on her other side, with Alexis on the end. Both of Eli's parents joined them, sitting farther down the table. Kale held no ill will toward Hank, but had told him he could never bring the rifle into Eli's house.

Kale's law firm was back on its feet. They'd hired on new lawyers, including Weyenberg. He'd even managed to win the case he'd been handling during Jackie's funeral. Kale would officially give up his apartment at the end of the month and live with Eli. Boxes were littered around the house, both Kale's new and Jackie's old.

Hank carved the turkey, impressively so, and passed out portions to everyone. Kale glanced at Riley and swore he'd never seen him so happy. It'd been a long time since Riley had been part of a real family unit too.

The banter at the table was friendly, laughter filled the room, the house no longer felt empty or sick. This was why Kale suspected Eli had insisted they host dinner, despite the packing boxes. He wanted the house to feel warm again.

Marge retrieved her so called famous chocolate cream pie for dessert as the front doorbell rang. Eli sprang up to answer. Marge portioned out the pie, giving slices to each of them.

§§§

Eli's heart skipped a few thumps as he saw Martin standing on his stoop. He'd expected it to be Selena. She'd promised to bring the baby over for a few hours, a make-shift custody arrangement they were still working on.

"Hi," Eli said, forcing the words out. He hadn't seen the man since Eli's suicide attempt, and Eli had no idea what business he would be having at his house.

"Is Kale here?" Martin asked. Eli glanced at the running car waiting at the curb. It looked like a woman was inside it.

"Yeah, come in," Eli said.

"Actually, I'll wait here," Martin said. "If that's okay."

"You're the one standing in twenty degree weather," Eli said. He shut the door and went to the dining room where everyone else was eating his mother's pie.

"We saved you a piece," Annabelle told him, handing him a plate with what had to be the smallest sliver of pie ever.

"Thanks," Eli said, noting everyone else had a slice three times as large. "Kale, the door is for you." He considered telling him who it was, but wasn't sure he wanted everyone to know. What if Riley wanted to see him? Or invite him inside? They liked each other, right?

"Don't eat mine," Kale warned. He abandoned his slice and went to the foyer. Eli took his old seat and stared at his pathetic slice. Despite the fact everything was moving forward with Kale, Eli still feared he would leave him for Martin. There was a bond there that wasn't going to go away. He'd seen it firsthand that night at the bus stop.

"Everything okay?" his father asked.

"Yeah, I'm just not hungry," Eli said. He pushed the pie away and collected some of the empty dishes. He took them to the kitchen and started washing.

"It's Martin, isn't it?" Alexis asked as she entered the room. She placed a stack of dishes on the counter.

"Yeah, it is." Eli dropped a plate and it crashed to the floor. Eli cussed.

"I got it," Alexis said. "Take a break, okay? He's not gonna leave you, Eli."

Eli nodded, but her words did nothing to ease the knots twisting in his guts. He went to the living room where he could view the front yard. Annabelle had a holiday special playing, one with a reindeer saving Santa. Eli leaned against the wall so he could best see out the window. Martin and Kale stood at arm's length. Eli could only see the back of Martin's head. Half of Kale's was blocked by it.

Kale nodded and the two of them hugged, actually hugged. Kale opened the front door and came back inside. He did his foot stomping routine on the rug as Eli approached.

"What did he want?" Eli asked. He knew it was none of his business, but the words were out anyway.

"He's moving to Minneapolis," Kale said. "He wanted to save me the trouble of hiring a private investigator to find him after I notice he's gone. He's going to open a new store for his sister. Wayne will eventually move down there too, he's just trying to find a job."

"He's moving?" Eli asked.

"Yes." Kale quirked an eyebrow at him. "Are you okay?"

"No, yes, I mean, no." Eli flung open the door and shouted to Martin, who had just reached the car his sister was waiting in. "Wait a minute!"

"What are you doing?" Kale asked.

Eli ignored him and dashed down the stairs to the basement. He knew exactly where it was and wrapped it in a dishtowel he grabbed from the hall closet so Kale wouldn't see. He bounded up the steps and out the door, pretending Kale wasn't glaring at him. He didn't realize he'd forgotten shoes until the chill of the frozen sidewalk chilled his feet. He was wearing socks, so it would have to do.

He reached the end of the curb and Martin rolled down the passenger window. Brandi was indeed the driver. She nodded at him.

"I wanted to give you this," Eli said. He handed the dishtowel to Martin. Eli wrapped his arms around himself, as the breeze cut through his sweater.

Martin looked at him with his too handsome face, looking even more like model quality now that the bruises from Kale's abuse were gone. Even Eli wanted to lean in and kiss those beautifully puffy lips.

Martin unwrapped the towel and exposed the single plate with a rooster on it. He heard the sharp intake of air as Martin realized what it was.

"I was only able to save the one," Eli said.

"No, this is, thank you. Thank you so much," Martin said. He looked up at him with tears in his eyes.

"You're welcome," Eli said. He backed away from the car, his feet numb and socks sticking to the cement. Martin smiled at him, yeah, that was a dental commercial quality smile, and Eli turned to retreat back to his house. Kale opened the door for him.

"What was that about?" Kale asked. Eli ripped his socks off and rubbed one of his feet.

"Not your business," Eli said. "Besides, you unearthed nearly all of my secrets, so it's about time for me to start marking new ones."

"I'm not a fan of your secrets," Kale said.

Eli grinned. "Maybe it's time I gave you your surprise then."

"Surprise?"

Eli looked at his dad. "Go get the basement ready."

"Are you finally going to explain why I haven't been allowed in the basement for the last week?" Kale asked.

"Yeah, come on." Eli grabbed Kale's good arm and led him to the stairs. Riley gave a cheer and pulled Annabelle with him. They bounded down the steps ahead of them.

"Riley knew?" Kale asked.

"Of course," Eli said. They reached the bottom of the steps and Eli turned to stop him. "Do you remember when you asked me what I'd collect if I had the money and space?"

"Yes," Kale said, worry in his tone.

"Well, you're about to see what I've been collecting," Eli said. He stepped back and let Kale enter. He kept his eyes locked on Eli. Then a trademark toot from an electronic model train came from the family room in the basement. Kale turned to view the source of the noise.

Hank stood to the side, operating the controls. Annabelle and Riley stood in the center of the track that looped around the entire room. The track was up on stacks of wood from various construction sets. Buildings of both dollhouse and cardboard variety were arranged around the three tracks with five different trains running on them.

"You collect trains," Kale said.

"Yeah, this isn't even all of them. I thought we'd set it up like a town, and when you get upset over losing a case you can destroy it, like King Kong."

"Or Godzilla!" Riley said.

"You want me to destroy your trains?" Kale asked.

"It's safer than breaking dishes, and I'll expect you to buy me new trains if you break them," Eli said. He watched a smile creep upon Kale's face.

"It does sound fun," Kale said.

"I thought you might like it," Eli said. Kale pushed him against the wall and leaned in as if to kiss him but stopped.

"I still want to know what you gave Martin."

"A secret I shall take to my grave," Eli said. Kale groaned and kissed him. The doorbell rang above, probably Selena, but it could wait.

EPILOGUE

The chairs were more uncomfortable than the ones used at Annabelle's school plays. Eli understood now why people would buy those cushions to use at sporting events. He shifted in the seat and Kale put a hand on his thigh to stop him.

"You're wiggling around more than Riley is," Kale said.

"Sorry," Riley said, from the other side of Kale.

"Sorry," Eli said, taking a moment to admire the crow's feet adorning Kale's face as he scowled at him. He opened the pamphlet for the graduation ceremony and distracted himself with reading the list of the events. He flipped to the list of valedictorians and grinned at the fact Annabelle's name was listed with two others.

"We did it," Eli said, more to himself than anyone.

"Did what?" Kale asked. He draped an arm around Eli's shoulders and leaned closer.

"Raised my daughter," Eli said.

"One down, one to go," Kale said. He nodded in the direction of Jezebel, who sat next to Eli. She had earbuds in and was watching who knew what on her phone. Her dark hair was colored pink at the tips. Yeah, they had their work cut out for them with Jezebel. "Better enjoy this graduation 'cause I'm betting she'll be a GED kind of girl."

"Watch it," Eli warned. The music started and the first speaker walked out onto the stage. The graduation was being held in a stadium downtown. Each high school got to host their event in two hours, with the building pumping out three graduations a day. The four of them sat six rows up on the north side, a perfect viewing location for Annabelle's alphabetical location in the class of five hundred.

"Camera on?" Kale asked. Riley held it up to show the red light. "Good job."

Eli settled back in his seat, no longer finding it quite as uncomfortable. His little girl was all grown up and starting her own life. Twelve years ago, he'd thought it was impossible, this day had been nothing but a dream.

Now it was his life, his family, and he'd never been happier. He could almost feel Jackie smiling down at him from heaven. Despite it all, in the end, he knew he'd made her proud.

"Don't you dare cry," Kale said. "I already know Riley is going too."

"I'm not." Eli wiped at his eye, removing the betraying droplet of water. "I love you."

"I know, me too," Kale said. He pulled him close and kissed his forehead. "You know, neither of us would be here if it wasn't for that brat sitting next to you," Kale said.

Jezebel yanked her earbud out. "I heard that."

"I know you did, I'm just reminding your father of how grateful I am your mother had him thrown in jail twelve years ago," Kale said. She stuck her tongue out at him, exposing a shiny piece of silver. "You pierced your tongue?" Kale's face went instant red.

Jezebel clamped her mouth shut.

"I'm going to kill your mother," Kale said. Eli ignored them and watched as Annabelle entered the arena. She looked up at them and smiled. As Kale reached across him to take Jezebel's phone away as punishment, Eli smiled back.

About the Author

Nina Schluntz is a native to rural Nebraska. In her youth, she often wrote short stories to entertain her friends. Those ideas evolved into the novels she creates today.

Her husband continues to ensure her stories maintain a touch of realism as she delves into the science fiction and fantasy realm. And their kitty, a rescued Abyssinian, is always willing to stay up late to provide inspiration.

You can find Nina on Goodreads, Facebook, and Twitter.

Her blog, mizner13.wordpress.com, has updates on any current or upcoming novels, plus her thoughts on her most recent reads and movie viewings.

OTHER BOOKS BY NINA R SCHLUNTZ

INFLUENCE of a GOD (Gods of Earth Series Book 1)
PROPHET of a GOD (Gods of Earth Series Book 2
MUSE of a GOD (Gods of Earth Series Book 3)
ENEMY of a GOD (Gods of Earth Series Book 4)
SYMBIOTE of a GOD (Gods of Earth Series Book 5)
RESURRECTION of a GOD (Gods of Earth Series Book 6)
Dragons and Healers (Enukara book one)
Immortal Black Dragons (Enukara book two)
The First Generation (Enukara book three)
Elemental Dragon Mages (Enukara book four)
The Second Generation (Enukara book five)
Dragon Devolution (Enukara book six)
Nosy Neighbors

Trademarks Acknowledgment

The author acknowledges the trademark status and trademark owners of the following wordmarks mentioned in this work of fiction:

Tums, GSK

Denny's, DFO, LLC

IHOP, IHOP Restaurants LLC

Old Spice, Procter & Gamble

Viagra, Pfizer Inc.

Vanity Fair, Condé Nast

Made in the USA
Columbia, SC
29 September 2022

67738914R10193